PENGUIN BOOKS

NEW WRITERS OF THE PURPLE SAGE

Russell Martin is the author of five nonfiction books, including the widely praised *Matters Gray and White* (1986) and, most recently, *A Story That Stands Like a Dam* (1989)—a history of the construction of Glen Canyon Dam and the decades-long environmental debate that has surrounded it— a book that received the Caroline Bancroft History Prize and was a finalist for the Western Writers of America Spur Award for Nonfiction Book of the Year. His first novel, *Beautiful Islands,* excerpted in this collection, was published in 1988, and a second, *The Shapes of Creeks and Rivers,* is forthcoming.

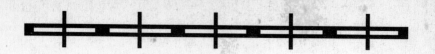

New Writers of the Purple Sage

An Anthology of Contemporary Western Writers

COLLECTED AND
WITH AN INTRODUCTION BY
RUSSELL MARTIN

PENGUIN BOOKS

PENGUIN BOOKS
Published by the Penguin Group
Viking Penguin, a division of Penguin Books USA Inc.,
375 Hudson Street, New York, New York 10014, U.S.A.
Penguin Books Ltd, 27 Wrights Lane,
London W8 5TZ, England
Penguin Books Australia Ltd, Ringwood,
Victoria, Australia
Penguin Books Canada Ltd, 10 Alcorn Avenue, Suite 300,
Toronto, Ontario, Canada M4V 3B2
Penguin Books (N.Z.) Ltd, 182–190 Wairau Road,
Auckland 10, New Zealand

Penguin Books Ltd, Registered Offices:
Harmondsworth, Middlesex, England

First published in Penguin Books 1992
1 3 5 7 9 10 8 6 4 2

PUBLISHER'S NOTE
Some of the selections in this book are works of fiction. Names, characters, places,
and incidents either are the product of the author's imagination or are used fictitiously,
and any resemblance to actual persons, living or dead, events, or locales is entirely
coincidental.

Pages 383–385 constitute an extension of this copyright page.

LIBRARY OF CONGRESS CATALOGING IN PUBLICATION DATA
New writers of the Purple Sage/collected and with an introduction by
Russell Martin.
p.   cm.
ISBN 0 14 01.6940 7
1. West (U.S.)—Literary collections.   2. American
literature—20th century.   3. American literature—West (U.S.)
4. Western stories.   I. Martin, Russell.
PS561.N48   1992
818'.54080803278—dc20   91–47851

Printed in the United States of America

Set in Goudy Old Style
Designed by Brian Mulligan

In memorium

Edward Abbey
1927–1989

Norman Maclean
1902–1990

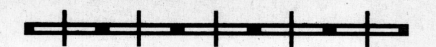

Loading a Boar

We were loading a boar, a goddam mean big sonofabitch and he
jumped out of the pickup four times and tore out my stockracks
and rooted me in the stomach and I fell down and he bit John
on the knee and he thought it was broken and so did I and the
boar stood over in the far corner of the pen and watched us and
John and I just sat there tired and Jan laughed and brought us a
beer and I said, "John it ain't worth it, nothing's going right and
I'm feeling half dead and haven't wrote a poem in ages and I'm
ready to quit it all," and John said, "shit young feller, you ain't
got started yet and the reason's cause you trying to do it outside
yourself and ain't looking in and if you wanna by god write pomes
you gotta write pomes about what you know and not about the
rest and you can write about pigs and that boar and Jan and you
and me and the rest and there ain't no way you're gonna quit,"
and we drank beer and smoked, all three of us, and finally loaded
that mean bastard and drove home and unloaded him and he bit
me again and I went in the house and got out my paper and
pencils and started writing and found out John he was right.

—David Lee

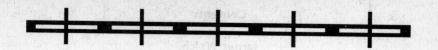

Contents

Introduction
xiii

William Kittredge
"Home"
1

Gretel Ehrlich
"Madeleine's Day" and "McKay"
From *DRINKING DRY CLOUDS*
14

Deirdre McNamer
From *RIMA IN THE WEEDS*
24

Rudolfo A. Anaya
Iliana of the Pleasure Dreams
37

N. Scott Momaday
"Remote as the stars are his sentiments just now"
From *THE ANCIENT CHILD*
49

James Welch
From *THE INDIAN LAWYER*
60

Pam Houston
"How to Talk to a Hunter"
80

Charles Bowden
From *DESIERTO*
87

Ivan Doig
From *RIDE WITH ME, MARIAH MONTANA*
108

Thomas McGuane
From *KEEP THE CHANGE*
124

Lisa Sandlin
"Invisible Powers"
145

Barbara Kingsolver
"Why I Am a Danger to the Public"
158

Linda Hogan
From *MEAN SPIRIT*
173

Robert Mayer
"The Dreams of Ada"
198

Gary Paul Nabhan
"Harvest Time" from *ENDURING SEEDS*
219

Denise Chávez
"The Last of the Menu Girls"
231

Tim Sandlin
From *SKIPPED PARTS*
255

Ron Carlson
"The H Street Sledding Record"
269

Joanne Greenberg
"Offering Up"
278

Russell Martin
From *BEAUTIFUL ISLANDS*
296

Terry Tempest Williams
"Whimbrels" from *REFUGE*
320

David Quammen
"Strawberries under Ice"
336

David Long
"The New World"
351

Notes on the Contributors
373

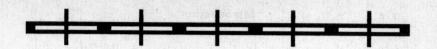

Introduction

The Navajos say they slipped into the world through a hollow reed high on the slopes of the Mountain Around Which Moving Was Done, better known nowadays as Hesperus Peak, tallest summit of the La Plata range in far southwestern Colorado. I have no quarrel with this claim, but neither can I say much about its veracity. I do know I entered the world through the rather more conventional route down at Mercy Hospital, 7,000 vertical feet and 15 horizontal miles off to the southeast. And although the Navajos have lived here roughly 500 years longer than I have, we share this much in common: none of us seems to be giving much thought to leaving.

I was born into this American outback during the last days of the administration of Harry Truman. This was not the absolute end of the earth back then, but it was close enough to make you sort of skittish. Back then, this Four Corners country didn't seem to be good for much besides passing through, and the kids who had the strange fortune to be born here grew up assuring themselves that once they had put in their eighteen years they could get away. Careers and culture and all those lusty, worldly women the magazines put you in mind of were parts of other, better places. You could encounter them in New York and in Chicago, couldn't you? Surely in mythic Los Angeles.

I don't remember being desperate to get away; I suppose I simply assumed that that would be the case. I'd be a *somebody*—sure I would—and somebodies didn't live in frowsy towns tacked onto the meager soil of a part of America that didn't matter. Life was elsewhere, it seemed, so I guess I grew up with my bags subconsciously packed. Yet except for some fortunate wanderings, I never did get away. Somehow, I never encountered that long-imagined place that mattered more than this one.

From the cabin on top of a rocky little bluff where I work (well, where I sit and type and very seldom get sweaty or run out of breath), I can see the outskirts of the town in which I grew up, bounded in the south by the high northern escarpment of Mesa Verde, its vertical cliffs suspending it above the valley that spreads and rolls below.

In the distant southwest are the low, dim summits of the Luka-chukais in Arizona and, closer at hand, the dark, sentinel hump of Ute Mountain, alone above the surrounding desert—a big, wonderful breast of a mountain that is part of Colorado, but only by inches. And in the east, draped now with the first autumn snow, the Mountain Around Which Moving Was Done and its companion peaks in the La Platas poke two and a half miles up into the cloud-scattered sky, sealing off the land that lies beyond them, keeping the rest of the world away.

I would be lying if I claimed that after all these years I still climb up the bluff and drink in the view like a tonic every morning, but there are those days when the light is low and glancing, or somehow the long cliff face of the mesa seems to have crawled a mile closer in the night, when I truly see this place's splendor. And every day, even when all I notice is that this is simply the same old place—forty years now of these relentless landforms—there is a kind of safety, a kind of groundedness in that recognition. *Oh yes, this place, I remember this place.* In a world with few constants, perhaps that is worth something in the end.

I don't mean to imply, however, that nothing has changed here in the four decades since Ike entered the White House. Oil and gas booms and busts, a burgeoning environmental movement, an influx of tourists, and the withering of a kind of hide-bound provincialism have brought this region—sometimes kicking and screaming—into the end of the twentieth century. It isn't the most isolated spot on the American map anymore, and, God knows, it's a place that's far from perfect.

The Anasazi, the first long-term inhabitants of this particular pocket of the American West, successfully survived and thrived here for more than a millennium before their society collapsed. The tenure of the Navajos has been half as long already, but the immigrant European attempt to create a civilization on this soil is little more than a century old. We haven't gotten very good at building towns—true communities—to date, and heaven knows we worked hard to subdue and scar our part of the wild West before some among us began to realize that we were in danger of destroying it. Agriculture is in trouble today, and mining is almost extinct. The oil business is trying to rebound from a battering bust, and tourism and a strange new industry they tend to call "retirement" seem to be the best hopes for some sort of sustained economy.

Kids still grow up here fashioning plans to leave. You cannot plan to become a biochemist or a ballet dancer and have any hope of living out your life between these mountains and the mesa. But you can become a doctor, a teacher, an archaeologist, or an engineer—even a farmer or a fellow who works cows from the back of a big-hearted horse—and still stake your allotted years to this rumpled and rock-sculpted region.

Or, if you're the sort of person who eschews honest work, you can simply sit on a bluff and write. When the words won't come and you're in danger of driving yourself crazy, you can walk outside and survey the territory: the valley dotted with cottonwood trees turning now from green to gold, scattered with fields and pastures, with too many trailer houses and too often too little hope; the proud, high hump in the west; the ragged line of cliffs in the south; and in the east, the snow-clad mountain you have always moved around, the mountain that reminds you of home.

The dry-dirt reality and the far more ephemeral *idea* of home are anchored to a wide variety of places for the writers of the interior West whose work is sampled in this collection. For some of them, home is a small and smoky university town cut by the cold Clark Fork in the mountains of far western Montana. Others are at home in and around a city that sprawls like a strange suburban oasis at the base of Arizona's sere Santa Catalina mountains, their *picacho* summits nearly as sharp-tipped as needles, their slopes stippled with saguaro cacti that are surely as old as time. Some are scattered among the squat piñon and juniper trees that drape the round shoulders of New Mexico's Sangre de Cristo range—the melodramatic Blood of Christ mountains—red and rich with pathos for a few moments at every sunset. One among this group, an immigrant into the mountain West, has come to, and considered, and made a home for herself in the tawny scrublands that roll between the Bighorns and the wind-swept Absarokas in a particularly unpeopled part of the unpopulous state of Wyoming. Another simply remains at home, like generations of Mormon forebears before her, beside a vast and salty inland sea, at the place that Brigham Young knew was the place where his people could shape and make a home.

These writers live in fabled contemporary towns: Jackson, Park City, and Santa Fe. They live in wide spots in the dusty road that really aren't much in the way of towns at all: places like Ajo, Kittredge, and McLeod. They live near creeks and rivers, some of them, that are alive with trout and the magic of moving water, streams that matter as much as family. They live near alpine peaks or fragrant hayfields or bold, bald-rock canyons, each of which offers its own sort of solace, its own peculiar ability to sustain and somehow offer refuge. One of this group—perhaps one of the best of them at limning the many ways in which this dry and often difficult region has come by now to be home—has lived in exile in soggy Seattle for some twenty years.

The interior West—the part of the West that encompasses the Rocky Mountains and the arid basins, plateaus, and plains that flank them on either side—is a place of many places, and you can't begin to pretend that it is one region, singular and homogenous unto itself. Just because you know you're at home, say, in the Douglas Fir forests of the Bitteroot range up by the Canadian border, it doesn't by any means follow that you'd belong as well in a cottonwood *bosque* beside the Rio Grande. Or imagine instead that home has always been a spot in southern Utah where the earth blew eastward to Colorado sometime before your time and all that remains is rock—striped and stunning and standing-up rock. If that were the case, you might not too readily settle down in Campbell or Crook or Weston counties, Wyoming, where only a single, spectacular, forever mysterious rock is exposed— the one called Devil's Tower—rising above the rolling steppe like a lighthouse.

The interior West—from northern Montana to southern New Mexico, from Idaho's thin panhandle to sonoran Arizona, from the big-basin heart of Nevada eastward up and over the twisting spine of the Rockies and into, but not too far into, the Dakotas, Nebraska, Kansas, and Oklahoma—is probably really three regions—or ten or twelve of them if you take your topography, your flora and your fauna fairly seriously. But let's say for simplicity's sake that the interior West includes the Northern Rockies, the desert Southwest, and a vast sort of transition zone that lies between them and somehow connects one to the other.

When you think of the Northern Rockies, think of upland country tending to be timbered and cut by ten thousand creeks, a wintery region, brooding oftentimes, evocative of the might of storms and the fireside security of shelter. Think of graying, well-built beaver-slides standing like sentinels in mowed pastures; think of high, cirque-bound snows that seldom melt. Of the southern terrain, imagine a place where green specifically means the presence of water—only a tiny, precious trickle of it, perhaps—and where otherwise only buffs and grays and browns color the country. Imagine rock, stacked up when the earth was young and exposed in adolescence, rock blanched by the midday sun yet grandly lit by glancing light at dawn and dusk. Imagine a kind of clean and well-kept emptiness; yet, too, a place where whatever is derelict seemingly lasts forever—a rabbit's bones or a fifties-era billboard. Think of a steel windmill, its rudder broken away, standing tall beside a tank that doesn't hold a trace of water; think of feeling thirsty.

The northern part of the region is a place that is curiously more communal than the south. It boasts better bars, a stronger tradition of support for organized labor, and decidedly more towns that look as though their residents take some pride in them than does the desert south. Grange halls, community centers, and little pioneer museums with donated homesteading displays are far more indicative of the north than of the sand-swept southern country, where the West's famed "rugged individualism" can take an almost misanthropic turn. In the Southwest, true communities are most often ethnic—the centuries-old pueblos of New Mexico, for instance, or the nearby villages first populated by Spanish immigrants whose tenure is almost as long. Otherwise down this way, we tend to live in a wonderful but often debilitating isolation from each other, and that holds true as much for those who live on Phoenix's mean and mighty hot streets as it does for the denizens of the distant back of beyond.

But if the northern and southern reaches of the interior West are so substantially different from each other, I can hear you asking, then why try to link them geographically or literarily? What can they truly claim in common? Well, it seems to me that the high, contorted ridgeline of the Continental Divide does tie together some essential similarities. It seems to me that these states held high by the Rockies do share common patterns of settlement by their indigenous peoples, similar patterns too of immigration and exploitation, and it appears certain as well that their futures hold similar fates.

First a kind of wonderland so sparsely populated that its people must have seemed somehow incidental, the interior West next felt the surge of seekers of fortune, people in search of riches of every sort: gold and grass, pelts, and, in later days, petroleum. The entire region, perhaps inevitably, became a kind of colony, a place whose wealth was channeled elsewhere and that suffered, therefore, a colony's classic sense of inferiority as well as its gnawing, troubled urge to assert its independence. For the people who became determined to stake a psychic claim to the region, to turn it into a home, that independence, that sense of separateness and *specialness*, was tied to the scale of the land, its immensity and its strange and rugged beauty. What it lacked in culture and community, what the West seemed unlikely ever to possess in the way of a spot on the nation's center stage, it made up for, north to south, with space, with room enough for its people to know—even in the midst of a life-long stream of calamities—a kind of niggard optimism, a sort of spatial hope.

At the close of the twentieth century, the West's frontier legacy of boom and bust still hasn't abated. Immigrants continue to barrel into the region, certain that it harbors those things that their lives have always lacked, and they continue, most of them, to end up disappointed. Western towns like the one I live nearby still swell with each new oil and gas discovery, with each new powerplant that somehow *has* to be built, then shrink back into a quiet and chronic depression once the quick gains have been gotten. The cities, the urban and suburban areas where most of the West's people actually live, continue to spread toward ever farther horizons, and the wilderness that once consumed this place continues to wither away. Yet somehow, despite the fact that many of its patterns continue unchanged, the West seems to be coming of age. Its people, and its contemporary writers in particular, I think, seem to realize that our mythic history—call it our cowboy heritage—simply isn't enough to hang our hats on forever. The colonial era is still far from over, but that doesn't seem to mean any longer that the West has to be trapped within a set of stifling colonial conventions. We're beginning to understand that we don't have to be in any sense one-dimensional—those of us who live amid this landscape—whether as awe-shucks kinds of cowboys or land-poor peasants who've never seen Pocatello, let alone Gay Paree, or as grease-stained roustabouts stuck on a God-forsaken rig somewhere out on the edge of the earth. Perhaps we've collectively lived here long enough now that we've proved to ourselves that we can be many things: artists, scientists, ascetics, even. And it seems certain now that we can fashion as many kinds of homes here as there is vast and varied land in which to set them.

In 1983, back when I wrote the introduction to the first *Writers of the Purple Sage* collection, the interior West appeared to be on the verge of an energy boom of such dramatic proportions that the region was sure to be utterly transformed. And it seemed to me then that the new western writers were "chronicling this uneasy shift, the sometimes melancholy slide of one epoch into another." Well, that boom quickly busted, as I and everyone else should have known it would, and I doubt very much now whether we have entered into an era that is entirely different from those that have come before it. Nine years following the publication of that first collection, it seems instead that what we've undergone is only a kind of welcome maturation, the realization that change is as constant here as the wind, and that people similarly have been lamenting the end of the West for 150 years, ever since the buffalo were slaughtered and the first rolls of barbed wire were strung across the grasslands. And instead of writing stories, novels, and memoirs that bemoan the crashing changes—its filling up with people and the shrinking of its space—it appears that the region's writers are paying rather more attention to the issue of home, at once simple and enormously complex, to the questions of why and how we stay anchored here despite that sweep of change.

As I began to collect pieces for a 1990s update of this anthology, one that might accurately reflect the current state of this sagebrush school of American literature, I wasn't concerned with themes or trends in subject matter or common kinds of perceptions among the many contributors. Diversity, in fact, seemed to be the only consideration of much editorial merit. I wanted the collection to reflect the geographic, ethnic, and stylistic diversity of the region's writers, to demonstrate as well that western stories aren't always set in bleak trailer houses, or in dark bars thick with smoke and macho pretensions, or in automobiles involved in desperate sorts of getaways out on lonesome highways. Some of these stories have those kinds of settings, to be sure; those places, those predicaments indeed are part of the contemporary western experience. But so too are stories set in an insular alpine monastery, in the dank wards of an Albuquerque hospital, in a southern New Mexico mining town polarized by a violent strike, even amidst the gentrified urban avenues of Salt Lake City—and those stories, too, are included here.

Among the few true requirements for this collection, it seemed essential that it include samplings of the work of the many writers who have immigrated into the interior West and made it a vital setting and subject for their work, as well as those writers who, for better or worse, were born here and somehow decided to stay; to spotlight the burgeoning number of women who are taking stock of this region and more fully defining it with their words; to make the case that the region's already renowned writers indeed deserve their reputations; and to demonstrate as well that a whole cadre of lesser known and even unknown writers are artists who are similarly possessed of substantial stuff. But curiously, as the collection came together (stories, novel excerpts, memoirs, and essays by eleven native writers and twelve immigrants into the region, written by nine women and fourteen men), a kind of thematic unity nonetheless did seem to emerge amid the otherwise eclectic mix.

A surprising number of these selections seem to be concerned, at heart, with that self-same question of home. There is, of course, the wonderful recollection by William Kittredge (the de facto dean of this group of contemporary western writers) of a personal place and time in which home meant "owning it all," and there are Gretel Ehrlich's linked stories concerned with the physical and psychic calamities of coming home to Wyoming at the end of World War II. The notion of home too is at the heart of the excerpt from Ivan Doig's most recent novel, a Winnebago-based peregrination around centennial Montana and an investigation into the kind of home it has become a hundred years after statehood; and home too is very much at issue in a piece from one of Tim Sandlin's wry, acerbic, off-beat novels, this one a coming-of-age, coming-cognizant story about a boy who wouldn't mind feeling like he belongs in a wacky western community where he's fairly certain he doesn't. David Quammen's eloquent explanation of ice floes and glaciation and how a particular place can somehow become "damn near humanly habitable" addresses the subject directly, as does an early chapter from Terry Tempest Williams's remarkable memoir about her mother's death, the drowning of a vital bird sanctuary, and the fundamental process of seeking refuge in the face of tragedy and tumult. Story after story, the selections seem to concern themselves not just with place, with prototypical *western* places, but also with the ways in which particular landscapes can and do crawl into your heart and make themselves immensely important, somehow essential, even as they often make you crazy—shelters, harbors, homes.

Two writers whose work was included in the first volume of this anthology—Edward Abbey and Norman Maclean—have died in the years since it was published. In a career that spanned three decades, Abbey's large, desert-devoted, boisterous body of work, together with his passionate, anarchist's persona, made him somehow larger than life, the West's one true contemporary literary legend. Maclean, a native Montanan whose professional life was spent almost entirely in the English department at the University of Chicago, serendipitously, almost magically, built his considerable reputation as a writer solely on the strength of a single book of stories, and on one virtually perfect story in particular. "A River Runs Through It," a first-person tale about fly-fishing and family, about art and discipline and grace, may not be matched by western writers—or writers anywhere—for a very long time to come. With the passing of these two men, two vital and widely resonant western voices sadly have been stilled.

Eleven other writers whose work helped shape that first collection are included here a second time: Rudolfo A. Anaya, Ivan Doig, Gretel Ehrlich, William Kittredge, David Long, Thomas McGuane, Robert

Mayer, N. Scott Momaday, David Quammen, and James Welch, their bodies of work expanding substantially and importantly during the intervening years. Twelve others, writers of great promise whose careers are just beginning, as well as several veteran writers who are authors of many books, are included for the first time, and it is a particular pleasure to present samples of their work: Charles Bowden, Ron Carlson, Denise Chávez, Joanne Greenberg, Linda Hogan, Pam Houston, Barbara Kingsolver, Deirdre McNamer, Gary Paul Nabhan, Lisa Sandlin, Tim Sandlin (unrelated and a thousand miles separate), and Terry Tempest Williams.

Missing from this collection, because physical constraints prevent it from matching the true breadth of the region's writing community, are well-established, well-respected writers such as Ralph Beer, Olive Ghiselin, William Hjortsberg, John Nichols, Alan Prendergast, Jim Sagel, Leslie Marmon Silko, Annick Smith, Stephen Trimble, and Ann Zwinger. Newer writers such as Rick Bass, Sandra Dallas, and Douglas Peacock, who, it already seems certain, will produce many fine books among them, are missing as well and their absence is equally lamentable. Sadly, mystery writers such as Rex Burns, James Crumley, and Tony Hillerman couldn't be included here, nor could important regional poets like Joy Harjo, Simon Ortiz, and Robert Wrigley; and absent too are writers with strong connections to this western country whose lives and work are now focused elsewhere: Rick DeMarinis, Richard Ford, Patricia Henley, Marilynne Robinson, and Elizabeth Tallent. And there are many more, of course. And lists like these do none of the writers any justice, except to point out vividly how rich this sagebrush school is, flush with lyrical voices that describe the look and the lay of the western land, the convoluted, crazy, and yet still splendid lives its people lead—their anglings toward answers and the certainty that answers are hard to come by.

Bill Kittredge—our grand old literary man, as I have mentioned, a teller of sparkling tales who somehow sizes up this region in ways that tend to leave the rest of us a little dazzled—wrote not long ago that "if you wanted to know why I live in Montana, I would tell you it was because Montana is the place where I feel most securely connected to luck." Although we have corresponded from time to time, I've never met Bill Kittredge. An awful lot of territory separates the two of us: him up in the fir-forested northern country where gaunt gray clouds scud across the landscape for fully half of every year, me down on the cusp of the great and sere southwestern deserts. Yet he and I are near neighbors nonetheless, citizens of the same plundered but still open and still optimistic province, similar practitioners too of the tenuous business of linking words in the hope of something transcendent. And I think I know what he means about being connected to luck in our separate western places. I think it has something to do with understanding that coming to terms with a particular piece of the planet, coming to depend on it like some difficult but steadfast lover, letting it take you in with a knowing and forgiving kind of comfort, is about all any of us can hope for come the end of the complicated day. I think luck is a lot like home.

—R.M.
Dolores, Colorado

New
Writers of
the Purple Sage

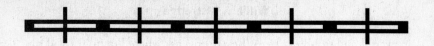

WILLIAM KITTREDGE

Home

I

In the long-ago land of my childhood we clearly understood the high desert country of southeastern Oregon as the actual world. The rest of creation was distant as news on the radio.

In 1945, the summer I turned thirteen, my grandfather sentenced his chuckwagon cow outfit to a month of haying on the IXL, a little ranch he had leased from the Sheldon Antelope Refuge in Nevada. Along in August we came in to lunch one noontime, and found the cook, a woman named Hannah, flabbergasted by news that some bomb had just blown up a whole city in Japan. Everybody figured she had been into the vanilla extract, a frailty of cooks in those days. As we know, it was no joke. Nagasaki and then VJ Day. We all listened to that radio. Great changes and possibilities floated and cut in the air. But such far-off strange events remained the concern of people who lived in cities. We might get drunk and celebrate, but we knew such news really had nothing to do with us. Not in the far outback of southeastern Oregon.

When I came home from the Air Force in 1958, I found our backland country rich with television from the Great World. But that old attitude from my childhood, the notion that my people live in a separate kingdom where they own it all, secure from the world, is still powerful and troublesome. When people ask where I'm from I still say southeastern Oregon, expecting them to understand my obvious pride.

Jack Ray was one of the heroes of my boyhood. A slope-shouldered balding little man, Jack dominated the late rough-house craziness at our mid-July country dances. The Harvest Moon Ball.

"He can hit like a mule kicking," my father used to say after those dances, winking at us kids and grinning at my mother's back while she served up a very late Sunday breakfast of steak and fried mush and biscuits and thick sausage gravy.

At that time I was maybe five or six years old, and I would have been asleep in the back seat of our car for a couple of hours when the shouting and fighting started around midnight. So I recall those scenes with a newly awakened child's kind of strobe-light clarity, a flash here and there, all illuminated in the headlights of 1930s automobiles. The ranch women would be crowded outside onto the porch where they could see, some wife weeping, the men out closer to the battle in the parking lot, passing bottles.

But what I see mainly is Jack Ray getting up off the ground, wiping a little trickle of blood from the corner of his mouth, glancing down at the smear on his hand, his eyes gone hard while some sweating farm boy moved at him again; and torn shirts, the little puffs of dust their feet kicked there in the headlights. At that point my memory goes fragile. There is some quick slippery violence, and the farm boy is on his knees. Jack Ray is standing above him, waiting, wheezing as he breathes.

It's over, everybody knows, and soon it is. Two more grunting punches, and the farm boy is down again, and Jack Ray steps back, his eyes gone soft and almost bewildered in the light as a little shudder moves through the crowd, and someone shouts, and the bottles pass again. I see Jack Ray, there in those headlights, smiling like a child now that it's finished, the farm boy up on his knees, shaking his head.

No harm done, the air clear. I see it over and over, summer dance after summer dance. I see the kind of heroism my boyhood educated me to understand and respect.

And I hate the part that comes next. I grew up and ran the haying and combine crews on our ranch, and there eventually came a time when I hired Jack Ray to work for me. He had worked a lot of seasons for my father, and such men always had a job with us. Jack was maybe fifty by that time, and crippled by his life, the magic gone, a peaceable man who seemed to have turned a little simple. He did what he could, chores around the cook house, and once in a while he drank. After a bout in town which earned him some time in the county jail, he would show up grinning in the bunkhouse. "Well, hell, Jack," I would say, "it's a new day."

"Kid," he would say, "she's a new world every morning."

Looking backward is one of our main hobbies here in the American West, as we age. And we are aging, which could mean we are growing up. Or not. It's a difficult process for a culture which has always been so insistently boyish. Jack Ray has been dead a long time now. As my father said, he drank his liver right into the ground. "But, by God," my father said, "he was something once."

Possibility is the oldest American story. Head west for freedom and the chance of inventing a spanking new life for yourself. Our citizens are always leaping the traces when their territory gets too small and cramped.

Back in the late '50s, living with my wife and our small children in our little cattle-ranch house, when things would get too tight on a rainy Sunday afternoon in November I always had the excuse of work. "I got to go out," I would say, and I would duck away to the peacefulness of driving the muddy fields and levee banks in my old Ford pickup. Or, if the roads were too bad, I would go down to the blacksmith shop and bang on some damned thing.

Whenever I find myself growing grim about the mouth; whenever it is damp, drizzly November in my soul; whenever I find myself involuntarily pausing before coffin warehouses, and bringing up the rear of every funeral I meet. . . . Then he runs away to sea. *Ishmael.*

". . . lighting out for territory," says Huckleberry Finn, with his broken-hearted optimism, right at the end of his get-away down the Mississippi.

And it wasn't just the run-away boys in books. John Colter left Ohio at the age of thirty, to head up the Missouri with Lewis and Clark in 1804. He stayed west another five years, earning his keep as a fur trapper in pursuit of the beaver. One fearsome Montana winter he took a legendary walk from Fort Lisa on the Yellowstone, traveling through what is Yellowstone Park to circumnavigate the Tetons—about a thousand miles on snowshoes through country where no white man had ever been before. A thing both wondrous and powerful drove him. Maybe it was a need so simple as being out, away.

Imagine those shining snowy mountains burning against the sheltering endless bowl of clean sky, and Colter alone there in Jackson Hole. We will not see such things again, not any of us, ever. It's gone. We know it is. Only one man ever got to be Colter. Not even Bridger or Joe Meek or Jedediah Smith had a world so absolutely to themselves. Except for some natives, who maybe never thought they were alone.

In 1836 Narcissa and Marcus Whitman came west with Eliza and Henry Spalding. The first white women had crossed the Rockies. Along the way they witnessed one of the last fur-trapper rendezvous, on the Green River in Wyoming. Think of those Presbyterian women among the inhabitants of wilderness. Less than ten years later Marcus Whitman was leading one of the first wagon-trains west from St. Louis to the Oregon country.

The New York newspaper editor Andrew Greely worried about the exodus, wondering what those families could be seeking, leaving behind the best of climates and agricultural lands, schools and churches and markets: "For what, then, do they brave the desert, the wilderness, the savage, the snowy precipices of the Rocky Mountains, the early summer march, the storm-drenched bivouac, and the gnawings of famine? Only to fulfill their destiny! There is probably not one among them whose outward circumstances will be improved by this perilous pilgrimage."

Anybody sensible, Greely suggested, would stop ". . . this side of the jumping-off place." The only practice stupider than such migration, he said, was suicide.

It's easy to understand his puzzlement. The wagon-trains were predominantly middle-class ventures. Poor folks couldn't afford a wagon, much less provisions. The basic outfitting cost up toward a thousand dollars. And in those long-gone days that was some real money. But seemingly sensible people persisted in selling their good farms, and heading west.

Imagine half the population of Ohio picking up sticks, selling out, and heading for one of our latter-day mythological frontiers, Alaska or Australia. Greely was right, it was crazy, it was a mania.

What was pushing them? Lots of things. Among them a quite legitimate fear of mortal corruption and death. Cholera. By the spring of 1849 an epidemic had reached St. Louis. Ten percent of the population died of the disease. The road west from Independence was likened to traveling through a graveyard.

But mostly, we have to believe, they were lured West by promises. Promises of paradise for the taking. Free land, crystalline water, great herds of game roaming the natural meadowlands, good fishing, gold, all in unfettered abundance, a new world every morning.

What compelled men to believe promises of paradise on earth with such simpleminded devotion? Well, for openers, a gut yearning for the chance of becoming someone else, and freedom from the terrible weight of responsibilities, freedom too often equaling free, without cost.

My own great-grandfather on my father's side left Michigan in 1849 to travel down the Mississippi and across to Panama, where he hiked west through the jungles on the route Balboa had blazed, and caught a ship north to California and the gold camps. After a long and bootless career of chasing mineral trace in the mountain streams, first in the central Sierra and then up around the foothills of Mount Shasta, he gave it up and turned to ranching and school teaching in one place after another around the Northwest, until in 1897 he died white-trash poor in the sagebrush backlands near Silver Lake, Oregon, leaving a family determined to shake his suicidal despair.

It wasn't just the gold that he never found—such instant boomer riches were to have been only the beginning. The green and easy dreamland fields of some home place were to have been the ultimate reward for his searching, the grape arbor beside the white house he would own outright, where he could rest out some last serene years while the hordes of grandchildren played down across the lawns by the sod-banked pond where the tame ducks swam and fed and squawked in their happy, idiot way. The pastoral heaven on this earth—some particular secret and heart's-desire version of it—has time and again proved to be the absolute heart in American dreams. All this we promise you.

2

Childhood, it has been said, is always partly a lie of poetry. When I was maybe eight years old, in the fall of the year, I would have to go out in the garden after school with damp burlap sacks, and cover the long rows of cucumber and tomato plants, so they wouldn't freeze.

It was a hated, cold-handed job which had to be done every evening. I day-dreamed along in a half-hearted, distracted way, flopping the sacks onto the plants, sorry for myself and angry because I was alone at my boring work. No doubt my younger brother and sister were in the house and warm. Eating cookies.

But then a great strutting bird appeared out from the dry remnants of our corn, black tail feathers flaring and a monstrous yellow-orange air-sack pulsating from its white breast, its throat croaking with popping sounds like rust in a joint.

The bird looked to be stalking me with grave slow intensity, coming after me from a place I could not understand as real, and yet quite recognizable, the sort of terrifying creature which would sometimes spawn in the incoherent world of my night-dreams. In my story, now, I say it looked like death, come to say hello. Then, it was simply an apparition.

The moment demanded all my boyish courage, but I stood my ground, holding one of those wet sacks out before me like a shield, stepping slowly backwards, listening as the terrible creature croaked, its bright preposterous throat pulsating—and then the great bird flapped its wings in an angry way, raising a little commonplace dust.

It was the dust, I think, that did it, convincing me that this could not be a dream. My fear collapsed, and I felt foolish as I understood this was a creature I had heard my father talk about, a courting sage-grouse, we called them prairie chickens. This was only a bird, and not much interested in me at all. But for an instant it had been both phantom and real, the thing I deserved, come to punish me for my anger.

For that childhood moment I believed the world to be absolutely inhabited by an otherness which was utterly demonic and natural, not of my own making. But soon as that bird was enclosed in a story which defined it as a commonplace prairie chicken, I was no longer frightened. It is a skill we learn early, the art of inventing stories to explain away the fearful sacred strangeness of the world. Storytelling and make-believe, like war and agriculture, are among the arts of self-defense, and all of them are ways of enclosing otherness and claiming ownership.

Such emblematic memories continue to surface, as I grow older and find ways to accept them into the fiction of myself. One of the earliest, from a time before I ever went to school, is of studying the worn oiled softwood flooring in the Warner Valley store where my mother took me when she picked up the mail three times a week. I have no idea how many years that floor had been tromped and dirtied and swept, but by the time I recall it was worn into a topography of swales and buttes, traffic patterns and hard knots, much like the land, if you will, under the wear of a glacier. For a child, as his mother gossiped with the post-mistress, it was a place, high ground and valleys, prospects and sanctuaries, and I in my boredom could invent stories about it—finding a coherency I loved, a place which was mine. They tore up that floor somewhere around the time I started school, and I had the sense to grieve.

The coherency I found worn into those floorboards was mirrored a few years later, just before the war began, when I was seven or eight, in the summertime play of my brother and sister and cousins and myself, as we laid out roads to drive and rectangular fields to work with our toy trucks in the dirt under the huge old box elder which also functioned as a swing tree near the kitchen door to our house. It was a little play world we made for ourselves, and it was, we believed, just like the vast world beyond. In it we imitated the kind of ordering we watched each spring while our father laid out the garden with such measured precision, and the kind of planning we could not help but sense while riding with him along the levee banks in his dusty Chevrolet pickup truck. All the world we knew was visible from the front porch of our house, inside the valley, and all the work he did was directed toward making it orderly, functional, and productive—and of course that work seemed sacred.

Our play ended when a small rattlesnake showed up in our midst, undulating in sweeping little curving lines across our dusty make-believe fields. A young woman who cooked for my mother killed the snake in a matter-of-fact way with a shovel. But the next spring my mother insisted, and my father hauled in topsoil and planted the packed dirt, where we had played at our toylike world of fields, into a lawn where rattlesnakes would never come. We hated him for it.

These stories suggest reasons why, during childhood winters through the Second World War, such an important segment of my imagination lived amid maps of Europe and the Pacific. Maps delineated the dimensions of that dream which was the war for me, maps and traced drawings of aircraft camouflaged for combat. I collected them like peacetime city boys collect baseball cards, and I colored them in with crayons, my far South Pacific and Europe invaded and shaped by dreams and invisible forces I could not hope to make sense of in any other way.

In the spring of 1942, just before I turned ten years old, we opened every first-period class in our one-room Warner Valley schoolhouse singing *Praise the Lord and Pass the Ammunition*. We embraced the war. We heard it every morning on the Zenith Trans-Oceanic radio, while we got ready for school, and during recess we ran endless games of gunfighter pursuit and justifiably merciless death in the playgrounds. Mostly we killed Hitler and Mister Tojo.

Fall down, you're dead.

When it came your turn to play Nazi, you were honor bound to eventually fall killed through the long adult agony, twisting and staggering to heedless collapse in the dirt. Out in our land-locked, end-of-the-road, rancher valley, the air was bright and clean with purpose.

Always, at least in memory, those running battles involve my cousins and my younger brother and my even younger sister, and a black-and-white dog named Victory. Out back of the house in the summer of 1942 we circled and shot our ways through groves of wild plum in heavy fruit, and we swung to ambush from gnarled limbs in the apple orchard where the blue flies and the yellowjackets were mostly interested in having their way with the rotting fallen fruit: yellowjackets flitting to a hive in the hollow trunk of a Lombardy poplar along the irrigation ditch, burning the air with their going, and near to the secret, stinging, irreligious heart of my paradise.

In late September our dog named Victory was crushed under the rear duals of a semi-truck flatbed hauling hundred-pound burlap sacks of my father's newly combined oats across forty twisting miles of gravel road over the Warner Mountains to town and the railroad. My sister ran shrieking to the kitchen door, and my mother came to the roadside in her apron, and I was stoic and tough-minded as that poor animal panted and died. *Beyond the crystal sea, undreamed shores, precious angels.*

This was a time when our national life was gone to war against U-boats and Bataan and the death march, betrayal reeking everywhere. The death of that dog with cockleburrs matted into his coat must have shimmered with significance past heartbreak. We were American and proud, and we were steeled to deal with these matters.

So we unearthed a shallow grave in the good loam soil at the upper end of the huge rancher garden my father laid out each spring in those days, before it became cheaper to feed our crews from truckloads of canned goods bought wholesale in the cities. We gathered late-blooming flowers from the border beneath my mother's bedroom window, we loaded the stiffening carcass of that dead dog on a red wagon, and we staged a funeral with full symbolic honors.

My older cousin blew taps through his fist, my brother hid his face, and my six-year-old sister wept openly, which was all right since she was a little child. I waved a leafy bough of willow over the slope-sided grave while my other cousins shoveled the loose dry soil down on the corpse.

It is impossible to know what the child who was myself felt, gazing east across the valley which I can still envision so clearly—the ordered garden and the sage-covered slope running down to the slough-cut meadows of the Thompson Field, willows there concealing secret hideaway places where I would burrow away from the world for hours, imagining I was some animal, hidden and watching the stock cows graze the open islands of meadow grass.

On the far side of the valley lay the great level distances of the plow-ground fields which had so recently been tule swamps, reaching to the rise of barren eastern ridges. That enclosed valley is the home I imagine walking when someday I fall into the dream which is my death. My real, particular, vivid and populated solace for that irrevocable moment of utter loss when the mind stops forever. The chill of that remembered September evening feels right as I imagine that heartbreakingly distant boy.

It's hard for me to know where I got the notion of waving that willow branch over our burial of that poor dog unless I find it in this other memory, from about the same time. A Paiute girl of roughly my own age died of measles in the ramshackle encampment her people main-tained alongside the irrigation ditch which eventually led to our vast garden. A dozen or so people lived there, and true or not, I keep thinking of them as in touch with some remnant memories of hunting and gathering forebears who summered so many generations in the valley we had so recently come to own.

In the fall of 1890 a man named James Mooney went west under the auspices of the Bureau of Ethnology to investigate the rise of Native American religious fervor which culminated in the massacre at Wounded Knee on December 29. In Mooney's report, *The Ghost Dance Religion and the Sioux Outbreak of 1890*, there is a statement delivered by a Paiute man named Captain Dick at Fort Bidwell in Surprise Valley—right in the home territory I am talking about, at the junction on maps where California and Nevada come together at the Oregon border.

All Indians must dance, everywhere, keep on dancing. Pretty soon in the next spring Big Man come. He bring back game of every kind. The game be thick everywhere. All dead Indians come back and live again. They all be strong just like young men, be young again. Old blind Indians see again and get young and have fine time. When the Old Man comes this way, then all the Indians go to the mountains, high up away from the whites. Whites can't hurt the Indians then. Then while Indians way up high, big flood comes like water and all white people die, get drowned. After that water go away and then nobody but Indians everywhere game all kinds thick. Then medicine-man tell Indians to send word to all Indians to keep up dancing and the good time will come. Indians who don't dance, who don't believe in this word, will grow little, just about a foot high, and stay that way. Some of them will turn into wood and will be burned in the fire.

In the 1950s and '60s a Paiute named Conlan Dick lived in a cabin on our ranch in Warner Valley, and helped to look after the irrigation and fences. Conlan was reputed to be a kind of medicine-man in our local mythology, related to the man who delivered that statement. His wife, whose name I cannot recall, did ironing for women in the valley. And there was a son, a young man named Virgil Dick, who sometimes came to Warner for a few weeks and helped his father with the field work.

In the early 1960s my cousin, the one who blew taps through his fist in 1942, was riding horseback across the swampy spring meadows alongside Conlan. He asked if Virgil was Conlan's only child.

Conlan grinned. "Naw," he said. "But you know, those kids, they play outside, and they get sick and they die."

Story after story. Is it possible to claim that proceeding through some incidents in this free-associative manner is in fact a technique, a way of discovery? Probably. One of our model narrators these days is the patient spinning and respinning the past and trying to resolve it into a story that makes sense.

". . . they get sick and they die." Once I had the romance in me to think that this was the mature comment of a man who had grown up healed into wholeness and connection with the ways of nature to a degree I would never understand. Now I think it was more likely the statement of a man trying to forget his wounds—so many of which were inflicted by schoolyard warriors like us. A healthy culture could never have taught him to forgo sorrow.

In any event, Captain Dick's magic was dead.

All these stories are part of my own story about a place called Home, and a time in which I imagined we owned it all. The girl who died was named Pearl. I recall her name with that particular exactness which occasionally hovers in memories. She was of enormous interest to us because she so obviously disdained our foolish play with make-believe weapons and miniature trucks. Or so it seemed. Maybe she was only shy, or had been warned away from us. But to our minds she lived with adults and shared in the realities of adult lives in ways we did not, and now she was being paid the attention of burial.

Try to imagine their singing that spring morning. I cannot. I like to think our running brigade of warrior children might have been touched by dim sorrow-filled wailing in the crystalline brightness of her morning, but the memory is silent.

Maybe it's enough to recall the sight of people she loved, carrying her elaborately clothed body in an open home-built casket. Not that we saw it up close, or that we ever really saw a body, clothed or un-clothed.

They were making their slow parade up a sandy path through the sagebrush to her burial in the brushy plot, loosely fenced with barbed wire, which we knew as the "Indian Graveyard." I see them high on the banking sand-hill behind our house, and beyond them the abrupt two-thousand-foot lift of rimrock which forms the great western lip of our Warner Valley. That rim is always there, the table of lava-flow at the top breaking so abruptly, dropping through long scree-slopes clustered with juniper. As I grow older it is always at my back. The sun sets there, summer and winter. I can turn and squint my eyes, and see it.

From the flowering trees in the homesteader's orchard behind our house we watched that astonishing processional through my father's binoculars, and then we ran out through the brush beyond the garden, tasting the perfect spring morning and leaping along the small animal trails, filled with thrilling purpose, and silent and urgent. We had to be closer.

The procession was just above us on the sandy trail when we halted, those people paying us no mind but frightening us anyway, mourning men and women in their dark castaway clothing and bright blankets and strange robes made of animal skins, clutching at spring blossoms and sweeping at the air with thick sheaves of willow in new leaf. It is now that I would like to hear the faint sing-song of their chanting. I would like to think we studied them through the dancing waves of oncoming heat, and found in them the only models we had ever had for such primal ceremonies.

But this keeps becoming fiction. Ours was a rising class of agricultural people, new to that part of the world, too preoccupied with an endless ambition toward perfection in their work to care at all for any tradition of religion. No one in our immediate families had ever died, and no one ever would so far as we knew. None of us, in those days, had any interest in religion or ritual.

So I have this story of those shrouded people proceeding through my imagination. I feel them celebrating as that young girl entered into the ripe fruit of another paradise, lamenting the dole-food exigencies of their own lives, some of them likely thinking she was lucky to have escaped.

But I don't really have much idea what was going on behind the story I've made of that morning. It was as if those people were trailing along that sandy path toward tomorrow-morrow land themselves. Some of them, somewhere, are likely still alive.

In a book called *Shoshone*, the poet Ed Dorn tells of interviewing an ancient man and woman in a trailer house on the Duck Valley Reservation, a couple of hundred miles east of us but still deep in the high basin and range desert, along the border between Idaho and Nevada. They were both more than one hundred years old, and told Dorn they had never heard of white men until past the age of thirty. Which is possible.

It's easy to imagine those ancient people grinning in what looks to be a toothless old way in their aluminum-sided trailer house, with screens on the windows, on the Duck Valley Reservation. They must have understood the value of stories. Dorn says they demanded cartons of cigarettes before they allowed themselves to be photographed. The point is, they were willing to be part of any make-believe anybody could invent for them, willing to tell their stories and let us make of them what we could. But not for nothing. Stories are valuable precisely to the degree that they are for the moment useful in our ongoing task of finding coherency in the world, and those old people must have known that whatever story Dorn was imagining was worth at least the price of some smokes.

My father's catskinners bulldozed the shacktown Indian camp with its willow-roofed ramada into a pile of old posts and lumber, and burned it, after the last of those people had gone to wherever they went. Our children? In the fall of 1942, the same year that girl named Pearl was buried, they learned something about the emotional thrust of a warrior code as the news from the Zenith Trans-Oceanic radio was translated into singing in first-period music class, and they loaded that dead dog named Victory in a red wagon, and trailed him toward burial at the upper end of the garden. And I waved sweeps of willow over the ceremony while my cousin blew taps through his fist.

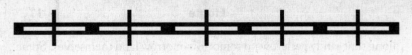

GRETEL EHRLICH

Madeleine's Day

From DRINKING DRY CLOUDS

I don't know what took me over that September day—the day Henry came home from being a prisoner of war in Japan—but I sped off on my horse and hid behind a hill. It was a cruel thing to do and perhaps my cruelty did not end there since it has a way of striking again and again. He had not come straight home from the Camp, but from the decks of the ship, *Missouri*, where he and other officers witnessed the signing of the surrender, then stateside from a Seattle hospital. What I'm getting at is that I was expecting him to be in better shape than he was, but that's getting ahead of the story.

As soon as I saw him standing at the gate and heard his two-fingered whistle, I hurried back to him, yet when we finally embraced, his presence was like a wind trying to blow me away. Was it his fear or mine? I don't know, but no matter what we did we could not seem to get close. For months I had been rehearsing our first night together, our first meal. That's what four years of war reduces you to—menus and place settings—but I finally decided on T-bone steaks, fried potatoes with a little onion, the wild asparagus I picked last spring and a lemon meringue pie.

After he put his things down, he followed me into the kitchen. I had already sweated two half moons into my shirt because there was nothing and everything to talk about. It either sounded too trivial or too serious for the first night at home. I took up the slack by cooking.

14

When it came time to eat he was hungry but couldn't make himself cut into the steak.

"I haven't had anything like this for a long time," he said. "I want it, but my stomach's afraid."

I guess I hadn't anticipated this problem, in fact I hadn't anticipated anything at all. His coming home was all that had mattered, and it was only natural to welcome him with a big spread because less would have seemed paltry.

He ate a few forkfuls, smiled at me, slowly pushed away, and threw up halfway to the back door.

That was the first and last time for many months that we tried to have a real dinner. What was wrong with me, why hadn't I known it would be like this?

I cooked up some rice and chicken broth and fed him in bed like a baby. After, he slept and I sat at the kitchen table and ate my enormous, stupid meal alone.

For the next few months I couldn't bring myself to share the same bed. That first night I stayed up late and thumbed through our old wedding pictures, though I knew it was into the future I should have been looking. My mother had warned me about "re-entry problems" which she said I must face with the same bravery I'd faced running the ranch alone, but I found this more difficult by far.

I slept on the couch then went out early the next morning to move cows. It was time to start bringing them closer to the ranch for winter. On my return I found Henry waiting for me, showered and dressed, thin and pale.

"I'm sorry about last night," he said. "It was a magnificent dinner. It's what I would have asked for."

He wanted to ride so I caught a horse, a gentle one I had bought during the war, and we rode out to the pasture so he could see the cattle. It occurred to me that many of these mother cows had been born while he was away. As he asked me about them, who their mother had been and where I'd bought bulls, it was like having a visitor at the ranch. Nothing of the old feeling was there, of the shared effort it takes to bring a herd along through winter and calving and summer storms. Only one thought ran through my head: these were the cattle McKay and I had raised.

Henry was too weak to ride fourteen-hour days in bad weather, and I had no idea how long that would go on. So he occupied his days making my small vegetable garden into a bigger one, hauling wheelbarrows of manure one by one and raking it in. One day he worked right through a September storm, heavy snow breaking branches all around and no matter how much time he put in, it would be eight months before he could plant seeds. He looked like a living skeleton.

It was then that I understood why war zones are called "theatres" because they frame a kind of play acting or, worse, deceit, that can stain a human life forever: the deceit of hate on hearsay—hating an enemy one doesn't know—and the deceit of a disrupted marriage inside of which a dark cavity grows. Yet, as the weeks went by I think I gained patience because I knew that in the natural geography of a marriage, love goes all over the place and the vows suspend disbelief until two people hook up again or go their separate ways.

One day I rode in early. The sky had been clouding over and a cold wind was pushing down from the Arctic. Henry always said he could hear the polar bears yawning when a north wind blew. But that day it was only him I heard.

"Don't come in here," he yelled as I opened the gate.

He was weeping, not in short bursts but in a low drone. I went to him anyway. He had on only a T-shirt, and it had begun to snow. I held him for a long time. He wedged the hoe between us as if to fend me off, to drive comfort away.

"So many of them died no matter what I did," he said. But that was all.

It was around Thanksgiving when I found the food he had been hoarding under the bed: peanut butter, crackers, canned goods, coffee. Since that day in the garden I learned he and the other men had bribed a guard for vegetable seeds and grown a huge garden at the Camp and had been responsible for keeping everyone, guards and prisoners both, from starving. I didn't say anything about the food. What difference did it make? The slightest misunderstanding might upset his progress. He'd just begun to fill out his clothes.

At least that's what I thought was right, when truly, I had no idea. Nine weeks had gone by since he had come home. That's a long time to live with a stranger. Finally, I called Bobby Korematsu because he knew how to take care of people. McKay answered the phone. His voice surprised me and my face flushed. We hadn't talked for a long time.

"At least you could come over and see me once in a while," he said.

"I know. I'm sorry. It's just that Henry's not doing too well."

"You better come then," he said, and I did, that very day.

I wanted to take Henry because he had seen McKay only once and they had been—despite everything—such good friends, but Henry said, "No, you go." Maybe that's when the cruelty began, because I went ahead without him. He watched me leave, his hands and chin resting on the hoe handle. When I ran over to blow him a kiss, the skin around his eyes tightened. Was he the prisoner and I the guard? How easily he acquiesced, but what could I expect? He had not known anything else for four years.

It felt good to drive fast. I knew the dirt track between our ranch and McKay's without having to think. I opened the windows, unsnapped my jacket and breathed in the chilled air. Home, I'm going home, I found myself thinking . . .

Bobby was nowhere to be found, nor was McKay. Champ's blue roan was in the corral. He eyed me, arched his neck and snorted. Then McKay appeared and before I knew what was happening we were laughing and hugging and I pushed my knee between his legs.

"Ain't you a sight for sore eyes," he said.

"Ain't?"

"Don't start that . . ." he said, winking.

"Why are your eyes sore?" I asked. "Who have you been looking at?"

"Heifers," he said. "The kind with four legs."

Then we embraced, only this time I wasn't laughing and a hard knot came all the way up through my body from my stomach into my throat like an old cow's cud made of tears. I bit my lip.

"Come on inside," McKay said, gently leading me into the house as he had done that night so many years ago, the night I found out Henry had been taken prisoner of war.

McKay poured coffee and added a shot of brandy. I watched him watch me drink. He saw into me. I said I missed him which is what we always say to each other, only usually, it's him saying it to me.

Are we so weak-hearted that we can only dive backward to what we know, to what we were? Or was history twisting me like a flower following the sun of McKay? Bobby never did come back that afternoon, and I'm not sure if I can say what happened. In some ways nothing did and that was the beauty of it. Since the end of the war, the whole world had become addicted to resuming normality. Few of us had been able to keep up the pace. "Normal times" were always a couple of lengths away and we secretly knew our valiant efforts had been failures.

I'd thought certain things had come to an end in my life, specifically, the cat-and-mouse game I'd always played with McKay, and in a way it had. But something else had taken its place, something even now I'm not sure of. Before, I was always reacting to him: pulling away or throwing myself into his life. Now, we were both too tired for such things.

That afternoon we sat quietly together at the kitchen table, nothing else. Yet, I felt I belonged there. McKay was his usual brooding, beautiful self. The wind howled and the stovepipe rattled in the ceiling. After a long time, he started pacing, circling me noiselessly as if marking out on the floor the distance that had kept us apart, trying to trample it away.

I left at four in the afternoon. I'd already been gone longer than I should have, and it was beginning to snow.

I found Henry in the bathroom. In front of him were boxes of food, opened, half-eaten. He gave me a fearful look as if I might scold him. I don't know how long I stood there staring at him and he at me, like two deer frozen in front of headlights. I remembered his story about being parachuted onto an island with no food. How in his hours of waiting for the maneuver to begin, he drew pictures of roasts and pies in the sand with a stick because it was Christmas Day.

He stuck his hand into a jar and took out a handful of pickled beans. When he offered them to me, I could no longer contain myself and burst out laughing.

"I'm hungry," he said in a small voice. Had my laughter hurt him?

I went into the kitchen and brought back a pie, a round of Swiss cheese, a loaf of homemade bread, and carved bite-sized pieces of each, lowering myself down on the bathroom floor so that our legs were entwined and facing each other this way, we ate. The dogs scratched on the door. They wanted to join in so we let them.

"This tastes so good," Henry said, our eyes locked, mouths full of food, we trembled with laughter, trying not to choke.

Finally, he was still. His green eyes softened. When I opened my arms, he leaned toward me, almost falling as if I was sky and he was jumping from a plane.

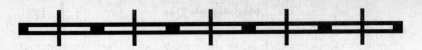

GRETEL EHRLICH

McKay

From DRINKING DRY CLOUDS

The day after Pinkey's funeral I had the Rural Electric lineman come out to the ranch and hook us back up to electricity. I was tired of dim rooms and old-fashioned ways. That had to do with the war years and the strange happiness I felt, with the way having less turns into surfeit, and the crazy love was offered and taken without thought for the next day. Now I'm trying to get a new start with my brothers home and in the absence of Pinkey, Madeleine and Mariko, and I thought having things lit up a little brighter might be one way.

But this morning the lights went off. Bobby and I fiddled with the switch and the fuse but to no avail. We called the lineman and he came back out only to say nothing was wrong because when he flicked the switch, the lights came on. Later, Bobby heard a crash in the dining room: a window had blown open and all the bottles in the liquor cabinet had tipped sideways. This evening the lights went out again. Bobby, Champ, Ted, and I were eating when the room went dark. "The sonofabitch is haunted," Champ finally said, pushing his chair back from the table. I got up to look around but what was there to look for? Then I found that one of the fuses was dead, so I replaced it and we had lights again.

Just before I went to bed that night I had an idea. I went to the liquor cabinet, poured a shotglass of Cobb's Creek and set it out on

20

the table because I had the distinct feeling that Pinkey was messing around. "How can you be so much trouble even when you're dead?" I asked aloud looking heavenward which was probably the wrong direction to look, and from that night on I always kept the whiskey glass filled.

That was the first night of the big storm, hard winds filled with snow. Forty inches fell in the first week followed by twenty more, followed by seven, then ten. Snow up to the window sills and drifts higher than my shoulder, smoothed and hardened so I could walk right over the tops of them. Had to doze out lanes for the cattle, lanes to water, lanes to the house and barn and corrals. Nights were hard. I felt cooped up, only these weren't necessarily the people I wanted to be cooped up with, not after what I'd had, not after Madeleine and Mariko. Sometimes I'd walk at night down long tunnels of snow, talk to the horses, or stand in the barn and look out over the white world below. "I almost had a child." That's what I found myself saying one night. What I meant, of course, was the child I had fathered with Madeleine which she had lost while riding—years ago. I was sure it was a girl which pleased me because it meant I'd have two Madeleines in my life. At the same time, no day went by without thinking of Mariko.

How many years has my heart been split like this—split in two like a dowser's rod—hunting—bending down over hidden water? Mariko wrote from Paris. She sent photographs of her new paintings with a note attached—anything more would have been incriminating: She would have had to talk about feelings. This, from a woman who jumped out of a moving train and walked back ten miles to make love to me in an open field in view of the highway, our fingers smearing mud over each other so that after, we looked as if we had painted ourselves. And at parting—no words, no promises, no goodbyes, just those mud marks, those scars.

Now snow has covered all that. It's weight has suffocated even Pinkey's beyond-the-grave escapades. Ted is housebound, studying to go back to medical school, and Champ—the "human bomb"—as we like to call him because of his temper, has settled down to braiding rawhide reins like so much occupational therapy. But a step forward is a step forward. The day he broke his cane across his colt's hocks, sending him into the barbed wire, I felt the blow against my own legs as though he'd hit me. Five canes later—canes he broke over the backs of chairs, over his own knee—his fury gradually subsided and now we work together feeding hay from a wagon pulled by a team with no more and no fewer resentments and quarrels than we had before the war.

Pleasure is never a constant thing. It surges through me as if my body were a hollow piece of straw. And so it was the few times Madeleine came to see me that winter. I couldn't help but notice she was more attractive than ever, her long copper braid intertwined with streaks of gray. I grabbed her, twirled her, went down on my knees, put my head against her and listened. Her stomach growled. "I'm hungry," she said laughing. "You always make me hungry."

I cooked for her. She watched me breaking eggs one-handed into a pan, cutting bread for toast, stoking the cookstove fire. Once her turquoise eyes filled with tears, then dried. "How's it going?" I asked. She twirled her wedding ring. She said everything bewildered her. "Maybe it would have been better if Henry had died. He's suffering so . . ."

When I touched her face she batted my hand away. "Stop trying to ruin my life," she snapped. We stood facing each other. "I'm not," I said. "I'm not trying anything." She spread her hands against my chest pushing, then pulling me toward her. "I'm not trying anything," I said again. I was in her arms and her head was against my chest. "Your heart beats irregularly," she said to me.

That was the last time I saw her until New Year's Eve when Bobby invited her and Henry for dinner. All morning he decorated the house with sprigs of pine and some white flowers he'd forced into bloom. Champ's girlfriend had already arrived and she lurked about the house when they weren't in the sack together. She didn't have much to say for herself and I was glad because I didn't feel like talking. Ted and Bobby cooked while Champ and I fed cows then we took our weekly baths.

When Madeleine and Henry came to the front door I couldn't help suppress a wild grin. I had a bottle of champagne and some glasses in my hand and I poured them a drink on the spot to keep the tossing and turning of jealousy and pleasure from showing. Henry and I embraced. He still looked thin. "But hell, I'm on the gain, two-point-four pounds a day just like a steer," he said, spilling his champagne onto my shoulder. Madeleine's hair was down and loose like water mixed with sun and I thought of Mariko's waist-length hair like black bamboo. In the kitchen Henry's hand shook as he raised his glass: "*Kampai*," he said. "Welcome home," Bobby chimed in and when I told him he looked "damned good," his mouth pulled to one side. "Like hell I do," he said, then we broke into laughter.

After dinner we all danced a little bit, taking turns with the two women, then grouping together, Ted, Champ, his girlfriend, Madeleine, Henry and me, and sometimes Bobby. Just before midnight we went outside to toast the New Year. I was already drunker than I wanted to be and once, when I closed my eyes, the ground moved backwards from under my feet and I stumbled head-on into a juniper tree. Then and there I relieved myself and when I turned back I saw Madeleine and Henry kissing—a prolonged, passionate kiss—and beyond, framed by the living room window, Champ and his girl danced by.

I sat in the jeep parked near the tree and turned on the engine and lights. They were aimed right at Henry's back and I could see Madeleine waving to me over his shoulder like a Hollywood star. I released the clutch. The jeep bumped toward them, then I slammed on the brakes because I thought I saw Pinkey coming toward me, but just then, Champ came to the door and yelled, "Happy New Year," and when I looked back I couldn't see Pinkey anymore.

I let the jeep go forward again. Once I heard Madeleine yelling at me, then Henry stepped in front of me with his hands out until the hood touched his fingers and bent them. He pulled back and ran behind the juniper with me on his tail. I could hear Champ laughing. Around and around we went. Hell, I never got close enough to run him down.

When I woke I was fully clothed on top of my bed. I held my hand over my eyes. The light hurt. It seemed to me that most of my life I'd left a space in my bed for someone else—for Mariko, for Madeleine, for someone who might marry me—but it was unoccupied still. For a long time I lay there listening—Madeleine and Henry were gone, Champ and his girl were probably elsewhere. I collapsed my weight into the unused part of the bed. How cold it felt against my groin. Holding a hand over my eyes I imagined a body under me—Mariko's, Madeleine's—and beside us, a child.

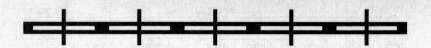

DEIRDRE McNAMER

FROM

Rima in the Weeds

October 22, 1962

The Hi-Line Investors Corp.—Skeet Englestad, Johnny Medvic, Ken Peterman, Doc Hansen, Earl Vane, and Dick Reitenbush—huddled over coffee, the day of the big blockade, to decide, finally and forever, what to call their new steak house.

The chin-to-chin showdown with Castro had them all stirred up, and they spoke with the hushed urgency of generals. Their first choice of a name, the one they'd been running with, wasn't going to work. The Tiki Room? Suddenly it was safe and ordinary, like something named by wives. And this was no ordinary bar and restaurant. This was part of the overall ability of the United States of America to call a bluff.

Here's why. This particular supper club would be a rendezvous point for the boys who manned and serviced the Minutemen—150 nuclear missiles the Air Force was burying, right this moment, beneath twenty thousand square miles of Montana prairie. It would be an officers' club, in a sense. Part of this country's military capability. You could look at it that way. And now, with the Cuba deal, you had an actual military operation under way—those missiles were Kennedy's ace in the hole—and there was just no way, given the situation, that Tiki Room seemed right.

———

The Hi-Line Investors were three wheat farmers, a chiropractor, a banker, and the city clerk and recorder. They all lived in Madrid, a town of two thousand, give or take, on the Montana Hi-Line, the sparsely settled rail corridor across the plains, near Canada. What they had in common, besides the fact that they'd all grown up in Madrid, was the war: the Second World War. Everyone except Earl Vane had done a stint, stateside or overseas, and they remembered it as the most alert, the most achingly clearcut time of their lives. To them, these new missiles were an extension into the future of that old exhilarating preparedness. A reminder of danger and a fast heart. The Minutemen. The prairie became a cover for hair-trigger weaponry. It buzzed. It joined the larger world.

Sure it was a gamble, this restaurant. Especially since it was five and a half miles south of town, out on the prairie where the missiles were. But what wasn't a gamble that was worth a damn in the first place? And it was chancy, sure, to stage the grand opening in the winter. But you needed time to get the kinks out before the spring and summer rush.

Right now, the name was the thing.

A military term seemed the way to go. Right for the times, and right as a hats-off type of thing to these missile people. The Firing Range? You'd have your double meaning there, with this suggestion of a kitchen range and steaks and such.

The Rocket?

You want to show these boys from the base that you appreciate their business, that five thousand missile workers is a goddam shot in the arm for your local economies. That a few naysayers don't represent the sentiments of any particular community at large. They will say these things, a few of our local people, about being a target for the Russians, and why should the Madrid area be a target for the Russians. Why are people in this area more expendable than people in someplace like Seattle, Washington? is the kind of thing they will say and write in letters and so forth. They will say they don't want to be a light bulb on some Russian general's map.

But you've always got these people, the naysayers. A decent person is proud to be a target if it's in the service of his country. You can be an ordinary area with a population of two people per square mile that no one knows about, especially since the oil fell off, or you can step out there and be counted. Where would we be if no one had volunteered for the war? Where would we be, for that matter, if no one took a chance on a new business? Where would we be if no one was willing to stand up to Khrushchev and put themselves on the political map?

The Target?

There's the matter of a name with some spunk. But there's also the consideration of your outdoor sign to go with the name. You want something simple and big, without expensive lettering. Something that makes you say the name to yourself, right off. Something that people don't have to sit around and figure out.

From an investment standpoint, there won't be beaucoup bucks for the decor. There will be a serviceable building that has a California-type atmosphere inside. An officers'-club-type atmosphere, with some booths and some candles in glass bowls. For a nice mood. But the line has to be held on expenditures, because these guys will be here for, what, a year more, the construction people, and then you'll just have the people who are in charge of the missiles, the ones who sit down there in those little rooms beneath the grass and the crops. And your maintenance people. And hopefully, by then, a stable local clientele. But it's a gamble, you bet. The point being, keep the upfront expenses down.

A military type of name. Something with some pizazz, some pride to it. Something that lends itself to an officers'-club type of idea. Then a sign, to go with it, that you're going to notice. A sign that doesn't cost an arm and a leg to light up after dark.

March, that year, was full of wind that rolled across the world with a sound as clean and lonely as rushing water. It rocked the stripped cottonwoods, hurried clouds across the sky, sprayed gravel against bare legs. You walked into it with a forward tilt.

Margaret Greenfield lay in bed, listening. At night, the wind was an ocean that whooshed forward, ebbed for the span of a train whistle or a dog's bark, whooshed again. She let it wash over her, safe on shore in a way that did not, then, feel temporary.

She lay beneath her warm blankets and the wind died a little. And then it sounded as if it were ruffling a huge sheet. This made her think of her mother's wedding veil. Margaret's parents, Roy and MaryEllen, had gotten married eleven years earlier, in the windy spring of 1951, a year to the day before Margaret was born. As soon as MaryEllen stepped out of the church, a gust blew the veil straight off her head. One black-and-white snapshot in the album shows her standing on the church steps, laughing, her shiny dress blown tightly around her hips, her pretty hand grabbing for the veil. Another shows the veil alone against the branch-crossed sky, a square of gauzy white, solitary and willful. And then more pictures: the veil wrapped around a bare branch; two men in suits climbing a single ladder, cigarettes clenched in their teeth. And another, the last, of the two men again. One is hatless and grinning; the other has a shadow over his face. They are on the ground, the veil stretched triumphantly between them. By then, MaryEllen has disappeared from the pictures. She has gone off to be a wife.

Margaret didn't know why a certain kind of wind at night made her think of the veil in the air. It was just one of those cases where two things stuck together. Whenever she smelled a Big Hunk candy bar, for instance, she thought of the movie *Cat People*. She must have eaten a Big Hunk when she saw it at the Rialto. But she had eaten them at other movies too. Who knows why they were linked to a specific one? A single nougaty whiff, and she could see every scene. She could see Irena, the beautiful, shy woman with a panther inside her that took over when she was made jealous or passionate. It was an old, simmering curse. When the panther sprang to life, Irena couldn't help what she did. She couldn't remain human if she tried.

To raise money that spring, Margaret's catechism class sold plastic cylinders with a figure of the Virgin Mary inside. They were beige and looked, on the outside, like foot-long rockets. A seam ran from base to tip, and it parted like cathedral doors to reveal the praying woman inside. They cost two dollars a piece. Anyone who sold three of them got to name an African pagan baby who would be baptized by missionaries when the money was sent in. Margaret sold six and named her babies Audrey and Gidget.

Trudging on Saturday mornings from door to door, selling the Virgin rockets, Margaret gathered evidence of something she already felt in her bones—that Madrid, where she lived, was not just a gappy little town on the northern Montana plains. Far from it! It was a place of layers and mysteries, of hidden rooms and muffled dramas.

Selling the rockets, she saw, through a slat in a venetian blind, an old man in red boxer shorts vacuuming a carpet. She heard Mr. Badenoch, the meek grade school principal, singing in a heart-breaking voice from beneath a car in his garage, and she watched a three-legged dog with a bow on its collar hop through a tunnel in some bushes.

She was invited into a living room where everything was covered in plastic—the lamps, the couch, even an arrangement of plastic flowers. A woman in a pink apron sat her on the crackling couch. The wind moaned beneath the eaves as the woman poked through a change purse for money. A young man in an old man's bathrobe and slippers padded through an adjoining room carrying binoculars.

She saw an immense salmon-colored Cadillac waiting for her to cross an intersection and remembered suddenly that she had seen it in a dream with palm trees and warm sand that trickled through her fingers, a dream so happy she woke laughing.

But this was the most mysterious of all: One morning she knocked lightly on the door of a yellow ranch-style house on Skyline Boulevard, her rockets in a shoe box under her arm, and heard a woman's distant cry. "So who *are* you, anyway?" she heard. "Who *are* you?" It seemed to come from behind several doors, from behind thick castle walls. It seemed to be shouting at a deaf person, a crowd, the entire town. "I have no idea," it wailed, "who you could possibly be."

On the day of the airplane ride, the second Saturday in April, Margaret woke to silence. No wind, none at all. Not even the usual breeze. This put a flutter of apprehension beneath her rib cage. If there was no wind, not even a breath of it, what would lift the small plane off the ground? What would boost it into the sky? She climbed out of bed carefully and tried to feel nonchalant. She phoned her best friend, Rita Kay, who had arranged the plane ride—the first for both of them—and asked whether she had any worries about the strangely silent skies. Rita Kay hooted at her.

"It doesn't take wind," she said. "It takes air. And there's always air. At least there was the last time I checked." This was a new expression of Rita Kay's: "the last time I checked." She had borrowed it from her older brother, Eugene, a small teenager who had already wrecked two cars, and she said it in a blithe, proprietary way that wounded Margaret a little.

It was a glittering, suspended morning. Sun shot off the small patches of ice left from the last cold snap of the season. The silent air made the sparrows too loud. Rita Kay's father fiddled with the radio dial as he drove them to the airport, skimming the tops of voices and music the way the plane would soon skim above the solid, comforting earth.

The rides were part of a fund-raising effort to repave the airport runway. Rita Kay had seen the ad in the paper and pestered her parents, and Margaret's, until they said yes. Now she bounced triumphantly on the seat, picking slivers of pink polish off her tiny fingernails. Margaret pressed her nose against the cold window and devoured scraped-looking stubble fields with her eyes, noticing for the first time how anchored and substantial they looked.

The airplane was intensely red and white and black, and it was parked just outside the doors of the metal hangar at the Darrell Johnson Memorial Airport. Bob Ronechek, the pilot, squatted beside it in a large plaid overcoat, examining one of the wheels. A large sign on the hangar wall said WEEKEND RIDES. $10 FOR 20 MINUTES YOU'LL NEVER FORGET.

Rita Kay's dad pointed at the sign. "Aren't you getting a little carried away, Bob?" he said. Bob laughed and shrugged his big plaid shoulders.

The minute he slammed the doors shut, Margaret knew she was trapped in a horrible mistake. It was the sound of the doors, light and plastic. Incredibly light. She was sealed inside a toy, and a man she didn't even know was going to aim it straight into the sky.

I should jump out now, she thought. It will be embarrassing, but I'll be alive. The only doors, though, were in the front, and Margaret had been placed in the back. Rita Kay sat in the co-pilot's seat next to Bob and craned her neck out the window. She turned and grinned at Margaret. Bob pushed a button that made the plane roar and shake. He placed headphones over his ears and muttered into a microphone.

He checked the seat belts. Too late. Margaret shut her eyes and consulted her vision of heaven.

For as long as she could remember, everyone up there had been peering over a bank of snowy clouds, monitoring the world with gentle smiles. The old God was flanked by his immediate family and friends, who watched with him: Mary, a pretty blue oval; Jesus, thin and pale-eyed, resting his young man's beard on the old man's shoulder; the Holy Ghost, wings stretched like a quivering silver canopy over their heads. And then all the rest, fanning out to the edges of the sky, tall to short, babies on the end, saints and martyrs and grandparents and orphans, robed and peaceful, looking down with encouraging eyes at her, Margaret, and the rest of the heavily turning blue world.

She knew the vision was too pretty and simple, like a Christmas card—that the details were probably more obscure and elaborate—but the feel of it remained. They were a big surprise party that would welcome her with quiet cheers when she died, providing she had not somehow pitched herself into a canyon of soul-killing sin. That's why it wasn't so bad to die young. You had less time to mess things up. When they wanted you, you should be happy to go.

"Not yet," she hissed at them angrily, surprising herself. Bob put a second pair of earphones on Rita Kay, who squealed with pleasure. The little plane began to move slowly toward the runway, rocking a little from side to side. Margaret stared at the floor. She imagined rows of powerful, hurt eyes. Then she gathered herself and spoke again. "I do *not* want to be with you. Stop looking at me." Bob glanced over his shoulder and lifted one earphone away from his head. "You want something?" he shouted. She shook her head. No, she mouthed. Nothing.

Bob slowed the plane, turned it a quarter turn, stopped it. He turned a handle on the ceiling, then pushed a lever, and the motor roared more alive. The sound grew, a terrible winding up until it screamed like a monster mosquito. The little capsule felt as if it would explode. One more notch and the seams would burst, spitting them all onto the concrete.

At the last moment, he pulled the lever in again, and the sound trailed away. They crawled to the runway. He checked their seat belts again and did a jaunty thumbs-up. He pushed the lever, and the engine started to climb, but this time they were moving with it. Faster, faster.

The ground blurred. Everything blurred. And then, just as it seemed they would never make it, that they would go roaring into a fence or a field and explode in flames, the earth dropped away from them like a stone, releasing them to the liquid sky. Small tears seeped from the corners of Margaret's clenched eyes.

The little plane circled and climbed. Then Bob lowered the nose so that it felt horizontal and announced above the roar that they were circling back over Madrid. Margaret opened her eyes and looked down, expecting an intricate little city, somehow made roofless by the plane's spying height. Finally, she could peak down pathways, into shaded corners, over hedges, through doorways. It would take hours to see everything down there on earth. Her home.

But Madrid lay on the immense animal back of the earth like the pieces of a miniature board game or a smashed raft. It was thin and gappy and had a dull, cardboard look to it. Nothing stood out except the oil tanks and the Lutheran church steeple and the Saddle Club arena. The rest was just shadowless little boxes and the gray lines of streets. If a town could be bald, Madrid was that. Bald and terrifyingly small.

"How 'bout that, girls?" Bob yelled above the roar of the engine. Rita Kay had her nose and hands pressed to the window. Her yellow fluff of hair looked electric. "I see my house!" she screamed. "I see Debbie!" Debbie was her elderly Persian cat.

"You can't see Debbie," Margaret said in a low voice. "You can't see anything." She felt sheer, bone-hollow disappointment. There was nothing wonderful about Madrid. The whole place looked flimsy and temporary.

"What?" Rita Kay shouted, snatching her eyes away from the window for a second to look at Margaret. Margaret shrugged dismissively. She tried to feign eagerness by looking out her own window. Beyond the town were great stretches of buff-colored grass and striped wheat fields, dark fallow soil alternating with pale stubble, reaching in shallow waves to the skyline. A couple of cars inched like bugs along Highway 2, and some freight cars sat by a gleaming clump of miniature grain silos.

Her vision reached so far that the horizons curved downward. And there was nothing sheltering on that earth except the row of mountains on the far western edge of everything. Madrid was lost at sea, Margaret thought, and didn't even know it.

The ground rose up to them. The little wheels bumped it hard, jumped a little, bumped again. Then they slowed and the engine died, and they were parked in front of the hangar. Done.

"Can I steer next time?" Rita Kay said coyly to Bob. Her cheeks were bright pink.

"Why not?" He turned in his seat. "How did you like the ride?" he said to Margaret. "You look a little green around the gills."

"Fine," she said, looking out the window.

He let them out, and Rita Kay ran to her father, a short, smiley man who sat in the car, listening to the radio. She began to chatter. Margaret fixed a mild smile on her face and waited to get home. Up there in the plane, during the span of a few terrible minutes, she had felt everything change. She had pushed herself away from heaven, from those faces who wanted her to come to them and be happy forever. And she had seen the bareness of earth, how it really was when you got a good look. Where did she belong now? Where did she want to be?

Riding her bike, a few weeks later, Margaret passed the Thorpes' large grassy yard. The sun had shone hard for several days, and then there had been an afternoon of rain. The Thorpes' lawn was dotted with mushrooms. Margaret slowed her bike and got off. She turned and wheeled it slowly past the grass again, studying it.

Some mushrooms were poison; some weren't. She thought she knew, from science, what the most poison ones looked like. But there was one kind that mimicked a safe mushroom, and it could grow anywhere. She stood over three mushrooms growing near the sidewalk and examined them. They looked safe. They also looked like the ones that looked safe but weren't.

Then Margaret did something so strange she felt she was doing it in her sleep. She glanced around, saw no one, knelt quickly to the sidewalk, and put her nose to the tip of one of the mushrooms. She sniffed its dried-leaf scent. Then she very deliberately ran her tongue over its velvety surface. And she very deliberately took a delicate bite from its edge. And swallowed it.

She stood up slowly. Slowly, she climbed back on her bike and began to pedal toward home. She held herself very straight, imagining the moonlike particle, tooth-marked, entering her stomach. Was she the same as before? Or was she on the edge of death? She tried to feel her body from the inside, tap it for clues. But her racing heart drowned out everything else. It could go either way. She might live to be a grandmother. She might collapse before she had traveled three more blocks.

Never had she ridden her bike like this. Her fingers fit perfectly in the grooves of the plastic grips. Her leg muscles stretched and tightened in a perfect, gliding rhythm. Her own stiff wind blew her bangs straight up. A small dog darted to the edge of the sidewalk and veered back, but Margaret had already swerved and straightened. Her reflexes were faster than the speed of thought. She pumped faster, eyes as wide as she could make them, fear zinging joyfully up her backbone.

The mushroom dissolved in her stomach and she felt it seep into her bloodstream just as she skidded, fish-tailing, into the long driveway. She threw her bike down and ran into the open garage to stand behind the tall box the new refrigerator had come in. She stood, hidden, until her heart quieted. She gave the mushroom time to do its work. Nothing happened. She was alive.

Inside the house, her mother handed her a peanut-butter-and-jelly sandwich, and Margaret burst into tears.

Through the long summer, she felt the slow growth of this runaway force inside her. She craved danger and fled from it. She cried, sometimes, for no reason. And her legs ached at night. She didn't know what it was. She saw Rita Kay almost every day, but Rita Kay wasn't interested, the way she used to be, in make-believe scenarios that went on for days. She didn't want to play jungle girl, or career girl, or movie-star divorcée, which she pronounced div-or-cee-ay because it was French. She wanted to ride bikes or swim. She wanted to talk about boys.

Margaret found an old pile of *Time* magazines in the basement and leafed through them at night in her bedroom. She always read the Medicine section first.

She read about an aircraft mechanic in California who could stop his heart for seconds at a time, whenever he wanted to. His fear was that he might not be able to start it again, but so far he always had. "Although yogis have claimed to be able to control the heart," *Time* said, "there are no well-documented cases in medical literature of an individual stopping his heart at will. What enables Mechanic Swenson to turn the trick is still a mystery."

She read about a family dinner at Orville Fjeldt's farm near Idaho Falls. Grandma Fjeldt served some beets that a neighbor had brought over. She thought the beets weren't sour enough, and she said so, out loud. Something was wrong, but she couldn't put her finger on what it was. As it turned out, the beets were too sweet because they contained a deadly toxin.

"Last week, because of the beets, Orville Fjeldt was dead," the article said. "So were his brother Kenneth Fjeldt (after lingering more than a week in an iron lung) and daughter Ramona, fifteen." A photo of Kenneth Fjeldt in an iron lung accompanied the story. The caption said, "Grandma wanted more vinegar."

The new fifth-grade teacher, Miss Schmidt, walked into class on the highest spike heels Margaret had ever seen. She had pale skin and red hair and didn't smile. She was very young, and from Massachusetts.

Miss Schmidt began each day calmly, severely. But inevitably something happened that made her excited or angry, that caused her cheeks to flush wildly. Sometimes it was a stumbling answer or a thrown spitwad. Other times, she would stare out the window at the playground, and the town, and the prairie beyond and get angry about nothing at all.

"Do you know how this town got its name?" she demanded one day. "This town got its name because a big fat railroad official picked it off the globe." She was shouting a little. The class kept silent, watching her. "Like this."

She walked briskly to the corner of the room, her spiked heels clicking, grabbed the big globe from its shelf, and placed it on her desk so they could all see clearly. Her face was blazing and sickly.

"Like this," she snapped, and she put the back of one hand dramatically over an eye. With the other, she spun the globe. She waited a second or two, then let her finger pounce. Bending over the frozen globe, she peered at her finger. "Aha!" she said, her voice deep now, like a fat man's. "Glasgow! Let's name this railroad stop Glasgow!"

Susie Appelt tittered, because she used to live down the road in Glasgow. Their teacher was spinning the globe again, jabbing. "Aha! Well, we've got a bunch of little towns near this finger. Where's the closest big town? Yes! Here we are. Le Havre. How about if we just call the next one Havre? Is that all right?" Margaret and everyone else nodded carefully. The wind made the windows shudder and clanged the cable on the flagpole outside.

Then, without even spinning the globe, Miss Schmidt dove with her index finger straight down to Spain. "Madrid!" she cried. "There's a good name! There's a dandy!" She fixed her pale eyes on the children. "Is Madrid a good name for this little outpost on the prairie? This little fort?"

"Yes," said Julie Jackson softly. Two boys giggled.

Miss Schmidt ignored them. She stared out the window again. No one moved. "Is anything wrong with Madrid?" she whispered, turning back to them. Then her eyes filled horribly with tears and she ran out of the room.

The next day, severe and contained, she told them the Russians had missiles in Cuba that were pointed right at the United States, ready to go. President Kennedy had told Khrushchev to get them out of our backyard or else. Not only were the missiles pointed at the United States, but most of them were probably pointed at Montana, at Madrid, because of the big missile system that Malmstrom Air Force Base was installing beneath the Montana rangeland and wheat fields at this very moment. Margaret felt her blood pick up.

She went home for lunch and found her mother grim-faced, listening to the radio. Margaret wondered aloud if Madrid was a target for all those Cuban missiles that were ready to blast off. Her mother looked at her, and her eyes filled with tears. "Oh, honey," she said, and hugged Margaret tight. "Say a little prayer. This will turn out all right." Then her face, which was round and sweet and comforting, got braver looking. She tilted her chin up a little. "Eat your cheese dream," she said. "Don't worry." Cheese dreams were grilled cheese sandwiches made out of French toast, with syrup poured over the top. They were Margaret's favorite meal, and she knew she was eating them, right then, because of what was happening in Cuba.

She wasn't worried, though. She was thrilled. She said a little prayer, but she didn't really mean it. All day, she heard the excitement in her own voice. She thought she could hear the faint underground buzz of Madrid's own missiles, ready too.

She liked the idea of the missiles and all those wires connecting them, even though Susie Appelt's horse had fallen into one of the ditches they had dug for the cables and still favored a hind foot. The missiles made the ground you walked on seem important.

But then she walked into her house after school and smelled baking cookies and furniture polish, and she remembered an incinerated bird she had seen inside the shell of Rev. Olson's burned-down house, and she was washed with remorse and fear. Not yet, she thought.

Remembering, vaguely, a saint's story, she pocketed a small bottle of her favorite cologne, Intimate, and peddled her bike to the large garden behind the hospital. There, she poured the whole bottle over the feet of the statue of the Virgin Mary. And she prayed, earnestly this time, that everyone would calm down.

The garden was empty. The last frail, wine-colored leaves clung to the bushes. She watched the cologne drizzle across the stony toes of the Virgin and plunk into the dirt below. And as the earth soaked up the liquid, she closed her eyes. She seemed, then, to be standing not on the broad firm ground but on a very high rail just wide enough for her feet. If she tipped off one side, she would land in a pile of straw. If she tipped off the other, the straw would be knives. She was up there alone, the wind in her ears. Her mother didn't see the danger. Rita Kay didn't. No one did.

She stood for a long time like that. A squirrel chucked. The bushes whispered. She felt herself begin to lean. She put her arms out for balance. Then she felt herself falling and her eyes jumped open, catching her just in time.

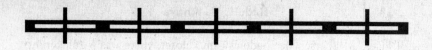

RUDOLFO A. ANAYA

Iliana of the Pleasure Dreams

liana stirred in the summer night, then awakened from her dream. She moaned, a soft sigh, her soul returning from its dreams of pleasure. She opened her eyes, the night breeze stirred the curtains, the shadows created images on the bare adobe wall, an image of her dream which moved, then changed and was lost as the shadows moved away from dream into reality.

In the darkness of the night, smelling the sweet fragrance of the garden which wafted through the open door, lying quietly so as not to awaken Onofre, her husband, she lay smiling and feeling the last wave of pleasure which had aroused her so pleasantly from her deep sleep. It was always like this, first the images, then the deep stirring which touched the depths in her, then the soft awakening, the coming to life.

In the summer Onofre liked to sleep with the doors and windows open, to feel the mountain coolness. Her aunts had never allowed Iliana to sleep in the moonlight. The light of the moon disturbs young girls, they had said.

Iliana smiled. Her aunts had given her a strict religious upbringing, and they had taught her how to care for a home, but they had never mentioned dreams of pleasure. Perhaps they did not know of the pleasure which came from the images in her dreams, the images which at first were vague, shadows in a place she did not recognize, fragments of faces, whispers. The shadows came closer, there was a quickening to her pulse, a faster tempo to her breathing, then the dream became clear and she was running across a field of alfalfa to be held by the man who appeared in her dreams. The man pressed close to her, sought her lips, caressed her, whispered words of love, and she was carried away into the spinning dream of pleasure. She had never seen the man's face, but always when she awakened she was sure he was standing in the garden, just outside the door, waiting for her.

Yes, the dream was so real, the flood of pleasure so deep and true, she knew the man in the dream was there, and the shadows of the garden were the shadows of her dreams.

She rose slowly, pushing away the damp sheet which released the sweet odor of her body. Tonight the man had reached out, taken her in his arms and kissed her lightly. The pleasure of his caress consumed her and carried her into a realm of exhilaration. When she awakened she felt she was falling gently back to earth, and her soul came together again, to awaken.

She walked to the window quietly, so as not to awaken her husband. She had never told him of her private world of dreams, and even when she confessed her dreams to the priest at Manzano she could not tell him everything. The dreams were for her, a private message, a disturbing pleasure she did not know how to share. Perhaps with the man in the dream she could share her secret, share the terrible longing which filled her and which erupted only in her dreams.

She leaned against the door and felt the cool breeze caress her perspiring body. Was he there, in the shadows of the garden, waiting for her? She peered into the dark. The shadows the moon created were as familiar as those she saw in her dreams. She wanted to cry out to understand the dream, to share the pleasure, but there was no one there. Only the soft shrill of the night crickets filled the garden. The cry of the grios foretold rain, the clouds would rise over the mountain, the thunder would rumble in the distant sky, and the dry spell of early summer would be broken.

Iliana sighed. She thought of her aunts, Tia Amalia and Tia Andrea. Why had they not explained the dreams of pleasure? They were women who had never married, but they had said marriage would be good for her. All of the girls in the village married by eighteen and settled down to take care of their families. Onofre was a good man, a farmer, a hard worker, he did not drink, he was a devout Catholic. He would provide a home, they said, and she would raise his children.

The girls of the mountain valley said Onofre was handsome but very shy. He would have to wait many years and marry a widow, they said, and so they were surprised when Iliana married him. Iliana was the most beautiful girl in the valley. It was a marriage of convenience, the young women whispered to explain the match, and Iliana went to her marriage bed with no conception of what was expected of her. Onofre was gentle, but he did not kiss the nape of her neck or whisper the words of pleasure she heard in her dreams. She vaguely understood that the love of Onofre could be a thread to her secret dreams, but Onofre was abrupt, the thread snapped, the fire of her desire died.

She was unsure, hesitant, she grew timid. They ate in silence, they lived in silence. Like an animal that is careful of its master, she settled around the rhythms of his work day, being near when it was time to be close, staying in her distant world the rest of the time. He too felt the distance; he tried to speak but was afraid of his feelings. Sitting across the table from her he saw the beauty of her face, her hands, her throat and shoulders, and then he would look down, excuse himself, return to his work with which he tried to quench the desires he did not understand.

There is little pleasure on earth, the priest at the church said. We were not put on earth to take pleasure in our bodies. And so Onofre believed in his heart that a man should take pleasure in providing a home, in watching his fields grow, in the blessing of the summer rains which made the crops grow, in the increase of his flocks. Sex was the simple act of nature which he knew as a farmer. The animals came together, they reproduced, and the priest was right—it was not for pleasure. At night he felt the body of Iliana and the pleasure came to engulf him for a moment, to overwhelm him and suffocate him. Then as always the thread severed, the flame died.

Iliana waited at the window until the breeze cooled her skin and she shivered. In the shadows of the garden she felt a presence, and for a moment she saw again the images of her dream, the contours of her body, the purple of alfalfa blossoms. A satisfaction in the night, a sensuous pleasure welled up from a depth of soul she only knew in her dreams. She sighed. This was her secret.

How long had it been in her soul, this secret of pleasure? She had felt it even in the church at Manzano where she went to confession and mass. She had gone to the church to confess to the priest, and the cool earth fragrance of the dark church and the sweetness of the votive candles had almost overwhelmed her. "Help me," she whispered to the priest, desiring to cleanse her soul of her secret even as the darkness of the confessional whispered the images of her dream. "I have sinned," she cried, but she could not tell him of the pleasures of her dreams. The priest, knowing the young girls of the village tended to be overdramatic in the stories of their love life, mumbled something about her innocence, made the sign of the cross absolving her, and sent her to her small penance.

Iliana walked home in deep despair. Along the irrigation ditch the tall cottonwood trees reminded her of strong, virile men, their roots digging into the dark soul of the earth, their branches creating images of arms and legs against the clear sky. She ran, away from the road, away from the neighboring fields; over the pine mountain she ran until exhausted she clutched at a tree, leaned against the huge trunk; trembling she listened to the pounding of her heart. The vanilla smell of the pine was like the fragrance of the man in her dreams. She felt the rough bark, like the rough hands of Onofre at night. She closed her eyes and clutched at the tree, holding tight to keep from flying into the images of her dream which swept around her.

Iliana remembered her visit to the church as she returned to her bed, softly so as not to awaken Onofre. She lay quietly and pulled the sheet to her chin. She closed her eyes, but she could not sleep. She remembered the images at the church and felt again how she was overcome when she pressed close to the tree. It was the same tonight in her dream, the immense pleasure which filled her with a desire so pure she felt she was dying and returning to God. Why?

She thought of her aunts, spinsters whose only occupation was to care for the church at Manzano. They swept, they sewed the cloths for the altar, they brought the flowers for mass, they made sure the candles were ready. They had given their lives to God; they did not speak of pleasure. What would they think if they knew of the dreams that came to Iliana?

Release me, Iliana cried. Free me. Leave me to my work and to my husband. He is a good man, leave me to him. Iliana's tears wet the sheet, and it was not until the early morning that she could sleep again.

"We can go this afternoon," Onofre said as they ate.

"Oh, yes," Iliana nodded. She was eager to go to the church at Manzano. Just that morning her aunts had come to visit her. They were filled with excitement.

"An apparition has appeared on the wall of the church," Tia Amalia said.

"The face of Christ," Tia Andrea said, and both bowed their heads and made the sign of the cross.

That is what the people of the mountain valleys were saying, that at sunset the dying light and the cracks in the mud painted the face of Christ on the adobe wall of the church. A woman on the way to rosary had seen the image, and she ran to tell her comadre. Together they saw it, and their story spread like fire up and down the mountains. The following afternoon all the people of the village came and gathered in the light of dusk to see the face of Christ appear on the wall. Many claimed they saw the face; some said a man crippled by arthritis was cured and could walk when he saw the image.

"I see! I see!" the old man had shouted, and he stood and walked. The people believed they had experienced a miracle. "There!" each shouted in turn as the face of Christ appeared. The crown of thorns was clear, blood streamed down the sad and anguished face. The women fell to their knees. A miracle had come to the village of Manzano.

The priest came and took holy water and blessed the wall, and the old people understood that he had sanctified the miracle. The following evening people came from miles around, from the mountain villages and ranches they came to see the miracle. Those who saw the face of the savior cried aloud or whispered a private prayer; the women on their knees in the dust prayed rosary after rosary.

People from the nearby villages came; families came in their cars and trucks. The women came to pray, eager to see the image of Christ. Their men were more guarded; they stood away from the church wall and wondered if it was possible. The children played hide-and-seek as all waited for the precise moment of dusk when the image appeared.

The young men came in their customized cars and trucks, drinking beer, eager to look at the young women. Boys from the ranches around the village came on horseback, dressed in their Sunday shirts and just-pressed Levis; they came to show off their horsemanship to the delight of the girls. A fiesta atmosphere developed; the people were glad for the opportunity to gather.

The men met in clusters and talked politics and rain and cattle. Occasionally one would kick at the ground with his boot, then steal an uncomfortable glance at his wife. The women also gathered in groups, to talk about their children, school, marriages and deaths, but mostly to talk about the miracle which had come to their village and to listen to the old women who remembered a prior apparition when they were young. A young woman, they said, years ago, before cars came to the mountains, had seen the image of the Virgin Mary appear, on a wall, and the praying lasted until the image disappeared.

"One never knows which is the work of the devil or the work of God," an old woman said. "One can only pray."

A strange tension developed between the men and the women who went to see the miracle. It was the women who organized the rosaries and the novenas. It was the women who prayed, kneeling on the bare ground for hours, the raw earth numbing their knees and legs. It was they who prayed for the image to appear, their gaze fixed on the church wall, their prayers rising into the evening sky where the nighthawks flew as the sun set red in the west.

The priest grew concerned and tried to speak to the men, but they greeted him quietly, then looked down at the ground. They had no explanation to share. The priest turned to the women; they accepted him but did not need him. Finally he shut himself up in the church, to pray alone, unsure of the miracle, afraid of the tension in the air which had turned the people in a direction he did not understand. He could not understand the fervent prayer of the women, and he could not control it. The people of this valley in the Sangre de Cristo mountains, he had been warned, were different. Now he understood the warning. The image had come to the wall of the church and the people devoutly accepted it as a miracle. Why had he been sent to the church at Manzano? He belonged in the city, where the politics of the church were clear and understood. This transformation in his parishioners he did not understand. He opened the chest where he kept the altar wine and drank, wondering what it was he had seen in the lines and shadows when he looked at the wall. He couldn't remember, but he couldn't look again.

In the afternoon Onofre and Iliana drove over the ridge of the mountain to the church at Manzano. Onofre drove in silence, wondering what the visitation of the image meant. Iliana rode filled with a sense of excitement. Perhaps the image on the wall of the church was a sign for her. She would see her savior and he would absolve the pleasure dreams; all would be well.

Iliana smiled, closed her eyes and let herself drift as the rocking of the truck swayed her gently back and forth. Through the open window the aroma of the damp earth reached her nostrils. She smelled the pregnant, rich scent of the soil and the pine trees. She remembered the dapple horse she used to ride across the meadow from her Tia Amalia's house to her Tia Andrea's.

When they arrived at Manzano, Iliana opened her eyes and saw the crowd of people around the church. Cars and trucks lined the dirt road. Together Onofre and Iliana walked toward the group by the church.

Onofre felt awkward when he walked in public with his wife. She was a young and beautiful woman. He did not often think of her beauty, except when they were with other people. Then he saw her as others might see her, and he marveled at her beauty.

"It's the Spanish blood of her mother which gives her her beauty," her aunts were fond of saying.

Her oval face reminded Onofre of a saint he had seen once in a painting, perhaps at the cathedral at Santa Fe. Her face, the dark eyelashes, the dark line of the eyebrows, the green eyes. She was exquisite, a woman so beautifully formed that people paused to watch her. Onofre felt the eyes of the young men on his wife as they walked, and he tried to shake away the feeling of self-consciousness as he walked beside her. He knew the men admired the beauty of his wife, and he had been kidded about being married to an angel.

Iliana was aware of her beauty; it was something she felt in her soul. Everything she did was filled with a sensuous pleasure in which she took delight, and as they walked toward the church she took pleasure in feeling the gaze of the men on her. But she cast down her eyes and did not look at them, understanding that she should not bring shame to her husband.

Instead she looked at the children who played around the church; the gathering had become a fiesta. Someone had brought an ice machine to sell flavored ice. Another person had set up a stand to sell rosaries and other religious items, and a farmer was selling green chile and corn from the bed of his truck. There were people Iliana did not recognize, people from as far away as Taos and Española.

As Iliana and Onofre passed, friends and neighbors greeted them, but when the young bachelors of the village saw her a tension filled the air. Her beauty was known in the mountain villages, and at eighteen she was more beautiful than ever. All of the young men had at one time or another dreamed of her; now they looked at her in awe, for underneath her angelic beauty lay a sensuality which almost frightened them.

"Onofre must be treating her right," one young man whispered to his friend. "She is blossoming."

How lucky Onofre is, they thought. He so plain and simple, and yet she is his. God is not fair, they dared to think as they tipped their cowboy hats when she passed. All were young and virile men of the mountains, handsome from their Spanish and Indian blood, and all were filled with desire when they saw Iliana.

They called Onofre a lucky man, but the truth was that each one of them had had a chance to court Iliana. Each one of them had seen her at school; they saw her at church on Sundays, and each day they saw her beauty grow. They could not touch her, even in the games they played as children, they dared not touch her. When they grew into young manhood a few of them sought her out, but one glance from her eyes told them that Iliana was a young woman filled with mystery. They turned away, unwilling to challenge the sensuous mystery they felt in her presence. They turned away and married the simple girls of the village, those in whom there was no challenge, no mystery to frighten and test them.

Now, as Iliana passed them, she felt the admiration of the young men of the mountains. She smiled and wondered as she stole a glance at their handsome faces if one of them was the man who appeared in her dreams.

Her aunts were there; indeed, they had been there all day, waiting for the setting of the sun, waiting for the image of Christ to appear. They saw Iliana and drew her forward.

"We're pleased you arrived," they said. "Come, hija, it's almost time." They pulled her away from Onofre, and he sighed with relief and stepped back into the crowd of men.

The women parted as the two aunts drew Iliana forward so she could have a good view of the church wall. Already candles were lighted, a rosary was being prayed. The singing of the Hail Marys fell softly on their ears, and the sweet scent of paraffin filled the air. The women drew close together, prayed; the crowd grew quiet as the sun set. The cracks of the old plaster on the wall appeared thick and textured as the sun touched the horizon of the juniper-covered hills to the west. If the image appeared, it would be only for a few minutes, then it would dissolve into the gray of the evening.

Iliana waited. She prayed. Pressed between her aunts and the women, she felt their fragrances mix with the wax smell of the candles. So it had been at the church, the distinctive aroma of women co-mingling with the sanctity of God. The hush of the crowd reminded her of the hush of the church, and she remembered images and scenes. She remembered the pleasure that came with her first blood, the dapple horse she rode from the house of one aunt to the other . . . the field of alfalfa with purple blossoms and the buzzing of the honey bees, the taste of the thick, white paste at school, the tartness of the first bite of an apple, the fragrance of fresh bread baked in the horno behind her Tia Amalia's house, the day the enraged bull broke loose and tore down the horno until there was only a pile of dirt left, and the fright-ened women watching from their windows, cursing the bull, praying to God. She swayed back and forth on her knees, felt the roughness of the pebbles, heard the prayers of the women, felt the flood of disconnected images which dissolved into the smell of the mountain earth after a summer rain, the welcome smell of piñon wood burning in the fireplace and flavoring the air, the feeling of pleasure which these sights and sounds and memories wove into her soul. . . .

She closed her eyes, and pressed her hands to her bosom to still the pounding of her heart, to stop the rush of heat which moved up from the earth to her knees and thighs. Around her she heard the women praying as if in a dream. Beads of sweat wet her upper lip as the images came to tease her; she licked at the sweat and tasted it.

Then the crowd grew still, the magic hour had come. "Look," one

of the aunts whispered. Iliana opened her eyes and looked up at the
lines and shadows on the wall.

"You see!" the other aunt said.

Iliana, in reverie, nodded, smiled. Yes, I see, she wanted to say
aloud, her gaze fastened on the scene on the wall. She saw a figure,
then two. Arms and legs in an image of love. Yes, it was the image
of her dream. Iliana smiled and her body quivered with pleasure.

"Dear God," she cried, overwhelmed by the pleasure of the waves
which rolled through her body. "Dear God," she cried, then Iliana
fainted.

In her dream she walked on purple blossoms, and the sweet aroma
rose like sweet wine and touched the clouds of summer. Red and mauve
and the crimson of blood. In the darkness of the field the man waited
by the dapple horse. The waves of pleasure dissipated, the thread broke
before she reached the man.

Tia Amalia touched camphor to her nose and Tia Andrea patted
her hand vigorously. Iliana awoke and saw the shadows of the women
around her. Beyond the women Iliana caught a glimpse of the wall,
dark now, the congealing of shadows and lines no longer held the
secret she had seen.

"A miracle," her aunt whispered. "You saw the face of Christ! You
are blessed!"

"Blessed be the Lord Jesus Christ," the chorus of the women
responded.

"When you fainted you smiled like an angel," her aunt said. "We
knew you had seen the miracle."

"Yes," Iliana whispered, "I have seen the face of God." She struggled to rise, to free herself from the press of the women. On their
knees they prayed, in the darkness, and when she rose they looked up
at her as if she was part of the miracle.

"Onofre," she cried. She pulled away from the cluster of women,
away from the ring of candles which danced and snapped in the rising
wind of night. What had become of Onofre?

Onofre, who in his quiet way had gazed at the wall, now stood
waiting in the dark. He stood alone, confused, unsure, not understanding the strange messages of his blood. He had looked at the wall,
but he had not prayed to see the image of Christ, he had prayed that
Iliana would understand his dreams of the warm earth he worked daily.

He had seen the men leave, taking away the exhausted children, the limp bodies of the boys and girls who moaned in their dreams as they were carted home. Chairs and blankets were brought for the women; they would pray all night. The men would return to work the following day.

The wind rose in the dark night, it moaned on the pines of the mountain, it cried as it swept around the church and snapped at the candle light, creating shadows on the church wall. The women huddled in prayer. Iliana stumbled in the dark, wondering why she had seen the image of pleasure on the wall and not the face of Christ. Was it the devil tempting her? Or had the image on the wall been the answer she sought?

"Onofre!" she cried in the dark. The cold wind made her shiver. She found the truck, but Onofre was not there. In the dark she crossed the road, drawn by the dark, purple scent of alfalfa. She ran across the field, stumbling forward, feeling the weakness in the pit of her stomach give way to an inner resolution she had to follow. "Onofre!" she cried, feeling as if she had awakened from a dream into another dream, but this dream was one she could live in and understand.

In the middle of the field she saw the image of the man, the man who stood in the dark holding the neck of a horse, the dapple horse of her dreams. Heart pounding she ran into the arms of Onofre. She felt his strong arms hold her, and she allowed herself to be held, to feel the strength of his body, his muscles hardened by work, his silence instilled by the mountains.

"I did not see the face of Christ," Iliana confessed.

"Nor I," Onofre said.

"What then?" Iliana asked.

"A dream," Onofre said, unsure of what she meant, sure of his answer.

"Have I done wrong by dreaming?" Iliana asked.

Onofre shook his head. "I remember the old people saying: Life is a dream. . . ."

"And dreams are dreams," Iliana finished. "There is a meaning in my dreams, but I don't understand it. Do you understand your dreams, Onofre?"

"No," he smiled, the first time in a long time he had smiled at his young wife. Holding her in the dark in the middle of the field, the desire he felt was new, it was a desire rising from the trembling earth, through his legs into his thighs and sex and into the pounding of his heart.

"Sometimes at night I awaken and go to the open door," he said. "I look at the beauty of the night. I look at you lying so peaceful in the bed. You make soft sounds of contentment. I wish I could be the one who draws those sounds from you. Then you awaken, and I step into the shadows, so I won't frighten you. I watch as you go to the door to look at the garden. I know you have awakened from a beautiful dream because you are alive with beauty. At those times, you are all the beauty on earth."

"We need to share our dreams," Iliana said. Onofre nodded. They looked at each other and understood the secret of dreams was better shared.

"It is time to go home," Iliana said.

Yes, it was time to go home, to sleep, to unravel dreams. Arm in arm they walked across the field of alfalfa, walking together with much pleasure, stirring the purple blossoms of the night.

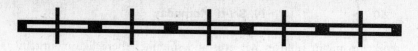

N. SCOTT MOMADAY

Remote as the stars are his sentiments just now

From THE ANCIENT CHILD

There was a music in Grey's mind, a music made upon banjos. Never had she to quest after visions.

Her hands were trembling. The note was printed in minute letters on a bit of cigarette paper, folded several times. She held it concealed between the index and middle fingers of her right hand. She had pressed her fingers so tightly together that she could no longer feel the note. Was it there?

Grey smiled brightly at J. W. Bell, who obviously appreciated her appearance. And well he might. She had brushed her hair until it shone like obsidian. She had lain naked in the sun the day before, so that her skin was burnished and retained the merest glowing heat. She wore the long white dress with third button, just above her breasts, missing, and no undergarments, so that the full shape of her body should be visible and her movements perfectly unimpeded in the flowing folds. She had crumpled and kneaded the dress in order to take the stiffness out of it. It had become not yellow with age, nor yet was it white, but the color of tea and cream, and this certain softening of the once hard and unadulterated whiteness gave to her complexion an accent like the touch of reflected firelight. She had shaped her nails, brushed her teeth with baking soda, and gargled Lilac Vegetal, diluted with water from the well. She had looked all morning at—rather into—a thirty-carat turquoise stone, a Lander's stone, that its reflection might hold in her eyes and shimmer there like mountain rain. She had brushed her beaded moccasins with sprigs of cedar and sage, and she had patted her breasts with crushed juniper berries and rose hips and the pollen of sunflowers. She stood graceful and tall and comely.

"Oh, Mr. Bell," she intoned, "I *do* thank you for your kindness to me. It's my brother, you see. Adam owns a newspaper in Philadelphia, and he would *so* like to hear that I had met Mr. William Bonney on my sojourn in the glorious West."

She fluttered her eyelashes, and Bell blushed. Over his shoulder she caught sight of the other guard, Bob Olinger. His was a face, she told Billy afterward, that she would never forget. Hate was a living thing in his eyes; she would always, from that moment on, think of hatred as a dull opalescence in the eyes of *this* man. Olinger smiled and spat. It would remain in her mind as one of the strangest smiles she had ever seen. Afterward, too, she would try to imagine Olinger as a child, as his mother's child, but innocence and a mother's love she could not lay at his place. He had never been a child, she thought; he had not been born of woman. He was a mutation, an awful accident of nature, an incomprehensible act of God, like a pestilence. He stood in the presence of death and evil. Yes, there was the scent of death in his hair, on his skin, at his mouth. But in this moment when she beheld him for the first and last time, she could not know that it was his own death that defined him precisely, ominous, impending, imminent. It was too far down in her intuition to grasp, but it made for a terrible fascination nevertheless. She could not know that he would die violently on this very day, in less than an hour. A subtle sweet-and-sour scent of death permeated the room, a faint putrescence.

She was distracted, and her fingers had begun to ache. Bell made an awkward gesture of presentation, and she turned to Billy. Oh, he had become so thin and pale! His cheeks were hollow, and his mouth was drawn. But he regarded her evenly, with a stiff, formal respect.

"Howdy, ma'am," he said.

Howdy, ma'am? She bit her tongue to keep from laughing and extended her hand. He took it lightly in his own, bowing slightly. The shackles seemed excessively large and cumbersome on his flat, slender wrists.

"I want to thank you for coming here today," he said. "I won't forget, no, ma'am."

She released the note into his hand. The thing was accomplished. She could not bring herself to say anything to him directly. Her heart was pounding, and her talent for seduction and intrigue evaporated in the heat of the moment. Bell's blush was gone; she dared not look at Olinger.

"Gracious me," she said sweetly, and she nodded curiously, turned, and took her leave. Her moccasins scarcely sounded on the stairs. Billy shuffled to the window, his leg irons ringing, and watched her cross the street below. The air outside smelled of lilacs and wood smoke.

When he turned, Olinger was looking at him, the strange smile still on his face, a double-barreled shotgun in his left hand, balanced delicately as on the tips of his fingers, the muzzles bobbing and weaving slowly, almost imperceptibly, never trained, but never wide of Billy's body. The shotgun was Olinger's signature.

For twelve days now Billy had listened to Olinger's taunts. They had begun on the ride from Mesilla, when Billy had been chained to the back seat of the ambulance, Olinger facing him. Two other guards were inside, three on horseback outside. They were all heavily armed, and they were a deadly dangerous lot of men. Any one of them, but most especially Olinger, would have been glad to dispatch the soul of Billy the Kid to hell. That ride, which lasted seven days, had shaken Billy. He was not afraid—it wasn't fear—but sickened by the circumstances. He wanted to be free, but he was shackled hand and foot. He wanted to be among his friends, but everyone in his immediate reach was a deadly enemy. He wanted to be left alone, but he was subjected to relentless observation, suspicion, and public humiliation. Above all, he was the victim of Olinger's sadism.

Never had Grey to quest after visions. She sat on a chair in front of Wortley's Hotel, across the street from the Lincoln County Courthouse. It was a bright April day, verging on noon. The sky was blue; there were clouds in the distance like feathers floating. The music of commerce in Lincoln had come to a stop: siesta. The bustle of the morning—and her mission—had been excitement and restoration; rarely had she felt herself so much alive. But, too, she was grateful for this lull. A delicious breeze touched her forehead. The good scents of food cooking—beans and chili and tortillas—made for a pleasant hunger in her, not a hunger to be satisfied at once but one to be borne for a time, savored like the food to come. The broad, dusty main street of the town of Lincoln, New Mexico Territory, reached away into summer. She thought of something she had once read:

> Great Streets of silence led away
> To Neighborhoods of Pause—

Sitting, the white dress drew up tightly at the breasts and arms. She unbuttoned the throat, the first two buttons. She closed her eyes. When she opened them again, a good many people had gathered in the street. There was no longer siesta. A sudden gust set a whirlwind careening in the street. There had been a shot.

She had not to quest after visions.

"Why don't you leave him alone, Bob?" Bell said. "Hell, he ain't doin' you no harm. He cain't, hardly."

Olinger spat on the floor at Bell's feet without taking his eyes off Billy the Kid. The smile was still there, crooked, without mirth. He bent his knees slightly and hunched his shoulders, making a bow of his body, and raised the shotgun and aimed it between Billy's eyes. He exerted ever so little pressure on the front trigger; his excitement was coming to an intensity almost unbearable. Spittle formed at the corners of his smile; his hands began to shake. Billy stood so still that he seemed in a trance. He did not blink, and he held his eyes, in which there was no expression, upon Olinger's. The tension was too much for Bell.

"Goddammit, Bob, stop it!"

"Pow!" Olinger's breath exploded. Bell flinched, but Billy did not. "Hey, lookit there! Lookit there, Bell! The Kid ain't got no head! Good God to Hallelujah! Would you lookit that!" He was animated now, warming to the performance, dancing in place, emitting hysterical laughter. "Lookit that, would yuh? Lookit, Bell! Lookit that there bloody stump between his shoulders there. Looks like a chicken's neck, don't it, what's head has been wrung off. Would you just lookit, Bell? The Kid's bloody, hairy brains is splashed all over the wall yonder, all

around the window there. Hey, a goodly gob must have splashed down in the street for the dogs and chickens."

"Stop it, Bob," Bell said, but there was no authority in it; he knew that Olinger would go on.

"Hey, ol' Godfrey Gauss's dog, it must be around. Shit, that there dog *loves* brains. An' Bell, you know Widow Mora's chickens, them rangy things what's always peckin' in the road? Why, them dumb critters'll eat anything. Hey, one day I seen them chickens peck the eyes right out of a sheep's head!"

"Aw, for God's sake," Bell said with disgust.

"Kid, I'd sure like to spill your brains out there in the street an' watch the chickens peck your eyes into jelly; it would pleasure me for certain, it would." He spoke directly to Billy, who had not moved, who appeared not even to breathe.

"I had you figured for a man who liked to watch chickens, Bob," Billy said. His voice was low and perfectly even.

"Sooner watch you floppin' headless on the floor, Kid. Like to see you gropin' for your face, find it gone, find nothin' but the bloody stump. Like to see you flop and wiggle around for a spell."

"Well, if you don't blow my head off, Bob, I guess you'll just have to come to the hangin'."

"Lookin' forward to it, Kid."

"To tell you the truth, Bob, I can take it or leave it. It don't seem half as exciting as the little scene you've just laid out."

"I ain't so sure, Kid. Once down to El Paso I seen a man hanged, a man named Ficker, or Flicker, not much bigger'n you. When he hit the end of that rope, his head was just ripped right off—damnedest thing you ever seen! But I guess it happens. I 'spect we'll leave them irons on you, so's you'll have some honest weight. You got a kinda scrawny girl's neck, anyway. Shit, I 'spect there'll be one helluva pop at the end of that rope. I'll just bet you snap right in two. An', Kid, they ain't gonna be in no hurry to bury you, I'll wager. I reckon they'll cart the big part of you off first and leave your head lyin' there, an' shit, I'll bet anything them chickens'll come along and peck your eyes out. Them dumb critters love eye jelly."

"It don't sound like much of a card game, Bob," Billy said and smiled.

"May, Friday the thirteenth," Olinger said. "Fifteen days."

"It ain't a bad day to die."

"I want to see the big half with the stump flop around on the ground like a chicken with its head wrung off."

"I had you figured," Billy said.

It was time for Olinger to go to lunch. He said something to Bell, placed his shotgun in a room that served as an armory, a closet on the landing halfway down the stairs, and went out. Billy turned to the window again. He counted Olinger's steps as he crossed the street diagonally northeastward to the Wortley Hotel—105 steps. On a chair in front of the hotel Grey sat in her white dress. She was the picture of repose. She was a girl in a painting. She was his mother on that day in early spring, 1873, in Santa Fe, when he and his brother Joe witnessed her marriage to William H. Antrim. She was, in his heroic and chivalrous intelligence, a woman to admire, to serve, to stand for, to protect, to cherish, and to die for. Such women are very delicate, very beautiful, he thought to himself—really, women of taste and breeding and refinement, so far beyond him that he could only stand in awe of them. Suddenly he thought of a nun, Sister Blandina, whom he had met at Trinidad and who had prevailed upon him to spare the physicians. *There* was a woman of mercy and charity and grace and goodness, a woman of perfect virtue. That saintly Italian woman, that woman of God, he could not have imagined her beneath her habit. He could not have imagined that she moved her bowels or broke wind or that her breath or her feet ever stank.

In front of the Wortley Hotel, Grey belched.

There had been a shot.

The scents of lilac and wood smoke had faded, and again there was a little stench of death in the room. Billy, facing the window, unfolded the note. It read: OUTHOUSE.

There had been a shot.

Billy turned. All of his instincts came to bear upon his next step. In a moment he became the creature he was best at being, an organism of inexorable purpose; his concentration was so great as to be irresistible. It was as if he already had the gun in his hand. Remote as the stars were his sentiments just now—Grey, Paulita, his mother in her wedding dress—remote beyond reckoning. He would have put bullets in the eyes of Sister Blandina, had she stood in his way.

"Hell, I'm sorry, Bell, I gotta take a pee."

J. W. Bell led Billy the Kid, straining against his chains, down the stairs and into the yard. He watched him enter the privy.

"Don't take too long," he said, and then was sorry he had said it; there was no need. He stood close by, cleaning his nails with a pocketknife. All was well. Everything was proceeding according to the established order. Except for the girl, this was a day like yesterday and the day before, and the day before that. He was not one to be bored by the ordinary. He liked everything in its place.

Bell, like so many others, had developed a liking for Billy the Kid. Billy was always ready to laugh, to joke, to pass the time in an agreeable way. He was, in fact, an attractive man. He gave a good account of himself. He was unassuming. Although famous—or infamous—he did not "put on airs," as Bell said. He seemed always to expect the best in people. He was well spoken. He liked, or was prepared to like, everyone, especially women, in whom he seemed to awaken the maternal instinct. He played a fair hand of poker, and he was known never to forget a kindness. Bell had nothing against the Kid personally. Billy was a man, scarcely more than a boy, with whom Bell could be comfortable—more than comfortable: giving, loyal, compassionate. Bell neither condoned nor understood Olinger's vicious behavior toward Billy. It was a vague and fatal notion in Bell's mind that Billy the Kid was less dangerous than he was said to be.

There had been a shot.

The gun was a Colt .44, single-action. Billy, urinating loudly for Bell's sake, checked to see that it was fully loaded. It felt like a heavy bird in his hands, then lighter, a goose that was mounting on the wind, streaking off into a distance that reached beyond the rim of the world. With his small white hands he handled it as a bear might handle a fish, with some sense of ancient respect, playfully and skillfully. Then he placed it inside his belt, under his shirt.

With difficulty he mounted the stairs to the level of the armory, Bell just behind him. There Billy drew the gun, turned, and leveled it at Bell's face.

Billy waited for a long moment, letting Bell take stock of the situation. Then he said, "I've got the upper hand, Bell. The whole show is mine now. I want you to do *exactly* as I say. The Lord knows

I don't want to kill you." His voice was again low, even, almost a whisper, and he spoke slowly, enunciated carefully.

"Oh, God!" Bell said. He tried desperately to restore order to his mind. He could not, and he was then beside himself. His impulse was to run. He struggled with his fear and humiliation. In the foreground of his awareness was the realization that he had made a grave mistake, unspeakably grave: he had allowed Billy the Kid to turn the tables on him. For a fraction of a moment he heard his own hysterical laughter, like Olinger's, in his ear. No one in the history of the world had done what he had just done; no one had ever forfeited his mortal advantage so foolishly, so decisively. Beyond the mask of his station and age, he began to cry. His own gun was of no use. There was no one else on the stair, in the building, as far as he knew. He was absolutely alone with this man, this dangerous and desperate man, this cold-blooded killer, this most-wanted outlaw. He wanted to vomit. None of this was real to him; it was like a dream, a nightmare. In this very moment he had grown old. His surprise and confusion and shame were overwhelming. He spun and bolted. His boots struck the stair, four steps below; his next step would strike the landing. There was a blind corner; the lower flight descended at a 90 degree angle. If only he could turn the corner, he would be safe. The Kid could not negotiate the stairs easily in his chains. He could not possibly pursue, Bell must have thought. But if indeed these considerations did happen upon Bell's stricken consciousness in the last moment of his life, they were idle.

As Bell lurched, Billy the Kid said to himself, "Don't do it, Bell, please." And in the same instant he pulled the trigger. The gun bucked, and Bell's body slammed against the wall, slumped on the landing, then tumbled out of sight. He was, somewhere in that infinite series of motions, dead.

Billy hobbled to the body, took the keys, and made his way awkwardly to the armory, opened it, and withdrew Olinger's shotgun. There was no hurry; he set the next few events to his own clock. He was on time; all the motion of the town of Lincoln, at midday, on April 28, 1881, was on time. He made his way to the window overlooking the main street, the only street of the town.

There had been a shot.

Olinger looked up. There had been a shot. He brought his sleeve quickly to his mouth and moved his chair backward, standing up. Others in the dining room had heard it too. They cocked their heads. For a moment there was a stasis, a silence thick and unwieldy, strange. Then each one returned to his meal, except Olinger. In that silence he was confounded. There had been a shot. He shook his shoulders and went out into the street. A girl in a white dress sat in a chair in front of the Wortley Hotel. He took notice of her and nodded, but she was looking away. She was in repose, a seated woman in a white dress. She was like no one and nothing else in Lincoln. She was like a painting by Renoir, a soft and lovely composition against a hard landscape, with its dry earth colors. It was strange to Olinger that he, a brittle man, more nearly an animal than a man, without the least advantage or sensitivity where the beautiful was concerned, should somehow be moved by the girl in the white dress. But he hadn't time to ponder. He hurried across the street, eighty-nine steps. The voice in the window above stopped him in his tracks. "Hello, Bob." It was familiar and reassuring; everything was as it ought to be. Olinger looked up into the twin muzzles of his own shotgun. In that moment Olinger saw Billy the Kid in extraordinary detail, saw into the blue, expressionless eyes, saw the dark brows and the long curly hair with definition, saw the mouth barely open and the teeth protruding, saw the fine, articulate hands on the gun, perfectly still, saw the little bony wrists, raw with the rub of the handcuffs. And the black eyes of the shotgun, peering into his soul. There was no depth to them, or there was depth unending; they were the blackness of the void beyond the stars. In them Olinger could see eternity. Had the girl seen him walking to his death? He could not be sure, nor did it matter, really. He had seen her. Even at this most extreme moment of his life, he was acutely aware of having seen her. She was something to see. And now, looking up at the man who was going to take his life, he held on, meagerly, to the vision of the girl. He felt nothing for her, nothing to which he could give a name. It was only that she in her remote loveliness, unattainable, untouchable, stood for some cipher in the sum of his existence. He had never imagined what his last vision of the world might be; his life had been a paltry thing. He wondered that in his mind's eye, at the ultimate hour, there should be a girl in a white dress.

Billy pulled the first trigger. The load struck Olinger in the middle, dividing him nearly in two. His body was blown into the street, face down, bent at a hideous angle. Billy pulled the second trigger, and the other load exploded into Olinger's back. The body jerked violently.

Talk, a hectic murmur, was coming up from the street now. Billy made his way down to the yard behind the courthouse. There was Godfrey Gauss, the caretaker. Billy instructed the old man to bring him a horse. For a long time the old German man labored to catch a horse in the adjacent pasture. At last he succeeded. The horse was a skittish mare that belonged to Billy Burt. "Tell Mr. Burt I'll return the horse," Billy said. Gauss saddled the mare and tied it to a fencepost. Billy had been trying to remove the leg irons, but he could not. At gunpoint, old man Gauss chopped the chain in two with an ax. Billy tied the loose ends of the chain to his belt.

At last, in the bright spring afternoon, Billy the Kid led the mare out into the wide street, where the residents of Lincoln had been gathered since midday. Billy had taken his time. He had armed himself; he had secured a horse and broken his shackles; he had left two men dead. All in all, it was one of the most intense and exhilarating days of his young life. He had never been higher. The good citizens of Lincoln, New Mexico Territory, respectfully awaited the appearance of El Chivato. Bets were laid and liquor was drunk, but quietly, discretely; there was a solemnity in the town, an air of grave celebration, as on a Day of the Dead. Billy had been wounded and could not ride; he had been killed; he was searching the courthouse for a hidden treasure; he was praying for the souls of Bob Olinger and J. W. Bell; he was composing a letter to Lew Wallace, Governor of the Territory, begging pardon.

Shortly after Olinger had been shot down in the street, there was a brief commotion. In front of the Wortley Hotel a girl in a white dress leaped upon a large sorrel stallion and raced away, her long hair flying and her immaculate dress whipping up like meringue high on her dark thighs. Collectively, the townspeople caught their breath.

Billy the Kid appeared at last. He bade a small boy step forward and hold his horse. Then he walked up one side of the street and down the other, shaking hands. "*¡Gracias, gracias!*" he said again and again. "*Adios.*" And there was bestowed upon him the best wishes of the people. *"¡Hasta luego, Billee! Vaya con Dios. ¡Bravo, bravo! ¡Bien hecho, Billee!"*

With difficulty because of the heavy chains, which, though broken, were still affixed to his ankles, Billy mounted the horse and urged it to a gallop at once. *"¡Salud!"* he shouted. *"¡Salud y amistad! ¡Adios, mi amigos, amigos de mi corazón, adios!"*

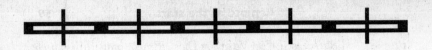

JAMES WELCH

FROM

The Indian Lawyer

It had happened a little less than a year ago in the library on the high side. He felt the shank go in and it surprised him. He knew in a split second what had happened but it surprised him and then it pissed him off. He was the cautious type and he had let himself get stuck like a fish just off fish row. A couple of guys on the unit had given him a little shit for that. Harwood, the old con, getting stuck like some fish. He had to know that the Indians were going to try it some time. In the library yet. He hadn't been on the job for three weeks when it happened. But he got nine days in the infirmary out of it. That wasn't too bad. He even managed to score some Tylenol 3, which he sold to the inmate who brought the mail.

But then he had to go to max. In the old days he would have gone to a Protective Custody Unit, which had its good points, but he would have picked up a jacket, probably as a snitch although he had never snitched anybody off. Once you got labeled you might as well serve the rest of your shift in PC, because somebody in population would get you. But that was the old days. Now they made you go to max for protection and there were some bad dudes there. It was the new policy to discourage inmates from vegetating in PC. There were no treatment programs, no school, no jobs in the PC units, just the opportunity to fuck the dog all day. Ah well, it might have been tempting in the old days to go PC, to avoid all the hassles in the yard, the chow hall, the other units. But he was better off in population as long as he stayed away from the fucking Indians.

Harwood closed his eyes and snorted, almost laughed. Here he was, thinking about staying away from the Indians, and Little Dog was sitting right next to him. But Little Dog was all right. He didn't really run with the rest of them. He ate with them and sometimes watched television in the dayroom, but most of the time when he wasn't working he stayed in his house and read. He'd been busted back six months ago from the dairy dorm for paraphernalia. They hadn't found the shit.

Little Dog's house, or cell, was only a couple of doors down the corridor from Harwood's. One morning he dropped by to borrow some toothpaste and Harwood had glanced up and down the corridor, looking for the setup. Nothing seemed out of the ordinary, just the usual migration to the showers, and so he squeezed some toothpaste on Little Dog's toothbrush. Little Dog smiled and said thanks, but Harwood didn't go to the showers that morning. Since then he'd decided that Little Dog was okay, that he wasn't interested in the Indian games.

"What are you, some kind of fence, Harwood?"

Harwood sat up straight in the metal chair, pulling his long legs in. He didn't look up.

"How about it, Harwood?"

"Yeah, some kind of fence, Beasley."

"We gotta keep this area free of shit, Harwood, in case we need an emergency exit. I guess your legs classify as shit, don't they?"

Harwood folded his arms across his chest and smiled. He knew Beasley. Most of the time Beasley was assigned to the library; in fact he had been on duty the day Harwood got stuck. He had wanted to write Harwood up for fighting but he was talked out of it by another officer. Everybody knew Beasley.

"Hey, Little Dog—remember that time down in the chow hall when I wrote up one of your soul brothers? Do you remember what he did?"

"Farted."

"That's right. He farted in the chow line. You know what that's called, Larry? Insolence. That's what I put in the report. Insolence. Class Two. Let's see." Beasley scratched his head. "What happened to him? I can't remember."

"Locked him down. Fifteen days." Little Dog was studying the papers on his lap. His GED. Certificates of successful completion of the addictive diseases program, aggression control, World of Work, Twelve Steps. He hadn't gone through the Intensive Treatment Unit for chemical dependency—that might be a sticking point—but he had done all right this time in. No way they could deny him parole.

"You know what Harwood is, Larry? A walking Class Two. A walking, talking, farting Class Two. Oh, he thinks he's getting away with it, pulling down those easy gigs. What was it before the library, Harwood—that's right, you were a bookkeeper over in Prison Industries. Hear that, Larry? You smokes get sent out to the dairy dorm, bust your asses out there in the cold, and Harwood here is a bookkeeper. And now he's up for parole. I don't know—sounds to me like there's a lot of prejudice—"

The door to the hearing room opened. Harwood and Little Dog looked up.

"Wait right there, Bill. We'll get a disposition sheet out to you in a couple of minutes." The hearings officer closed the door behind him.

"How'd it go?" said Harwood.

Shanley threw himself down in the chair, leaned back, and exhaled.

"How about it, Shanley?" Beasley had his feet up, scraping the bowl of his pipe with one of the keys that dangled from a chain at his waist. "You gonna celebrate the Fourth with the kids? That'd be nice, wouldn't it, take the little ones to the lake, eat hot dogs, drink a little beer, maybe mess around with the wife a little."

"I don't know," said Shanley. He looked at Harwood and his eyes were wide. "I'm damned if I know what went on in there. I think I did okay—I answered all their questions, damn it!"

"That's all you can do," said Harwood. "Don't worry, you're a first-timer, you've done all right." Shanley didn't belong in the close units on the high side. He should have been in the letter units on the low side. Low security. As usual the prison was overcrowded, so they stuck a guy like Shanley in with the heavies. Harwood had tried to watch out for him, to teach him the ropes, but Shanley was just too innocent. As a result he'd been bulldogged numerous times, raped twice, and Harwood suspected he was having his wife send him money to pay off the heavies, probably the Indians, since they controlled the unit. All because he didn't belong on the high security side. At least Harwood had made sure he didn't become somebody's old lady.

"Well, what's it going to be, Shanley, long sheet or short sheet? We're going to miss you down there in the kitchen. You got a real touch with those sweet rolls. I almost hope they set you back. How long you been in, Shanley?"

"Thirteen months, twelve days, not counting sixty days jail time."

"Hooo," Beasley breathed. "That's a pretty good stretch for checks. You must have been laying some pretty serious paper. What's that on—five years? You know, most guys, they'd give a suspended or deferred, slap their wrist a little—but you, you must be some kind of badass. Like Harwood here. How long you been down this time, Harwood, five, six years?"

"Close to seven, Beasley. That's on a forty-year beef reduced to thirty by Sentence Review. Fifth felony, second armed robbery, persistent offender, declared dangerous. And an escape, two years consecutive to the thirty. Anything else you need to know, Beasley?"

"Hey now, don't get testy, Harwood. I'm just making conversation, that's all, trying to ease the tension. I know you guys are a little nervous when you come up. You're a little nervous, aren't you, Larry?"

Little Dog knew better than to get drawn in. He'd done all right this time and he wasn't about to blow it by telling Beasley to fuck off. He wanted to go home. It'd been nearly four years and it had been three years before that. In fact, he'd been on the outside only two years out of the last eleven. He was tired of the joint and tired of the juvenile home and foster homes. He was ready to go back to the reservation and live with his grandmother. He held up his GED diploma. "See this, Officer Beasley? This is my ticket. I got a good training program waiting for me on the res and I'm going to make it."

Beasley laughed. "That's the spirit, Larry. Hell, nothing's going to stop you this time. You just lay off the sauce, you'll be okay. See that, Harwood?"

The door opened and the hearings officer entered the small holding room. He waved a piece of paper and smiled. "Short sheet, Bill. You did a good job."

Shanley let out a deep breath and slumped back on the chair. He had done some hard time. He accepted Harwood's hand, his eyes glittery. "When can I leave?" His voice was small, apprehensive.

"Well, I'm going to have to read you out, check out that job plan once more. It's a little shaky, but I don't see why we can't get you out of here the end of next week. I'll come by your unit tomorrow. We'll get the ball rolling then."

Shanley stood and the tears came. He couldn't help them. He tried to read the disposition sheet. He turned away from the others.

"Want to sit here for a while, Bill, kind of get it together?"

"I'm all right." Shanley wiped his eyes with his sleeve. He shook the hearings officer's hand. "Thanks."

"You earned it. Good luck." The hearings officer turned to Little Dog. "Larry?"

Little Dog straightened his papers and stood, following the officer into the hearing room. The door chunked behind them.

Shanley looked down at Harwood. "Thanks—thanks for helping me. I don't know if . . ." His voice caught and his "Good luck" was barely a whisper.

Harwood listened to Shanley's steps echo down the hall. It was late in the afternoon and the building had turned quiet. A couple of officers talked in low tones in the muster room next door and Harwood couldn't see or understand them. Beasley was reading the newspaper, his feet up on the desk. Suddenly Harwood felt empty inside. He knew it was hopeless, an exercise in delusion. That morning he had actually felt good. He had gotten his library job back and he spent the morning unpacking a couple of crates of books from some church group in Billings. They weren't the kind of books he would have read, mostly inspirational, self-help stuff, but he had unpacked them and glued on the little envelopes that held the checkout cards. Then he spent the afternoon up to three-quarters of an hour ago typing the names and titles on the checkout cards. It was a good mind-numbing job and he thought of Patti Ann and he thought he would get a chance to be with her shortly. That's how much he deluded himself. They had been married for nine years and he had spent seven and a half of them locked up, counting jail time and prison time. At least he had that going for him. Maybe they would think he had served enough time; maybe they'd cut him a little slack because he'd been shanked. His prison record was pretty good—no write-ups the last couple of years; he'd completed ADSP and the follow-up program even though he didn't have a drinking or drug problem; he'd gone through aggression control; he'd even had several one-on-one sessions with the shrink, Larson, to see why he liked to point guns at people. He knew he

interested Larson because he wasn't like most of the other inmates—
he was bright and clean-cut and had a degree in economics as well as
an A.A. in bookkeeping. He'd been interviewed by a couple of student
psychologists who also couldn't figure out why he pulled the shit he
did. He liked Larson, he was an old pro, and Harwood had tried to
level with him, but he just couldn't explain his motivation. It came
out sounding like he was a thrill-seeker or some bullshit thing like
that. Larson figured it had something to do with power, he'd told
Harwood that much, but he couldn't understand what was behind it.
Most of the other inmates were pretty easy to figure out, the patterns
were there—poverty, abuse, history of criminality in the family, im-
pulsiveness. But Harwood was something else. He came from a good
family, he had a normal childhood, and he hadn't committed a crime
until he was twenty-four. By that time he'd been working two years
in the accounting department for a small chain of grocery stores in
Montana and Idaho. He'd gotten good evaluations. Things were looking rosy. So why now, at the age of thirty-seven, was he doing his
second stretch for armed robbery? Harwood used to laugh and throw
up his hands at Larson's frustration. If you couldn't laugh you'd end
up crying. There was a lot of laughing in the joint.

Harwood put all that old business out of his mind and concentrated
on Patti Ann. What was it—a little over a month since she had last
come down to see him? Jesus! Harwood looked at his watch. 4:35. She
was here now, waiting for him in the visiting room. Waiting to see if
he made it. He glanced over at Beasley. Shit, if it had been any other
officer Harwood could have him call over to the visiting room and tell
Patti Ann he would be a little late. Ah, Christ, it didn't matter. The
news wasn't going to be good anyhow. Harwood shook his head and
wished there was a window to look out of. There were never enough
windows.

What would she be wearing today? Maybe that white dress with
the little straps. Yeah, she'd be wearing that, it was his favorite. Sexy
and innocent-looking at the same time. And the high heels, the bur-
gundy ones. He liked the way her legs looked in that outfit. She'd be
nice and tan, slender but healthy-looking. God, she was probably going
nuts wondering what was happening to him. She knew his hearing
was today but she didn't know it would be the last one of the day.
She'd driven all the way over from Helena and if they were lucky

they'd get half an hour together. It wasn't going to be a very happy visit, so maybe it was just as well. She can come back next month, thought Harwood, when things were back to normal.

He heard the muffled sound of laughter from the hearing room and then the door opened and Little Dog came out beaming.

"We'll do your release papers tomorrow, Larry. We should be able to get you on a bus by the end of next week, maybe sooner. It's all been cleared with your parole officer. Okay?"

"Sooner the better. I'm going to make it this time. I'm done with this shit."

"Just don't set your sights too high, Larry, at least not initially. One day at a time, just like the old song. Get adjusted out there. Good luck to you." The hearings officer shook Little Dog's hand, then turned to Harwood. "Come on in, Jack."

The first thing Harwood noticed was the carpeting, wall to wall. He hadn't walked on carpeting in seven years. Then the bank of windows that looked across the courtyard to a twenty-foot-tall cement wall. Some view.

"You want to sit here, Jack?" The hearings officer pointed to a chair across the table from the three board members. It was set back a way from the table. "Jack, these are the members of the board who will conduct your hearing—Mr. Berglund, Mr. Higgins, and Mr. Yellow Calf. Jack Harwood."

"How you doing, Jack?" The man in the middle leaned forward with a smile.

Harwood glanced down at the nameplate. Peter Higgins. He was the chairman, the one you had to look out for, that was the word in the yard. He came down hard on the bullshitters, so shoot straight. "Not bad, Mr. Higgins."

"Good, that's good. Let's see—" Higgins picked up a loose-leaf notebook. "Five felonies, two armed robberies, one escape. Two probation violations, one parole violation. That sound about right, Jack?"

"Unfortunately, that's correct."

"Unfortunately? What do you mean, unfortunately? Fortune has nothing to do with it. You're up to your ears in the life of crime, Jack. You're a big-time hood."

Harwood shrugged.

"Okay, instant offense, holding up a savings and loan in Helena, two fall partners. Where are they now, Jack?"

"Hartpence is still here, Williams got out a couple of years ago. Williams did good time."

"He also rolled over on you guys, didn't he? I seem to remember reading that he cut himself a deal with the county attorney's office. You remember that case, Bob?"

Berglund had been rolling his necktie around a pencil. The question caught him by surprise. "Williams. Yeah, we paroled him two years ago. He snitched these guys off and Judge Howard gave him a reduced sentence. He was the driver."

Higgins looked down at the thick notebook. It held all the cases the parole board was to hear at the prison that month. The other members of the board had identical notebooks. As they studied them, Harwood took the opportunity to glance behind him. The hearings officer and the executive secretary were talking. Flaherty, that was the secretary's name, Walt Flaherty. He was a good guy. He treated the inmates well, answered their questions, didn't act like a honcho. Harwood looked out the windows. A yard crew was working on the small strip of grass in the courtyard. Seven of them.

"Have you ever had a gun stuck in your face, Jack?"

Harwood was surprised at the suddenness of the question but not the question itself. He remembered his first parole hearing. He knew they liked to come from all angles, trying to trip you up.

"Just once, Mr. Higgins. One of the arresting officers this last time pointed his revolver at me. I guess both of them did but the other one was behind me."

"Can you imagine how that poor woman in the savings and loan felt, some jackass comes along and sticks a gun in her face? She must have been terrified. She probably still has nightmares!" Higgins's voice was beginning to rise. "All because a big-time hood like you is too damn lazy to go out and earn his money like decent human beings, like that woman!"

Remorse. That was the key. "I think about it all the time, Mr. Higgins, believe me. If there was anything I could do—I just thank the Lord—"

"This was your second armed robbery, Jack. Why don't you tell us about the first one." Berglund had a calm, level voice. He was a rancher from Miles City, a tall balding man who had put in several years in the state legislature, who had pushed for better treatment programs in the prison and who had been a key player in getting the funds to build the new prison. Now, he liked to joke, his appointment to the parole board was punishment for his past political sins.

"There's not much to tell, Mr. Berglund," said Harwood. "I didn't need the money, I was a decent hardworking human being—" Harwood glanced at Higgins. "I guess it was just an impulsive thing, you know, one of those things you do—"

"Impulsive?" Higgins's voice was strained with wonder. "You call going to a bar, buying a sawed-off shotgun, picking up a fall partner at his home way out in Rimini, returning to Helena, gassing up your car, then holding up the Colonial Inn—impulsive?"

Harwood glanced over at Sylvester Yellow Calf. He was leaning back in his swivel chair, studying the notebook in his lap. He was a big man, good shape, good-looking. Harwood had never seen an Indian in a suit and tie before. He knew Yellow Calf was a lawyer in Helena and a former basketball player. In fact, Yellow Calf had played for the University of Montana while Harwood went to school there. Harwood didn't pay much attention to sports but the fact that Yellow Calf was a lawyer in Helena did intrigue him. That was Harwood's turf, that was where Patti Ann lived.

"I guess 'impulsive' is the wrong word for it, Mr. Higgins. I don't know, maybe 'fascination' would be a better one. I kind of became fascinated with serious crime, not just shoplifting or writing a bum check. I don't know, maybe it became kind of an obsession, I just knew I had to try it. So my friend and I held up the Colonial."

"How much did you get?"

"A little over two thousand."

"And how much from the savings and loan?"

"Twelve."

"Okay, Jack, the million-dollar question—why? And don't give me any more of that fascination bullshit. You might be able to con a couple of student psychologists but you're talking to us now." Higgins swept his arm around the room. "We're all adults, nothing goes beyond this room, you know that. So why not level with us?"

Harwood hesitated. For the first time since deciding that he wasn't going to make parole anyway he felt a kind of pressure to answer the question well. Were they taking this hearing seriously? Jesus, he might actually have a chance. "Okay, I'll try to explain it all, Mr. Higgins. That first time was pretty much like I said. I'm sure it's in your records there—I had graduated from UM and had taken a job in the accounting department of the grocery chain. I was in training and not making a lot of money but I was getting by, I was single then. I didn't have much going for me socially so I started hanging around this particular bar in Helena. I never had a drinking problem but it was a place to go, to spend the evenings. To make a long story short, I met a couple of guys I shouldn't have. They'd done time over here and they were into some petty shit, mostly burglaries. One night I went with them —that was the night we hit the Steinhaus, got over four hundred in cash, a thirty-eight that was behind the bar, and a couple of cases of booze. Those guys were pretty elated but I was scared shitless. They tried to give me some of the money but I wouldn't take it. I stayed away from that bar for a couple of weeks. I thought I was through with it. But one night I met them in the parking lot at Buttrey's. I don't to this day know why but I let them talk me into riding around with them. They were drinking beer and started talking about doing time here in Deer Lodge. They told me all about the way guys are bull-dogged, beaten up for not playing con games. I was fascinated—there's that word again, Mr. Higgins—and kind of scared. It was like there was a reason for telling me about this scary shit. There seemed to be a threat behind it. Anyway, we hit the Cenex that night and got a bunch of tools and some cash. One of the guys said there was supposed to be a lot of cash around but we couldn't find it. Turns out the sixty dollars we did get was money from a football pool. I don't know, a week or so later one of the guys and I robbed the Colonial."

"That's a pretty major step, Jack, going from burglary to armed robbery," said Berglund. He was shaking his head. "I don't understand how a fellow like you could get involved in burglary, much less robbery. As far as I can tell, you had no juvenile record, no priors. Let's see, the judge gave you five, five, and twenty, all concurrent, and suspended fifteen." He looked up from his notebook. "That's a curious sentence, Jack, kind of harsh and lenient at the same time."

"I did fourteen months on it, built up a lot of good time. I was earning day for day toward the end." Harwood smiled. "I thought I learned a pretty good lesson there."

"And what happened?"

"It's a fairly old story. My employer wouldn't take me back because I was a criminal, and I couldn't get bonded, so my career as an accountant was over almost before it started. I couldn't even get a job as a boxboy with that chain. I ended up paroling out to a housepainting outfit in Helena and made some decent money that summer. But it wasn't a career."

"Isn't that about the time you got married?"

"Yeah, I painted her house that summer. She was in the process of getting a divorce and she was fixing up the house in order to sell it. I helped her do some other stuff on my time off, then I helped her move when she sold it. We got married that winter—nine years ago." Harwood looked at the backs of his hands, which were resting on his knees. "She's a good woman."

"Doesn't she work for the state?"

"Human Resources—she's in records."

"Children?"

Harwood knew they had this information in their notebooks, but this was part of their game. "She miscarried twice, had to have a hysterectomy after the second time. I was already in here when that happened. It was a pretty bad time for her. That's when I decided to walk away. I wanted to go to Helena to be with her."

Higgins had been leaning back in his swivel chair, studying Harwood's reactions to Berglund's questions. He glanced over at Sylvester Yellow Calf, who had Harwood's jacket spread before him. He was reading a trial transcript. Higgins looked beyond Yellow Calf to the twenty-foot-high wall on the other side of the courtyard. It was sliced in half by the shadow of the administration building. Higgins's stomach growled. Last case of the day, and it was a tough one. He listened to Harwood explain his escape and how he was picked up in Helena two days later at the hospital. It appeared that he did just want to be with his wife, because he had to know that would be the first place they would look for him—and there he was. He was still in his prison khakis when the cops walked in on him. That escape was probably the reason he was still in the joint. Escapes were mandatory consecutive sentences.

They could have paroled him before now without the escape. It was hard to get a handle on Harwood. In some ways he was about as decent an inmate as they'd heard today, for several months for that matter. The word was that Harwood took some of the weaker inmates under his wing—no sex, no bulldogging, just protection. And he was certainly a lot brighter than your run-of-the-mill inmate. And that's what irked Higgins. Pissed him off, in fact. He didn't have to pull this crap. He should be out taking care of his wife, going to work, paying taxes. Peter Higgins felt his jaw tightening and he had to tell himself, Easy, go easy.

Berglund was beginning to wind down. He was old and had a weak heart. He'd only been back from triple-bypass surgery for three months and Higgins worried about him. At least the new hearing room was air-conditioned, not like the old one where you had to keep the doors closed and locked for security reasons and it got to be an oven in there. This was pretty plush. Even the flags looked crisper in here.

Sylvester Yellow Calf laid the file on the table and waited for Berglund to finish questioning the inmate. He too could tell the old man was about finished for the day. His usually level voice was becoming flat and tinny. And they had put in a long day, seen a lot of inmates. Sylvester sneaked a look at his watch. 5:10. Not too bad. He probably was going to make it back to Helena by 6:30. Took about an hour if you hustled. He hated cocktail parties and he should be laughing at himself for being anxious about this one. But it was a big one.

Finally, Bob Berglund slumped back with an audible, grateful wheeze. He automatically reached in his shirt pocket for a cigarette before he remembered they weren't there anymore. He'd had to give them up.

Sylvester looked at the inmate, Jack Harwood, almost for the first time since he had glanced up when Harwood entered the room. Clean-cut, short hair, no headband, no bandanna, no tattoos. His khakis were ironed, maybe even starched, and the running shoes looked brand-new.

"Mr. Harwood, I've been reading the transcript of the savings and loan robbery trial. Just a couple of things, let's see." Sylvester flipped back a couple of pages. "Here we are—in response to a question by the prosecuting attorney you state that you have no desire to cooperate with the court, that what's done is done, and here, I quote: 'I've already ruined my fucking chance for a decent life, you're going to flush me anyway, I'm not taking anybody else down.' Then you refused to answer any more of the prosecuting attorney's questions. Just a couple of things, Mr. Harwood. First, why did you request a jury trial if you weren't going to cooperate with anyone, including your own attorney—and second, what did you mean by the statement 'I'm not taking anybody else down'? That almost sounds like there were more of you than got charged for the robbery."

Harwood laughed, softly, to the whole table. "I may have been a little melodramatic there. That prosecutor was a bulldog. No, there were just the three of us—Hartpence, Williams, and me."

"You're sure? No other accomplices?"

"That's the way it went down, just like on your police report there."

"It also says in the transcript that only three thousand dollars was recovered—that's out of twelve thousand. What happened to the rest of the money?"

"That's always puzzled me, Mr. Yellow Calf. I can't imagine what happened to the rest of it. We put the athletic bag with the money in it in the trunk of Williams's car. When they busted Williams the next day, they only found the three thousand." Harwood laughed and lifted his eyebrows as though the joke was on him.

"C'mon, Jack, you were the man. Those other guys didn't have enough brains between them to make a good breakfast. All right, tell me this—tell me what you think happened to the money."

Harwood began to realize that things were getting out of control. It was clear that Higgins didn't like him, and now this Indian was getting smart. Harwood almost laughed again but caught himself. Be sincere, be straight, level with them. As much as you can.

"You're not going to believe this, you're not going to want to believe this—" Harwood glanced quickly at Higgins, who was examining his fingernails. "I don't think Williams got away with it. He knew the consequences—Hartpence is a pretty mean dude." Now Harwood looked into Yellow Calf's eyes. "I can only guess it was the cops. They're the only ones besides Williams who had access to the car and the money. That's the only way I can figure it."

"For Christ's sake, Harwood!" If so much wasn't on the line, it would have been comical to see Higgins explode. He was a small man with a shiny face and round eyes that always seemed full of helpless fury. He had abandoned his clip-on tie earlier that afternoon and now even his neck was bright red.

Yellow Calf jumped in quickly. "Jack, you don't expect us to believe this, do you? You know, as Mr. Higgins has already pointed out, all we want out of you guys is the truth. You have already been to trial, you've been found guilty, you're serving your time. We can't do anything to you if you tell us the truth. We just want the truth. Do you understand that, Jack? Do you want to try again?"

Things were definitely fucked. Just like that. Even Berglund was looking at him with mild disgust.

"You've done pretty well in here, Jack. No write-ups the past two years, you've completed some programs, you're working. You were kind of a smartass early on but you've cleaned up your act considerably. That's to the good—but there are two or three areas we need to address in considering your case. One, you picked up a felony, the escape, while you were in here. That doesn't look good. That makes it hard for us to parole you on your first appearance. And law enforcement doesn't want you back in the Helena area. We have notes from the county attorney's office, the sheriff's department, the police department. But mostly they—and we—believe that you got away with the rest of the money, the nine thousand dollars. That's not a hell of a lot of money, Jack, but you put us in a very awkward position. How will it look to law enforcement, to the people in Helena, if we just parole you without your having to account for the money?"

"I sure wish I knew what happened to that money, Mr. Yellow Calf, I'd sure tell you." The jig was now up. Harwood had tried to sound sincere, to act sincere, but he knew Yellow Calf had detected the small sarcasm in his voice. Practically seven years in the joint and he still couldn't tell them. But what if he did? What would happen? What about the statute of limitations? Didn't that run out in seven years? He'd have to look that up tomorrow in the library. One thing about a prison library, it has a good legal section. And good jail-house lawyers. For a couple of packs of cigarettes he could have one of them review his case. Be kind of fun to ask this Indian lawyer right now about the statute of limitations, get a little free legal advice from the adversary. But even as Jack Harwood thought this, he felt his spirits sinking rapidly.

"Anything else you'd like to tell us, Jack?"

Harwood stared at Yellow Calf. Yeah, I've been shanked by the fucking Indians. Don't I get some points for that, some good time, combat pay, a Purple Heart? Harwood wanted to tell this Indian fucking lawyer that. It seemed only human to take that into consideration, but he knew the board wouldn't. They had that information in their notebooks but for some reason they chose not to bring it up. Neither would he. Neither would he forget Sylvester Yellow Calf.

He turned to the chairman and smiled. "I guess that's about it, Mr. Higgins. I'd like a chance out there. Things have changed and I'd like to see what it's like."

Higgins had regained his composure. Now he just sounded weary. "You want to step outside? We'll get a disposition sheet to you in a minute."

Harwood stood and thanked the board, smiling, brisk. He waved to Walt Flaherty. "See you in the yard, Walt." The old con code—don't let them see you sweat. Just like in the commercial.

Patti Ann Harwood sat at a small round table in the visiting room, watching the families—the parents, the children, the wives, the girl-friends. It was getting late and most of the children had grown tired of seeing their fathers, their stepfathers, their mothers' boyfriends. Some had gone outside to play; others twisted and whined on plastic chairs; still others, the smaller ones, slept on jackets or small blankets on the concrete floor. The initial enthusiasm had long since worn off and the conversations were by turns desultory and intimate.

Patti Ann had been sitting, waiting, for an hour and forty minutes. She knew Jack would probably be a little late but this was ridiculous. She'd already had the duty officer call over to the hearing room. Jack was the next case, but that had been at least an hour ago. It was bad enough having to see him like this, once a month because he wouldn't let her come any more often, but now there were only twenty minutes left. There was so much to say—Patti Ann caught herself—there was usually nothing to say because to say things out loud made each visit more painful than the last. Patti Ann could feel herself slowly, inex-orably slipping to the edge of Jack's life. What could he tell her of his life in the prison? What could she tell him of the outside world that didn't fill him with regret, even pain? The small talk—she had become pretty good at it but it didn't go anywhere. When she left the prison after each visit she felt insignificant. She didn't have a family with Jack, she didn't have a life with Jack. She lived alone, a prison widow.

She dug into her purse, found her cigarettes and plastic lighter. As she lit up she glanced around the room at the other women. Years ago she had scorned them and pitied them. Most of them were unattractive—fat or skinny, hard-looking or puffy, stringy hair or pathetic, glamorous bouffants; some of them had tattoos on their knuckles and arms; most of them were on general assistance, relief, child care. These were the ones who came to visit most often. They lived in downtown Deer Lodge, sometimes two to three families to an apartment. Some of them worked but most found it more profitable to stay on assistance. That way, too, they could visit their men at every opportunity.

In the beginning Patti Ann had looked down on them, especially those who met their men in prison through sisters or girlfriends or former boyfriends and husbands, pen-pal organizations, church groups. These were the saddest to Patti Ann. Losers on the outside and losers on the inside. They fulfilled their men's needs while they were in prison but when they got out the men usually dumped them. Who needs an unattractive divorced woman with two kids that aren't even yours?

Even now Patti Ann could see these women scattered around the visiting room. And today she didn't feel very different from them. She was nervous and fitful, mildly depressed. At first when she heard that Jack was scheduled for his parole hearing this month she had been elated, despite his cautions. She had walked around her apartment looking at the furniture, the pictures, the rugs, the small things, trying to see them as Jack might when he walked in for the first time. She had even bought a bright new comforter for the double bed. Then she thought of looking for a new larger apartment until she realized that he had been living in a cubicle smaller than her bedroom. Jack had called a couple more times and spoken to her with a quiet sobriety and she did come to realize that he might not make it. But he had been in for seven years—how could the parole board turn him down? She had waited for him, they had to know that. If she could have had a child perhaps she could have waited forever, but all she had was herself, every night in the small apartment, herself.

Patti Ann had been watching a family, and the inmate smiled at her and waved. It took a second for her to realize that the gesture was directed at her. She smiled awkwardly and tried to place him—slight, sandy hair, a little obsequious even at this distance. Yes, Stanley, Stanley—no, Shanley, Bob? Bill? The little guy that Jack tried so hard to protect. Jack had introduced her to him last winter. Now he gave her the thumbs-up and she remembered that he was up for parole too. He had made it. She smiled and nodded, and then she smiled and nodded to his wife, who was also slight—in her sleeveless blouse, tight jeans, and sneakers, she looked like somebody's little sister, but there were three children at the table.

Above the murmur of the late-afternoon conversations Patti Ann heard the electric gate roll open. She was surprised that she was that attuned to the nuances of prison noises. She looked toward the open door and she saw Jack enter the visiting room. He dropped his pass on the duty officer's table and looked at her. He did not look happy.

She stood and watched him pick his way between tables, once stepping over a sleeping child, and she moved forward and hugged him and gave him a small kiss, the kind the officers allowed. She knew before asking but she asked anyway.

"They turned me down," he said, and he lowered himself wearily onto a plastic chair.

"But why?" she said. "How could they . . ."

He unfolded a sheet of paper and handed it to her and then sat back and watched her read it. "Nature of crime," he said. "Also, they don't parole repeat violent offenders on their first appearance."

"But you're not violent, that's ridiculous!"

"Seven years ago I stuck a gun in someone's face. That makes me violent. Listen, we've been all through this. I warned you, didn't I? I told you not to get your hopes up. You've seen how this system works. You make a couple of mistakes and they make you pay. They don't care how long it takes, just so long as you pay." Harwood leaned forward, shook a cigarette out of her pack, and lit it. "So I'm paying," he said glumly.

"Well, what do you have to do now? What else?"

"It's on there, near the bottom." Harwood nodded toward the piece of paper on the table. He noticed the full ashtray. She was smoking too much again.

Patti Ann picked up the disposition sheet. Under Recommendations, in longhand, it listed reduced custody, continued clear conduct, advanced aggression control. But it was the top of the sheet that caused her heart to sink. Parole denied, pass to discharge of sentence. Such clinical, dispassionate language—a couple of phrases that probably meant nothing to the parole board but meant everything to Jack, and to her. She set the piece of paper aside and sighed an almost contented sigh. Parole denied. And she suddenly recognized the source of her earlier depression. It startled her, the utter simplicity—she had been afraid that Jack would be paroled, that he would come home to her apartment, to her life! She had made a life. She had a routine, a couple of friends, she sewed in the evenings and she had been to bed alone more than she had with Jack or any man. She looked at Jack as though he were an object and she saw a familiar face, a small smile fading as the eyes narrowed in puzzlement.

"What's wrong?" he said.

She shook her head and tried to smile. Today, for the first time since he went in, she saw an inmate sitting across the table, wearing khakis and running shoes like the rest of them. He even had that look, that edgy don't-get-too-close look that some of the longtimers had. But it was the uniformity of it all, the cinder-block buildings, the maze of sidewalks, the guard towers, the dirt parking lot in front of the administration building, the inmates in their khakis and blues and watch caps, the officers in their blue blazers and maroon ties, the glint of the ribbon wire on top of the endless Cyclone fences—all of it was colorless in its monotony and now she saw that lack of color in her husband and it scared her and made her angry.

"Jack," she said. She leaned forward and put her hand on his knee. "I need you out of here. Things are getting too odd for us. I can't deal with you being in here and me out there. Every time I drive home from here, I look at the streams, the pines, the mountains—the world just seems too big, too much to handle every day. I think I won't see you again." She lowered her head and looked at her hand. "It frightens me so much when I think that someday I might like it that way."

Harwood covered her hand with his own. He glanced at his wristwatch. They had only ten minutes left. "You have to be strong for a little while longer. I know this is a blow but we have to weather it out. We can if we stay strong."

Patti Ann looked up into his face and it was familiar again but it would always be changed by what she had seen earlier. She had seen what prison actually does to a man; she had seen the dull gray edges of resignation, and she wondered if she could ever look at her husband again without seeing that. She sighed and nodded her head.

Harwood stubbed out his cigarette and leaned away from her. "You smoke too much, you know that?"

She smiled, then laughed softly. He had said that to her when he first met her, when he painted her house. The world was different then.

"You're also very pretty. You didn't wear my favorite dress, though. How about it—next time?"

"Okay." She had deliberately not worn that dress. It was an innocent-looking sundress, a little short with delicate shoulder straps, hardly striking on the street, but in here she felt naked and vulnerable. Part of her discomfort came from the way Jack had stared at her last time, as though he were one of the gang and she a prime piece. Now he was memorizing her from top to bottom and she tried to understand his unabashed lust, but all she could feel was a vague shame at the unnaturalness of it. She was his wife.

She became aware of a change in the noises that surrounded them and she glanced around and saw that visiting hours were over. The women were gathering kids and toys, some were giving their men a last-minute thrill, a squeeze here, a tongue there, a small packet of dope. But most seemed just weary and relieved that it was over for another day.

Harwood stood and took her hand and brought her to her feet. Amid the milling, he hugged her close and kissed her hard. She felt his hand on her butt and just as quickly it was gone and he was walking her out the door to the electric gate.

"I need you to do me a favor," he said quietly as they waited for the other visitors to assemble at the gate. "There's this guy on the parole board, his name's Sylvester Yellow Calf—an Indian, a lawyer from Helena. You can look him up in the phone book. I want you to find out something about him, if he's married, what law firm he's attached to, what kind of law he practices. Find out who his friends are, what does he do for a social life, things like that. I know this is asking a lot, but I need to know something about him."

Patti Ann had been looking through the metal gate at a shadowy mountain that loomed above the administration building. Although it was late August a small crevice near the top contained a wedge of snow that was turning blue as the light went off it. Behind the right shoulder of the mountain she could see a column of smoke. Now she turned toward Jack, but he was looking straight ahead at the electric gate. Just then the gate buzzed and began to slide open. Jack squeezed her hand and turned to go back across the yard to his unit. She had begun to move with the crowd through the gate when she heard him call her name. She turned but she was caught up in the moving throng.

"I want you to meet him," he called. "Soon. Make an appointment with him, bump into him in the grocery store, anything—just meet him. I'll call you."

By then she was through the gate and she stepped to one side. "Why?" she cried, but Harwood smiled and waved as he walked briskly back to his unit.

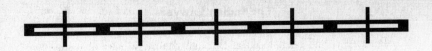

PAM HOUSTON

How to Talk to a Hunter

When he says "Skins or blankets?" it will take you a moment to realize that he's asking which you want to sleep under. And in your hesitation he'll decide that he wants to see your skin wrapped in the big black moosehide. He carried it, he'll say, soaking wet and heavier than a dead man, across the tundra for two—was it hours or days or weeks? But the payoff, now, will be to see it fall across one of your white breasts. It's December, and your skin is never really warm, so you will pull the bulk of it around you and pose for him, pose for his camera, without having to narrate this moose's death.

You will spend every night in this man's bed without asking yourself why he listens to top-forty country. Why he donated money to the Republican party. Why he won't play back his messages while you are in the room. You are there so often the messages pile up. Once, you noticed the bright green counter reading as high as fifteen.

He will have lured you here out of a careful independence that you spent months cultivating; though it will finally be winter, the dwindling daylight and the threat of Christmas, that makes you give in. Spending nights with this man means suffering the long face of your sheep dog, who likes to sleep on your bed, who worries when you don't come home. But the hunter's house is so much warmer than yours, and he'll give you a key, and just like a woman, you'll think that means something. It will snow hard for thirteen straight days. Then it will really get cold. When it is sixty below there will be no wind and no clouds, just still air and cold sunshine. The sun on the windows will lure you out of bed, but he'll pull you back under. The next two hours he'll devote to your body. With his hands, with his tongue, he'll express what will seem to you like the most eternal of loves. Like the house key, this is just another kind of lie. Even in bed; especially in bed, you and he cannot speak the same language. The machine will answer the incoming calls. From under an ocean of passion and hide and hair you'll hear a woman's muffled voice between the beeps.

Your best female friend will say, "So what did you think? That a man who sleeps under a dead moose is capable of commitment?"

This is what you learned in college: A man desires the satisfaction of his desire; a woman desires the condition of desiring.

The hunter will talk about spring in Hawaii, summer in Alaska. The man who says he was always better at math will form the sentences so carefully it will be impossible to tell if you are included in these plans. When he asks you if you would like to open a small guest ranch way out in the country, understand that this is a rhetorical question. Label these conversations future perfect, but don't expect the present to catch up with them. Spring is an inconceivable distance from the December days that just keep getting shorter and gray.

He'll ask you if you've ever shot anything, if you'd like to, if you ever thought about teaching your dog to retrieve. Your dog will like him too much, will drop the stick at his feet every time, will roll over and let the hunter scratch his belly.

One day he'll leave you sleeping to go split wood or get the mail and his phone will ring again. You'll sit very still while a woman who calls herself something like Patty Coyote leaves a message on his machine: she's leaving work, she'll say, and the last thing she wanted to hear was the sound of his beautiful voice. Maybe she'll talk only in rhyme. Maybe the counter will change to sixteen. You'll look a question at the mule deer on the wall, and the dark spots on either side of his mouth will tell you he shares more with this hunter than you ever will. One night, drunk, the hunter told you he was sorry for taking that deer, that every now and then there's an animal that isn't meant to be taken, and he should have known that deer was one.

Your best male friend will say, "No one who needs to call herself Patty Coyote can hold a candle to you, but why not let him sleep alone a few nights, just to make sure?"

The hunter will fill your freezer with elk burger, venison sausage, organic potatoes, fresh pecans. He'll tell you to wear your seat belt, to dress warmly, to drive safely. He'll say you are always on his mind, that you're the best thing that's ever happened to him, that you make him glad that he's a man.

Tell him it don't come easy, tell him freedom's just another word for nothing left to lose.

These are the things you'll know without asking: The coyote woman wears her hair in braids. She uses words like "howdy." She's man enough to shoot a deer.

A week before Christmas you'll rent *It's a Wonderful Life* and watch it together, curled on your couch, faces touching. Then you'll bring up the word "monogamy." He'll tell you how badly he was hurt by your predecessor. He'll tell you he couldn't be happier spending every night with you. He'll say there's just a few questions he doesn't have the answers for. He'll say he's just scared and confused. Of course this isn't exactly what he means. Tell him you understand. Tell him you are scared too. Tell him to take all the time he needs. Know that you could never shoot an animal, and be glad of it.

Your best female friend will say, "You didn't tell him you loved him, did you?" Don't even tell her the truth. If you do, you'll have to tell her that he said this: "I feel exactly the same way."

———

Your best male friend will say, "Didn't you know what would happen when you said the word 'commitment'?"

But that isn't the word that you said.

He'll say, "Commitment, monogamy, it all means just one thing."

The coyote woman will come from Montana with the heavier snows. The hunter will call you on the day of the solstice to say he has a friend in town and can't see you. He'll leave you hanging your Christmas lights; he'll give new meaning to the phrase "longest night of the year." The man who has said he's not so good with words will manage to say eight things about his friend without using a gender-determining pronoun. Get out of the house quickly. Call the most understanding person you know that will let you sleep in his bed.

Your best female friend will say, "So what did you think? That he was capable of living outside his gender?"

When you get home in the morning there's a candy tin on your pillow. Santa, obese and grotesque, fondles two small children on the lid. The card will say something like, From your not-so-secret admirer. Open it. Examine each carefully made truffle. Feed them, one at a time, to the dog. Call the hunter's machine. Tell him you don't speak chocolate.

Your best female friend will say, "At this point, what is it about him that you could possibly find appealing?"

Your best male friend will say, "Can't you understand that this is a good sign? Can't you understand that this proves how deep he's in with you?" Hug your best male friend. Give him the truffles the dog wouldn't eat.

Of course the weather will cooperate with the coyote woman. The highways will close, she will stay another night. He'll tell her he's going to work so he can come and see you. He'll even leave her your number and write "Me at Work" on the yellow pad of paper by his phone. Although you shouldn't, you'll have to be there. It will be you and your nauseous dog and your half-trimmed tree all waiting for him like a series of questions.

This is what you learned in graduate school: in every assumption is contained the possibility of its opposite.

In your kitchen he'll hug you like you might both die there. Sniff him for coyote. Don't hug him back.

He will say whatever he needs to to win. He'll say it's just an old friend. He'll say the visit was all the friend's idea. He'll say the night away from you has given him time to think about how much you mean to him. Realize that nothing short of sleeping alone will ever make him realize how much you mean to him. He'll say that if you can just be a little patient, some good will come out of this for the two of you after all. He still won't use a gender-specific pronoun.

Put your head in your hands. Think about what it means to be patient. Think about the beautiful, smart, strong, clever woman you thought he saw when he looked at you. Pull on your hair. Rock your body back and forth. Don't cry.

He'll say that after holding you it doesn't feel right holding anyone else. For "holding," substitute "fucking." Then take it as a compliment.

He will get frustrated and rise to leave. He may or may not be bluffing. Stall for time. Ask a question he can't immediately answer. Tell him you want to make love on the floor. When he tells you your body is beautiful, say, "I feel exactly the same way." Don't, under any circumstances, stand in front of the door.

Your best female friend will say, "They lie to us, they cheat on us, and we love them more for it." She'll say, "It's our fault. We raise them to be like that."

Tell her it can't be your fault. You've never raised anything but dogs.

The hunter will say it's late and he has to go home to sleep. He'll emphasize the last word in the sentence. Give him one kiss that he'll remember while he's fucking the coyote woman. Give him one kiss that ought to make him cry if he's capable of it, but don't notice when he does. Tell him to have a good night.

Your best male friend will say, "We all do it. We can't help it. We're self-destructive. It's the old bad-boy routine. You have a male dog, don't you?"

The next day the sun will be out and the coyote woman will leave. Think about how easy it must be for the coyote woman and a man who listens to top-forty country. The coyote woman would never use a word like "monogamy"; the coyote woman will stay gentle on his mind.

If you can, let him sleep alone for at least one night. If you can't, invite him over to finish trimming your Christmas tree. When he asks how you are, tell him you think it's a good idea to keep your sense of humor during the holidays.

Plan to be breezy and aloof and full of interesting anecdotes about all the other men you've ever known. Plan to be hotter than ever before in bed, and a little cold out of it. Remember that necessity is the mother of invention. Be flexible.

First, he will find the faulty bulb that's been keeping all the others from lighting. He will explain in great detail the most elementary electrical principles. You will take turns placing the ornaments you and other men, he and other women, have spent years carefully choosing. Under the circumstances, try to let this be a comforting thought.

He will thin the clusters of tinsel you put on the tree. He'll say something ambiguous like, Next year you should string popcorn and cranberries. Finally, his arm will stretch just high enough to place the angel on the top of the tree.

Your best female friend will say, "Why can't you ever fall in love with a man who will be your friend?"

Your best male friend will say, "You ought to know this by now: Men always cheat on the best women."

This is what you learned in the pop psychology book: Love means letting go of fear.

Play Willie Nelson's "Pretty Paper." He'll ask you to dance, and before you can answer he'll be spinning you around your wood stove, he'll be humming in your ear. Before the song ends he'll be taking off your clothes, setting you lightly under the tree, hovering above you with tinsel in his hair. Through the spread of the branches the all-white lights you insisted on will shudder and blur, outlining the ornaments he brought: a pheasant, a snow goose, a deer.

The record will end. Above the crackle of the wood stove and the rasp of the hunter's breathing you'll hear one long low howl break the quiet of the frozen night: your dog, chained and lonely and cold. You'll wonder if he knows enough to stay in his dog house. You'll wonder if he knows that the nights are getting shorter now.

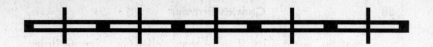

CHARLES BOWDEN

FROM

Desierto

S torm clouds scud low off Tonto Rim and the air rushes raw with cold fingers across the desert. The men walk slowly into the Gila County courthouse, the Levis worn, the fingers scarred, hands big, guts hanging over their belts, their shirts all with metal snaps. The faces are well creased by memories of sun and wind, the hats, they are different here, deliberately out of fashion, crown high and barely dented, brim pulled down fiercely in front and back. They nod to each other and barely speak. There is little need, the blood goes back three, four, five generations. The men under the hats share these things: they hate lions, they kill lions. And they love lions. These matters will never be spoken, but in the Rim country most of what is, is never said. Or it will not be at all.

They have killed hundreds, lassoed them, shot them, tracked them with hounds up the rock and into the trees. Shot down the mothers, brought home the kittens and raised them in cages. Crossed their yards each morning, the cats standing up, the blank green eyes reaching through the bars.

"You wonder what they're about," one rancher says. "You watch your ten-year-old kid walk past the cage and then look into those eyes."

I am sitting in the back of the room and do not speak but watch. I have driven up here in order to listen to the lion world. To consider nature, that fine word we feel more than understand. Ignore drugs, ignore them absolutely. Forget development, Charlie, finance, wine in goblets with fine stems, the voices on the phone with whispers of deals, testimony, fissures of bankruptcy streaking across the country club faces. Of course, there is no Mexico in this part of the desert, it is safely kept out of sight and mind. There is also the matter of love. And I have come to meet Harley Shaw, the one man in the state paid to think about lions.

My interest goes back to a time I cannot remember, perhaps when as a boy I hunted all day in the desert for deer and then as light began to fail turned back toward camp and followed my tracks. For more than a mile, I saw the dusty print of a lion in the outlined tread of my boots. Probably it started at that moment, realizing something I had never seen had followed me and watched me for hours. It may have been the Yaqui barrio that clung near the freeway in the city. I would go down there as a boy and stay all night to watch the dances. The Yaquis have songs, songs I did not understand until decades later, but songs that I heard and that seeped somehow into my imagination.

The Yaquis have a lot of songs and there is one about a female mountain lion. No one sings this song much up on Tonto Rim.

> Flower lion, flower lion,
>   walking in the wilderness, flower lion.
> Flower lion, flower lion,
>   walking in the wilderness, flower lion.

There are also songs about deaf mountain lions. And mad lions. But that is the flower world.

When I was a kid I sat in the Yaqui village late one night in the house of a man who talked in Spanish or Yaqui, neither of which I understood. His face was pleasant and blank to my eyes. The house was bare and simple, naked light bulbs hanging from the ceiling, a white porcelain sink standing free and gleaming like a treasure in the corner. The hours crawled by. After a while the man, he was the village headman with a secure job on a highway crew, offered me a jar of chiltipíns, small red balls of explosive pepper. I did not know what they were and threw a fistful into my mouth. The man laughed silently as I bolted for the faucet.

Later, I sat under the ramada of an old man in his eighties. He swept out the church for the priest. When he smoked a cigarette, the end was soaked from his hungry lips. As a young man he had been a warrior in the Yaqui wars that raked Sonora until the '30s. Now he made flutes from cane. I still have one.

There is a place that is the desert—except that it is the desert made perfect. The deer are there, as they are here, and the flowers. This place is called *sea ania*, there the people are called *Surem*. The Yaqui learned of this place when a man who herded sheep and goats began to envy the hunters he saw decked out in the hides of many animals. He made a bow, fashioned an arrow, and went into the forest. He saw two large antlered deer rasping their horns together and a third, a smaller deer, moving around them. Then he understood: the large deer were making the music and singing, the small deer was dancing. He learned the songs and from that moment on the wall fell between this world and the flower world, the *sea ania*.

They say, for those who know the way, it lies to the east beneath the dawn.

One night at the dances I see this man. He is crawling across the dirt plaza toward the big wooden cross. It is black, mesquite smoke drifts on the March winds, the ground shakes with the stomping of the dance. The Yaquis huddle in a village of shacks less than a mile from the freeway. They are surrounded by the night moans of the city, a pudding of cement and tract houses that has flowed across the desert floor and trapped a half-million Americans in its grid of streets. The dancers do not hear the city, the man crawling does not hear the dance. He is drunk, he is a disgrace, he has, I suppose, violated the sacred rituals of the tribe's Easter. The dancers are in the flower world, the other reality where deer explain the nature of life to Yaquis.

They can do this but I cannot. The village has these problems, the heroin dealers, the lack of money, and of course the drunks. These matters cannot enter the flower world. The drunk has crawled on another ten years, he is covered with dust and strange grunts and cries pour out of his foamy mouth. No one says anything to him. No one tries to stop him. He does not exist in the flower world. So he does not exist.

Men who are not dancing sit on benches and smoke cigarettes. They wear deer heads. The drunk is struggling to his feet now, he is at the big cross that dominates the plaza. He cannot keep his head erect, he weaves and staggers forward. I am the only human being in the village who will look at him, but then he and I are not in the flower world. He lunges forward, drapes his outstretched arms on the cross. There, the silhouette against the fire: crucifixion.

Before the Spaniards arrived, all the people divided into two groups—the *Surem* and the *Yoemen*. A young *Surem* girl listened to a talking tree and when her people heard the tree's prophecies they decided to hold a dance. When it ended the *Surem* went into the earth. They are enchanted. Some argue that they became ants or dolphins, others say they still look human—they are just magical. To this day, a *Yoemem* will stumble on a *Surem*, a visitor from the enchanted world, the flower world. Such a meeting may kill the *Yoemem*.

This is the way Felipe Molina reports the matter in a book. He is a Yaqui living near Tucson. He also notes, "for that reason, my grandfather and especially my grandmother disapproved of me going into the desert alone."

Perhaps, that is where the interest in lions began. For years, decades, I find their tracks, their dung, their lairs. But I never see one. I look for almost twenty-five years before I so much as catch a glimpse, the green eyes burning in the night.

Harley Shaw stands up in the Gila County courthouse and explains some new rules on killing lions and reporting the killing of lions and the how and the why of it. He is the bridge in this room between the men out on the land and the people who never see the land but make the rules for it. The walls of the room are decorator-selected soft tones and there is no clue within this chamber that this is the ground that spawned fables of the West. Zane Grey, a dentist, sought out this place to hunt and fish and pump the memories of local people for tales, odd yarns that he could stretch into short books for insurance salesmen bored with their jobs and their women back in Pittsburgh. The Pleasant Valley War left blood just to the north, the grizzly staged a last stand here. Just on top of the Rim in the town of Young with Moon's Saloon on the main dirt drag, the village hugging the edge of Pleasant Valley. In the '50s a woman tells me the boys were lounging out in front knocking back some cool ones when the first motorcycle to ever beat its way out of Tonto Basin came rolling down the street. They shot its tires out so as to have a better look.

The lions have never left, never given ground.

When Harley Shaw went to college, he wrote a paper in his freshman English class on Ben Lilly, a legendary hunter who died in 1936. Lilly started in Alabama and worked his way west slaughtering bears, coyotes, wolves, and lions. Once he guided for Theodore Roosevelt. He married twice, but these ventures did not work out. His first wife went insane, his second wife he abandoned. He was a solitary man, a religious man, who followed his hounds on foot six days a week subsisting on a little parched corn. At sundown on Saturday, he tied his dogs—Ben Lilly would not hunt on the Sabbath. If a dog failed to perform up to his standards, he beat it to death. He ended up in Arizona's Blue River country exterminating the last holdouts among the grizzlies and wolves. His name still conjures up tales in that region. For hunters, Ben Lilly is truly a legend—Texas folklorist J. Frank Dobie once wrote a book stating just that in the title, *The Ben Lilly Legend*. Shaw as a boy was fascinated by wildlife and so Lilly, the premier killer, was a link to the natural world for a boy growing up in the valley east of Phoenix.

Now Shaw is older and he is Arizona's expert on mountain lions. He remembers his fascination with Lilly and a soft grin graces his face. Harley Shaw has spent eighteen years following the lions on foot, on horseback, behind dogs, from airplanes.

He has never killed one.

Like us, lions kill. In the Southwest, their house occupies about 150 square miles on the average, and they move patiently through its many rooms. They are 5.5 to 7.5 feet long, the weight ranging from 75 to 190 pounds. We seldom see them: perhaps if lucky, once in a lifetime. But they always see us. They like to watch, they will follow us at that slow walk for hours. They almost never attack—in Arizona perhaps once a decade according to our records. They seem not to regard us as a suitable source of food. But the kill is the thing and what they like is something around a hundred pounds and alive. Studies in Arizona find about one out of every five kills is a calf. They eat what they kill, not what others have killed. We have studied this matter and we have numbers to comfort us. Every ten and a half days, an adult will kill. Or, if a mother, every 6.8 days. In certain regions, at certain times, under certain conditions. Because we really know very little about them, very, very little. Our major contact with them has always been on bloody ground, the kill.

I am standing in a patch of chaparral on the edge of Salt River north of Globe and the rancher is angry in that slow, hard way that ranchers vent their emotions. The voice is flat, almost monotone, the face placid. In one month he has lost thirty-four calves to them with calves worth hundreds of dollars apiece. But it is more than the money. It is the kill, the neck punctured by those large teeth, the small animal ripped open like an envelope. It is logical to argue that he was merely going to raise the calves to a certain weight and then ship them off to eventual slaughter. But this fact does not abate a rancher's anger. The calves were under his care, *his care*, and he has been violated by a force he never sees but whose presence he constantly suspects. He calls in the expert hunters and has seven of them taken off his land. That was months ago, but still he is not at peace. The fury of finding those dead calves in the morning light will not leave his eyes. He reaches the conclusion that many others have who stumble into their country: they like the killing.

And perhaps they do.

We will never find out.

We do not know how to ask.

It is just before Christmas. A mountain lion workshop clogs the lobby of a fine old hotel with 150 biologists, guides, animal control folk (trackers, trappers, poisoners, and hunters), plus a handful of conservationists, all tossing down drinks during the get-acquainted cocktail hour. A rumor floats through the room, one brought here by a government hunter from California. A woman, about fifty-one, has been found. The skull said to be punctured by a large tooth mark. The other whispered signs offer unmistakable evidence of a kill. The autopsy, well, that's the kicker, the autopsy, according to the rumor, suggests that the woman was alive while being eaten.

The kill.

I have come here with my simple question: What is it like to kill with your mouth? The biologists turn away when I ask. There are things about the wilds, we are not supposed to say.

And this brings us down to perhaps the fundamental fault line between us and lions. Our basic contact with mountain lions is the kill and yet what little we know suggests this is not the major portion of a mountain lion's life. Harley Shaw has studied lions in Arizona for eighteen years and he is the host of this big workshop. He is fifty-one now, the hair and trimmed beard silver, a bearlike man who is not tall, the eyes and voice very alert and deliberate. At times, he can be a bundle of statistics and graphs and scat samples and radio-collared plottings of lions. But now he is sitting down and just talking.

"Lions," he says, "more than other animals, have time for contemplation. They lay up, seek high places and vistas. So you wonder what goes through their minds."

You certainly do.

As soon as we knew they were around, we tried to kill them. When the Jesuit priests hit Baja at the end of the seventeenth century, they ran into a culture, one now vanished which we recall as the Pericue, that refused to slay lions. Imagine it is three hundred years ago and Father Ugarte, a large man and a strong man, wants the lion dead. The cat comes in the night, slaughters the mission stock at his outpost in southern Baja, then vanishes. The Indians will not kill the beast —if they do, they say they too will die. The priest is riding his mule on a narrow path, he sees a lion, throws the stone, the animal dies. He places the warm body across his mule, rides back to the mission, and shows off his trophy. The Indians watch, the priest does not die. See, he says, now you are free, now you can kill the lions.

We have not stopped since that moment. As a people, we've had a hard time abiding lions because they want what we want: meat, especially venison, lamb, and beef. Take Arizona. Between 1918 and 1947, 2,400 lions were killed in Arizona. Mainly, they were taken out for killing stock. Legendary men emerged like Uncle Jim Owens of the Grand Canyon country who is said to have bagged 1,100 cats in his lifetime. A man named Jack Butler is reported around 1929 to have killed fifty-eight in eighteen months in the Sowats and Kanab Wash area around the Canyon. Government animal control people tried poison, traps, dogs, bullets—everything in their arsenal. In 1947, the state legislature took a look at the situation and decided to offer a bounty, one that floated between $50 and $100 for the next twenty-two years. They were moved to add this incentive because decades of lion killing had not seemed to dent the lion population. When the bounty finally became dormant in 1969 (it is still technically on the books ready to come to life if desired) another 5,400 lions had been knocked down.

All over the West (with the exception of Texas) attitudes about lions began to change in the sixties, and first one state and then another shifted them from varmints to game animals, started issuing hunting tags, and generally tried to manage them just like deer, bighorn sheep, elk, and antelope. Arizona made this shift in 1970 when it allowed one lion per hunter per year, stopped funding the bounty system, and gave control of the beast to the Game and Fish Department. Stock-killing lions could still be taken out by ranchers if they contacted the government.

What is the net result? No one's really sure. There are somewhere between two thousand and three thousand lions in Arizona—nobody has any good way to count them. The hunt has now been limited to six months a year, and Game and Fish is busily studying their new charges. Each twelve months between two hundred and four hundred of the cats are killed (the state figures run around two hundred, but some critics figuring in estimates of unreported rancher kills tend toward the high end). And after a century or more of slaughter they are still out there. In the American West there is no place where lions are endangered. They have survived without our help, they have survived in the face of our hatred. . . .

Almost no one has ever seen a lion kill. There are millions of people living in the desert, they are crawling up every canyon, the families are picnicking under the willows by every mountain stream, the bull-dozers claw at every roll of the bajadas, the satellites spin by day and night with giant glass eyes watching everything that moves. But still almost no one has ever seen a lion kill.

But we can guess some things from the kills we find. Harley Shaw has seen many kills, made his notes, puzzled out the action that is now dry blood, broken bones, empty eyes with flies buzzing in the air. He has written a book, *Soul Among Lions*, and then rewritten the book and then rewritten the rewritten book. He has drifted into an obsession. The thing floats around as a manuscript, the publishers look, consider, hesitate. It is not a normal book by a normal biologist. The facts are all there, the slender scraps of fact we have sifted from the world of the lion. But there is a feeling gnawing at Harley as he studies his field notes and tries to understand how the cats eat. He has gotten too close, and he knows it. "I have begun," he writes, "to dislike the ways humans view themselves." He has begun to see the world through a lion's eyes—he cannot see that world, he has learned too much, sensed too much to ever think he can see that world, but he has a feel for its presence and that has changed how the things now look through his eyes. Now he is there, he is so close, it is all in his notes, in his mind, in his senses as he thinks about lions, and it is not nearly enough, barely a beginning. He has about studied himself out of a profession, biologist. As he notes dryly of his work, "You will be forced to reexamine your beliefs."

They are out there right now, looking down at us from the sierras, cruising silently across the desert floor, lying up on a cliff and watching, waiting for the glimpse of the right thing. They cannot run, cannot really run at all, and everything must be a brief sprint. The lion drops down, creeps, slides, it must get within fifty feet or less if it is to succeed. The lion is alone, in this act almost always alone, a single force that must always do its work alone.

This colors the act.

The object of desire should be around a hundred pounds or less. The lion weighs seventy, eighty, ninety, perhaps a hundred pounds—sometimes a lot more, but not usually. The animal is not as large as the feeling the name *lion* conjures up in our minds and hearts. The lion does not seek a fight, a combat. This would be a dangerous choice. The broken rib, the torn muscle, and that half step is lost, the microsecond of speed and grace vanishes, and then the hunger comes and weakness follows that and the thing spirals into death. So the fight must be avoided.

The object is close now, a deer, browsing, alert, but as yet unaware. The skin of the deer is a fur almost gray in this light. It drifts among the chaparral, a ghost that is alive. The sun is up and warm on the gray fur but still it eats, feeling safe in the cover of the brush. It begins to happen, the lion is close, belly to the ground, and now it surges, slithers forward, and nears. The cat rises up on its hind feet and those big front paws with sharp claws sink into the deer's back and the animal

goes to ground instantly. The mouth opens—feel the warm breath?
—and the jaws settle around the back of the neck and the teeth
penetrate the muscles near the base of the skull.

There are nerve endings at the base of the big teeth, very sensitive
endings, and as the fangs plunge and tear through the warm flesh these
endings pick up that gap between the vertebrae and the teeth slide in,
the lion swings its jaws, the neck snaps. Death washes across the deer's
face. Harley has seen many kills and if the lion is an adult, an experienced killer, it is over very fast, it seems—the sites show little if any
signs of struggle. With younger cats—and it takes a lioness almost two
years to train up her kittens to a good and proper kill—it may be
messier. Attacks on humans usually involve cats under two years, those
who have not mastered the feel of the kill and the risks of the kill.
Sometimes when a doe is killed, the fawn lingers around and is killed
later. There is speculation that such objects provide training for kittens.

What happens next the biologists can only guess, but this is the
guess: the lion leaves the kill, goes off a short ways, and lies down for
perhaps an hour. The stalk, the leap, the teeth probing for that gap
between the vertebrae, the rush of hot blood against the tongue, all
these things have stimulated the lion and it is not a proper time to
eat until calm returns to the well-muscled body.

Now it is ready and rises and walks slowly back to the deer. The
lion drags it across the ground to some place that suggests safety,
perhaps under a tree or a rock. It is time to feed. First, the cat clears
the hair with its teeth from the deer where it will be entered—typically
just behind the ribs, Harley notes. The procedure here is thorough,
much the way humans prep for surgery. The claws flash, the deer is
opened up. First the heart, liver, and lungs are devoured, then, it
seems, the back legs with the meat on the interior of the legs taken
first. The stomach and intestines are pulled out and ignored. Eight to
ten pounds of flesh may be swallowed at this first feeding.

Then the animal is covered. The cat will toss up grass, brush, soil,
rocks, something, to cover the kill. Why, we can only speculate—to
hide it from other animals? to keep the meat cool to delay spoiling?
Harley once found a mule-deer kill on solid rock. The cat had placed
a single twig on the animal.

The lion retreats, perhaps a couple of hundred yards, and beds
down. It will lay up where it can see and come back often to check

the kill. What does it do while lying up there, the desert a vista before it, or the oaks of the canyon a carpet unrolling in front of it? This is not a small matter. The kills come every three to ten days in the desert. It depends, in part, on how long the meat lasts before going bad. Or so we suspect. We really have no clear ideas why lions abandon kills. There are just little glimpses. One cat in Idaho stayed and fed off an elk kill for nineteen days. What goes through the brain for nineteen days as the meat is engorged and then come the quiet hours sprawled up high, the eyes staring out at the big empty?

Normally, the lions will not eat carrion. If they do not kill it, they do not eat it. This has made them hard to poison. The wolves, they are gone from the Arizona desert. The grizzlies are gone. The lion is not.

Of course, kills vary. If the animal is large, the lion cannot reach up and sink those claws in deeply. Then the teeth go to the throat—Harley has a photograph in color, everything very red and bloody, of an elk's windpipe with a big puncture in it, the hole a memory of the cat's tooth. Then the lion kills by suffocation. But this is to be avoided. Those who follow the cats, whether to study them or kill them, agree on one thing: a lion is not likely to leap from a ledge or drop down out of a tree onto the back of a large animal. Such a ride is dangerous and for lions danger is not the drug it seems to be for human beings. They will kill anything: steers, horses, sheep, elk, desert sheep, deer, javelina, people. They must eat. But all things being equal, the object of desire will not be too large, it will not struggle, the claws will grip the shoulders, the mouth will open, the teeth, those wonderful teeth with sensitive nerves at the base, will probe and find that gap between the vertebrae and the neck will snap. Death descends like a summer shower, the lion walks off and rests. Then an area will be cleaned of hair for the incision. . . .

The lobby is fine soft couches, lamps casting warm yellow light, good wood in the tables, a fireplace that swallows large logs. On the ceiling beams, delicate floral abstractions open and spin across the painted surface. The floor is tile and cool to the eye. A woman plays the grand piano and sings the songs that you hum in elevators but can never name. One hundred and fifty lion people mill about this lobby. They drink, form small knots of conversation, eye each other's name tag.

They have come from all over the United States and Canada, wherever the lion still hunts. Harley Shaw is the host. He wears a dark sportcoat with leather patches and looks like a professor of Elizabethan poetry with his silver hair, trimmed silver beard. This is the world of the *per diem* people, those who work in state agencies, federal agencies, who plunder government for grants so that they can continue their researches in universities. These are the lions' official modern keepers. Everyone standing here with a glass of wine or bottle of beer in hand cashes checks signed in blood by the big carnivore that courses the mountains and flats leaving carcasses in its wake. This is not part of the rumble of conversations.

The lobby is filled with people who focus on the killing, men dressed in tight Levis, wearing cowboy boots, the faces weathered, the hair trimmed, that careful mustache, the deliberate hat with the brim exactly bent. These men speak little if at all, they are ranch people, sometimes descended from lion-killing families. Now, as the West shrinks and business takes the land for esoteric tax purposes, they hang on as federal and state killers of the wild things that make up the West that has always held them in its thrall.

They traffic in stories, anecdotes, glimpses of the trail and the hunt. Harley moves easily with them: they know what he wants to know. Science here searches folklore like a hungry scavenger seeking a clue that will destroy the mysteries. There was this cat in the Big Bend area of Texas that took to attacking people in the park, so it was captured and shipped to Florida where a big state project seeks to salvage the last few panthers huddled in the Everglades under the glow of the hot, cocaine night skies. Now the problem lion lives in a cage in a research center. Captive lions not subjected to mobs in zoos tend to be very shy and try to crawl under things when they see people. This one stares the biologists straight in the eye, gets up and presses against the wire. So they do an X-ray, find a dark mass in the brain, and speculate it may be a tumor or a viral blob. They consider killing the lion, cutting open its head and looking at the brain. There has to be some reason why it does not cower in our presence.

There are many things to be explained. Recently, a lion was killed on the road near Fresno, California, and others are seen often on the local golf course even though it is fifteen miles across the big agribusiness fields to the sierra.

Death, that is the only place in which we can get near. Why do we want to get near? Why do we crave to get so very, very near? That is not a question to be asked, it is forbidden. We have our excuses. I will tell them to you. There is this thing called depredation—that means the lion eats things we want to eat, kills things we wish to kill. The calf stares blankly up at the hot sky, neck broken, underbelly ripped open, body gnawed, bones crushed like small sticks. The sheep scattered willy-nilly, twenty, thirty sheep dead, so dead, and only one or two even eaten. The rest, just killed, wantonly we say, killed for sport we say. Killed for reasons we cannot comprehend. And if we do not act, act right now, the lion will be back at nightfall and kill again and again and again. Depredation, we say.

Besides depredation, we say science. We want to answer the mysteries of life, curious questions of gestation, digestion, population densities, nurture, movement, prey selection, social organization. Diet. We want to put radio collars on them, we want to dart them with drugs and take their vital signs, spend many hours sorting out the remains in their scat. Weigh them, measure them, consider blood type, disease vectors. Learn how to determine their age by putting calipers to their teeth. Science, an excellent screen for our desires.

Besides science, there is envy. That is the one we will not speak of. Not at all, seldom if ever. Envy. We go where they are. We take a truckload of dogs, pull the horses in a trailer behind us. The hounds are released, we saddle up and ride. We carry guns. We carry our food, cover our body with fabrics in order to endure the weather. Sometimes we have radios so that the hunters can communicate constantly. It has taken us years to train the dogs, hundreds and hundreds of hours on the trail. And if we are lucky, we may tree a lion. The cats, they are out there alone, they carry their culture inside their bodies, they move anywhere, set up a universe wherever they decide to lie up. When hungry, they kill and dine day after day after day. They breed—meeting by some miracle of scent like two lonely ships in an endless sea—train up their young, push on.

I am having a drink and I tell a woman of the kill, the special nerves at the base of the teeth feeling the gap between the vertebrae. She says, "I want to feel that."

"Be a lion?" I ask.

"It doesn't matter," she says. "I'm willing to be either."

That envy. And from that envy comes our love. It is not a normal love, or perhaps it is, but at any rate it is not the love we normally admit to. It is not a desire to share or nurture or protect. It is much stronger than that, more powerful in its effects. It is a desire to join them.

So of course, we must kill them, kill every damn one of them.

The Greek restaurant is near the University and this is a quick break for a faculty member. A big new road may knife through some barrios, here are the plans, here are the arguments—stop the road. His hair is blond, his eyes alert behind the glasses, the issues crisp. Development versus neighborhoods, cars versus whatever, the present versus the past. And of course, his house, which sits in a barrio about to be amputated by the new road.

Before the road, there was Don Jesús, a Yaqui who had taught the man I'm having lunch with some deer songs for a book. A curious thing happened when he was doing the book with a Yaqui who lived in Arizona. They'd been down there in Sonora and Don Jesús took sick. The professor and his Yaqui friend could not stay with the old man because they had to get back to the States. They drove north to Arizona and their homes and that night they both had dreams. The faculty member woke up his wife to tell her that he had dreamed of Don Jesús. The Yaqui also dreamed. In his dream, he is watching a woman making tortillas and sees the image of the Virgin of Guadalupe on one, an angry cloud appears on the horizon and the rain comes down. The drops are on fire. The man's uncle tells him such a rain comes once every few centuries and he begins to sing a deer song. The stanzas tumble out and the uncle becomes Don Jesús.

Down on the Rio Yaqui, people say that during Don Jesús's last hours his heart was over Arizona and from that fact the dreaming came. The rain of fire is another matter.

The songs do not seem to end. The voices speak a strange language, one that sounds hard to the ears. The flower world beckons, but who can believe in it? The *Yoemem* sing.

> Where the enchanted spotted mountain lion ate,
>   a fawn's head was found.
> An enchanted, enchanted buzzard

was not hovering there.
An enchanted, enchanted big coyote
was sounding there.

They see a thin line between us and them. And they guard this line with guns, poison, and words. We are standing, beers in hand, and the talk flows with missionary ease. Darrel C. Juve works for the Department of Agriculture in Arizona but he does not farm. He kills. The term is Animal Damage Control and what he does is patrol that thin line between us and them.

He's in his late forties now and his world is plain. "A lion," he says briskly, "is nothing but a big housecat. Curious."

It's not just the lions, no, no, there are coyotes out there, bears, and if you look up, my God, the birds. Juve speaks without a smile, his eyes scanning people to see if they understand, if they can handle his message. Ravens? They kill. They kill calves, they kill steers. Drop down from the sky and peck their eyes out, blind them, and then comes the hard death with these black birds pecking, pecking, pecking.

We've made some progress. Take the wolf, he's gone. "There's a good reason," he almost snaps, "why they were wiped out in the West." And then he pauses to make sure his next words truly sink in: "They destroyed millions of dollars of livestock." His face has that tension in it, the tension flooding a man who knows, who really knows, and yet has learned that others will shun his knowing.

He's got eleven people under him, the calls come in each day, there is no way to keep up, no way at all. The lions complaints alone would bury his force if they dealt with all of them. People, he continues, have lost touch with reality. Only four percent of the population produces the food for the other ninety-six percent, and now you see people going into supermarkets and tossing a nice plastic-wrapped chunk of meat in their baskets and they have no idea where or how that piece of flesh got there.

"People don't understand," he says with cold anger, "that for them to eat, something has to die. We try to attach sentimentality to animals without ever thinking about what is really going on out there. *Humane* is not a word spoken by Mother Nature. The mass media depict wild animals in unrealistic terms."

He is struggling now, trying to rein in his feelings, to make the words seem like a reasonable position, one arrived at after much research, the product of cool detachment by a scholar sitting in his study before the fire and musing over a glass of fine sherry. But he cannot maintain the tone.

"They," he flames up again, "they think there is a 'balance of nature'—that's bullshit. There is no balance out there."

Out there. The heart of darkness. The ground where we are not in control. Wait, twist the lens, see it zoom into focus? Yes, that ground, the world seen through a lion's eyes, the warm blood-soaked breath flowing out the cat's open mouth. We deny it, we abolish it with fine shots in calendars, with musings about the intricate relationships between all living things. We avert our eyes so that we can always see Eden. Juve, ah, he insists on the teeth at the throat, on those long beaks tearing at the eye of a terrified calf. He wears glasses, Levis, an oval belt buckle inlaid with a coyote (made by a convict, he explains). His brown hair is trimmed, the face seldom smiles, the voice is almost always urgent, the words clipped. He is the man with the mission. He has been Out There. An image rises up from the snap of his sentences: Nature is this teeming, unruly bitch at the gates of our lives, ready at an instant to violate our humanity. She waits out there by the picket fence so white against the green lawn. You stroll out, open the gate, and suddenly she walks out of the desert, dressed smartly, the lips full and inviting, the eyes dangerous with desires. Her hair is black, the teeth very even, the cheekbones strong, the voice, well, you can hear no voice, you merely sense a kind of purring coming off her body. She moves toward you, seems almost to glide, you turn, smile, tip your head silently forward as to say hello. Her dress rustles, a soft silky kind of sound, the hair is long and stirs with the breeze. She is at your throat, the teeth tear and warm blood cascades down your body. Out there.

That is one mountain lion. Harley Shaw thinks the lion exists through human eyes, and the different eyes see different lions: stock killer, hunter's trophy, curious biological machine for studies by scientists, noble beast of the sierra and bajada. It all depends on who you are. For Harley, the lion exists in a very strange place: he says he cannot conceive of them except in front of hounds. Dogs have shaped his lion world, they are the door or window or what-have-you that permits him to go to the lion world.

He does not think this view has any particular merit. It just is that way for him. Out there, that black place full of sun, is very hard to reach, in the case of the lion almost impossible, and we can only stay a very short while—idle moments standing under a tree while the dogs bay, the wait for the dart to drug the cat, the quick measurements and sampling, your hands running over the warm fur, then retreat, the groggy animal staggering off and vanishing. Flies are buzzing around a kill, you measure scratch marks, you are being watched, you can sense this fact, feel it, but you cannot see. The lion?—the lion is that excited sound in the dogs' throats, the lion is that long slash on the deer's shoulder. The lion is something you make up to fill a big empty spot inside you.

She is standing before an auditorium of lion people, the hair blond, the dress blue, the face smooth and open. The room is dark and the light at the lectern splashes up on her and she seems like a spirit, a clean-smelling angelic form, reading thoughts to the soiled and the human. Slides flash on the screen as row after row of biologists and lion hunters slump in their seats. She is from New England, from some institute or foundation, and the slides express her feelings about the wilds. Big color images of the desert in a real estate ad, huge close-ups of lions with their big tawny faces seeming dignified and noble and innocent. The mouth on the cats in these slides is always closed, the teeth a secret kept from the camera. Of course, there are two kittens sitting on the snow. She reads a poem by D. H. Lawrence, "Elegy to a Mountain Lion." Out There vanishes.

Can we call this love? Juve, like many men who kill animals, has ready explanations for the killing. There is a need. The coyotes, they'll take your dog. The bear, he will eat your calf. The lion, he murders everything he meets. The ravens, they are at the eyes. They must be stopped.

But there is another level in their words. The talk will drift, the drinks will take hold, the pretense of positions will become too great a weight to carry day and night, and then the talk will change. For a century we have been cleaning up the desert, setting this house in order. We have the records, incredible records where everything is columns of bounties paid, wages paid, damages reported, poisons bought and spread, traps set and accounted for, skins piled up and assessed, skulls sent to natural history collections. We have a record.

The wolf? Ah, the wolf was easy to take out, he was not that smart. He could not adapt, not at all. The wolf lost, and because he lost to us, he lost our respect. You can hear this behind the words, you can. He lost our respect. The grizzly, he was easy too. Big, stupid, and now gone, and never ever coming back to the desert. We will not permit it. He does not deserve it. We took him out. The coyote, my God, the coyotes, they cannot be beaten, we kill them with guns, traps, poisons. Still they keep coming, and coming. The coyote is our enemy, we must fight him if it takes forever. And then you can hear a kind of love come into the words. The coyote is worthy of our respect. And the lion, nothing seems to touch the lion. They are out there, walking slowly in their kingdoms, and we kill them, kill hundreds of them a year in the desert and still they keep walking slowly across their king-doms. The men slumped in their seats in the auditorium, the Levis skintight, the black cowboy hats hugging their heads, brims bent low in the front and the back, the large oval belt buckles recording that good day at the rodeo, these men who kill lions worship them. You can hear it in their words, in the horror which they describe of the sheepbeds after a bloody night, the rich language that flows from their mouths when they recount the long, deep rips in a calf's small soft body. The feeling is also there when they speak of the hunt. The cat is so hard to find—if it is hot and dry, the hounds can find no scent; if they find scent the ground is so broken and difficult, the cat sees so well, senses everything, moves so silently, broods without whimpering, slaughters without being seen, lives without our knowing. Except for the blood.

You can hear a kind of love in their words. Without the cats they would not know who they are, would not have a clue. For the lion is something that exceeds their grasp, they have tried everything and still he exceeds their grasp and from this fact, the love comes. The lion has kept the world from getting too small. The men who kill lions are ever vigilant to maintain this reality. Some men hunt lions with trucks, the dogs riding on the hoods until a track is struck, the lead dog wearing a radio collar with a beeper and when a cat is treed and the lead dog bays, the collar lets off a special beep and then the hunters zero in thanks to the radio. This, the men who love to kill lions, this they want outlawed, this they want stopped. They also oppose the winter hunt in the crisp snow because it makes things too easy—

"Murder," one snaps with contempt. There are other abominations they oppose. Will-call hunts, where a guide trees a lion, leaves his hounds and a friend under the cat, and then calls that doctor or dentist in the next state who will pay $2,000 or $3,000 for the trophy, and the client then hops a jet and within a day is under the tree, fires once, the cat falls dead, and the hunt is successful. There are also men who trap lions, then cage them, and when a rich man wants to hunt, release this captive just ahead of the hounds. All these things the men who love to kill lions hate. They will admit this fact, they will say it in their low monotones, their lips barely moving, the sentences very short, often merely fragments of sentences.

Love, that word cannot be said. You can feel it, but no one will say it. Who will admit to loving something that will not love you back? There is that rumor floating around the room as we stand and drink, a whispered thing where the men huddle and clutch the beer bottles in their hands. In another state, the whispers go, a woman has been found. She is dead, middle-aged, there are the marks, the right marks on her body. She has been killed by a cat. The autopsy, people almost whisper, suggests that while she was yet alive, the lion fed on her. This can be determined, the murmurs continue, determined from the hemorrhaging. Alive. The rumor floats around the room, an electric current reviving the tired air. Months later, the story will become a vapor, a thing that never happened, that does not check out. But of course, that does not really matter. For there will be new rumors, new tales. They are necessary, the menace is essential to us for reasons we can barely state. The mountains would have a new frightening emptiness if we could not imagine the soft padding of those clawed feet, the unflinching eyes scanning our every move, the muscles rippling under the tawny fur. He is out there. Out There. Love.

But no one will say that word.

Harley Shaw sips his coffee in the saloon. He is very calm, very careful. There are things he thinks about but finds difficult to say, almost dangerous to say. Much of this is in the book that he toiled over. He seems small now as he sits and sips his coffee out of a clear glass cup. The book (and he has finally found a publisher) contains his odyssey—the break that spun him out of turkey studies into lion studies, the early years training the hounds, learning from the lion men, collaring the cats, charting their wanderings. The bad time when he caught a mother and her kittens and a lion kitten died. The sinking—that is what it feels like when he talks or when he writes—the sinking into the idea of lions and then the country of lions and then into some place we do not have a word for. He tries to find the word. He uses that German concept, *umwelt*, the idea that any species is the product of the entire universe and encapsulates the entire universe in its being. Yes, the *umwelt*.

He has worked himself out of what was going to make him Mr. Somebody. That is the problem. The hounds are gone now. He no longer follows them in the saddle, listening for the bay, riding hard over the ridges to see a treed cat. The darts are no longer fired, the chemicals slowly dribbling into the blood, the lion's eyes getting glazed. The radio collars are still. Harley no longer clamps them around the cats' necks. Here he becomes hesitant, careful in what he says. He utters circumspect sentences like "I am not opposed to darting lions if we're gaining some new knowledge." He cannot turn his back on knowledge, that is his business, his job. Gaining that little kernel of fact, writing that journal article—"deep down you know you're doing it to gather knowledge and if there is any immortality it is that you are leaving something that may change things."

But this time he is the thing changed. He has run out of reasons to bother lions. He has run out of the arrogance to think he can penetrate their world. He hates the bureaucracy he works for, he has turned against his own species. He thinks lions should be left alone. To kill.

"You follow them step by step," he explains softly, "and then you relate to them."

The saloon is richly oiled walnut, the barmaids wear fine black slacks, white ruffled shirts, black ties at their delicate throats. They stand by the back bar slowly polishing fine glasses. Their skin is very white, the hair perfect, the movements silent as a cat's. The word *lion* seems as alien as the word *love* in this room. We sit in a cell designed to seal out the air, the scent, the scat, the tracks, the warm blood coursing across the tongue, the tooth seeking ever so surely the gap, the twist. The neck breaks.

How many are there? We don't know. How are they organized? We can guess. How many types, how many subspecies? We still argue. How do they decide what to kill? We speculate. How long do they live? There is no counting. What do they matter? We have no idea.

Harley backs away from the questions. "We should go camping," he says. Maybe in the dark hours, the fire crackling, our tongues loosened by liquor, the blackness protecting our faces, maybe then our minds will be freed from our roles, maybe then we can talk.

You can love something that is not beautiful, that is not useful, that is not easy. That is not safe. But you cannot know it.

Harley is talking again, even more softly. He admires things that can be solitary, he says. There have been some bad marriages, hard nights, solitary is not a thing to be despised if it can be endured. He sees the lion clearly now in his mind, the beast floods the room with its scent, the big pads move silently across the saloon floor.

"Out there," he says suddenly, "out there alone without tools, without shelter, without food. Down deep I have an image of myself as being totally wild. And I know I never will."

Out there.

Love waits. With long teeth.

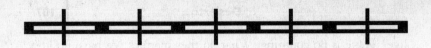

FROM

Ride with Me, Mariah Montana

T he Teton country is quite the geography. Gravelroading straight west as the Bago now was, we had in front of us the rough great wall of the Rockies where gatelike canyons on either side of Indian Head Rock let forth the twin forks of the Teton River. The floorlike plain that leads to the foot of the mountains is wet and spongy in some places, in others bone-dry, in still others common prairie. And even though I usually only remark it from a distance when I'm driving past on a Great Falls trip, Pine Butte itself seems like a neighbor to me. It and its kindred promontories make a line of landmarks between the mountains and the eastward horizon of plains— Heart Butte north near the Two Medicine River, Breed Butte of course between Noon Creek and English Creek, Pine Butte presiding here over the Teton country like a surprising pine-topped mesa, Haystack Butte south near Augusta. Somehow they remind me of lighthouses, spaced as they are along the edge of that tumult of rock that builds into the Continental Divide. Lone sentinel forms the eye seeks.

We drove in sunny silence until I said something about how surprising it was to have a swamp out on a prairie, causing Riley to get learned and inform me that the Pine Butte swamp actually was underlain with so much bog it qualified as a fen.

"That what you're going to do here, some kind of an ecology piece?" I asked.

"Sort of," Mariah said.

"Sounds real good to me," I endorsed, gandering out at the companionable outline of Pine Butte drawing ever nearer and the boggy bottomland—in Montana you don't see a fen just every day—and the summits of the Rockies gray as eternity meeting the blue August sky. This area a little bit reminded me of the Moiese buffalo range where we'd started out, nice natural country set aside, even though I knew the Pine Butte preserve wasn't that elaborate kind of government refuge but simply a ranch before the land was passed on to the Conservancy outfit, which must have decided to be defender of the fen. I couldn't help but be heartened, too, that the news duo at least had progressed from getting us butted by buffalo to moseying through a sweet forenoon such as this. "Great day for the race," I chirped, even. Oh, I knew full well Mariah had heard that one a jillion times from me, but I figured maybe Riley would fall for it by asking "What race?" and then I'd get him by saying "The human race"—but huh uh, no such luck. Instead Riley busied up behind me and announced, "Okay, gang, we've got to start watching along the brush for the state outfit. Should be easy enough to see, there's a crane on the truck they use to hoist the—"

"I'll watch out this side," Mariah broke in on him and proceeded to peer out her window as if she'd just discovered glass is transparent.

Dumb me. Even then I didn't catch on until another mile or so down the road when I happened to think out loud that even though we were going to be with ecology guys we'd all need to watch a little bit out in country like this, because the Pine Butte area is the last prairie habitat of—

The stiffening back of that daughter of mine abruptly told it.

"*Grizzlies?*" I concluded in a bleat. "Has this got to do with *grizzlies?*"

"Just one," said Mariah, superearnestly gazing off across the countryside away from my stare.

"That's way too damn many! This isn't going to be what I'm afraid it is, is it? Tell me it isn't."

Of course neither of this pair of story-chasing maniacs would tell me any such thing and so the nasty hunch that had been crawling up the back of my neck pounced.

"Bear moving!" I slammed on the brakes and right there in the middle of the county road swung around in my seat, as mad as I was scared—which is saying a lot—to goggle first at Mariah who ought to have known better than this and then at Riley whose goddamn phone call this morning all too clearly led into this. "Jesus H. Christ, you two! Anybody with a lick of sense doesn't want to be within fifty miles of moving a grizzly!"

"I reckon that's why the job falls to us," Riley couldn't resist rumbling in one of his mock hero voices. "What's got you in an uproar, Jick? The good news is you don't have to chauffeur the bear in the Bago. The state Fish and Game guys load him into a culvert trap."

I didn't give a hoot if they had portable San Quentin to haul a grizzly in, I wanted no part of it and I then and there let Mariah and Riley know exactly that. Didn't they even read their own newspaper, for Christ's sake? Only days ago a hiking couple in Glacier Park had encountered a sow grizzly and her two cubs, and survived the mauling only because they had the extreme guts and good sense to drop to the ground and play dead. And not all that far from where we right now sat, several—*several*—grizzlies lately kept getting into the geese and ducks at the Rockport Hutterite Colony until the Hutterites managed to run them off with a big tractor. The Bago, I emphasized, was no tractor.

Which did me about as much good with those two as if I'd said it all down a gopher hole.

Riley was mostly the one who worked on me—Mariah knew good and well how ticked off I was at her for this—and of course argument might as well have been his middle name. "The bear is already caught in a steel cable snare, the state guys will conk him out with a tranquilizer gun, and then they'll haul him in a chunk of culvert made of high tensile aluminum he'd have to go nuclear to get out of. Where's the problem?" he concluded, seeming genuinely puzzled.

The rancher portion of me almost said back to him, the problem is the grizzly, you Missoula ninny.

Instead, in spite of myself, my eyes took over from my tongue. They scrutinized the brush-lined creek as if counting up its willows like a tally with wooden matchsticks, they probed each shadowed dip of the Pine Butte fen, they leapt to every ruffle of breeze in the grass. Seeking and seeking the great furry form.

All the while, Riley's bewilderment was stacking up against the silent bounds of me and Mariah, who was keeping ostentatiously occupied with her camera gear. "Gang, I don't know what the deal is here," the scribbler owned, "but we can't just sit in the middle of this road watching the seasons change."

"Are you two going to this bear whether or not I'm along?" I managed to ask.

Say for Riley that he did have marginally enough sense to let Mariah do the answering on that one.

"Yes," she said, still without quite ever looking at me. "The Fish and Game guys are waiting for us."

I jammed the Bago into gear and we went on down the road for, oh, maybe as much as a quarter of a mile before Riley's bursting curiosity propelled out the remark, "Well, just speaking for myself, this is going to be something to remember, getting a free look at a grizzly, hmm?"

When neither of us in the cab of the motorhome responded, he resorted to: "You, ah, you ever seen one before, Jick?"

"Yeah."

"But up close?"

"Close enough." I glanced over at Mariah. Her face carefully showed nothing, but I knew she was replaying the memory, seeing it all again. Who could not? "I killed one once."

"The hell!" from Riley in his patented well-then-tell-me-all-about-it tone. "There on Noon Creek, you mean?"

"In the mountains back of the ranch, yeah." As sudden as that, the site near Flume Gulch was in my mind, as if the earth had jumped a click in its rotation and flung the fire-scarred slope, the survivor pine tree with its claw-torn bark, in through my eyes.

Greatly as I wished he would not, Riley naturally persisted with the topic. "You run across him by accident or track him down?"

"Neither."

"Then how'd you get together with Brother Griz?"

"I baited him."

Strong silence from behind me.

At last Riley said: "Did you. My dad did some of that, too, whenever he'd lose a calf. But black bear, those were. We didn't have grizzlies in the Crazy Mountains any more." Those last two words of his said the whole issue. Originally the West had been absolutely loaded with grizzly bears, but by now they were on the endangered species list.

"I'm not one of those Three S guys, if that's what you're thinking,"

I told Riley stonily. Law on the side of the grizzly notwithstanding, there still were some ranchers along these mountains who practiced the policy of shoot, shovel and shut up. Better a buried bear who'd be no threat to livestock or the leasing of oil rights than a living exemplification of wilderness, ran that reasoning.

"Riley never said you were," Mariah put in her two bits' worth.

Actually, except for her contribution being on his behalf it was just as well she did ante herself into this discussion, for my ultimate say on the grizzly issue needed to be to her rather than to some scribbler. I spoke it now, slowly and carefully:

"I don't believe in things going extinct. But that includes me, too."

I knew Riley was grinning his sly grin. "A grizzly couldn't have said it any better, Jick," issued from him. I didn't care. From the tight crinkle that had taken over her expression I could see that my words had hit home in Mariah, complicating what she had been remembering, what we both were remembering, of that time of the grizzly twenty-five years before.

It started with a paw mark in the pan of the slop milk Mariah had given the chickens.

Why that pan caught her eye so soon again after she'd done her morning chore of feeding the poultry flock, I do not know. Maybe even at ten years old as she was then, Mariah simply was determined to notice everything. When she came down to the lambing shed to find me I was surprised she and Lexa hadn't left yet for school, but nowhere near so surprised as when she told me, "You'd better come see the bear track."

I dropped to one knee there in the filth of the chicken yard, mindful only of that pale outline in the pan. My own hand was not as steady as I would have liked when I measured the bear's print with it. The width of the palmlike pad was well over six inches, half again wider than my hand. That and the five clawmarks noticeably off the toes distinguished what kind of bear this was. Not just a grizzly but a sizable one.

Considerations of all kinds swarmed in behind that pawprint. No sheep rancher has any reason to welcome a grizzly, that I know of. A grizzly bear in a band of sheep can be dynamite. So my mind flew automatically to the bunches of ewes and lambs scattered across the ranch—late April this was, the tail end of lambing season—like clusters of targets. But before that thought was fully done, the feel of invasion of our family was filling me. The creature that slurped the chickens' milk and tromped through the still-damp pan had been here astride the daily paths of our lives. Marcella merely on her way out to the clothesline, Mariah simply on her way to the chicken house, Lexa kiting all over the place in her afterschool scampers—their random goings surely crisscrossed whatever route brought the grizzly, coming out of hibernation hungry and irritable, in to the ranch buildings. Nor was I personally keen to be out on some chore and afterward all they'd ever find of me would be my belt buckle in a grizzly turd.

So when I phoned to the government trapper and his wife said he was covering a couple of other counties for the rest of the week, I did not feel I could wait.

It was the work of all that day to pick and prepare the trap site. Up toward Flume Gulch I was able to find the grizzly's tracks in the mud of the creek crossing, and on the trail along the old burn area of the 1939 forest fire I came across what in every likelihood was the same bear's fresh dropping, a black pile you'd step in to the top of your ankle. I chose the stoutest survivor pine there at the edge of the old burn and used the winch of the Dodge power wagon to snake a long heavy bullpine log in beside the base of the tree. Around the tree I built a rough pen of smaller logs to keep any stray livestock from blundering in, and even though the other blundersome species wasn't likely to come sashaying past I nonetheless nailed up a sign painted in red sheep paint to tell people: LOOK OUT—BEAR TRAP HERE. Then I bolted the chain of the trap to the bullpine log and set the trap, ever so carefully using screw-down clamps to cock its wicked steel jaws open, in the middle of the pen and covered it with pine swags. Finally, from the tree limb directly over the trap I hung the bait, a can of bacon grease.

One thing I had not calculated on. The next day was Saturday, and I got up that next morning to two schoolless daughters who overnight had caught the feverish delusion that they were going with me to check the bear trap.

They took my "No" to the court of appeal, but even after their mother had upped the verdict to "You are not going and let's not hear one more word about it," their little hearts continued to break loudly. All through breakfast there were outbreaks of eight-year-old pouts from

Lexa and ten-year-old disputations from Mariah. As the *aws* and *why can't we*'s poured forth, I was more amused than anything else until the older of these caterwauling daughters cut out her commotion and said in a sudden new voice:

"You'd take us if we were boys."

Mariah should have grown up to be a neurosurgeon; she always could go straight to a nerve. Right then I wanted to swat her precocious butt until she took that back, and simultaneously I knew she had spoken a major truth.

"Mariah, that will do!" crackled instantly from her mother, but by Marcella's frozen position across the table from me I knew our daughter's words had hit her as they had me. Mariah still was meeting our parental storm and giving as good as she got, at risk but unafraid. Beside the tense triangle of the other three of us, Lexa's mouth made an exquisite little O in awe of her sister who scolded grownups.

That next moment of Marcella and I convening our eyes, voting to each other on Mariah's accusation, I can still feel the pierce of. At last I said to my fellow defendant, "I could stand some company up there. How would you feel about all of us going?"

"It's beginning to look like we'd better," Marcella agreed. "But you two"—she gave Lexa a warning look and doubled it for Mariah—"are staying in the power wagon with me, understand?"

When we got up to Flume Gulch, we had a bear waiting.

Its fur was a surprisingly light tan, and plenty of it loomed above the trap pen; this grizzly more than lived up to the size of his tracks. The impression the caught animal gave, which shocked me at first, was that it was pacing back and forth in the trap pen, peering over the stacked logs as if watching for our arrival. Then I realized that the bear was so angrily restless it only seemed he was moving freely; in actuality he was anchored to the bullpine log by the chain of the trap and could only maneuver as if on a short tether. I will tell you, though, that it dried my mouth a little to see how mobile a grizzly was even with a hind leg in a steel trap biting to its bone.

We must have made quite a family tableau framed in the windshield of the power wagon. Lexa so little she only showed from the eyes up as she craned to see over the dashboard. Mariah as intent as an astronomer in a new galaxy. Their mother and I bolt upright on either side trying not to look as agog as our daughters.

"I better get at it," I said as much to myself as to Marcella. Something bothered me about how rambunctious the bear was managing to be in the trap. Not that I was any expert on grizzly deportment nor wanted to be. Quickly I climbed out of the power wagon and reached behind the seat for the rifle while Marcella replaced me behind the wheel and kept watch on the grizzly, ready to gun the engine and make a run at the bear in event of trouble. Mariah craned her neck to catalogue my every move as I jacked a shell into the chamber of the rifle and slipped one into the magazine to replace it and for good measure dropped a handful of the .30–06 ammunition in my shirt pocket. "Daddy will show that bear!" Lexa piped fearlessly. Daddy hoped she was a wise child.

Armed and on the ground I felt somewhat more businesslike about the chore of disposing of the bear. Habits of hunting took over and as if I was skirting up the ridge to stay above a herd of deer below, in no time I had worked my way upslope from the trap tree and the griz, to where my shot would be at a safe angle away from the spectating trio in the power wagon. All the while watching the tan form of trapped anger and being watched by it. Great furry block of a thing, the grizzly was somehow wonderful and awful at the same time.

I drew a breath and made sure I had jacked that shell into the chamber of the .30–06. All in a day's work if this was the kind of work you were in, I kept telling myself, aim, fire, bingo, bruin goes to a honey cloud. Hell, other ranchers who had grazing allotments farther up in the Two Medicine National Forest, where there was almost regular traffic of grizzlies, probably had shot dozens of them over the years.

Abruptly and powerfully the bear surged upright and lurched toward the standing pine tree, as if to shelter behind it from me and my rifle. The chain on the trap was only long enough for the bear to get to the tree, not around it. But as the animal strained there I saw that only its toes of the left rear foot were clamped in the jaws of the trap, not the rear leg itself, which awfully suddenly explained why the bear seemed so maneuverable in the trap pen. *Next thing to not caught*, the trapper Isidor Pronovost used to say of a weasel or a bobcat toe-trapped that way, barely held but unable to escape, and such chanciness seemed all the mightier when the caught creature was as gargantuan as this grizzly.

I will swear on all the Bibles there are, I was not intentionally delaying the bear's execution. Rather, I was settling the barrel of the .30–06 across a silvered stump for a businesslike heart shot when instead the grizzly abruptly began climbing the tree. Attacking up the tree, erupting up the tree, whatever way it can strongest be said, branches as thick as my arm were cracking off and flying, widowmakers torn loose by the storm of fur. The dangling bait can sailed off and clanked against a snag not ten feet from me. The fantastic claws raking furrows into the wood, the massively exerting hulk of body launching and launching itself into that tree. The trap dangling from the bear's rear toes was coursing upward too, tautening the chain fastened into the bullpine log.

Awful turned even worse now. The log lifted at its chained end and began to be dragged to the tree, the bear bellowing out its pain and rage at the strain of that taut pull yet still mauling its way up the tree. I stood stunned at the excruciating tug of war; the arithmetic of hell that was happening, for the log's dead-weight on those toes could—

Then I at last realized. The grizzly was *trying* to tear its toes off to get free.

All prescribed notions of a sure heart shot flew out of me. I fired at the bear simply to hit it, then blazed away at the region of its shoulders again, again, as it slumped and began sliding down the tree trunk, claws slashing bark off as they dragged downward, the rifle in my arms speaking again, again, the last two shots into the animal's neck as it crumpled inside the trap pen.

All those years after, I could understand that Mariah was uneasy about that memory of the toe-caught but doomed grizzly. What the hell, I was not anywhere near easy about it myself, even though I yet believed with everything in me that that particular bear had to be gotten rid of. I mean, six-inch-wide pawprints when you go out to feed the chickens? But I knew that what was bugging Mariah was not just the fate that bear had roamed into on our ranch. No, her bothersome remembering was of us, the McCaskills as we were on that morning. Of the excitement that danced in all four of us after I had done the shooting—Marcella with her worldbeating grin, Lexa hopping up and down as she put out her small hand to touch the pale fur, Mariah stock-still but fever-eyed with the thrill of what she'd witnessed, myself breaking into a wild smile of having survived. Of our family pride, for in honesty it can be called no less, about the killing of the grizzly, with never a thought that its carcass was any kind of a lasting nick out of nature. Late now, though, to try to tack so sizable an afterthought into that Flume Gulch morning.

Clearly this day's grizzly already knew that matters had become more complicated. The snared bear stood quiet but watchful in a pen of crisscrossed logs—much like the one I built—under a big cottonwood, a respectful distance between it and the two state men beside their truck when the motorhome and the three of us entered the picture.

Riley forthwith introduced himself and then Mariah and me to the wildlife biologist, and the biologist in turn acquainted us with his bear-management assistant, a big calm sort who apparently had been hired for both his musclepower and disposition. After we'd all handshook and murmured our hellos, the immediate next sound was Mariah's camera catching the stare of the bear. Inevitably she asked, "How close can I go?"

No sooner was the utterance out of her mouth than the grizzly lunged through the side of the pen, lurching out to the absolute end of the cable it was snared by. That cable was of steel and anchored to the tree and holding the bear tethered a good fifty yards away from the five of us, but even so . . .

"Right where you are is close enough until we get the tranquilizer in him," the biologist advised. He gave a little cluck of his tongue. "I've been at this for years and my heart still jumps out my throat when the bear does that."

Mine was halfway to Canada by now. I got calmed a little by reminding myself that the assistant bear mover had in hand a .12-gauge semi-automatic shotgun with an extended magazine holding seven slugs, armament I was glad enough to see.

Riley went right on journalizing. With a nod toward the bear he asked, "What have we got here?" I sent him a look. *We?*

"A sub-adult, probably about a two-year-old," the biologist provided and went on to explain that a young bear like this one was a lot like a kid on the run, no slot in life yet and getting into trouble while it poked around. More than probably it had been one of the assailants on the Hutterites' fowl. Mischief this time was spelled v-e-a-l, a white-faced calf killed in the fence corner of the rancher's pasture we were now in.

This contest too is tribal. Ignore the incidental details that one community is four-footed and furred and the other consists of scantily haired bipeds, and see the question as two tribes in what is no longer enough space for two. Dominion, oldest of quarrels. The grizzly brings to the issue its formidable natural aptitude, imperial talent to live on anything from ants to, as it happens, livestock. But the furless tribe possesses the evolutionary equivalent of a nuclear event: the outsize brain that enables them to fashion weapons that strike beyond the reach of their own bodies.

Riley did a bunch more interviewing of the biologist and the biologist talked of the capture event and the relocation process and other bear-management lingo, Mariah meanwhile swooping around with her camera doing her own capturing of the bear-moving team and Riley and for whatever damn reason, even me. Even she couldn't help generally glancing at the snared grizzly, as we all kept doing. Yet somehow the bear's single pair of eyes watched us with greater total intensity than our five human pair could manage in monitoring him. And a grizzly's eyes are not nearly its best equipment, either. Into that black beezer of a nose and those powerful rounded-off ears like tunnels straight into the brain, our smells and sounds must have been like stench and thunder to the animal.

The majority of my own staring went to the rounded crown of fur atop the bear's front quarters, the trademark hump of the grizzly. Not huge, just kind of like an extra bicep up there, an overhead motor of muscle that enabled the grizzly to run bursts of forty-five miles an hour or to break a smaller animal's neck with one swipe. Or to rip off its own trapped toe.

My throat was oddly dry when the question came out of me. "What do you bait with?"

The biologist turned his head enough to study me, then sent Riley an inquiring look. Who, goddamn his knack for aggravation, gave a generous okaying nod. Just what my mood needed, the Riley Wright seal of approval.

"Roadkills," the biologist told me. "I collect them. Heck of a hobby, isn't it? This one's a deer, good bear menu."

Now that he'd obliged Riley's notebook and Mariah's camera, the biologist said, "We'd better get this bear under way. First we dart him off."

With doctor gloves on, he used a syringe to put the tranquilizer dose into a metal dart and then inserted the dart into what looked almost like a .22 rifle. The assistant hefted the shotgun and with their respective armaments the two bear men edged slowly out toward the grizzly, the biologist saying to us in reluctant tone of voice, "This is always a fun part."

When the pair neared to about thirty yards from him the bear *really* lunged now. At the end of the cable tether it stood and strained. My God, even the fur on the thing looked dangerous; this griz was browner than the tan one I'd shot, and the wind rippled in that restless dark field of hair.

Clicking and more clicking issued from Mariah's camera while the biologist and his guardian eased another ten yards closer to the bear. Riley alternately jotted in his notebook and restlessly tapped his pen on it. I wonder now how I was able to hear anything over the beating of my heart.

When he was no more than twenty yards from the bear, the biologist raised his dart rifle, leveled it for what seemed a long time, then fired, a compressed air *pfoop*. The dart hit the grizzly high in the hind quarters. As the Fish and Game men rapidly walked backwards to where we were, the bear reared up behind, thrashed briefly, then went down, lying there like a breathing statue as the paralyzing drug gripped it.

The bear men stood and waited, the shotgunner never taking his eyes off the bear, the biologist steadily checking his watch and the animal's vital signs. After about ten minutes the biologist said, "Let's try him."

He reached in the back of the truck for a long-handled shovel. Going over beside the hairy bulk with a careful but steady stride while the helper trailed him, shotgun at the ready, the biologist took a stance and rapped the near shoulder with the end of the shovel handle, not real hard but probably plenty to start a fight if the other party is a grizzly.

When the bear just lay there and took that, the biologist announced: "Okay, he's under."

Christamighty, I hadn't known there was even going to be any doubt about it or I for sure would have watched this part of the procedure from inside the metal walls of the motorhome.

There was a surprising amount of business to be done to the sedated bear. Weighing it in a tarp sling and scale that the state pair rigged from the stoutest branch overhead. Checking its breathing rate every few minutes. Fastening a radio collar—surveillance to see whether this was going to be a repeat offender—around its astonishing circumference of neck. Putting salve into its eyes to keep them from drying out during this immobilization period. And of course as the biologist said, "the *really* fun part," loading the thing into the culvert cage. All of us got involved in that except Mariah. For once I was thankful for her cameramania as she dipped and dove around, snapping away at the two state guys and Riley and me huffing and puffing to insert the three-hundred-pound heap of limp grizzly into the tank-like silver trap. Every instant of that, remembering the fury exploding up that tree of twenty-five years ago, claws slashing bark into ribbons and broken branches flying, I was devoutly hoping this bear was going to stay tranquil. Sure, you bet, no question but that it was snoozing as thoroughly as drug science could make it do. Yet this creature in our hands felt hotblooded and ungodly strong, and all this time its eyes never closed.

Heaven's front gate could never sound more welcome than that clang of the door of the trap dropping shut when we at last had the bear bedded inside. "Nothing much to this job, hmm?" the panting Riley remarked to the biologist.

The state men then employed their crane to lift the cage onto the flatbed truck and soundly secured it with a trucker's large tie-down strap.

"Well, there," I declared, glad to be done with this bear business.

Almost as one, Mariah and Riley looked at me as if I was getting up from supper just as the meat and potatoes were put on the table.

Good God, how literal could they get, even if they were newspaper people. I mean, the movers had the bear all but under way. Did we need to watch every revolution of the truck's wheels, tag along like the Welcome Wagon to the grizzly's new home, to be able to say we'd seen bear moving?

By Mariah and Riley's lights, indubitably. Out our caravan proceeded to Highway 89 and then south and west down thinner and
thinner roads, to a distant edge of the Bob Marshall Wilderness. As
we went and went, maybe the bear was keeping his bearings but I sure
as hell couldn't have automatically found my way back to the Pine
Butte country.

      Exile is the loser's land. Others set its borders, state its terms,
enforce the diminishment as only the victors know how; the
outcast sniffs the cell of wilderness.

The motorhome had been growling in low gear for what seemed
hours, up and up a mountain road which had never heard of a Bago
before, until at last the truck ahead swung into a sizable clearing.

"Here's where we tell our passenger adios," the biologist came over
to us to confirm that this at last was the release site, sounding several
hundred percent more cheerful than he had all day. The idea now,
he told Riley and Mariah, was to simply let the bear out of the culvert,
watch it a little while to be sure the tranquilizer was wearing off okay,
and allow it to go its wildwood way, up here far from tempting morsels
of calf etcetera.

He could not have been any readier than I was to say goodbye to
the grizzly. The back of my neck was prickling. And though I couldn't
see into the culvert trap, I somehow utterly knew, maybe the memory
of the bear I had killed superimposing itself here, that the ruff of hair
on the young grizzly's hump was standing on end, too.

"You folks stay in your vehicle," the biologist added, somewhat
needlessly I thought, before heading back to the truck. The state pair
themselves were going to be within for this finale of bear moving, for
they could operate the crane from inside the cab of the truck to lift
the trap door. Except for rolling her window down farther than I liked,
even Mariah showed no great desire to be out there to greet the bear
and instead uncapped a long lens and fitted it onto her camera.

The remote control debarkation of the bear began, the state guys
peering back through the rear window of the truck cab to start the
crane hoisting the culvert door so the bear could vamoose. We waited.
And waited.

It was Mariah, scoping over there with her lens, who said it aloud. "Something's fouled up."

The truck doors opened and the two bear movers stepped out, the helper carefully carrying the shotgun. Reluctantly but I suppose necessarily, I rolled my window down and craned my head out, Riley practically breathing down the back of my neck.

"Equipment," the biologist bitterly called over to us as if it was his personal malady. "Murphy's Law seems to have caught up with the crane—probably some six-bit part gave out. This won't be as pretty but we can do the release process manually."

The pair of men climbed onto the flatbed of the truck. The shotgun guard stationed himself back by the truck cab while the biologist carefully climbed atop the trap and began the gruntwork of lifting the aluminum door up out of the slotted sides.

From the trap there was the sound of great weight shifting as the grizzly adjusted to the fact of freedom out there beyond the mouth of daylight. The big broad head poked into sight, then the shoulders with the furred hump atop them. I breathed with relief that we were about to be through with that haunting passenger.

The bear gathered itself to jump down to the ground but at the same time aggressively bit at the edge of the trap door above it. By reflex the biologist's hand holding that edge of the door jerked away.

The grizzly was all but out of the trap when the heavy door slammed down on its tailbone.

As instantly as the grizzly hit the ground it whirled against what it took to be attack, snarling, searching. The men on the truck froze, not to give the bear any motion to lunge at.

With suddenness again, the bear reared up on its hind legs to sense the surroundings. It saw the man on top of the culvert trap.

The grizzly dropped and charged, trying to climb the side of the truck to the men.

"Don't, bear!" the biologist cried out.

BWOOMWOOM, the rapid-fire of the shotgun blasted, and within the ringing in my ears I could hear the deep peals of echo diminish out over the mountainside.

Both shotgun slugs hit the grizzly in the chest. Stopping-power, the human tribe calls such large calibre ballistics, and it stopped the life of the bear the instant the twin bolts of lead tore into his heart and lungs. The bear slumped sideways, crumpled, and lay there in the clearing. Above the sudden carcass the two bear men stood rooted for a long moment. For one or maybe both of them, the shotgun had bought life instead of death by mauling.

Of all of Mariah's pictures of that day, here was the one that joined into Riley's words.

But as the shotgunner still held the gun pointing toward the grizzly, these survivors, too, seemed as lifeless as the furred victim.

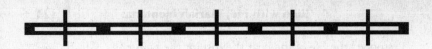

THOMAS McGUANE

FROM

Keep the Change

I n the dream it was summer and when he awakened he remembered the lazy sound of a small airplane and the sight of a little girl too far away to see clearly, picking chokecherries on the side of a ravine. The prairie spread into the distance and its great emptiness was not cheerful. It woke him up with sharp and undefined sadness. He tipped his watch, lying on the table beside the bed, so he could see its dial against the vague light coming in the window. It wasn't quite five yet. He lay back and felt the warmth of Astrid beside him. He knew he had to see Clara. He couldn't wait. He had thought his situation with Ellen would sort itself out and an appropriate introduction would ensue. But it seemed now that might never happen. He couldn't wait any longer.

He would go to the end of the Keltons' road and watch Clara get on the school bus. He arose slowly and began to dress. His stealth awakened Astrid. "What is it, honey?"

"I've got to get receipts for those cattle. I'm meeting the brand inspector at the scale house."

"When will you be back?"

"Before lunch." He felt something sharp from the deceit.

Joe left the truck almost two miles away from the Keltons' road just as the sun began to come up. He hurried along the oiled county road straight toward the lime and orange glow that in a matter of minutes would be the new day. When the sun finally did emerge, Joe was safely concealed in the scrub trees opposite Ellen and Billy's mailbox. He had a feeling he couldn't uncover. Waiting for his little girl to catch the school bus, he was as close to whole as he had felt in memory. It was several blissful moments before the absurdity of his situation, his concealment, his uncertain expectations, dissolved his well-being. The chill of morning crept in. Finally, the yellow school bus rose upon the crown of the hill and went right on through without stopping, as though it never stopped here. Did Ellen invent Clara? Joe thought of that first.

He crossed the county road and started up the ranch driveway, walking as quietly as he could so that he could hear if anyone approached. As he went along, presumably getting closer, his nervousness increased and he began to picture alert dogs bounding at him, a family bursting from the front door to confront a stranger.

By the time the house was visible, a modest white frame house, neatly tended, a few yards from its barns and outbuildings, Joe could see in a small grove of wild apple trees the perfect place to hide. A rooster crowed. And when he got inside the trees, his concealment was so perfect that he arranged his sweater against a tree trunk as a pillow and prepared to spend however long it took to watch every single human being who lived in that house, who used its front door, who walked in its yard, who did its chores.

The rooster crowed again and in the near distance a bull bellowed rhythmically. Past the house was a small corral. A solitary paint horse rolled and made a dust cloud, then stood and shook. In the sky above the house, just now ignited by sunrise, were clouds which must have hung there in the windless air all night long. Joe felt himself drift into this serenity as though, not merely hidden, he was incorporeal and free as a spirit.

The door opened and a little girl ran out, pursued by Billy. He overtook her, turned her, and rebuttoned her cloth coat. He pulled her straw hat down close on her head and she tipped it back again. He pulled it down and she tipped it back. He swept her up. He held her at arm's length where she hung like a rag doll with a grin on her face. She acted almost like a baby with Billy though she was far too old for that. Above all, she clearly resembled her father, Billy Kelton. Joe scarcely had time to track his astonishment. It was enough that

Billy's olive skin was there and the distinctive, inset brown eyes. But the minute Clara spoke, asking Billy to let out some chickens, Joe knew from her crooning voice that Clara was feeble-minded. Billy planted her where she stood and went into a low shed. There was an immediate squawking from within and then four or five hens ran into the yard. Clara ran after them. Billy came out and deftly swept up a small speckled hen. Clara took it in her arms. Billy removed her hat, kissed the crown of her head, and replaced the hat. He went back into the shed while Clara stood bundling the hen and rubbing her cheek against it. The little chicken sank her head between the shoulders of her wings. Billy emerged with some eggs held against his stomach with his hand.

"Let's eat, kid. Put your friend down."

"I want take my hen!" Clara crooned.

"Mama won't let us, angel," said Billy, wincing sympathetically.

"My friend!" she pleaded.

"Okay, go on and take her in the house," said Billy gently. "What d'you think Mama's gonna say? I'll tell you what Mama's gonna say. Mama's gonna say take that chicken on out of here."

Clara shrugged and followed Billy toward the house, defiantly carrying her hen. Billy went in and Clara hesitated. When the coast was clear, she set the hen down and made a haughty entrance to the house. The speckled hen shot erratically back to the shed. Joe didn't move. He felt compassion sweep over him, not for Clara, whom he did not know, but for Billy in all his isolated, violent ignorance. It was this Joe had waited for: something that would cross his mind like a change of weather and leave a different atmosphere behind.

The sun couldn't quite penetrate the pale gray sky. It looked as if it might rain; if it did, it would be a cold rain, close to snow. Everything about the morning said the season was changing fast. When Joe awoke, he felt a lightness that approached giddiness, almost a gaiety. It seemed so beyond sense that he thought he must immediately put it to use.

He got on the telephone and began calling truckers to haul his yearlings to the sale yard. He got a mileage rate, a loaded rate, and a deadhead surcharge. He arranged a dawn departure. The only thing to slow this cattle drive down was going to be the speed limit.

He spent the next day on horseback. Overstreet's nephews came up from their ranch as they had done for the branding and helped him gather his pastures. A small herd formed, then grew as he traveled forward, downhill and toward the corrals. The horses loved this and tossed their heads, strained at their bits, ran quartering forward, and generally hurled themselves into the work of sweeping the land of beef. Every now and again, a herd-quitter gave the men the excuse of a wild ride to restore the yearling to the mass of its fellows. By nightfall, the dust-caked nephews with the thin crooked mouths of their grandfather had started down the road home on lathered horses, and the cattle were quiet in the corrals. Overstreet himself was there to count the yearlings, mouthing the numbers and dropping his arm decisively every ten head. Looking at the backs and heads of the crowded cattle, the myriad muzzles and ears, the surge of energy, Joe was reminded of the ocean when it was choppy. He thought he knew why Overstreet was being so helpful.

Joe put his hot horse in a stall out of the wind and gave him a healthy ration of oats, which roared out of the bucket into the tin-lined trough. The little gelding always looked like he was falling asleep while he ate, and Joe watched him a moment before going out to check his gates.

Joe had become so preoccupied with getting the cattle shipped that his communications with Astrid almost came to a stop. She seemed to sense something and they rather politely stayed out of each other's way.

They loaded the cattle in the morning by the yard light. The metal loading chute rocked and crashed under their running weight. Joe went inside the trailer to help swing the partitions against the crowded animals. Their bawling deafened him. At the end of each load, the rope was released from the pulley and the sliding aluminum door flew down to a silent stop in the manure.

The first truck pulled off while the second one loaded. There were three frozen-footed steers that were crippled and hard to load. They went up last and the two trucks pulled out, their engines straining in low gear at the vast contents of living flesh going down the ranch road in bawling confusion. From beneath the bottom slats, the further green evidence of their terror went on flowing. Joe watched the back of the trailers rocking from side to side with the mass and motion of big trawlers in a seaway. In a moment, the red taillights had curved down past the cottonwoods and disappeared.

By three that afternoon, the cattle went through the sale at seventy-one and a half dollars a hundredweight and the money was sent to Lureen's account in Deadrock. And of course the ranch was Joe's. Mainly, it filled in the blanks in the painting of the white hills. A homeowner, a man of property. He sat in the living room with the deed in his lap. He showed it to Astrid. He fanned himself with it. He tried to make it a joke, but she didn't laugh and neither did he. He wondered what Smitty would do with the money.

Sometime after midnight, Joe was awakened from sleep by someone knocking on the door. Once he saw the clock and knew how late it was, he was filled with sharp panic. He got up without turning on the lights and eased into the kitchen. In the window of the door, he could see the shape of someone standing. He thought first of not answering the door and then wondered if it might not be a traveler, someone with car trouble, or a sick neighbor. And so he went into the kitchen and turned the light on. The minute he did that, the figure outside the door was lost. He opened the door on the darkness and said, "What is it?"

There was no reply. Joe had made out the shape of the figure. It looked like his father. The glow from the yard light, so recently cloudy with insects, was sharply drawn on the cold night. Joe wanted to say, "It's a clean slate." Surely this was a dream. It must have been a traveler.

Joe closed the door as quietly as he could but left it unlocked. There was no sound anywhere. He went back to bed and lay awake. He felt the cold from the blackened window over the bed. He had begun to suspect that by coming here at all, he had taken back his name. He remembered the sense of paralysis having a particular name had given him in the first place. He had loved moving into a world of other people's names. He had even tried other names and had felt a thrill like that of unfamiliar air terminals and railway stations, places where he could abandon himself to discreet crowd control. Finally, this took such vigilance it was wearying. He wanted his own name. And yet, the ride home through spring storms, through unfamiliar districts, had a quality that was independent of where he was coming from and where he was going. He had a brief thrill in thinking that all of life was about two things: either move or resume the full use of your name. But the idea slipped away when he tried to grasp it.

It was still dark when he got in the truck and filled it up at the fuel tank next to the barn. Then he began to drive. He drove to White Sulphur Springs, Checkerboard, Twodot, Judith Gap, Moccasin, Grassrange, Roundup, and home, four hundred miles without stopping.

By the time Joe pulled up in front of the house, he was exhausted. The lights shone domestically in the dark, illuminating parts of trees and the white stones of the driveway. It seemed that a placid, sunshot existence must be passing within.

Joe opened the door and Ivan Slater rose inelegantly from the deep, slumped couch while Astrid, standing a certain distance from one undecorated wall, tried to hang the moon with a smile that was both radiant and realistic.

"What are you doing here?" Joe demanded. "Where did you come from?" He smelled a rat. Ivan had been called in as Astrid's chief adviser before.

"Joe." She may have said something before that but Joe didn't hear it. Then she said, "I need to talk to you."

"I know," Joe said, noticing that whatever was in the air suspended Ivan's promotional bearing so that he stood exactly where he had arisen, taking up room. It was exactly the moment one would ordinarily say, "Stay out of this."

"Joe, let me run this by you," said Ivan. "Astrid isn't suited for this, somehow. She has asked me to help her get resituated. I'm Astrid's friend and this is what friends are for. P.S. We're not fucking."

"That's fine, I hate her," said Joe experimentally.

"Now Joe," Ivan said, "you've had a long drive."

"You knew I wouldn't stay," Astrid said. "What's this about, anyway? I don't know. But I do know I'm getting out of here. And it's a joke to claim you hate me."

"The fucking Cuban geek," Joe offered.

"Punch him in the nose, Ivan," said Astrid.

"That will do," Ivan said to Joe without emphasis.

"Take the dog with you," said Joe to Astrid. "That's the worst dog I ever saw. It'll be perfect for your new home."

"Okay, but don't generalize about me. And what is this about a new home?"

"I used to like dogs," Joe explained maladroitly.

"I had a lot to offer. I still do. Not for you, obviously. But who does? All I need to know is that it's not me. And I loved you. So, good luck. Good luck with the place. All the luck in the world with the cows. Enjoy yourself with the land. Happy horses, Joe."

"I used to like women!"

"I'm not like that dog, Joe," Astrid said.

"Don't jump to conclusions. I want you both out of here right away. I need a quiet place to sleep."

"Joe, it's late," Ivan said. "You're not in your right mind. As if you ever were, in fact."

"This advisory role you cultivate, Ivan, is unwelcome just now. I dislike having my time wasted."

"You're not that busy," sang Ivan. Joe sighed and looked at the floor. He wanted to collect his thoughts and he feared a false tone entering the proceedings. He wanted to leave off on a burnishing fury and empty out the house. It was hard to see that he'd had the intended effect; Ivan was scratching his back against the doorjamb. Astrid was smiling at a spot in midair. She was a fine girl. They had feared all along that they couldn't survive a real test. It had been lovely, anyway. It was a provisional life.

While they packed Astrid's things, Joe watched TV. As luck would have it, it was a feature on farm and ranch failures with music by Willie Nelson and John "Cougar" Mellencamp. He remembered leaving the deed in the truck. He might have left the windows open. Pack rats could get in and eat the deed. The wind could get the deed.

They came into the living room with their suitcases.

"This is pretty interesting. It's about farm and ranch failure," Joe said. "Can you go during the commercial?"

"No," said Astrid, "we're going now. Were you serious about that dog?"

"What next!" said Joe without taking his eyes off the screen.

"May I see you a moment, Joe?" Astrid stood in the doorway to their bedroom. Ivan studied the backs of his fingernails in the open front door, buffing them occasionally on his left coat-sleeve. Joe met

Astrid in the bedroom and she shoved the door shut. She gave him a long look and took a deep breath.

"Let me tell you something, sport," she began, "you don't fool me with this tasteless display we've just witnessed."

"I don't."

"No, you don't."

"What sort of display would have struck you as less tasteless?"

"A sincere remark or two about your plight. A word of hope that you'll come to life soon. Your life."

"All whoppers!"

"I'm just gonna step back, and let you choose."

She went out the door. Joe followed her. Ivan was still in the same spot. When Joe went over, Ivan deployed his hand as a kind of hand-shake option, Joe's choice. Joe shook.

Ivan and Astrid went into the night. He heard them call the dog and when he saw the lights wheel and go out, and he knew the dog was gone, he at last realized how blithely things were being taken away from him. He went to bed and contained himself as well as he could, but the pillowcase grew wet around his face.

His sleep produced the need for sleep, for rest, for deep restoration from this masquerade of sleep in which all the tainted follies had opportunity for festivity and parade. He had Astrid in his arms and his inability to distinguish love and hate no longer mattered because she wasn't there in the light of day.

The cool spell passed and it was hot again. Joe was going to take a good long look at the white hills. He was going to start at the beginning. He got in the truck and drove toward the drought-ravaged expanses east of town where the road looked like a long rippled strip of gray taffy; on the farthest reaches of the road, looking as small as occasional flies, were the very few vehicles out today. Dust followed a tractor as an unsuccessful crop was plowed into the ground. Joe could picture the cavalry crossing here, following the Indians and their ghost dogs. Sheep were drifted off into the corners of pastures waiting for the cool of evening to feed. Ribbed cattle circled the tractor tires that held the salt. Old stock ponds looked like meteor craters and the weeds that came in with the highway gravel had blossomed to devour the pastures.

It was neither summer nor fall. The sky was blue and the mountains lay on the horizon like a black saw. A white cloud stood off to one end of the mountains. In a small pasture, a solitary bull threw dust up under himself beneath the crooked arm of a defunct sprinkler. The thin green belt beneath the irrigation ditches contrasted immediately with the prickly pear desert that began inches above. The radio played "Black roses, white rhythm and blues." Astrid used to say, "I thought Montana was so unlucky for you. I can't understand why you want to go back." And he had said with what seemed like prescience and laudable mental health, "Yes, but I'm not superstitious!" And she'd said, "Wait a minute. You were pretty clear on this. You said it was unlucky for you and it was unlucky for everybody else."

Joe said, "That's my home!"

He stopped the truck at the bottom of a long, open draw and walked for almost an hour. At the end of that walk, he reached the gloomy, ruined, enormous house that he had long ago visited with his father, the mansion of the Silver King, a piece of discarded property no longer even attached to a remembered name. It was a heap out in a pasture and if you had never been inside it the way Joe had and felt in the design of its chambers the anger and assertion of the Silver King himself, the mansion didn't look good enough to shelter slaughter cattle until sale day. Grackles jumped and showered in the lee of its discolored walls and the palisade of poplars that led from the remains of the gate seemed like the work of a comedian.

Joe walked to the far side of the building and sat down close to the wall out of the wind. The mud swallows had built their nests solidly up under the eaves and wild roses were banked and tangled wherever corruption of the wall's surface gave them a grip. Concentric circles in the stucco surrounded black dots where stray gunfire had intercepted the building, adding to the impression that it was a fortress. Joe thought about how his father's bank had repossessed the property. His father was gone—even the bank was gone! He was going to go in.

A piece of car spring in the yard made a good pry bar, and Joe used it to get the plywood off one of the windows, leaving a black violated gap in the wall. He made a leap to the sill, teetering sorely on his stomach, then poured himself inside. He raised his eyes to the painting of the white hills.

Joe walked across the ringing flags to get a view of the picture. He could feel the stride the room induced and imagined the demands of spirit the Silver King made on everything. Such people, he thought, attacked death headlong with their insistence on comfort and social leverage. It was absolutely fascinating that it didn't work.

But the painting was still mysterious; it had not changed. "The only painting I've ever understood," said Joe's father after he had showed it to his son. "Too bad it's fading." The delicacy of shading in the overlapping white hills, rescued from vagueness by the cheap pine frame, seemed beyond the studied coarseness Joe's father leveled at everything else.

It was a matter of dragging an old davenport across the room and bracing it against one corner of the fireplace. He stepped up onto one arm, then to its back and then up onto the mantel. He turned around very slowly and faced the wall, to the left of the painting. By shuffling in slow motion down the length of the mantel he was able to move himself to its center.

There was no picture. There was a frame hanging there and it outlined the spoiled plaster behind it. It could have been anything. It was nothing, really. Close up, it really didn't even look like white hills. This of course explained why it had never been stolen. Joe concluded that no amount of experience would make him smart.

His father must always have known there was nothing there. The rage Joe felt quickly ebbed. In his imaginary parenthood, he had begun to see what caused the encouragement of belief. It was eternal playfulness toward one's child; and it explained the absence of the painting. It wasn't an empty frame; it was his father telling him that somewhere in the abyss something shone.

He was driving a little too fast for a dirt road, tools jumping around on the seat of the truck and a shovel in the bed beating out a tattoo. He was going to see Ellen, sweeping toward her on a euphoric zephyr. He knew how intense he must look; and he began doing facial exercises as a preparation for feigning indifference. The flatbed hopped across the potholes. Antelope watched from afar. "Hi, kiddo," he said. "Thought I'd see how you were getting along." He cleared his throat and frowned. "Good afternoon, Ellen. Lovely day. I hope this isn't a bad time." He craned over so he could watch himself in the rearview mirror. "Hiya Ellen-baby, guess what? I'm gonna lose that fucking ranch *this week*. YAAGH!" A sudden and vast deflation befell him and he slumped in the front of the truck and slowed down. When he got to the schoolyard, the children were gone and Ellen was walking toward her old sedan in her coat.

She saw Joe and walked over toward him. She said, "Well, what do you know about that?"

"I wanted to see you," said Joe.

"Here I am."

"Have you been thinking?"

"About what? My phone bill? My cholesterol?"

"Your phone bill."

"I think about it every time I lift the Princess Touchtone to my ear. Incidentally, my husband and I are anxious for you to know how happy we are to have worked everything out. I realize I'm kind of repeating myself. But it seems we have to do that with you. Joe, I don't want to be this way."

"Can we take a short drive?" Joe asked.

"How short?"

"Five minutes."

"I guess it can be arranged," said Ellen and climbed in. Joe noticed how closely she followed the rural convention of going from an amorous interest to a display of loathing; in the country, no one broke off an affair amicably. Ellen looked out at the beautiful fall day, directing a kind of all-purpose disgust at falling aspen leaves. This was the sort of thing Astrid never put him through.

Joe drove back toward town and quickly approached its single stoplight; he was heading for the open country to show her the white hills, both the painting and the ones beyond, and explain enough about his life that he could, if necessary, close this chapter too.

"Where are we going?" Ellen asked in alarm. "Stop at this light and let me out." The light began to turn red. Ellen tried the door handle. Some pedestrians had stopped to look on. Joe ran the light. Ellen pushed the door open and shouted, "*Help!*" and Joe hit the gas. The bystanders fluttered into their wake. He watched in the rearview mirror as they started to go into action.

"We'll just take a little loop out toward the Crazies and I'll drop you back at the school. What in God's name caused you to yell that?"

"I wanted to be dropped off. Joe, you have to learn to take hints a little better than you do."

"I'm going to show you something and we're going to talk."

"About what? My husband and I are back together. We have resolved our differences. We're happy again. We're a goddamn couple, got it?"

"Why did you lie to me about Clara?"

She studied him for a moment in a shocked way. Then he saw she wouldn't argue.

"Billy and I had hit this rough spot in the road."

"I still don't follow you."

"It was Daddy's idea actually. He had worked it out on the calendar. I have to admit, it wasn't that far-fetched. But he's got that big bite missing from his ranch and he kind of put two and two together."

"You ought to be ashamed of yourself."

"Whatever." She turned to him suddenly. She made little fists and rolled her eyes upward. "You don't need to understand me. Billy knows everything there is to know about *me*, and he loves *me*."

Joe wished he had time to think about this. She had a point. It was about lives that were specific to each other. It wasn't about generalities. It wasn't about "love." "Love" was like "home." It was basic chin music.

Joe drove along slowly, as though adding speed would only substantiate the appearance of kidnap. Since he was pouring with sweat, he now merely wished to add a few amiable notes and get Ellen back to the schoolyard. This had all turned into something a bit different from what he had hoped for. At that very moment, he began to realize how much he wished he had Astrid advising him right now. She would say something quite concrete like "Hit the brakes" or "Don't do anything stupid. That way nobody will get hurt."

"Here they come," said Ellen.

"Here comes who?"

"Look in the mirror."

A small motorcade had formed a mile or so back; a cloud of dust arose from them and drifted across the sage flats. Joe picked up speed but couldn't seem to widen the gap. Perspiration broke out on his lip. "Are you going to clear this business up with that mob, if they catch us?"

"Let me get back to you on that," said Ellen with the faintest smile. Ellen had become so strange. It was more than indifference—it was a weird fog. He imagined her thinking how badly she wanted to get shut of this jackass and back to the husband and daughter she loved. This perception reduced Joe's account to virtual sardine size. He felt too paltry to go on taking the wheel.

He flattened the accelerator against the floor. The truck seemed to swim at terrific speed up the gradual grade toward the hills. A jack rabbit burst onto the road ahead of them, paced the truck for fifty yards and peeled off into the sagebrush. Nothing Joe did seemed to extend the distance between himself and the cluster of vehicles behind.

"Have you been doing any fishing?" Ellen asked.

"I really haven't had the time."

The truck skidded slightly sideways.

"Somebody said there's a Mexican woman staying with you." So that was it. A bird dove at the windshield and veered off in a pop of feathers.

"An old girlfriend," Joe said candidly. "It's a very sad thing. She couldn't stick it out. She'd had enough, and she was very patient in her own way. If she'd lied to me more I'd be with her today."

Ellen mused at the rocketing scenery.

"I've got a teacher's meeting in Helena," she said wearily. "On Tuesday. That's another world."

"Who will substitute for you?"

"An old lady who doesn't make the kids work. It makes me look like a bum." Somehow, Joe got the truck into a wild slide going down a steep grade into a gully. The truck turned backward at about sixty miles an hour. "This is really making me moody," said Ellen. They plunged into a grove of junipers and burst out the other side in a shower of wood and branches. Some of the foliage was heaped up against the windshield and it was a little while before Joe could see where he was going. The vigilantes were still bringing up the rear in a cloud of dust. One of them dropped back, a plume of steam jetting from the radiator.

It was hopeless. He couldn't outrun them in this evil, weak farm truck. All he wanted was a brainless chase that could last for weeks. He stopped, backed and turned around. Deadrock was visible in the blue distance. The machines advanced toward him. "You've really got a bee in your bonnet," Ellen said.

"Shut up, you stupid bitch, you rotten crumb."

"I *see*," said Ellen. "The idea being that I got you into this?"

Joe said nothing.

"After the big rush, I am now a 'stupid bitch.' This may be the first serious conversation we've had since we met. Are you telling me that it is possible I could mean more to you than pussy or golf lessons? Let's have it, Joe. I could actually rise in your esteem to the status of 'stupid bitch.' Oh, this *is* romantic. I had really misjudged the depth of feeling around here. And I've gone back to my husband when I could have enjoyed these passionate tongue-lashings."

At the approach of massed cars and trucks, Joe just stopped. Twenty vehicles wheeled all around them and skidded to a halt, dumping a small crowd of armed civilians, the State Farm agent, a mechanic still in his coveralls, a pharmacist in a white tunic of some kind, a couple of waitresses. They were still pouring out and a few guns had been displayed, when Ellen threw open her door and cried, "This is all a terrible misunderstanding! It was supposed to be a joke!" She climbed out of the truck. One of the mechanics, in coveralls and a gray crewcut that showed the crown of his head, came to the truck and held a gun to Joe's temple. Joe looked over to see Billy Kelton emerging from a Plymouth Valiant he should have recognized. "A complication," Joe said. "Here comes Billy."

"Son," said the man in the crewcut in a startlingly mild voice, "this is where she all comes out in the wash." Joe had a sudden feeling of isolation as Ellen walked over and joined her husband at a distance from the cluster of people and vehicles. Billy shoved her away from him and began to walk toward Joe's truck. Joe wondered what the shoving meant, in terms of a margin of safety, of an exploitable ambiguity.

"That's Billy," said Joe's guard. "He's getting ready to have a fit."

"What's he going to do?"

"Do? He's going back to Vietnam!"

The mechanic smiled like a season ticket holder. The blood beat in Joe's face. Joe thought that was the time to grab the gun but he just thought about it with a kind of longing, knowing he wouldn't have any idea what to do with it.

Billy came over with a bakery truck driver at his side, a blond-haired man with long sideburns and an expression of permanent surprise. "Something to tell the grandchildren, ay?" Billy said to the mechanic. "Get him out for me, would you?"

The mechanic opened the door and dragged Joe out. He and the man from the bakery held his arms, shoving him up against the car. Billy got so close, Joe could only focus on one of his eyes at a time. But it was enough for Joe to recognize that Billy didn't have his heart in this. Twice he had punched Joe years ago and apparently that was enough. "Time is hastening, Joe. You need to cut it out." Billy turned and spoke to the others. "You guys can go." They hesitated in their disappointment. "Go on," he said more firmly. They began to move off. "The show is over," he said, making what Joe considered an extraordinary concession.

"Is that it?" asked the mechanic.

"That's it," said Billy without turning back. "Ellen, take my car back to the house."

"He really didn't do anything, Billy."

"Probably not. Just go on back now with Vern and them."

Ellen moved away from them. A breeze had come up and the clouds were moving overhead rapidly. The air was cold enough that the exhaust smell of the vehicles was sharp. Billy turned to Joe once more. "We'll just let Ellen go on back to town with Vern and them. If she goes, they'll all go. They're upset because they couldn't lynch you. You and your family sure been popular around here. All them boys banked with your dad."

"Which one is Vern?" asked Joe without interest.

"Fella with the flattop."

"Oh." Joe's eyes drifted over to Vern, who was returning reluctantly to a car much too small for him. Joe couldn't see how he could even get in it. But he elected not to report this impression.

"Let me drive," said Billy, opening the door to get in. Joe slid over.

"The keys are in it," Joe said with a sickly smile.

Billy was wearing old Levis and wingtip cowboy boots nearly worn through on top by spur straps. He smiled at Joe and started up the truck. Joe could see that the cars and trucks which had followed them were almost out of sight now. As the various members of the community who had come out to help returned to town in their cars, something went out of the air. Joe said, "I saw on the news they're having a potato famine in Malibu."

"I don't have too good a sense of humor today, Joe."

They drove on, and Billy was a careful driver. They took the road that went around to the south, which eventually connected to the ranch. "Am I the biggest problem you've got, Joe?" They both followed with their eyes a big band of antelope the truck had scared, all quick-moving does except for one big pronghorn buck who rocked along behind in their dust cloud.

"Not really."

Billy sighed. Joe looked out the windshield but saw nothing. Joe remembered one time he and Astrid were dancing to the radio and she called him "sweetheart." She had never called him that before and never did again. Everything takes place in time, Joe thought, wondering why that always seemed like such a heartbreaking discovery.

Suddenly, Joe wanted to talk. "My old man used to say, 'If you ain't the lead horse, the scenery never changes.' Now it looks like I might lose the place. I need to get out front with that lead horse. I feel like I've been living in a graveyard."

Billy looked at him. Joe watched Billy deeply consider whether or not the fraternization was appropriate. It was clear that there was insufficient malice in the air to warrant this drive on any other basis. What a day we're having here, thought Joe.

After a resigned sigh, Billy started to talk: "When I come home, I pretty much come home to nothing. Except that we already had a kid. And then we got married. Old man Overstreet never let me forget I come into the deal empty-handed, just had my little house. He always introduces me, 'This here's my son-in-law Billy. He runs a few head of chickens over on the Mission Creek road about two and a half miles past the airport on the flat out there.' Never *will* let me forget. And I ought to punch you but I can't really. Life used to be so simple."

It was a long way around. It seemed as if the mountains toward Wyoming stayed the same size ahead of them, sharp shapes that curved off toward the Stillwater. You could be under traveling clouds and off toward the mountains the clouds would seem stopped. And the mountains looked like a place you'd never reach. On top of that, nobody seemed to want to get there much anyway. Billy must have felt Joe look over because he turned on the radio only to get the feverish accordion of Buckwheat Zydeco shouting out the bright nights of New Orleans. He turned it off and said, "I want to go back to work."

It seemed to Joe to be the most glowing of all thoughts. It went with the day and it went with their situation.

"I don't seem to understand what it means to have something," Joe said. "I don't seem to get what I ought to out of it. I feel like that place still belongs to my dad."

"It ought to belong to whoever's been working on it."

"Which is you, I suppose."

"It was when Overstreet had it leased. When you took it back, I had to go up to the house. That was when me and Ellen started to have such a wreck. We ain't over it yet. We may never get over it. She was raised up to think I ought to have something, and I don't." Joe remembered long ago when Billy had punched him out at the railroad station, and he thought he might have understood even then how the dispossessed are quick with their fists. But now Billy seemed to have lost even that capability. Joe thought that at the narrow crossroads in which Billy Kelton lived, the use of his hands had been cruelly confined to a kind of unchosen service. Lack of his own ground indentured him to people smaller than himself.

"That place of mine," Joe said, "has got serious debt against it but a man who wanted to stay and fight it ought to be able to hang on to it." He stared at the beautiful prairie and wondered if anyone had ever owned it. "I don't want to stay and fight it. That's just not me."

Billy slowed the truck. "Have you seen my father-in-law's map?"

"The one with the missing piece?"

"Do you have any idea what it would mean if I had that little chunk of the puzzle? Even for five minutes?"

"I probably don't," said Joe. "But we're all so different."

Joe had dinner with Lureen at her house. She didn't feel like cooking, so Joe stopped off for some chicken, a carton of cole slaw, and some soft drinks. She greeted him in the doorway, then went right back inside and sat under the kitchen window with her hands in her lap. Looking at her, Joe wondered if it wouldn't be the kindest thing he could do to burn her house down.

Joe walked around opening cupboards, looking for dishes and uten-
sils and glasses, then set the kitchen table for the two of them. He
got Lureen to come over and they sat down to eat. She didn't seem
to want to eat much. Joe bit into a drumstick, then watched her over
the top of it while he chewed. He tried the cole slaw. It was sweet
and creamy like a dessert.

"Good chicken," he said.

"Delicious."

"You haven't tasted it yet."

"I will. Thank you for bringing it."

"Look at it this way," said Joe. "It's not beef! Ha-ha!" She took
it in listlessly. A bird hit the window and they both looked up.

"It's all right," said Joe. "Didn't hit that hard."

Then he noticed Lureen's tears falling in the cole slaw.

"You must have foreseen this," he said.

"I didn't, Joe."

He chewed on the drumstick, trying to have a perception.

"But didn't it ring kind of a bell after it happened?"

"No."

"It was a bit of a crooked scheme for all parties concerned," Joe
pointed out, actually enjoying this store chicken.

"*I know!*" Lureen wailed, throwing herself back in her chair.

"Long ago, my father, your brother, your *other* brother, told me
never to take my eyes off Smitty."

"It's going to be hard to watch him in Hawaii," Lureen sniveled
with an extraordinary, crumpled misery that Joe had not only never
seen before in her but never seen in anyone of her age.

The phone rang and Joe answered it. The lovely and cultivated
voice of a young woman explained that he, as the head of the household, was a finalist in a multi-million-dollar sweepstake. Joe cut her
off. "I'm not the head of a household," Joe said and went back to
Lureen.

"Wrong number," he said.

"Was it those sweepstakes people?"

"Yes."

"They're used to speaking with Smitty," she said and began to cry
again. Joe's heart ached to see his poor little aunt in this condition

even if she had brought it upon herself. He could see a tulip glow from the setting sun high in the kitchen windows. And then the perception came.

"Lureen, I'm going to tell you something and I want you to listen carefully." She stared at him like a child. "You know our Smitty," he said and she nodded her head up and down in a jittery fashion. "He'll spend all that money. You know that and I know that." He let this sink in. "And it won't take long." The nodding stopped. She was listening raptly. Joe was now ready to drop the panacea. *"And then he'll be back."*

Lureen stopped all motion. She looked at Joe's face with extraordinary concentration.

"Are you telling me the truth?"

"Yes."

"And it won't take that long?"

"Not that long at all."

"I ask myself if he's really secure in Honolulu. You read from time to time of racial problems there. The Hawaiians are quick to throw a punch and they are absolutely enormous."

And it's unrealistic to expect another thorough bombing by the Japanese, Joe thought. Lureen picked up a wing and seemed to admire it. "You're one hundred percent right about his inability to handle his finances," Lureen observed in a comparatively lusty voice. "I might just as well start resigning myself to the reappearance of his little face at the screen."

"Not a moment to lose," said Joe tonelessly. "Start resigning yourself today." He gave her a confirming gesture with his bare drumstick which was reminiscent of the heads of corporations Ivan admired so, the ones who promoted their own products on television. Then he looked up to the band of sky in the window. He had seen that band when his grandfather died and he had asked his grandmother if he'd left him any gold.

As the principal lien-holder, Darryl took in hand the matter of working out the closing, the ritual exchange of a dollar bill so crumpled it took two paper clips to attach it to the documents. Joe accepted that the substitution of a born-to-the-soil type like Billy Kelton for a drifter like himself was equal in favorable impact to keeping it out of the hands of an opportunistic schemer like Overstreet who never borrowed from banks anyway. The picture of this hard-working cowboy with an honorable service record holding a gun to Overstreet's head would be applauded throughout the community and give them something to discuss other than the *Dead End* sign the state had put up on the road into the cemetery. Overstreet paid Joe one visit, waving a checkbook and making one or two ritual threats which were windier than his usual succinct style. It had been years since Joe had heard the phrase "rue the day" and he mulled it over until the words dissolved into nonsense.

The mineral rights were briefly a hitch. Joe couldn't at first face that his father had long ago placed them in trust for a caddies' college fund in Minnesota. But when he realized this, he knew finally that his father had really said goodbye to the place even before his soul left his body in that four-door Buick. He borrowed Darryl's phone at the bank while the principals still sat around the contracts in a cloud of cigarette smoke, and called Astrid to explain his latest theory, that they could work it out. Astrid's reply was typical, almost vintage, Astrid.

He drove toward the ranch that was no longer his. It was hard not to keep noticing the terrific blue of the autumn sky. The huge cottonwoods along the river had turned purest yellow, and since no wind had come up to disturb the dying leaves, the great trees stood in chandelier brilliance along the watercourses that veined the hills. Joe had to stop the truck to try to take in all this light.

The branches were heavy with early wet snow. Joe looked out from his kitchen window and felt his unshaven face. The light on the snow-edged world was dazzling. He used to feel this way a lot, almost breathless. He quickly started a pot of coffee and returned to the window to look at the snow starting to shrink in the morning sun. There was a soft mound of it on his woodpile, and on the ends of the logs he could see that water from snow melt had sunk into the wood. A sudden memory came back across the years: his father cleaning grouse at the sink in the ranch kitchen, a raft of feathers on darkened water. "I wish I was a vegetarian," he'd laughed. "You never have to pick number-eight shot out of a tomato!" The sky was blue and the air coming from under the slightly opened window so cool and clean that he admitted to himself that his spirits were starting to soar. He thought he'd begin to get his things together. He stood in the window a moment more and looked out at the beautiful white hills.

What Astrid had said, more or less, was that they would pretty much have to see.

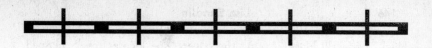

LINDA SANDLIN

Invisible Powers

Sonia is lying in bed with the covers knuckled under her chin, repeating the single mother's credo: *It's just you out there . . . It's just you out there.* It's her way of shoring up a tricky unilateral decision, telling herself she did the right thing. The alarm rang weeks, possibly months, ago; she needs to get up. But the chinks of the blinds say it's still night. It's February, and the one thing she can count on is that the floors will be cold right into April.

Yesterday, Sonia told her seven-year-old son he didn't need a baby blanket any longer. She'd dropped Nanket—the tattered satin scrap that was all that remained of his blanket—behind the washing machine. Outraged, Jesse presented her with a white face gone red in the middle, marched to his room, and locked the door.

So she's surprised when the bedroom door clicks open to a darting shadow, and Jesse bounds into the bed. He burrows underneath the covers.

"Hey, you're bouncing me all over the place. You're tearing my bed to pieces. Come out of there."

Has he forgiven her? Or just not remembered he's mad yet? Either way, Sonia's grateful for the reprieve. She ducks under the blankets and grabs a handful of synthetic nightgown. Somehow, she expected to see a gleam of skin, at least some eye white under there. It's just

145

black, perfectly black. Lifting the covers, she locates Jesse's clasped hands—circling his knees as though he is floating in black water.

"Watch this, Jess."

Sonia rubs her nightgown against the blanket to generate static electricity. The quick spark that shoots between them makes Jesse jump.

"Wow. Is that hot? Do it again, Mom." Jesse rolls up onto his hands and knees, focused on the wad of nightgown.

Jesse is huffing through his mouth; his warm breath smacks her cheek like a moist smoke ring. The air underneath the tunnel of covers is heavy with their breathing. She knows it's late, but she makes another spark, and another. She goes on making the sparks just to hear him laugh. His head falls on her arm briefly, and laughing, he does not take it away.

"How does it do that, Mom? Do it one more time," he says. His smile is slow with growing wonder.

Sonia smiles back. She cannot explain how it works; she only knows that it does. Like the way Jess could always tell—even in the dark with heavy eyes fluttering—when she tried to substitute a ringer for the misplaced Nanket. She swishes her nightgown with both hands. At once, the black space is shot with sparkles. The little lights leap and travel; they flicker for an instant and extinguish.

"I don't know what makes it work, bud. Something to do with the blankets."

Uh oh, she hadn't meant to say "blanket." Jesse's warm breath moves away from her; he retracts to the foot of the bed. Backing out of the covers, Sonia sees the clock says 7:09.

"Come on, Jesse, we gotta hit it."

Mounded, Jesse refuses to answer.

"Jess, we'll be late."

A hand snakes out to trap her by the wrist. "I'll breathe your hair on fire." It is his dragon-voice, the same voice he gives to the green plastic soldiers he arranges in V-formations before ticking them over one by one. The soldiers mostly say "C'mon, men." They have deep screams.

"You better give back my treasure," the voice goes on, "or I'll smush you with my tail. . . ."

Quickly, Sonia tickles him. "J-E-Double-S is a mess, can't say yes, why he's like that, I can't guess."

Jesse drops her wrist. "Say it again, Mom."

She does. To Sonia's relief, he rolls in the bed delighted, tossing back the covers. She holds onto a set of kicking toes, letting her arm be jerked around. But when she notices the time, Sonia sits back. She lowers her neck, allowing herself one minute to ease the kinks out.

She feels a tapping stroke on the top of her head. "Oh Mom," Jesse says. He is petting her like a cat when the phone rings.

Raking stiff fingers through her hair, shifting from foot to freezing foot, Sonia listens to Carol's muffled excuses. "Yeah," she says. "Sure, okay." The old nightgown is molded to her body with static electricity. Cursing silently, she seizes it with her free hand, wrestles it around, and stretches it as far out as it will go. The nightgown snaps right back, sticking to her stomach in layered wrinkles.

"What? What?" Jesse is standing there, poking her in the side.

Sonia drops the receiver on the hook. "We're out a babysitter, once a-gain. Carol's sick. Now I have to leave Risto's and pick you up at school and take you back there with me. You'll have to hang out until I get everything done."

Jesse's mouth crumples. He used to like to go to Risto's cabinet shop—there's a video machine, plenty of boards and nails to play with. But the novelty has worn off.

"It's just for a couple of hours, and then we'll come home."

Jesse just looks at her. Sonia is a small woman, dark and quick-moving. Jesse is small like Sonia, but with his father's ashy hair—a metallic blond without a trace of yellow. His gray eyes are smudged underneath with a sooty purple.

Allergies, the doctor says, those bluish marks beneath his eyes, but to Sonia they are the symbol of her son's vulnerability. She'd like to be rid of the fear that frames her enormous love for him; she gets so tired of carrying it around. But she doesn't know how to let go of it, doesn't even know if that is wise.

Sonia takes a Kleenex from the counter and cups her hands under her son's chin. "Look, bud, we have to." She meant to wipe his nose. Really, she did. Instead, Sonia finds herself daubing at the delicate shadowing beneath his eyes, as though the blue tint were a dye she could scrub away. Throwing out a hand to protect himself, Jesse scoots away from her and out the kitchen door.

After letting Jesse off at school, Sonia heads for Risto's cabinet shop, out in the industrial part of town. She drives with one hand, constantly twisting the radio dial to find a song she likes. Nothing about the day cheers her. The February sky is white with bunchy clouds, slotted and tinged with gray like an old mattress pad. A low fog has erased the mountains. Only the foothills remain, black with tall pine and aspen, speckled white with snow.

Sonia turns down Risto's dirt road, passing the gaping dumpster that marks his nondescript street from all the others. Hunched-up sparrows line the dumpster's metal rim, hiding their filament legs. Opposite them, a crow dips and flaps, reeling on big stiff feet.

Risto is levered against the Asteroids machine he bought for $50, banging buttons. His profile is all beard and fiercely slitted eyes; his springy black hair jiggles from the action. "*Oye*, Sonia!" he calls through the smashing and dinging. A second later he whips around, throws his fists in the air.

"Ta-da! 5,465, a new all-time record!"

Sonia inclines a shoulder to slide off her purse, catches it on the way down, and tosses it onto the desk. "Congratulations go out to Evaristo Duran. And January's income statement . . . another new all-time record."

Risto's fists sink into his pockets. "Ah, Ming the Merciless. And his lovely bookkeeper Sonia. Grumpy today?"

"The babysitter died."

"Not a hardy breed, your babysitters. Well, we'll put the kid to work."

"Where's everybody else?"

"Willy and Paul are installing. Juan checked out on a mental health day." For a second, he sags. Risto's losing weight; a smack on the seat of his baggy pants would take a while to reach flesh.

Then he flings it off. "Listen, I know somebody is going to walk in today with a killer job." He fingers the faceted crystal dangling by a long string from his desk lamp. Risto has a penchant for things like that, crystals, prisms; after explaining them in precise technical terms, he shakes his head. His eyes light up. It's as though the crystal's core harbors one last part—the thing that really makes it work—that he suspects is out of the province of science entirely.

Sonia plunks herself down, already reciting her tasks for the day. She's got to reconcile the bank statement, go through a week's time cards and invoices, figure out labor costs, compile a P&L. . . . The armrest of her old green desk chair clanks off onto the cement floor. Sonia glares at it, muttering, "I love omens." Then she scoops it up and sticks it back, grimly shoving the metal into its slot.

"So how do you like my new shirt?" Risto is down on dark colors, claims they're magnets for "*pinche*"-ness—everything ratty and stingy and shameful. His shirt, Sonia notes, is a yellow heartbreaker with gauzy stripes of red and green.

"Mr. Hock. MasterCard or Visa?" she asks him. Risto looks crestfallen.

"Oh, forget that." Sonia plucks at her own linty black sweater. "Must be these *pinche* clothes. You're the spitting image of a brown-eyed handsome man."

Suddenly jaunty, Risto pulls his desk chair over. "Eee, see how you are?" The teasing phrase is supposed to throw her back on herself, promote a good mood. It doesn't work, and he reaches across to close the ledger Sonia is thumbing through. Risto counts on his fingers.

"Every time I get down to sweeping the floor, somebody comes in with a job. Every time. Ten years, same story. What we're talking about here is emotional leeway. I've accumulated a respectable amount by now. And . . . you are looking at a superlative cleaner."

It's true, Risto is a superlative cleaner. When he finishes a sink, it's not simply clean, it's young again.

Locomoting sideways like a sand crab, he scoots his chair back over to his desk and leaps up. In the kitchenette, he takes out the soft scrub and begins to scour. He talks to Sonia over the whir of the adding machine, wheeling around just often enough to make her lose her place. When she finally tunes in on him, he's going on about George Washington Carver.

". . . and they said what can you do? You want an education and you got no bucks, pardon us, ha-ha, what can you possibly do for us?

'Clean,' George Washington Carver said, 'I can clean.' So they gave him a storeroom, and whoa! look out, it was all over. I mean, the guy had . . . he had . . ."

Risto's round, bearded face is glowing. He stands in the doorway to the kitchenette, palms offered. Behind him, thick china mugs hang in a gleaming row.

"What? So what was it he had?" This story reminds Sonia of something. Irritably, she scrubs dust from the calculator's light display until she remembers. It's like what Risto said when he got his back worked on by the psychic surgeon. He had felt a plucking as the man seized a red lump from his back and flung it into a silver bowl. But it was the man himself who got to Risto, not the miraculous lump, the size of a chicken's heart, or the white cloth wiping him that blooded to a dark pink. *He was like a bullet*, Risto kept saying, *the guy had only one purpose to him.*

"Yes?" Staring at him with mock patience, Sonia inadvertently hits the total button. The machine whirs through a series of zeros, *ack-ack-ack-ack.*

Risto squints at her, hands drooping. "Nosir, there is no joy in Mudville." Miffed, he turns back to the sink. "My mother told me that story."

His mother, the first Hispanic professor at a famous university, organized day-care centers for migrant workers in her spare time. Sourly, Sonia churns up a face—La Profesora Duran—wide and dark and Indian-looking, except for the clear spectacles, explaining to a little son the political leverage of humility. Sonia's mother dealt in that commodity, doling out government foodstuffs at the county office, always anxious lest a weevil leap out of the burlap bags.

Risto starts on the shelf above the cups. He's piling up coffee cans and filters, fast-food packets of salt and sugar and ketchup, so that he can wipe the shelf clean. Risto sings to himself, jouncing to his own rhythm, knees working. His sweet voice always disconcerts Sonia; he sings eerie street-corner harmony to unseen partners. *Why you wanta grieve me mama, everybody round us know, this how it ought to go, everybody but you. . . .*

Sonia has often wondered what it would be like to sleep with Risto—neither of them is married—but, just as often, she sweeps the thought away. She's efficient at this, and gives herself points for protocol. Besides, she takes lots of messages from women with no last names. But there's something in the wide scale of his nature that scares her, too. Things are fine the way they are. She lifts her shoulders in a silent sigh. Her neck pops.

The office doorknob grates and as Risto jogs past her, he shoots out, "Major contractor, 6000 square foot house, cabinets, doors—we do it all. C'mon, crystal." He scoops up a lined note pad.

The door bangs against the wall. Backing in, an old Indian couple wrestle between them a rocking chair with a broken arm. Its faded orange cushion, flat and buttonless, slaps lightly against the seat.

"Eh, how much to fix this up?" the old man asks. Tilting his face to address Risto, his eyebrows slide up hopefully; he smiles. The top of his headband—a green bandanna—has unfolded into a roosterish point. Behind him, with identical pleasant expression, his wife stands in a veteran ski jacket over a print dress, purse pressed against her round stomach.

"Needs a dowel in here to hold it, see? She don't want to get rid of it." He nods toward his wife. She looks at him. He speaks to her in Tewa, sounding to Sonia as if he is pronouncing only the middles of words.

"Ohhh, no, no." Suddenly laughing, her eyes disappear into crinkles of skin as she shakes her head. "Old . . . friend." She pats the rocker.

"Well, sir, repairs aren't exactly what we do here."

The old couple waits comfortably in silence.

Risto runs a hand over his hair, letting it spring back up, as he smiles fixedly at the old woman. "Ten dollars."

"You wait a minute, okay?" The man taps his wife, motions toward the door. He's still smiling. He looks as though he will continue to smile no matter what. The wife leaves and comes back, lugging a cooler, walking with a stiff lateral roll, putting all her weight first on one foot, then on the other.

With the expansiveness of a host, the old man half-turns to include Sonia. "We got some tamales—homemade. She made them. Elk."

Sonia looks at Risto, who would shovel the Asteroids machine to the bottom of an arroyo before he would look back at her. He will drill the rocker, slip in a dowel and glue it, rub on a little stain so that you can't see the break. Half an hour—elk tamales. Humming, Risto spins the crystal, sprinkling the shop with invisible powers.

"Why can't I bring it in? Please. I won't hurt anything. I'll just throw it to myself." Jesse has walked backwards on the balls of his feet all the way into the shop, ready at any second to retrieve the football locked in the car. "C'mon, Mom."

"Look, bud, this is a potentially dangerous place. You could knock some clamps down. Christ, you could knock some drill bits on you and they'd stick in your head like birthday candles."

"So?"

"So, that's my worst fear, my absolute worst."

"What?" Sullen, Jesse looks at her with unwilling interest.

"Drill bits in your head. Why don't you make a ship? I've got some boards all ready for you to use."

"I want to watch TV."

"There's lots of little pieces here. Animal legs. Make a horse. Make a herd of armadillos."

"Uck."

"Make some valentines."

"Sure, Mom. Wood valentines." Jesse squints at Sonia, arms folded.

She glances at Risto, who is muscling corbel material to the band saw, pretending not to listen.

"All right then, make the Empire State Building so I can jump off it because I've lost my job and can't feed you anymore," she hisses.

Jesse narrows his eyes further, put-upon. "Okay, I'll do a building." He waits until Sonia turns away before picking up the hammer.

Sonia sets her teeth, angry at herself for having lost patience with him. Before she sinks back down into the green chair, she brings one foot up and kicks her other leg, hard, in the shin.

Bent over the adding machine, she plows through the time sheets, sorting the labor job by job. The concrete floor vibrates beneath her feet to the hum of machinery. Risto's got the golden oldies station cranked, rocking out to La Bamba. As the whir of the big band saw dies off, Sonia hears his falsetto: *No soy marinero, soy capitán, soy capitán.*

The whish of an air hose announces that he's blowing the dust off his clothes. Finished with the corbels, Risto ambles into the office.

"Hey, be back in an hour, hour and a half. Whatever it takes. Got the bill ready?"

She scribbles the figures, adds tax, totals. "You sure they're going to pay you today?"

Risto shrugs. "Who knows what *pinche*-ness lurks in the heart of man?"

Sonia waves backward over her shoulder. Two times more through the sheets, and the last job is complete, numbers entered into the ledger. Grimacing, she fills each dismal sum into its correct slot on the P&L. And if Risto doesn't make any more money than this, she's going to be out of work anyway.

The radio is playing *Under the Boardwalk*. It is possibly the most inappropriate song Sonia can think of, for a dreary February day like this. She stands and bends over, letting her hands sway between her knees. "Jess-ee! We're outa here!"

Jesse does not dash in, liberated, as she expects. There's no sound of nailing. Sonia snaps off the radio and leans out the office door. The shop is quiet and empty.

The hammer and a fitful tower of boards sit on top of a workbench. Nails stick out all over, apparently whacked in for decoration. Craning to take in the whole shop, Sonia nudges the milk crate Jesse uses to stand on back underneath the bench.

"Jesse! We can go now."

She rubs her back just above the tailbone. "Je-ess, let's go!"

The shop stands around her, machines silent. From the wall a bikinied girl clutches a router and grins. Her hair fans backward in stop motion, frozen at the sides of her rosy face.

Where is he? He couldn't have gone anywhere, he'd have had to come through the office. . . . Sonia spins to see that the big roll-up door to the shop is lifted at the bottom, open to two feet of air.

Outside. . . . He must have gone out to play.

Sonia heaves up the door, which rumbles as it slides overhead. She takes in the vacant parking lot once, then, blinking, again.

Hers is the only car. She knows it's locked, but she jogs over to peer in anyway. Her wet palms mark the window glass. The football leans on its tip against the back of the seat.

Striding toward the road, Sonia shades her eyes with both hands to scan up and down. Weathered metal buildings and faded signs, dead cars, stacks of pipe, rusted-out machinery, the tarnished fiberglass swimming pool, weird as an ark, that looms up next to the plumbing supply—everything is inert.

Far down the road, a yellow backhoe is parked. Sonia can see— small as a toy—a hard-hatted head in the cab, just that one head, but she shouts for Jesse anyway. Marking the other end is the dumpster with its dotted molding of sparrows.

Yelling leaves her breathless. She pivots and dodges back through the roll-up door, scraping her head against its metal edge.

"Jesse! Jes-se!" She tries to think, tries to tamp it down, but a giddy circular motion is building inside her. The top of her head burns from the scrape; Sonia presses her hands against the throb while she turns around and around, calling.

The shop is so still. In this huge room full of hundreds of moving parts—gears, belts, motors, blades—nothing moves. Her son should be nailing wood scraps here, but he's not. There's no one in this room but her. She lets her hands fall.

Stooping faster and faster, Sonia searches behind everything: band saw, planers, table saws, workbenches. Each piece of machinery gets one flat glance before she flings herself on to the next one: he may be there, he may. Everything may, in the next instant, take shape and become normal again, softly moving with its usual life. Sawdust streaks Sonia's cheeks like face powder, clings to her sweater, her knees, the palms of her hands. Panting, she calls Jesse in a voice that is sucked away into nothing. No one answers. The machines remain, bizarre in their stillness.

Skirting the workbenches, she runs back into the office. She ducks to check under her desk, Risto's desk. She thrusts her head in the bathroom door. The toilet stands by itself—pristine and shiny white as Risto polished it.

Behind her the office doorknob rattles. It always does that when Jesse opens it; he turns it the wrong way. Sonia's fingertips are buzzing.

Her thought processes are reduced to a single hum—*pleasepleaseplease-please*. . . .

"Did we get paid or what? You-betcha-*que-sí!*" Risto waves an envelope. As he takes in Sonia, the awful slow motion of the shop engulfs him, too; the envelope winds down to his side, his white grin melts away into the darkness of his beard.

Sonia's voice is strange, watery—her words rise and sink, slide into each other without rhythm. "I can't find him. He's gone. I've called and called . . . he's gone. Somebody got him."

Some distant part of her sees that Risto has ahold of her arm, but she cannot feel the pressure of his grasp, only the heat. He's nodding toward the shop area; one hand smoothes the air. She cannot wait to understand him because he has gone unrecognizably motionless, like everything else, and the only thing to do is to have Jesse within reach again.

Sprinting, she hits the office door palms-out. The road's muddy ruts twist and cross like an expanse of wrecked track. Its narrow shoulders are coated with last week's snow. Fields behind the chain-link lie white and bare, humped where the snow has buried things.

For a split second, because she wants to throw herself in all directions at once, Sonia is stopped. Her feet have grown cold and light. Foothills waver in the mist, shifting, one black hill behind the other. Down by the dumpster a man heaves something in and lopes away.

Sonia screams Jes-seee! She is already on her way to the dumpster before she realizes that she has moved. At her approach, a fan of sparrows rises and floats away into the white sky.

Grabbing at the dumpster's iron rim, Sonia hoists herself to look. A stained mattress bowed into a horseshoe. Splintered plywood, coat hangers, rags, beer cans, sacks, newspapers . . . on top of the mound of garbage, protruding from an untied plastic bag, the toe of a small muddy tennis shoe. The toe rests sideways, slanted down. Just above it is a square bulge, as if another little shoe nestled there in the curve of an ankle. Sonia looks again and again as the shimmery outline of the tennis shoe distorts and reforms, refusing to disappear. There has always been, somewhere down in the midst of her fears for Jesse, a place for this shoe.

Half over the rim, Sonia seesaws, blanked. Her careful boundaries disengage and lift away like the wedge of sparrows.

She has become unattached. Nothing she sees makes any sense now. She cannot assemble the dumpster, the dirt road, her own fingered hand, into shapes that she comprehends. Sonia does not try to catch herself with her already outstretched hand, does not think of it. The metal rim gouges her body as she slips back down it. Her elbow bangs and she watches her arm bounce upward before it flails to her side.

As she runs, the road straightens and curves, straightens again. She has no sense of depth; her strides hit the hard mud in big loose jerks. At the far end of the road, a hard-hatted head extends from the silent backhoe, watching her run. A man and a woman crowd the door of the sheet metal shop, looking toward her. Sonia's fingers take up the middle of her mouth.

"Hey, Sonia!"

From the dull tones around her, she catches a beam: a little spectrum existing within all the whites and browns and grays. Her knee joints buckle and catch, buckle and catch. There is nowhere left to go but toward that color.

"Sonia!"

Rocks skid beneath her feet like marbles as she crosses the parking lot. Risto stands next to his truck, one hand cupped for yelling. When she's past the tailgate, she sees there beside him . . . hooked by the collar . . . Jesse.

"Found him pasted behind the bathroom door," Risto says. He releases Jesse's collar and tactfully turns away, bending to use the truck window for a mirror to brush at his beard.

Head cocked, Jesse's slouching, wiping his eye with a fist. Sonia grips her son's shoulders, his arms, fits trembling hands around the small barrel of his ribs. He is coated from foot to ashy hair with sawdust. One bright eye confronts her through the covering of dust, telling her he is the safe one there behind it, studying her from exactly where he should be. Jesse stares toward his mother with a quizzical, crooked smile, half-sorry, half-satisfied.

It's a reproach, that look. But right now it's too much to understand: she does not have the power to protect her son. First she has to understand this relief rolling through her, heating her face, that doesn't stop coming even when she knows she's about to start that ugly kind of crying. She lifts her head to see Risto leaning against the truck, watching her with eyes half-closed and alert. He murmurs *Hey, hey, see how you are.* . . .

She goes toward him with one clear thought. In this, at least, she has faith: Risto will hold her upright until she can finish with this violence she's done herself. Another step—his arms are already opening—her fingers reach out and close upon a fold of yellow shirt.

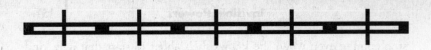

BARBARA KINGSOLVER

Why I Am a Danger to the Public

Bueno, if I get backed into a corner I can just about raise up the dead. I'll fight, sure. But I am no lady wrestler. If you could see me you would know this thing is a *joke*—Tony, my oldest, is already taller than me, and he's only eleven. So why are they so scared of me I have to be in jail? I'll tell you.

Number one, this strike. There has never been one that turned so many old friends *chingándose*, not here in Bolton. And you can't get away from it because Ellington don't just run the mine, they own our houses, the water we drink and the dirt in our shoes and pretty much the state of New Mexico as I understand it. So if something is breathing, it's on one side or the other. And in a town like this that matters because everybody you know some way, you go to the same church or they used to babysit your kids, something. Nobody is a stranger.

My sister went down to Las Cruces New Mexico and got a job down there, but me, no. I stayed here and got married to Junior Morales. Junior was my one big mistake. But I like Bolton. From far away Bolton looks like some kind of all-colored junk that got swept up off the street after a big old party and stuffed down in the canyon. Our houses are all exactly alike, company houses, but people paint them yellow, purple, colors you wouldn't think a house could be. If you go down to the Big Dipper and come walking home *loca* you still know which one is yours. The copper mine is at the top of the canyon and the streets run straight uphill; some of them you can't drive up, you got to walk. There's steps. Oliver P. Snapp, that used to be the mailman for the west side, died of a heart attack one time right out there in his blue shorts. So the new mailman refuses to deliver to those houses; they have to pick up their mail at the P.O.

Now, this business with me and Vonda Fangham, I can't even tell you what got it started. I never had one thing in the world against her, no more than anybody else did. But this was around the fourth or fifth week so everybody knew by then who was striking and who was crossing. It don't take long to tell rats from cheese, and every night there was a big old fight in the Big Dipper. Somebody punching out his brother or his best friend. All that and no paycheck, can you imagine?

So it was a Saturday and there was just me and Corvallis Smith up at the picket line, setting in front of the picket shack passing the time of day. Corvallis is *un tipo*, he is real tall and lifts weights and wears his hair in those corn rows that hang down in the back with little pieces of aluminum foil on the ends. But good-looking in a certain way. I went out with Corvallis one time just so people would have something to talk about, and sure enough, they had me getting ready to have brown and black polka-dotted babies. All you got to do to get pregnant around here is have two beers with somebody in the Dipper, so watch out.

"What do you hear from Junior," he says. That's a joke; everybody says it including my friends. See, when Manuela wasn't hardly even born one minute and Tony still in diapers, Junior says, "Vicki, I can't find a corner to piss in around this town." He said there was jobs in Tucson and he would send a whole lot of money. Ha ha. That's how I got started up at Ellington. I was not going to support my kids in no little short skirt down at the Frosty King. That was eight years ago. I got started on the track gang, laying down rails for the cars that go into the pit, and now I am a crane operator. See, when Junior left I went up the hill and made such a rackus they had to hire me up there, hire me or shoot me, one.

"Oh, I hear from him about the same as I hear from Oliver P. Snapp," I say to Corvallis. That's the rest of the joke.

It was a real slow morning. Cecil Smoot was supposed to be on the picket shift with us but he wasn't there yet. Cecil will show up late when the Angel Gabriel calls the Judgment, saying he had to give his Datsun a lube job.

"Well, looka here," says Corvallis. "Here come the ladies." There is this club called Wives of Working Men, just started since the strike. Meaning Wives of Scabs. About six of them was coming up the hill all cram-packed into Vonda Fangham's daddy's air-conditioned Lincoln. She pulls the car right up next to where mine is at. My car is a Buick older than both my two kids put together. It gets me where I have to go.

They set and look at us for one or two minutes. Out in that hot sun, sticking to our T-shirts, and me in my work boots—I can't see no point in treating it like a damn tea party—and Corvallis, he's an eyeful anyway. All of a sudden the windows on the Lincoln all slide down. It has those electric windows.

"Isn't this a ni-i-ice day," says one of them, Doreen Carter. Doreen visited her sister in Laurel, Mississippi, for three weeks one time and now she has an accent. "Bein' payday an' all," she says. Her husband is the minister of Saint's Grace, which is scab headquarters. I quit going. I was raised up to believe in God and the union, but listen, if it comes to pushing or shoving I know which one of the two is going to keep tires on the car.

"Well, yes, it is a real nice day," another one of them says. They're all fanning theirselves with something paper. I look, and Corvallis looks. They're fanning theirselves with their husbands' paychecks.

I haven't had a paycheck since July. My son couldn't go to Morse with his baseball team Friday night because they had to have three dollars for supper at McDonald's. Three damn dollars.

The windows start to go back up and they're getting ready to drive off, and I say, "Vonda Fangham, *vete al infierno*."

The windows whoosh back down.

"What did you say?" Vonda wants to know.

"I said, I'm surprised to see you in there with the scab ladies. I didn't know you had went and got married to a yellow-spine scab just so somebody would let you in their club."

Well, Corvallis laughs at that. But Vonda just gives me this look. She has a little sharp nose and yellow hair and teeth too big to fit behind her lips. For some reason she was a big deal in high school, and it's not her personality either. She was the queen of everything.

Cheerleaders, drama club, every school play they ever had, I think.

I stare at her right back, ready to make a day out of it if I have to. The heat is rising up off that big blue hood like it's a lake all set to boil over.

"What I said was, Vonda Fangham, you can go to hell."

"I can't hear a word you're saying," she says. "Trash can't talk."

"This trash can go to bed at night and know I haven't cheated nobody out of a living. You want to see trash, *chica*, you ought to come up here at the shift change and see what kind of shit rolls over that picket line."

Well, that shit I was talking about was their husbands, so up go the windows and off they fly. Vonda just about goes in the ditch trying to get that big car turned around.

To tell you the truth I knew Vonda was engaged to get married to Tommy Jones, a scab. People said, Well, at least now Vonda will be just Vonda Jones. That name Fangham is *feo*, and the family has this whole certain way of showing off. Her dad's store, Fangham Drugs, has the biggest sign in town, as if he has to advertise. As if somebody would forget it was there and drive fifty-one miles over the mountains to Morse to go to another drugstore.

I couldn't care less about Tommy and Vonda getting engaged, I was just hurt when he crossed the line. Tommy was a real good man, I used to think. He was not ashamed like most good-looking guys are to act decent every once in a while. Me and him started out on the same track crew and he saved my butt one time covering the extra weight for me when I sprang my wrist. And he never acted like I owed him for it. Some guys, they would try to put the moves on me out by the slag pile. Shit, that was hell. And then I would be downtown in the drugstore and Carol Finch or somebody would go *huh-hmm*, clear her throat and roll her eyes, like, "Over here is what you want," looking at the condoms. Just because I'm up there with their husbands all day I am supposed to be screwing around. In all that mud, just think about it, in our steel toe boots that weigh around ten pounds, and our hard hats. And then the guys gave me shit too when I started training as a crane operator, saying a woman don't have no business taking up the good-paying jobs. You figure it out.

Tommy was different. He was a lone ranger. He didn't grow up here or have family, and in Bolton you can move in here and live for about fifty years and people still call you that fellow from El Paso, or wherever it was you come from. They say that's why he went in, that he was afraid if he lost his job he would lose Vonda too. But we all had something to lose.

That same day I come home and found Manuela and Tony in the closet. Like poor little kitties in there setting on the shoes. Tony was okay pretty much but Manuela was crying, screaming. I thought she would dig her eyes out.

Tony kept going, "They was up here looking for you!"

"Who was?" I asked him.

"Scab men," he said. "Clifford Owens and Mr. Alphonso and them police from out of town. The ones with the guns."

"The State Police?" I said. I couldn't believe it. "The State Police was up here? What did they want?"

"They wanted to know where you was at." Tony almost started to cry. "Mama, I didn't tell them."

"He didn't," Manuela said.

"Well, I was just up at the damn picket shack. Anybody could have found me if they wanted to." I could have swore I saw Owens's car go right by the picket shack, anyway.

"They kept on saying where was you at, and we didn't tell them. We said you hadn't done nothing."

"Well, you're right, I haven't done nothing. Why didn't you go over to Uncle Manny's? He's supposed to be watching you guys."

"We was scared to go outside!" Manuela screamed. She was jumping from one foot to the other and hugging herself. "They said they'd get us!"

"Tony, did they say that? Did they threaten you?"

"They said stay away from the picket rallies," Tony said. "The one with the gun said he seen us and took all our pitchers. He said, your mama's got too big a mouth for her own good."

At the last picket rally I was up on Lalo Ruiz's shoulders with a bull horn. I've had almost every office in my local, and sergeant-at-arms twice because the guys say I have no toleration for BS. They got one of those big old trophies down at the union hall that says on it "MEN OF COPPER," and one time Lalo says, "Vicki ain't no Man of

Copper, she's a damn stick of *mesquite*. She might break but she sure as hell won't bend."

Well, I want my kids to know what this is about. When school starts, if some kid makes fun of their last-year's blue jeans and calls them trash I want them to hold their heads up. I take them to picket rallies so they'll know that. No law says you can't set up on nobody with a bull horn. They might have took my picture, though. I wouldn't be surprised.

"All I ever done was defend my union," I told the kids. "Even cops have to follow the laws, and it isn't no crime to defend your union. Your grandpapa done it and his papa and now me."

Well, my grandpapa one time got put on a railroad car like a cow, for being a Wobbly and a Mexican. My kids have heard that story a million times. He got dumped out in the desert someplace with no water or even a cloth for his head, and it took him two months to get back. All that time my granny and Tía Sonia thought he was dead.

I hugged Tony and Manuela and then we went and locked the door. I had to pull up on it while they jimmied the latch because that damn door had not been locked one time in seven years.

What we thought about when we wanted to feel better was: What a God-awful mess they got up there in the mine. Most of those scabs was out-of-towners and didn't have no idea what end of the gun to shoot. I heard it took them about one month to figure out how to start the equipment. Before the walkout there was some parts switched around between my crane and a locomotive, but we didn't have to do that because the scabs tied up the cat's back legs all by theirselves. Laying pieces of track backwards, running the conveyors too fast, I hate to think what else.

We even heard that one foreman, Willie Bunford, quit because of all the jackasses on the machinery, that he feared for his life. Willie Bunford used to be my foreman. He made fun of how I said his name, "Wee-lee!" so I called him Mr. Bunford. So I have an accent, so what. When I was first starting on the crane he said, "You aren't going to get PG now, are you, Miss Morales, after I wasted four weeks training you as an operator? I know how you Mexican gals love to have babies." I said, "Mr. Bunford, as far as this job goes you can consider me a man." So I had to stick to that. I couldn't call up and say I'm staying in bed today because of my monthly. Then what does he do but lay off two weeks with so-called whiplash from a car accident on Top Street when I saw the whole story: Winnie Hask backing into his car in front of the Big Dipper and him not in it. If a man can get whiplash from his car getting bashed in while he is drinking beer across the street, well, that's a new one.

So I didn't cry for no Willie Bunford. At least he had the sense to get out of there. None of those scabs knew how to run the oxygen machine, so we were waiting for the whole damn place to blow up. I said to the guys, Let's go sit on Bolt Mountain with some beer and watch the fireworks.

The first eviction I heard about was the Frank Mickliffs, up the street from me, and then Joe Gomez on Alameda. Ellington wanted to clear out some company houses for the new hires, but how they decided who to throw out we didn't know. Then Janie Marley found out from her friend that babysits for the sister-in-law of a scab that company men were driving scab wives around town letting them pick out whatever house they wanted. Like they're going shopping and we're the peaches getting squeezed.

Friday of that same week I was out on my front porch thinking about a cold beer, just thinking, though, because of no cash, and here come an Ellington car. They slowed way, way down when they went by, then on up Church Street going about fifteen and then they come back. It was Vonda in there. She nodded her head at my house and the guy put something down on paper. They made a damn picture show out of it.

Oh, I was furious. I have been living in that house almost the whole time I worked for Ellington and it's all the home my kids ever had. It's a real good house. It's yellow. I have a big front porch where you can see just about everything, all of Bolton, and a railing so the kids won't fall over in the gulch, and a big yard. I keep it up nice, and my brother Manny being right next door helps out. I have this mother duck with her babies all lined up that the kids bought me at Fangham's for Mother's Day, and I planted marigolds in a circle around them. No way on this earth was I turning my house over to a scab.

The first thing I did was march over to Manny's house and knock on the door and walk in. "Manny," I say to him, "I don't want you mowing my yard anymore unless you feel like doing a favor for Miss Vonda." Manny is just pulling the pop top off a Coke and his mouth goes open at the same time; he just stares.

"Oh, no," he says.

"Oh, yes."

I went back over to my yard and Manny come hopping out putting on his shoes, to see what I'm going to do, I guess. He's my little brother but Mama always says "*Madre Santa*, Manuel, keep an eye on Vicki!" Well, what I was going to do was my own damn business. I pulled up the ducks, they have those metal things that poke in the ground, and then I pulled up the marigolds and threw them out on the sidewalk. If I had to get the neighbor kids to help make my house the ugliest one, I was ready to do it.

Well. The next morning I was standing in the kitchen drinking coffee, and Manny come through the door with this funny look on his face and says, "The tooth fairy has been to see you."

What in the world. I ran outside and there was *pink* petunias planted right in the circle where I already pulled up the marigolds. To think Vonda could sneak into my yard like a common thief and do a thing like that.

"Get the kids," I said. I went out and started pulling out petunias. I hate pink. And I hate how they smelled, they had these sticky roots. Manny woke up the kids and they come out and helped.

"This is fun, Mom," Tony said. He wiped his cheek and a line of dirt ran across like a scar. They were in their pajamas.

"Son, we're doing it for the union," I said. We threw them out on the sidewalk with the marigolds, to dry up and die.

After that I was scared to look out the window in the morning. God knows what Vonda might put in my yard, more flowers or one of those ugly pink flamingos they sell at Fangham's yard and garden department. I wouldn't put nothing past Vonda.

Whatever happened, we thought when the strike was over we would have our jobs. You could put up with high water and heck, thinking of that. It's like having a baby, you just grit your teeth and keep your eyes on the prize. But then Ellington started sending out termination notices saying, You will have no job to come back to whatsoever.

They would fire you for any excuse, mainly strike-related misconduct, which means nothing, you looked cross-eyed at a policeman or whatever. People got scared.

The national office of the union was no help; they said, To hell with it, boys, take the pay cut and go on back. I had a fit at the union meeting. I told them it's not the pay cut, it's what all else they would take if we give in. "Ellington would not have hired me in two million years if it wasn't for the union raising a rackus about all people are created equal," I said. "Or half of you either because they don't like cunts or coloreds." I'm not that big of a person but I was standing up in front, and when I cussed, they shut up. "If my papa had been a chickenshit like you guys, I would be down at the Frosty King tonight in a little short skirt," I said. "You bunch of no-goods would be on welfare and your kids pushing drugs to pay the rent." Some of the guys laughed, but some didn't.

Men get pissed off in this certain way, though, where they have to tear something up. Lalo said, "Well, hell, let's drive a truck over the plant gate and shut the damn mine down." And there they go, off and running, making plans to do it. Corvallis had a baseball cap on backwards and was sitting back with his arms crossed like, Honey, don't look at me. I could have killed him.

"Great, you guys, you do something cute like that and we're dead ducks," I said. "We don't have to do but one thing, wait it out."

"Till when?" Lalo wanted to know. "Till hell freezes?" He is kind of a short guy with about twelve tattoos on each arm.

"Till they get fed up with the scabs pissing around and want to get the mine running. If it comes down to busting heads, no way. Do you hear me? They'll have the National Guards in here."

I knew I was right. The Boots in this town, the cops, they're on Ellington payroll. I've seen strikes before. When I was ten years old I saw a cop get a Mexican man down on the ground and kick his face till blood ran out of his ear. You would think I was the only one in that room that was born and raised in Bolton.

Ellington was trying to get back up to full production. They had them working twelve-hour shifts and seven-day weeks like Abraham Lincoln had never freed the slaves. We started hearing about people getting hurt, but just rumors; it wasn't going to run in the paper. Ellington owns the paper.

The first I knew about it really was when Vonda come right to my house. I was running the vacuum cleaner and had the radio turned up all the way so I didn't hear her drive up. I just heard a knock on the door, and when I opened it: Vonda. Her skin looked like a flour tortilla. "What in the world," I said.

Her bracelets were going clack-clack-clack, she was shaking so hard. "I never thought I'd be coming to you," she said, like I was Dear Abby. "But something's happened to Tommy."

"Oh," I said. I had heard some real awful things: that a guy was pulled into a smelter furnace, and another guy got his legs run over on the tracks. I could picture Tommy either way, no legs or burnt up. We stood there a long time. Vonda looked like she might pass out. "Okay, come in," I told her. "Set down there and I'll get you a drink of water. Water is all we got around here." I stepped over the vacuum cleaner on the way to the kitchen. I wasn't going to put it away.

When I come back she was looking around the room all nervous, breathing like a bird. I turned down the radio.

"How are the kids?" she wanted to know, of all things.

"The kids are fine. Tell me what happened to Tommy."

"Something serious to do with his foot, that's all I know. Either cut off or half cut off, they won't tell me." She pulled this little hanky out of her purse and blew her nose. "They sent him to Morse in the helicopter ambulance, but they won't say what hospital because I'm not next of kin. He doesn't have any next of kin here, I *told* them that. I informed them I was the fiancée." She blew her nose again. "All they'll tell me is they don't want him in the Bolton hospital. I can't understand why."

"Because they don't want nobody to know about it," I told her. "They're covering up all the accidents."

"Well, why would they want to do that?"

"Vonda, excuse me please, but don't be stupid. They want to do that so we won't know how close we are to winning the strike."

Vonda took a little sip of water. She had on a yellow sun dress and her arms looked so skinny, like just bones with freckles. "Well, I know what you think of me," she finally said, "but for Tommy's sake maybe you can get the union to do something. Have an investigation so he'll at least get his compensation pay. I know you have a lot of influence on the union."

"I don't know if I do or not," I told her. I puffed my breath out and leaned my head back on the sofa. I pulled the bandana off my head and rubbed my hair in a circle. It's so easy to know what's right and so hard to do it.

"Vonda," I said, "I thought a lot of Tommy before all this shit. He helped me one time when I needed it real bad." She looked at me. She probably hated thinking of me and him being friends. "I'm sure Tommy knows he done the wrong thing," I said. "But it gets me how you people treat us like kitchen trash and then come running to the union as soon as you need help."

She picked up her glass and brushed at the water on the coffee table. I forgot napkins. "Yes, I see that now, and I'll try to make up for my mistake," she said.

Give me a break, Vonda, was what I was thinking. "Well, we'll see," I said. "There is a meeting coming up and I'll see what I can do. If you show up on the picket line tomorrow."

Vonda looked like she swallowed one of her ice cubes. She went over to the TV and picked up the kids' pictures one at a time, Manuela then Tony. Put them back down. Went over to the *armario* built by my grandpapa.

"What a nice little statue," she said.

"That's St. Joseph. Saint of people that work with their hands."

She turned around and looked at me. "I'm sorry about the house. I won't take your house. It wouldn't be right."

"I'm glad you feel that way, because I wasn't moving."

"Oh," she said.

"Vonda, I can remember when me and you were little girls and your daddy was already running the drugstore. You used to set up on a stool behind the counter and run the soda-water machine. You had a charm bracelet with everything in the world on it, poodle dogs and hearts and a real little pill box that opened."

Vonda smiled. "I don't have the foggiest idea what ever happened to that bracelet. Would you like it for your girl?"

I stared at her. "But you don't remember me, do you?"

"Well, I remember a whole lot of people coming in the store. You in particular, I guess not."

"I guess not," I said. "People my color was not allowed to go in there and set at the soda fountain. We had to get paper cups and take our drinks outside. Remember that? I used to think and *think* about why that was. I thought our germs must be so nasty they wouldn't wash off the glasses."

"Well, things have changed, haven't they?" Vonda said.

"Yeah." I put my feet up on the coffee table. It's my damn table. "Things changed because the UTU and the Machinists and my papa's union the Boilermakers took this whole fucking company town to court in 1973, that's why. This house right here was for whites only. And if there wasn't no union forcing Ellington to abide by the law, it still would be."

She was kind of looking out the window. She probably was thinking about what she was going to cook for supper.

"You think it wouldn't? You think Ellington would build a nice house for everybody if they could still put half of us in those falling-down shacks down by the river like I grew up in?"

"Well, you've been very kind to hear me out," she said. "I'll do what you want, tomorrow. Right now I'd better be on my way."

I went out on the porch and watched her go down the sidewalk —click click, on her little spike heels. Her ankles wobbled.

"Vonda," I yelled out after her, "don't wear high heels on the line tomorrow. For safety's sake."

She never turned around.

Next day the guys were making bets on Vonda showing up or not. The odds were not real good in her favor. I had to laugh, but myself I really thought she would. It was a huge picket line for the morning shift change. The Women's Auxiliary thought it would boost up the morale, which needed a kick in the butt or somebody would be busting down the plant gate. Corvallis told me that some guys had a meeting after the real meeting and planned it out. But I knew that if I kept showing up at the union meetings and standing on the table and jumping and hollering, they wouldn't do it. Sometimes guys will listen to a woman.

The sun was just coming up over the canyon and already it was a hot day. Cicada bugs buzzing in the *paloverdes* like damn rattlesnakes. Me and Janie Marley were talking about our kids; she has a boy one size down from Tony and we trade clothes around. All of a sudden Janie grabs my elbow and says, "Look who's here." It was Vonda getting out of the Lincoln. Not in high heels either. She had on a tennis outfit and plastic sunglasses and a baseball bat slung over her shoulder. She stopped a little ways from the line and was looking around, waiting for the Virgin Mary to come down, I guess, and save her. Nobody was collecting any bets.

"Come on, Vonda," I said. I took her by the arm and stood her between me and Janie. "I'm glad you made it." But she wasn't talking, just looking around a lot.

After a while I said, "We're not supposed to have bats up here. I know a guy that got his termination papers for carrying a crescent wrench in his back pocket. He had forgot it was even in there." I looked at Vonda to see if she was paying attention. "It was Rusty Cochran," I said, "you know him. He's up at your dad's every other day for a prescription. They had that baby with the hole in his heart."

But Vonda held on to the bat like it was the last man in the world and she got him. "I'm only doing this for Tommy," she says.

"Well, so what," I said. "I'm doing it for my kids. So they can eat."

She kept squinting her eyes down the highway.

A bunch of people started yelling, "Here come the ladies!" Some of the women from the Auxiliary were even saying it. And here come trouble. They were in Doreen's car, waving signs out the windows: "We Support Our Working Men" and other shit not worth repeating. Doreen was driving. She jerked right dead to a stop, right in front of us. She looked at Vonda and you would think she had broke both her hinges the way her mouth was hanging open, and Vonda looked back at Doreen, and the rest of us couldn't wait to see what was next.

Doreen took a U-turn and almost ran over Cecil Smoot, and they beat it back to town like bats out of hell. Ten minutes later here come her car back up the hill again. Only this time her husband Milton was driving, and three other men from Saint's Grace was all in there besides Doreen. Two of them are cops.

"I don't know what they're up to but we don't need you getting in trouble," I told Vonda. I took the bat away from her and put it over my shoulder. She looked real white, and I patted her arm and said, "Don't worry." I can't believe I did that, now. Looking back.

They pulled up in front of us again but they didn't get out, just all five of them stared and then they drove off, like whatever they come for they got.

That was yesterday. Last night I was washing the dishes and somebody come to the house. The kids were watching TV. I heard Tony slide the dead bolt over and then he yelled, "Mom, it's the Boot."

Before I can even put down a plate and get into the living room Larry Trevizo has pushed right by him into the house. I come out wiping my hands and see him there holding up his badge.

"Chief of Police, ma'am," he says, just like that, like I don't know who the hell he is. Like we didn't go through every grade of school together and go see *Suddenly Last Summer* one time in high school.

He says, "Mrs. Morales, I'm serving you with injunction papers."

"Oh, is that a fact," I say. "And may I ask what for?"

Tony already turned off the TV and is standing by me with his arms crossed, the meanest-looking damn eleven-year-old you ever hope to see in your life. All I can think of is the guys in the meeting, how they get so they just want to bust something in.

"Yes you may ask what for," Larry says, and starts to read, not looking any of us in the eye: "For being a danger to the public. Inciting a riot. Strike-related misconduct." And then real low he says something about Vonda Fangham and a baseball bat.

"What was that last thing?"

He clears his throat. "And for kidnapping Vonda Fangham and threatening her with a baseball bat. We got the affidavits."

"*Pa'fuera!*" I tell Larry Trevizo. I ordered him out of my house right then, told him if he wanted to see somebody get hurt with a baseball bat he could hang around my living room and find out. I trusted myself but not Tony. Larry got out of there.

The injunction papers said I was not to be in any public gathering of more than five people or I would be arrested. And what do you know, a squad of Boots was already lined up by the picket shack at the crack of dawn this morning with their hands on their sticks, just waiting. They knew I would be up there, I see that. They knew I would do just exactly all the right things. Like the guys say, Vicki might break but she don't bend.

They cuffed me and took me up to the jailhouse, which is in back of the Ellington main office, and took off my belt and my earrings so I wouldn't kill myself or escape. "With an earring?" I said. I was laughing. I could see this old rotten building through the office window; it used to be something or other but now there's chickens living in it. You could dig out of there with an earring, for sure. I said, "What's that over there, the Mexican jail? You better put me in there!"

I thought they would just book me and let me go like they did some other ones, before this. But no, I have to stay put. Five hundred thousand bond. I don't think this whole town could come up with that, not if they signed over every pink, purple, and blue house in Bolton.

It didn't hit me till right then about the guys wanting to tear into the plant. What they might do.

"Look, I got to get out by tonight," I told the cops. I don't know their names, it was some State Police I have never seen, seem like they just come up out of nowhere. I was getting edgy. "I have a union meeting and it's real important. Believe me, you don't want me to miss it."

They smiled. And then I got that terrible feeling you get when you see somebody has been looking you in the eye and smiling and setting a trap, and there you are in it like a damn rat.

What is going to happen I don't know. I'm keeping my ears open. I found out my kids are driving Manny to distraction—Tony told his social-studies class he would rather have a jailbird than a scab mom, and they sent him home with a note that he was causing a dangerous disturbance in class.

I also learned that Tommy Jones was not in any accident. He got called off his shift one day and was took to Morse in a helicopter with no explanation. They put him up at Howard Johnson's over there for five days, his meals and everything, just told him not to call nobody, and today he's back at work. They say he is all in one piece.

Well, I am too.

LINDA HOGAN

FROM

Mean Spirit

Oklahoma, 1922

That summer a water diviner named Michael Horse forecast a two-week dry spell.

Until then, Horse's predictions were known to be reliable, and since it was a scorching hot summer, a good number of Indians moved their beds outdoors in hopes a chance breeze would pass over and provide relief from the hot nights. They set them up far from the houses that held the sun's heat long after dark. Cots were unfolded in kitchen gardens. White iron beds sat in horse pastures. Four-posters rested in cornfields that were lying fallow.

What a silent bedchamber the world was, just before morning when even the locusts were still. In that darkness, the white beds were ghostly. They rose up from the black rolling hills and farmlands. Here, a lonely bed sat next to a barbed wire fence, and there, beneath the protection of an oak tree, a man's lantern burned beside his sleeping form. Near the marshland, tents of gauzy mosquito netting sloped down over the bony shoulders and hips of dreamers. A hand hung over the edge of a bed, fingers reaching down toward bluegrass that grew upward in fields. Given half a chance, the vines and leaves would have crept up the beds and overgrown the sleeping bodies of people.

In one yard, a nervy chicken wanted to roost on a bedframe and was shooed away.

"Go on. Scat!" an old woman cried out, raising herself half up in bed to push the clucking hen back down to the ground.

That would be Belle Graycloud. She was a light-skinned Indian woman, the grandmother of her family. She wore a meteorite on a leather thong around her neck. It had been passed on to her by a man named Osage Star-Looking who'd seen it fall from the sky and smolder in a field. It was her prized possession, although she also had a hand-written book by the old healer, Severance.

Belle slept alone in the herb garden. The rest of her family believed, in varying degrees, that they were modern, so they remained inside the oven-hot walls of the house. Belle's grown daughters drowsed off and on throughout the night. The men tossed. The two young people were red-faced and sweating, tangled in their bed linens on sagging mattresses.

Belle frightened away the hen, then turned on her side and settled back into the feather pillow. Her silver hair spread over the pillow. Even resting outside in the iron bed surrounded by night's terrain, she was a commanding woman with the first morning light on her strong-boned face.

A little ways down the road toward Watona, Indian Territory, a forest of burned trees was just becoming visible in morning's red fire-light. Not far from there, at the oil fields, the pumps rose and fell, pulling black oil up through layers of rock. Across the way was a greenwood forest. And not even a full mile away from where Belle slept, just a short walk down the dirt road, Grace Blanket and her daughter Nola slept in a bed that was thoughtfully placed in their flower garden. Half covered in white sheets, they were dark-skinned angels dreaming their way through heaven. A dim lantern burned on a small table beside Grace. Its light fell across the shocking red blooms of roses.

Grace Blanket sat up in bed and put out the lamp. It smoked a little, and she smelled the kerosene. She climbed out from between her damp sheets. Standing in her thin nightdress, buried up to her dark ankles in the wild iris leaves that year after year invaded her garden, Grace bent over her sleeping daughter and shook the girl's shoulder. Grace smiled down at Nola, who had a widow's peak identical to her own, and even before the sleeping girl opened her eyes, Grace began to straighten the sheets on her side of the bed. "Make your bed every morning," they used to say, "and you'll never want for a husband." Grace was a woman who took such sayings to heart and she still wanted a husband. She decided to let Nola sleep a few minutes longer.

Lifting the hem of her nightgown, she walked across the yard, and went inside the screen door to the house.

Indoors, Grace pulled a navy blue dress over her head and zipped it. She fastened a strand of pearls around her neck, then brushed her hair in front of the mirror.

It was a strange house for a Hill Indian, as her people had come to be called. And sometimes, even to herself, Grace looked like an apparition from the past walking through the rooms she'd decorated with heavy, carved furniture and glass chandeliers. It seemed odd, too, that the European furniture was so staunch and upright when Grace was known to be lax at times in her own judgments.

She went to the open window and leaned out, "Nola! Come on now." She could see the girl in the growing daylight. She looked like an insect in its cocoon.

Nola turned over.

The Hill Indians were a peaceful group who had gone away from the changing world some sixty years earlier, in the 1860s. Their survival depended on returning to a simpler way of life, so they left behind them everything they could not carry and moved up into the hills and bluffs far above the town of Watona. Grace Blanket had been born of these, and she was the first to go down out of the hills and enter into the quick and wobbly world of mixed-blood Indians, white loggers, cattle ranchers, and most recently, the oil barons. The Hill Indians were known for their runners, a mystical group whose peculiar running discipline and austere habits earned them a special place in both the human world and the world of spirits.

But there were reasons why Grace had left the hills and moved down to Watona. Her mother, Lila Blanket, was a river prophet, which meant that she was a listener to the voice of water, a woman who interpreted the river's story for her people. A river never lied. Unlike humans, it had no need to distort the truth, and she heard the river's voice unfolding like its water across the earth. One day the Blue River told Lila that the white world was going to infringe on the peaceful Hill People. She listened, then she went back to her tribe and told them, "It is probable that we're going to lose everything. Even our cornfields."

The people were quiet and listened.

Lila continued, "Some of our children have to learn about the white world if we're going to ward off our downfall."

The Hill Indians respected the Blue River and Lila's words, but not one of them wanted to give their children up to that limbo between the worlds, that town named Watona, and finally Lila, who had heard the Blue directly, selected her own beautiful daughter, Grace, for the task. She could not say if it was a good thing or bad thing; it was only what had to be done.

Lila was a trader. That was her job at the Hill settlement. She went down to Watona often to trade sweet potatoes for corn, or sometimes corn for sweet potatoes. On her journeys, she was a frequent visitor at the Grayclouds'. Moses Graycloud, the man of the house, was Lila's second cousin. She liked him. He was a good Indian man; a rancher who kept a pasture and barn lot full of cattle and a number of good-looking horses. One day, when she mustered up enough strength, Lila took cornmeal and apples down to the small town, stopped by the Graycloud house, and knocked on the door.

As always, Belle was happy to see Lila Blanket. She opened the door for her. "Come in. Welcome." She held Lila's hand and smiled at her. But when she saw Lila's grief, her expression changed to one of concern. "I see you didn't come to trade food," she said. "What is it?"

Lila covered her face with her hands for a moment, then she took a deep breath and looked at Belle Graycloud. "I need to send my daughter to live near town. We've got too far away from the Americans to know how their laws are cutting into our life."

Belle nodded. She knew that a dam was going to be built at the mouth of the Blue River. The water must have told Lila this, about the army engineers and the surveyors with their red flags.

Lila was so overcome with sadness that she could hardly speak, but she asked Belle, "Can Grace stay with you?"

"Yes. I want her here." Belle put her hand on Lila's arm. "You come too, as often as you want. There's always an extra plate at our table."

On the day Lila took Grace to the Grayclouds, she kissed the girl, embraced her, and left immediately, before she could change her mind. She loved her daughter. She cried loudly all the way home, no matter who passed by or heard her. In fact, an old Osage hermit named John Stink heard the woman's wailing and he came down from his campsite, took Lila's hand, and walked much of the way home with her.

Grace Blanket had a ready smile and a good strong way with Belle's wayward chickens, but she paid little attention to the Indian ways. She hardly seemed like the salvation of the Hill Indians. And she was not at all interested in the white laws that affected her own people. After she finished school, Grace took a job at Palmer's store in town, and put aside her money. It wasn't any time at all before Grace bought a small, grassy parcel of land. She rented it out as a pasture for cattlemen, and one day, while Grace was daydreaming a house onto her land—her dream house had large rooms and a cupid fountain—Lila Blanket arrived in Watona, Indian Territory, with Grace's younger sisters. They were twins, ten years old, and the older woman wanted them to live with Grace and go to school. Their American names were Sara and Molene. And they had the same widow's peak that every Blanket woman had. They were wide-eyed girls, looking around at the world of automobiles and blond people. The longer they were there, the more they liked Watona. And the more Lila visited them, the more she hated the shabby little town with its red stone buildings and flat roofs. It was a magnet of evil that attracted and held her good daughters.

But the girls were the last of the Hill Indians ever to move down to Watona. Molene died several summers later, of an illness spread by white men who worked on the railroad. Sara caught the same paralyzing illness and was forced to remain in bed, motionless for over a year while Grace took care of her. By the time Sara was healthy enough to sit up in a wheelchair, both she and Grace wanted to remain in Watona. It was easier to wash clothing in the wringer washers, she reasoned, than to stir hot water tubs at home, and it was a most amazing thing to go for a ride in an automobile, and to turn on electric lights with the flick of a fingertip. And the delicate white women made such beautiful music on their pianos that Grace wanted one desperately and put away some of her earnings in a sugar bowl toward that cause.

There also were more important reasons why they remained; in the early 1900s each Indian had been given their choice of any parcel of land not already claimed by the white Americans. Those pieces of land were called allotments. They consisted of 160 acres a person to farm, sell, or use in any way they desired. The act that offered allotments to the Indians, the Dawes Act, seemed generous at first glance so only a very few people realized how much they were being tricked, since numerous tracts of unclaimed land became open property for white settlers, homesteaders, and ranchers. Grace and Sara, in total ignorance, selected dried-up acreages that no one else wanted. No one guessed that black undercurrents of oil moved beneath that earth's surface.

When Belle Graycloud saw the land Grace selected, and that it was stony and dry, she shook her head in dismay and said to Grace, "It's barren land. What barren, useless land." But Grace wasn't discouraged. With good humor, she named her property "The Barren Land." Later, after oil was found there, she called it "The Baron Land," for the oil moguls.

It was Michael Horse, the small-boned diviner who'd predicted the two-week dry spell, who had been the first person to discover oil on the Indian wasteland, and he found it on Grace's parched allotment.

With his cottonwood dowsing rod, he'd felt a strong underground pull, followed it straight through the dry prairie grass, turned a bit to the left, and said, "Drill here. I feel water." Then he smiled and showed off his three gold teeth. The men put down an auger, bored deep into the earth, and struck oil on Grace Blanket's land.

Michael Horse fingered one of his long gray braids that hung down his chest. "I'll be damned," he said. He was worried. He didn't know how he had gone wrong. He had 363 wells to his credit. There was no water on Grace Blanket's land, just the thick black fluid that had no use at all for growing corn or tomatoes. Not even zucchini squash would grow there. He took off his glasses and he put them in his shirt pocket. He didn't want to see what happened next.

When Grace Blanket's first lease check came in from the oil company, she forgot the cupid fountain and moved into a house with Roman columns. She bought a grand piano, but to her disappointment she was without talent for music. No matter how she pressed down the ivory keys, she couldn't play the songs she'd heard and loved when white women sang them. After several months, she gave up and moved the piano outside to a chicken coop where it sat neglected, out of tune, and swelling up from the humidity. When a neighboring chicken built a nest on the keys, Grace didn't bother to remove the straw and feathers.

After that, she only bought items she could put to good use. She bought crystal champagne glasses that rang like bells when a finger was run over the rim, a tiny typewriter that tapped out the English words she'd learned in school, and a white fur cape that brought out the rich chestnut brown in her dark skin. She wore the cape throughout her pregnancy, even on warmer days, so much that Belle Graycloud poked fun at her. "When that baby comes, it's going to be born with a fan in its tiny hands."

"That's all right," said Grace, flashing a smile. "Just so long as it's electric."

"Say, who is the father, anyway?" Belle asked. But Grace just looked away like she hadn't heard.

After Nola was born, Grace took the child back a few times each year to the world of the Hill society, and while Nola had a stubborn streak, even as an infant, she was peaceful and serene in the midst of her mother's people. As much as the child took to the quieter ways of the Hill Indians, they likewise took to her, and while Grace continued to make her way in life, enjoying the easy pleasures money could buy, not one of those luxuries mattered a whit to Nola. By the time she was five years old, it was apparent to everyone that Nola was ill-suited for town life. She was a gentle child who would wander into the greenwood forest and talk to the animals. She understood their ways. Lila thought that perhaps her granddaughter was going to be the one to return to the people. Nola, not Grace, was the river's godchild.

But what Lila didn't know, even up to the day she died, was that her daughter's oil had forestalled the damming of the Blue River, and that without anyone realizing it, the sacrifice of Grace to the town of Watona had indeed been the salvation of the Hill Indians. The dam would not go in until all the dark wealth was removed from inside the land.

That morning, as the sun rose up the sky, and Nola was still asleep, Grace went to the window and called out again, "Nola. Get up!"

Nola was dark and slender. Even with her eyes swollen from sleep, she was an uncommonly beautiful girl. She sat up like a small queen in her bed, with already elegant brown skin stretched over her thirteen-year-old bones. She climbed out of the bed, still sleepy, and went indoors. She slipped out of her nightgown, washed herself, and put on a Sunday white dress, and after Grace tied the bow behind Nola's thin waist, they walked together up the road to where Belle Graycloud slept in the middle of her herb garden with a stubborn golden chicken roosting on the foot of the bed, a calico cat by the old woman's side, a fat spotted dog snoring on the ground, and a white horse standing as close to Belle as the fence permitted, looking at her with wide, reverent eyes.

It was such a sight, Grace laughed out loud, and the laughter woke Belle.

Belle was indignant. "I knew someone was looking at me. I felt it. There ought to be a law against sneaking up on people like that. You gave me a fright."

Nola had slipped away to the house even while Belle talked. She was looking for her friend, Rena.

"Especially old people," Belle grumbled, rising from the bed. "Shoo!" She pushed the hen away from her bed.

Grace moved the cat. "Here, let me help you make the bed." She began to smooth Belle's sheets.

"Leave it," said Belle. "You know the saying. Maybe if I leave it in a mess, the young men will stop chasing me all the time." She pushed her dark silver hair back from her face. It hung like an ancient waterfall. Then she headed for the house, Grace alongside her. Behind them, the cat stretched and followed.

In the house, Belle's granddaughter, Rena, was already dressed. Rena had gold skin, the color of ochre, like a high yellow mulatto. It gave her, at first glance, a look of mystery. Her eyes, also, were gold-colored, and her hair. But she was still a child and she was impatient that morning as she walked around the creaky floor of the farmhouse, impatient to go with Nola and Grace to cut willow branches, impatient also for Grace to teach her how to weave the willow baskets, how to be that kind of an Indian woman.

In the kitchen, Belle's unmarried daughter, Leticia, took the perking coffeepot off the woodstove and set it on the table. "You sure you don't want some?" she asked Grace.

The girls passed by her in a hurry, and again the screen door slammed. Lettie opened the door behind them and called out, "Do you girls swear you won't soil your good church dresses?" She looked sharply at Rena. "You hear?"

"Cross my heart," said Rena, but she was already halfway down the walk. She looked back at Lettie who was dressed in a house dress and apron, but who nevertheless wore an expensive felted wool hat on her head. It was blue and a net was stitched to it.

"That goes for you, too," Lettie called out to Grace as Grace tried to catch up with the girls.

Grace turned and took a few steps backward before she blew a kiss to Lettie. Then she caught up with the girls. The sun lit her arms. For a change, she was in a hurry and the girls fell behind. Grace wanted to gather water willows and be done in time to put in a rare appearance at church, an appearance prompted only by the presence of a new, handsome man in town, and the only thing Grace knew about him was that he was a Baptist, so she knew where to find him.

Michael Horse drove a gold car. It matched his teeth. That Sunday morning, he was in his shirtsleeves. On his way to church, he drove past three Indian boys who were playing hooky from the House of Our Lord. They sat on a curb, sharing a fat brown Cuban cigar. They called it a stogie and blew gray smoke rings into the summer air. The boys wore lightweight Sunday suits, had taken off their jackets, and their shirt collars were opened. It was sweltering. One of the boys was Ben Graycloud, the grandson of Belle and Moses.

Horse was late for church, but even so, after he parked his car, he stopped for a moment in front of the boys and let them shake his hand the way their parents had taught them to do with elders. All of them were taller than he was. They tried to hide the cigar. Horse pretended not to notice the cloud of smoke one of them fanned with his hat.

There was a blue law on Sunday mornings and the town was quiet. Sinners and saints were in church, nonbelievers still in bed. The streets were almost empty of people, but dark, expensive automobiles were parked outside of the Oklahoma Indian Baptist Church. Michael Horse was proud of the fact that he owned the only gold car in town. It shined bright as a brick of bullion.

Not that the other cars were shabby. On South Street alone there were two powder-blue Ford roadsters with tooled leather seats, five

Lincolns, three Cadillacs, and every one of them belonged to the cash-paying Indians who were singing "Amazing Grace" inside the church.

Horse heard their voices. The congregation had risen up to sing. They rested the backs of their legs against dark pews and fanned their faces, he knew, with paper fans that had pictures of Jesus knocking on the door of a heart.

Horse went in and stood in the back of the church until the singers closed their hymnbooks, and in a rustle of clothing and a clearing of throats, he walked in and sat down in a pew not far behind Moses and Belle Graycloud.

As usual, the church was nearly full. Mixed-blood people were side by side in faith with their darker brothers and sisters. Though they wore dark, American suits, most of the men still braided their hair. Some of the younger women had lightened their hair to a brassy orange with hydrogen peroxide. Some of them wore makeup that was paler than their faces, imitating the white women's pictures in magazines, but Michael Horse wasn't fooled; they were Indians, and even if he hadn't known most all their parents and grandparents—and he did— he would have known by the way their bones moved, by the way they sat or talked, that they were from one of the tribes around Watona. It was in the way a person tilted her head when she laughed, or in the set of shoulders. He would have guessed Ben Graycloud just by the way the boy held the Cuban cigar between his thumb and middle finger like Moses had always done.

Horse was a good judge of people and he had what they called a sixth sense. He was also a dreamer.

At night, asleep, he saw a side of people that was more true than the poker faces some of them wore in public, more telling than blood-lines, and way more revealing than black suits or blue silk dresses.

He was lost in these thoughts when everyone rose up once again to sing a hymn. Horse searched absently in his shirt pocket for his little round reading glasses until Velma Billy, in the pew behind him, handed him a hymnal opened to page 261, "Rock of Ages." He smiled, "Thank you," and saw how her wire-framed glasses caught a yellow glint of sunlight from the stained glass window, and so did the cross she wore around her neck, resting in the soft center of her bosom. She didn't need the book. She knew the songs by heart.

In front of Horse, Moses Graycloud sang with vigor. He had removed the jacket of his hot, dark suit, and his shirt was damp with sweat. A medal of valor from the Spanish-American War was heavy on his chest. Moses was a very dark man and he was physically strong, even though he limped on damp, rainy days. Beside Moses was Belle. At first glance she looked small, but in spite of her slight stature, she was a giant on the inside, and hard to reckon with.

Horse watched her. Her steel-gray hair was damp from the heat, with loose strands plastered against the back of her neck. The sun came through the stained glass robes of Jesus and touched one side of her strong-boned face and warmed her hair. Now and then, she glanced over her shoulder toward the door, and once Horse caught her eye, and even though she was surprised to see him in church—Horse was not a Christian Indian—she nodded a hello at him before her eyes again watched the door.

Horse could not explain, even to himself, what he was doing in church that morning. Except for the gold car, he was one of the last proud holdouts from the new ways and he didn't want younger Indians to get the wrong idea about how old-timers lived in the world or that maybe he believed in the white man's God, but mostly he was embarrassed to be caught gazing at Belle. Michael Horse had a soft spot for Belle, but he wouldn't have said so.

That morning, the young Reverend Joe Billy was talking about toppling worlds. "The Indian world is on a collision course with the white world," Billy said.

Wasn't that the truth, Horse thought. It didn't even need to be said.

Joe Billy fanned himself with his sermon notes, "It's more than a race war. They are waging a war with earth. Our forests and cornfields are burned by them. But, I say to you, our tears reach God. He knows what's coming round, so may God speak to the greedy hearts of men and move them."

And he had hope, the kind of hope a young Creek Indian had when he'd gone to a seminary back East, in Boston, married a white society woman against her father's will, and returned home determined to save and serve his own Indian people.

Service and praying were in Joe Billy's blood; he'd inherited those traits from his father, Sam Billy, who'd been a medicine man for twenty-three years before he'd converted to the Christian faith.

At least a dozen of the Billy line were in church that morning, Horse noted. Velma Billy, with the "Rock of Ages" fixed permanently in her mind, was Sam's daughter. Joe Billy, Sam's favored son, saying, "So be it, my brothers and sisters." And when he said, "Amen" that morning, his voice put Horse in mind of Sam's.

Horse watched Belle Graycloud's shoulders rise and fall with every breath. He overheard her whisper to Moses. "Something's not right. I think the girls are in trouble."

Moses was what they called a logical man, and no matter how many of Belle's hunches proved true, he was hard put to believe her, so he smiled reassuringly at her and laid his hand over hers. Then the service was over, and the congregation began to spill out of the church, but each and every person stopped at the door and shook hands with the preacher's blond wife.

When it was Michael Horse's turn, she took hold of his hand and pumped it. "Why, hello, Mr. Horse." She sounded musical. Her name was Martha. She was skinny and frail, and sweating from the heat. Her yellow hair was in a tight, damp bun. Horse was shy. He stared down at her small hand. It was the color of the paper he wrote his journals on, all the way down to the pale blue lines of her veins.

"Come back soon, Mr. Horse," Martha Billy called out to him as he went down the step.

Outside the church that morning, Belle was giving her grandson Ben one of the glares that she had been famous for all her life. Ben got up from his roosterlike perch, left the other boys behind, and followed his grandmother.

Horse followed along with them. He was thinking that Belle's bones were never wrong and he'd felt it too, something uneasy in the air that day, like a dry, hot wind starting to blow over the scorched land.

Horse dropped behind Belle, behind her bountiful, gliding hips.

"I'm going straight home," she said to Horse over her shoulder. "If you want to come, you're welcome."

Horse accepted Belle's invitation. He fell into step with Ben. "You want to ride with me?" he asked Ben Graycloud. Ben brightened up. He looked at his grandmother for approval.

She turned back and was stern a moment. "You sure do smell like cigar smoke," she said with her owl eyes staring sharply into his, then she waved him away and said, "Go on if you're going. Git!" She didn't look back again.

Ben hooted and raced ahead of Horse. By the time Horse reached his gold convertible, Ben was already in the passenger seat, his hat pulled down over his eyes, one leg crossed over the other. He looked like a dandy. If they hadn't known him better, anyone would have thought he was a city boy in gabardine pants.

"Get out," Horse said. He sounded gruff. Ben looked up, surprised, but Horse had a big grin on his face and he was smiling and held up the key. "Slide over," he said to the young man.

Ben slid over to the driver's seat. He turned the car around, and he drove tall and proud past the dressed-up churchgoers while Michael Horse enjoyed the scenery. Maybe it was the light reflecting off the red sandstone buildings that day but people walking on the street looked rosy and golden. White dresses, in the light, were blushing. The men's black suits had a sheen about them, like burnished metal. The sunlit Indian people stood in line outside the stores, waiting for shopowners to turn the "Closed" signs around. Some of the women held red umbrellas above their heads and so they stood in ruby circles of light, scolding their children for playing in the white noonday heat. One Indian woman called to her daughter, "You're going to faint. Get in here." Under the circle of shade, she meant.

There were two dry goods stores in Watona. One of them was painted red. Palmer's Red Store, as it was called, sold yard goods and household things that appealed to the women. The other one was sky blue. The Blue Store sold hardware, hunting rifles, and had a thin, yellowed catalogue on a stand where women could order wallpaper and linoleum. It was also owned by Palmer, since the previous winter when the Indian owner disappeared. The last person who'd seen him was John Tate, Moses's brother-in-law. Just before noon, the shopkeepers covered their candy bins to keep children's thieving fingers away, then, at twelve sharp, they turned their signs around. Mr. Palmer, at the Red Store, opened the door with a jangle of keys, and stepped aside to let the Indian women enter. They went into the store, folded down their umbrellas, and fawned over lead-backed mirrors that were filled with their own faces. While older women haggled over the cost of lacquer boxes that played the Blue Danube, young girls bought paper fans for their friends to autograph and like most Sundays, the men and boys went their own ways into the Blue Store where they bought tobacco and rifles for hunting the last remaining bear and deer. And gunpowder was cheap.

But for Belle, Sunday was the day when she changed the racks in her beehives, cleaned out her chicken coop, or walked along the creek bed, gathering watercress and wild onion. "The earth is my marketplace," she would tell her family, and they understood what she meant for they ate the fruits of her labor.

When Ben drove the gold car up the road to his home and honked, Belle was outside standing beside a large azalea bush. She watched the distant roads where dust flew up as cars zigzagged back and forth across the land.

Horse got out of his car, looking off in the direction she was squinting. There was a bluebird flying, but it was nearly invisible against the blue sky and the dust from the roads. A few cardinals stood out like spots of blood in the distant trees.

"I'll be back," Horse said to Belle, and he went out to the barn to talk with Moses. Ben remained in the driver's seat, turning the wheel as if he were going somewhere. He imagined he was driving between the many cattle that dotted the pasture.

In the barn, Moses was at work shoeing one of his horses. He held the black mare's leg up on his thigh and cleaned the hoof, then took a nail from his pocket.

"How's your car running?" he asked Michael Horse. He tapped the metal shoe lightly with a hammer. The horse blinked at him with big black eyes.

"Good." Horse looked in the direction of his gold roadster. It ran like a charm.

"That's good. How are your teeth?" Moses breathed heavily, from the effort, and he glanced quickly up at Michael Horse.

"I went to the dentist in Tulsa last week." Horse bent down and watched Moses. "Say, do you need some help?"

"I'm almost done." Moses put the mare's leg down and wiped his forehead with his arm. He didn't mention the other man's bad reputation with horses. He breathed a little heavily. "You've got more money tied up in your mouth than I have in horse flesh."

Michael Horse laughed. "Isn't that the truth?"

They led the mare out of the barn. Moses limped. A hot wind had started blowing. It blew the horse's dark mane over to one side. Moses looked up at the sky. "You say we've still got a week or so before it rains?"

"Maybe two," Horse confirmed.

"The way my bad leg hurts, I'd say it's going to rain today." The dust blew up around them. Moses led the horse over to where Belle was standing. Her hands were on her hips, the breeze blowing her dress against her soft body. Moses clicked his tongue at the mare, but he did it for Belle's comfort more than for the horse, and he watched Belle all the while he patted the black-eyed horse and tossed a gray blanket over its back.

His plan was to ride the horse to the far pasture and set it loose, then walk back to the house.

"I'm going to stop by Mother's on the way back," he told her. That was what he still called the place where his twin sister Ruth lived with her husband, John Tate. She hadn't appeared in church that morning, and that troubled him.

"Here," Belle said, "I'll hold the reins," and she watched while Moses pulled himself up and threw his stiff leg over the horse. He tried to put her worries to rest. He said, "They'll be back before long. It's all right, Belle."

"It's hot for walking," Horse said. "Don't you want me to drive out after you?"

Moses smiled down from the mare. "It's my constitutional," Moses said. "If I stop moving this leg, I'll lose it." He looked elegant and tall astride the dark horse. He was at home. Michael and Belle watched him turn the black horse toward the road.

"What's up?" Michael Horse asked Belle, trying not to sound too prying. He'd been watching her nervous behavior.

"Grace and Nola came by this morning. They took Rena out to cut willows. Then they were going to soak them in saltwater, and be back in time for church." While she talked, Belle fidgeted with a pearl button on her dress. She glanced at Horse, then back out at the road where Moses was becoming smaller. "We haven't seen them since."

Horse was known for his predictions, so when he said, "They probably just lost track of time," Belle took his word for it. "Well then, maybe we should have a cup of coffee," she said. But still she worried. In the kitchen, while waiting for the coffee, she tapped her fingertips on the table.

Horse looked out the window in the direction Moses had gone, as if he were still there. "How is Ruth?" he asked.

Belle also glanced that direction, seeing the road grow small, the path, the distance across the Mill Creek and the dark solid old house where Ruth and Moses's mother had lived out her life, where John Tate moved in after he'd married the single, quiet twin of Moses.

It was only a short while later, as they sat at the table talking, a strong wind came up. It was a "turn wind," the kind that stirs things up for a few hours and then dies down. Earlier that summer, other unexpected turn winds had caused fierce and dangerous sandstorms.

"It looks like a bad one," Horse said. He smelled the air. "Maybe we'd better drive out to see if we can't find Grace."

Belle went upstairs to grab a headscarf and by the time she told Lettie where she was going and returned, a dark cloud had blown in. It cast a shadow over the land. The wind picked up. It swept through tall dry grasses, hissing.

Horse drove through the flying dust with Belle Graycloud sitting next to him. The wind whipped at her scarf. Nothing was staying put; stray pieces of paper flew up all the way from town, and when they reached the creek, it was already blown full of earth. It rushed, muddy and red, downhill between swaying trees toward where it joined the wide Blue River. Horse parked. Belle got out of the car and called the girls. She crooked an arm over her eyes to shield them from the flying sand. Held up that way, the skin on her inner arm looked soft and vulnerable in the storm around them. Michael Horse gave her a hand-kerchief to hold across her eyes. He was worried about his paint job. He put the top up on his car and Belle got back in.

By the time they reached Woody Pond, Belle's scarf had blown away and caught on a tumbleweed that rushed across the land. Wind whistled down from the hills, and then just as they rolled up the windows, sharp rain started. It began as a roar moving toward them, then it let up a little as the roaring arrived and passed by them.

Belle and Horse walked against the violent wind, leaning into it. Horse's black pants whipped up against his legs. Belle's hair flew away from her face like seaweed pulled in a furious rip tide. There wasn't a trace of the girls. She cried, "Rena!" from the top of her lungs, but the wind only blew her words back to her. She called again, "Grace!" but there was only the raging sound of the wind and Horse, standing next to her, had not even heard her.

They drove to Grace's house. The sky was the deep lead color of sea. At the front door, Belle beat the brass knocker, but no one answered. Belle picked her way through thorny bushes and peered into the wind-rattled window. Inside, everything was still and peaceful.

Gold angels were on the walls. A crystal chandelier hung from the ceiling. Glass swans sat on the mantle and they were swimming in a marble lake. The silence was like the calm eye of a tornado.

Belle went around back. Grace's bed was standing in the rose garden. The wind had whipped up the sheets. One billowed like a sail against the metal bedframe. Another was flat and wet, spread over several rosebushes nearby.

They were at a loss. The gas tank was nearly empty. They hadn't found a single clue to the whereabouts of Grace, and Horse's gold car was chipped from the flying gravel and debris. Finally, they gave up the search and returned to the Graycloud house.

"I'm sorry about your car," Belle said to Horse.

He smiled at her. "It's okay. I was getting tired of gold paint anyway." He looked in the mirror. "Maybe we should go out to get Moses."

"No. He'll be all right. He'll stay at Ruth's until the storm dies down."

Then she became silent, and at home again, Belle sat down on the steps, pulled her damp blue skirt down over her knees, and didn't bother to protect herself from the rain.

Michael Horse said nothing, but he turned when he heard the door slam, and when Belle's daughter, Leticia, ran out, holding her hat down on her head, screaming out over the wind, "Mama, come inside." She pleaded, "You can't sit out here all day in this weather."

Belle looked at her daughter. She said defiantly, "Who says I can't?" And her hair whipped angrily about her face, but then she gave up, sighed, and with Horse, she followed Lettie indoors.

It was quieter in the house. They shut the door and latched it, but Belle kept watch at the windows, still looking for the girls. A while later, Moses, wet and dirty, limped in. "That's a hell of a turn wind," he said, rubbing his sore right leg and hip. "Why didn't you come get

me?" To Horse he said, "What did I tell you about my leg and rain?
You're losing your touch, old man. You're getting worn out. It's raining
like crazy."

"It's true. I think I'm slipping," Horse said. He shrugged his narrow
shoulders. It would be better for him anyway if people stopped coming
to ask him to find their rings and their lost dogs.

"Why didn't you stay at Ruth's?"

Moses seemed like he didn't want to answer, but said, "Tate had
some of his friends over. Ruth was angry about it. I felt like an
intruder."

He'd never liked Tate. John Tate was a small, fussy man with only
one eye and every time Moses looked into it, he could see nothing
warm, nothing human.

Normally Belle would stand up for Ruth and Tate. She'd seen the
toll of loneliness on Moses's twin sister for way too many years, but
she was worried about the girls.

"I think we ought to get the sheriff." Belle said. She was anxious,
but Moses convinced her to wait. His reasons made sense. Grace
Blanket was famous in those parts, both as a basket-maker and as an
oil-rich Indian who was given to catting around. She had a sweet
disposition, a mind of her own, and a fondness for men and drink.

"She's gallivanting around somewhere with a new boyfriend,"
Moses said. "The two girls are eating gritty ice cream in some man's
rumble seat. I can see them now. Their hair is flying straight out
behind them in the stiff wind. They're having the time of their lives."

Grace had that kind of reputation. And it made sense, Belle finally
agreed, since two nights earlier, Grace had a public fight with her new
white boyfriend over another man. That scene, combined with the
one Moses's words just painted, allayed Belle's fears. Even Horse agreed
that Grace was sometimes brash and reckless, especially if she had a
drink under her belt.

"Say, Horse," Moses said. "There's a livestock auction over in
Walnut Springs. I have to go over there. Why don't you come along
with me?" He opened the icebox and took out a sugar bowl full of
cash.

Horse looked at Belle. He was a single man, so he was sensitive
to her worries.

"Oh, go ahead," she told them. "I'm sure everything's fine."

"Well, I guess it wouldn't hurt to go look." Horse seemed a little reluctant. He watched her.

"I'll stay here with Mama," Lettie assured them. Lou, Belle's other daughter, and her white husband had gone to Tulsa for the weekend. They were due home later that night.

Belle and Lettie waited. Belle went outside often, to watch. They were both alarmed, though they said almost nothing.

And that night, after the dark set in, the two girls came home. They were alone. They were filthy and their eyes were full of terror. Belle was standing outside, watching the long dark horizon, and still wearing her white apron when they arrived.

What had happened that morning was this: After dawn, before Grace and Nola Blanket walked up to Belle's white bedstead, they passed the oil field. An oilman named John Hale nodded at them. Hale was a lanky white man who wore a gray Stetson hat. He'd been a rancher in Indian Territory for a number of years before he invested in the oil business. He was known as a friend to the Indians. He'd always been generous and helpful to his darker compatriots, but Grace didn't care for him.

Once, feeling Hale's eyes on her, Grace glanced back, quickly, over her shoulder. Hale watched her, but she was a beautiful woman and it wasn't unusual for men to stop and stare, so she thought little about it.

On their way to Woody Pond that Sunday morning, the girls walked a little behind Grace. They whispered to each other the secret things girls share. Nola bent and picked a sunflower. She handed it to Rena. Rena pulled the yellow petals from the flower, looked at its black center, and said, "He loves me."

"Who?" asked Nola.

"How should I know? But it's grand to be loved, isn't it?" Rena smiled.

Grace walked faster. "Hurry! We'll be late for church!" The sun moved up in the sky. They had another mile to go. But the girls didn't keep up with her and they lagged farther behind and there were more distances between Grace and the girls than just that stretch of road; there was a gap in time between one Indian way of life and another where girls were sassy and wore satin ribbons in their hair.

They turned and walked up the red dirt path to the pond. Grace gave each of the girls a small knife. "Cut those thin ones." She pointed to the willows she wanted for her baskets, and in their chalk-white dresses, the girls bent and pared them off, then handed the cuttings to Grace. She put them, one at a time, neatly in the sling she carried looped up over the padded shoulder of her dress.

It was hot and the white sun had risen further up the sky when Grace heard a car. It wasn't unusual for whiskey peddlers to drive past Woody Pond on Sunday mornings, nor was it odd for drivers on their way home from the city to stop there and rest.

The car kicked up a cloud of dust. When it cleared, Grace saw the black Buick. She smiled at first, thinking it belonged to Moses Graycloud, and that he was picking them up because they were late for church, but then her hand froze in the air.

The men in the car turned their faces toward her, as if something was wrong.

They talked while they watched her. She thought she saw a pistol, then thought she must have imagined it. The driver seemed to be saying "No" to the other man, and they drove in closer, still arguing. Hale was driving. Grace didn't know the passenger. He was a broad man with dark hair. She looked at them, then moved behind a tree. They turned the car around and drove slowly away down the road, but Grace remained nervous and watchful. "Hurry, it's getting late," she urged the girls. She glanced back toward the car. The girls worked faster. The sun was hot and the bees sounded dizzy, and then the car returned, and again the men's eyes were on Grace.

When the car braked, Grace panicked and held still, like a deer in danger, rooted to where she stood. Even the air became still, and not a hair on Grace's head moved as she stood still and fixed, a hand poised on the branches in the sling at her side. In desperate hope, she looked around for other Indians who might have been at the pond searching for turtles, or a Sunday morning rabbit hunter. But they were alone, and the girls felt Grace's fear, like electricity, rising up their skin, up the backs of their necks.

Nola looked around. "What is it?" she started to ask, but without turning toward her, Grace hissed at her, hoarse with a fear so thick that Nola dropped down to the ground. She hardly breathed. Grace scanned the oaks and hilly land. "Don't move!" she told the girls. "Whatever you do, don't follow me."

The car went by and turned around another time, with the men still looking, and in a split second before it returned, Grace whispered dryly, "Stay down. Stay there." Then she dropped her sling on the ground and ran, crashing through the bushes, away from the pond, toward town.

The girls fought their impulse to run. Even their own breathing sounded dangerous to them.

Grace was an easy target, and she knew it, but she wanted to, had to, lure the car away from the girls. She hoped and prayed she could turn and cut through rocky land a car couldn't cover, but the Buick followed her down the road, and when she ran faster, the car speeded up. Then she saw the rocky land and with relief, she veered off and cut through a field, and even from where they hid, the girls could hear the car turn and follow, grinding across the summer grass. The driver struggled with the dark steering wheel over stones and clumps of earth. In spite of her fear, Nola rose up to look, stood just enough to see her mother kick the shoes off her feet and race into the forest. As Nola watched, Grace disappeared in the dark green shadows of leaves and branches.

Rena was crying. She pulled Nola close to earth, tugging at her skirt. "Stay down."

The car braked, and Nola peered over the brush to see a man jump out. The driver remained inside, though, and the motor idled. Then in day's full light, a gunshot broke through air. Like a stone cracking apart, something falling away from the world.

The girls lay flat in the shallow water, hidden in the silty pond between the reeds. Nola covered her eyes with one of her muddy hands, but it was too late, she had already seen her mother run barefoot across the field, followed by the black car, and in her mind's eye she saw her mother wounded.

The car doors slammed shut. The girls heard the car begin to grind and jam once more across the field. They pressed themselves deeper into the marshy pond, still and afraid. Only their heads were out of the muddy red water. They barely breathed. Nola dropped her knife and searched the silt frantically, with shaking fingers, until she found it and held it tight and ready in her fist. Then the wind began to blow, hot and restless, drowning out the sound of the car. The men had propped Grace's body between them as if she were just a girlfriend out for a Sunday drive. They drove up to the pond where water willows were quaking in the wind, and when they lifted the woman out of the car, both of her dark braids came loose and fell toward earth. The wind blew harder. The men placed Grace's body behind a clump of wind-whipped black bushes, then they straightened their backs, turned around, and searched for Nola.

Nola could barely hear them speak over the sound of wind.

"I thought you said the girl was with her."

"She was."

Nola held her breath. She heard nothing else, for a sudden gust of wind whistled across the water and rattled the cattails. The girls were afraid to look. They heard the men search among the rushes, close to where they remained paralyzed with fright, but by then, the girls could not tell the difference between wind and the men's hands pilfering through the reeds.

The turn wind, a current from the south, blew grit up from the ground. The hillsides stirred with dust devils. Branches broke off the older trees.

As the hot wind quickened, tree branches began to creak. The storm drowned out the sound of the car and when the men drove away, the girls did not hear them. A mallard moved across the pond and took cover, hiding as the girls hid, in the blowing reeds.

A short while later, the car returned. Its motor sounded like the wind. The girls were sure the men were searching for children in Sunday dresses. One man got out and walked through the wind-swept grass toward Grace Blanket's body. From between the reeds, Nola could almost see his face. The wind blew his jacket open and away from his shirt. Behind him the trees bent. He placed a pistol in the dead woman's hand. Nola caught another glimpse of him. She couldn't tell who he was. She had never seen him before. He opened a bottle of whiskey and poured it on Grace Blanket's body, and the wind blew the smell of whiskey across the pond. The girls held their breaths while the man buttoned his dark jacket and laid down the empty bottle. He got back in the car and it rattled off toward town, erased by a storm cloud of dust.

The girls were drowning in the heat and wind of the storm. They didn't hear the sound of Michael Horse's gilt-colored car, nor did they hear Belle call out their names. They heard only the howling wind, and when it finally died down, they heard the horrible flies already at work on the body of Grace and then the afternoon sun turned red in the west sky, and then the long day was passing and the frogs began their night songs, and then it was night and the stars showed up on the surface of the dark pond. Nola crawled out of the water and up the bank of the pond on her elbows and knees. She half crawled toward her mother's body. Rena followed, shivering even in the heat. Her thin-skinned hands and feet were cracked open from the water. And in the midst of everything, the moon was shining on the water. Grace was surrounded by black leaves in the moonlight, and the whiskey smell was still thick and sickening. Grace was twisted and grotesque and her head turned to the side as if she'd said "No" to death. In her hand was the gun. The girl stood there for what seemed like a long time. She laid her head against her mother, crying, "Mama," and wept with her face buried in the whiskey-drenched clothing.

"Come on." Rena pulled Nola back into the world of the living.

Nola started to take the pistol. "Leave it," Rena told her, so Nola reached down and unclasped the strand of pearls from her mother's neck. With Rena's arm around her, she walked away, then looked back, hoping against all hope that her mother would move, that her voice would call out the way it had always done, "Come here, little one," but there were only the sounds of frogs and insects.

Rena took Nola's hand. They walked toward the Grayclouds' house, hiding themselves behind bushes or trees. The muddy weight of their dresses dragged heavily against their legs.

That night, the lights of fireflies and the songs of locusts were peaceful, as if nothing on earth had changed. How strange that life was as it had been on other summer nights, with a moon rising behind the crisscross lines of oil derricks and the white stars blinking in a clear black sky.

At the dark turnoff to the Grayclouds' house, sweet white flowers bloomed on the lilac bush. The mailbox, with its flag up, was half hidden by the leafy branches. The house, too, looked as it always did, with an uneven porch and square windows of light. The chickens had gone to roost for the night, and they were softly clucking, and out in the distance, the white-faced cattle were still grazing, looking disembodied.

When they passed through the gate and neared the front door, the girls saw something white at the azalea bush. They were startled. They stopped and stared, thinking at first it was a ghost. But then the ghost in its white apron stepped toward them and said, "Where's your mother, child?" and the ghost became solid and became Belle Graycloud. Between sobs that night, Rena tried to tell the story of what had happened, and before the loss of Grace turned to grief in the old woman, Belle raised her face to the starry sky and thanked the Great Something that the girls were alive.

Neither Belle nor Lettie Graycloud could sleep that night. They were still awake when Moses returned home from the livestock auction in Walnut Springs. He was wearing a new straw hat. Belle heard him whistling as he led a new palomino pony—they were the fashion that year—through the dark lot and into the barn.

She opened the door and called his name.

"I'm coming," he said from the darkness, then she saw him in the light from the house. He walked through the door and set his hat on the table. "What is it?"

She told him about Grace.

Moses was stunned with the news. He sat down heavily in a chair, and slumped over the table. He covered his face with his hands and was silent a long while, then he asked, "Did they see who did it?"

Belle shook her head. "All they know is that they drove a car like ours." She sat beside him. Her eyes were swollen.

He said, "Belle, I'm so sorry." He had doubted her. Then he said, "Black Buicks are everywhere." He took a deep breath, stood up, and put the new hat back on his head.

Belle was alarmed. "What are you doing?"

He answered slowly. "I'd better go talk to the sheriff."

She put up her hand to stop him. "I don't think you should."

He was puzzled. "Why not?"

She hesitated. She was weary and hoped she wasn't making a mistake. "Because, Moses, the killers didn't see the girls. I'm afraid that if they knew there were witnesses, they might come looking for them."

He turned it over in his mind, then took his hat off and, without an argument, he sat back down and rubbed the grit off his face.

Belle put her hand over his. She fingered one of the scars that crossed his knuckles. They sat that way, in silence for a while, Moses deep in thought, Belle too shaken to say more.

Then Moses pulled at one of his dark braids and said, "It was probably a lover's fight."

Belle studied his face. Moses was trying to push away his fear. It made her twice as cautious, as if to make up for him. "And if it wasn't?" she said, but before he could answer, she was on her feet. She took a pistol from a cabinet. It was a small handgun, one she used to frighten coyotes away from her nervous chickens. She loaded it. Moses said nothing.

Upstairs, the girls slept in Lettie's bed. It was hot. In the dim light of the lamp, they looked vulnerable in the large bed. Lettie watched over them. She also held a pistol. She straightened the sheet tenderly over them and smoothed the hair back from their damp faces. She wanted to hold them, to offer solace, but their breathing was deep and the waking world was dangerous, so she left them to the gift of sleep.

After a while, Belle relieved her of her watch, and the old woman set up her own silent vigil over the girls. But Lettie was overwhelmed with a feeling of loneliness, and around two in the morning, she returned to the bedside of the girls. She looked haggard. She wore a dark, worn robe. "Go on now, Mama," she said. "You need rest."

But Belle made no attempt to leave the room. "I can't sleep anyway," she said. Lettie was insistent, though, until Belle pulled herself up from the chair and went down the hall to her own room. She was restless, gripped in a hot fear, afraid for Rena and Nola.

She sat at the mirror. Out of habit, she brushed her long silver hair while she thought. In the dark, sparks flew and snapped through the air around her. She was sure something was afoot. She put the brush down.

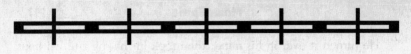

ROBERT MAYER

The Dreams of Ada

O n the morning of Labor Day 1984, police detective Dennis
Smith of Ada, Oklahoma—a pretty, Bible Belt town—asked
his wife, Sandi, how she would like to spend the holiday.

"Let's go look for Denice Haraway's body," Sandi replied.

The detective, a nineteen-year veteran of the police force, bald
almost in the manner of Kojak, agreed. Husband and wife got into
the family car and rode to the area near a packing plant on the western
edge of town. They climbed out and looked in fields and woodlands,
creeks and ravines, for the body of a lovely twenty-four-year-old college
senior who had disappeared without a trace from a local convenience
store four months before.

In time, in a dumping area strewn with old tires and abandoned
refrigerators, the detective saw a cardboard box with bloodstains on
the top. The blood, to his practiced eye, looked too fresh. He called
his wife over.

"Well, take the cover off!" Sandi urged.

The detective removed the lid. Inside the box, peering up at them
with mournful eyes, was the severed head of a deer.

If this morbid domestic image—Norman Rockwell by Charles
Addams—seems odd, it is only one curious scene in a haunting mystery
known in Ada as "the Haraway case"—a sanguineous web of reality

and illusion that is the most unusual murder case in the annals of Oklahoma law, perhaps one of the strangest in the land.

Consider these circumstances:

Six months after the young woman's disappearance, two "poor white" local boys were arrested and charged with robbery, kidnapping, rape, and murder. No witnesses to any killing had come forth, no body had been found, no murder weapon, no bloodstains: no physical evidence whatever that the girl who had disappeared was dead.

The arrests, and the trial nearly a year later, in which the state sought the death penalty, were based on videotaped confessions made by the suspects. The problem with this was that almost every verifiable statement on the tapes had been proved—by the police themselves—to be untrue.

The primary suspect insisted repeatedly that his taped confession —repudiated within hours—was based on a dream he had had about the case. Yet because of this "dream," he and his friend faced possible execution by the state of Oklahoma if they were convicted.

The mystery of what happened to Donna Denice Haraway gnawed at the God-fearing, picture-book town for seventeen months, and some feel gnaws at it still. Its almost mythic unraveling has worked its way into many an Ada dream.

The palindromic town, well known to crossword-puzzle addicts (city in Oklahoma, three letters), was named after a dark-haired girl, Ada Reed, daughter of the town's founder, back when Oklahoma was Indian territory. Now a city of about 17,000 people, county seat of Pontotoc County, ninety miles southeast of Oklahoma City, Ada is a small industrial hub, proud of its Main Street and its Main Street notions, set in an area of farmland, rolling hills, thick woodlands. This is quarter-horse country, where horses bred for quick bursts of speed are sold at periodic auctions. It is oil country, scores of pumps grazing like metal horses in every direction. Oil money built many of the magnificent mansions on upper-crust Kings Road. Ada is also a factory town. The gray turrets of the Evergreen feed mill tower only a block from Main Street like the superstructure of a battleship. The Brockway factory, a few blocks away, forges 1.3 million bottles and jars a day for Coke, Pepsi, and Gerber baby foods among others. Blue Bell jeans employs 175 local women to sew 45,000 pairs of Wranglers and Rustlers a week. Ideal cement is produced in the town, as are Solo plastic cups. The Burlington Northern Railroad track slices across Main Street, several freights a day shrieking to a halt in the innards of the feed mill.

Main Street dead-ends into East Central University, which makes Ada the modest cultural hub of the area. But Ada is perhaps most of all a religious town—mainly Baptist—where you can't buy a mixed drink without an annual "club" membership. There are fifty churches in the town (forty-nine Protestant, one Catholic) and four movie screens. If an architect were to construct a scale model of Middle America in the 1980s, he might well come up with Ada, Oklahoma. It is a town in which the Lord and the respectable predominate, but where there are enough illicit drugs, burglaries, rowdy teenagers dragging Main, and occasional violence to keep the police busy, to give the devil his due.

On Saturday night, April 28, 1984, just a few hours before the town would spring its clocks forward to daylight saving time, the devil was ascendant in Ada.

A few minutes after 8:30 that evening, two men and a high-school boy drove up to McAnally's, a convenience store that stands alone out on the highway at the eastern end of town. One of the men, Lenny Timmons, got out of his car and pushed through the double glass doors into the store. In the entrance he passed a young woman and a young man leaving. There was a small space between the two. There was no sign of a weapon. The woman did not appear frightened. The couple seemed to the witnesses like young lovers as they got into a gray-primered pickup parked out front and drove away.

Inside the store, its shelves brimming with candy bars, snack foods, paper products, Timmons saw schoolbooks open on the counter, a purse, a cigarette burning in an ashtray—but no clerk. After waiting several minutes to be helped, he looked behind the counter. The cashdrawer was open, empty. He called the police.

Sergeant Harvey Phillips was dispatched to the scene. In the purse he found a driver's license belonging to Donna Denice Haraway. The store manager was summoned from his home. He confirmed that Denice Haraway, as she preferred to be called, had been the clerk on duty, that a car still parked beside the store was hers. Before anyone could stop him, the manager cleaned up the counter. No fingerprints were taken.

Detective Mike Baskin and several highway patrolmen searched the area for the gray pickup, without success. Baskin telephoned Detective Captain Smith at home, awakening him.

"Treat it as a crime scene," Smith said.

The amount of money missing was estimated by the manager as $167.

Donna Denice Haraway has not been seen or heard from since.

The next day, Sunday, while Denice's mother and sister and stepfather waited, shaken and tearful, at police headquarters, her husband, Steve Haraway, also a senior at the local college, joined police, state troopers, members of the Ada Amateur Radio Club and the Ada Rifle and Pistol Club, as well as Haraway's Pi Kappa Alpha fraternity brothers, in a sweeping search of the 714 square miles of Pontotoc County. No sign was found of the woman or the truck.

The disappearance took place too late to make the Sunday edition of the town's only newspaper, the Ada *Evening News*. But on Monday afternoon it was the lead story. MISSING: LOCAL CLERK ABDUCTED, said the front-page headline. Below were the details as provided by the police, to one side a photograph of Donna Denice Haraway, with dark eyes, long hair falling well below her shoulders, a delicate chain necklace over her sweater.

In the days that followed, rumors blew through town: perhaps she had faked her own disappearance; perhaps she had run off with a lover; perhaps she was involved in drug trafficking. But to those who knew Denice Haraway, this seemed impossible. Shy with strangers, warm and sweet with friends, she was a responsible person, had worked in fast-food restaurants and convenience stores since she was thirteen to help support her family and to pay her way through school, always telephoning if she'd be late. She was due to graduate from East Central in a few months, had been student-teaching, studying for her exams. By all accounts her eight-month-old marriage, to the son of a prominent local dentist and Rotary Club member, was a happy one. She was not the kind of person to run off. On Monday morning, when she did not show up for her student-teaching position at Hayes Elementary School, many of her second-grade pupils cried.

By that time the police, theorizing that she had most likely been a rape victim, already believed she was dead. They knew that most rape victims who survive find their way to a road or a phone within a few hours.

The disappearance prompted young couples to buy handguns at the Ada Trading Post on Main Street. An artist from the Oklahoma State Bureau of Investigation (O.S.B.I.) drew composite sketches of two suspects, from descriptions supplied in large part by a clerk at J.P.'s Pak-to-Go, another convenience store up the road. That clerk said two men had been in her store, acting "weird," and had driven off in a gray-primered pickup minutes before Denice Haraway disappeared. When the sketches of the two men—both with shoulder-length sandy hair—appeared on television and in the *Evening News*, police received scores of phone calls. More than thirty callers said the picture on the right looked like a local boy, Billy Charley. More than thirty callers said the same picture looked like another local boy, Tommy Ward. Other callers gave dozens of other names.

Police questioned Charley, Ward, and others. Charley came in with his parents, who swore he had been at home that night. He was never a suspect again. Ward, a twenty-four-year-old Ada native, said he'd been fishing with a friend, Karl Fontenot. Police asked Fontenot to come in for questioning. When he did not appear, they did not pursue it. Neither Ward nor Fontenot owned a pickup, or any kind of vehicle.

One night, Denice Haraway's family spoke to a psychic, who told them where the body was: eight miles east of town, under a bridge over a creek, near a water tower, with the number seven hanging symbolically over the scene. Detective Dennis Smith, Smith's wife, and their two teenage sons piled into the family car with flashlights and picked up Mike Baskin. About eight miles east of town they saw a water tower, a creek, a bridge. The water tower was for Rural Water District 7. They got out and approached the bridge, and smelled the foul stench of death. Under the bridge they found the rotting carcass of a calf.

A year earlier, in nearby Seminole County, a young woman had disappeared under almost identical circumstances—missing from the convenience store where she was working, leaving behind her car, her purse, her keys. That case had never been solved. Four months before that, a young woman had been raped and murdered in her Ada apartment. The police believed they knew who had done it. But the man had never been brought to trial, for lack of evidence. Because of these two cases, there was great pressure on the Ada police to solve the Haraway case.

But spring became summer. The class of '84 was graduated from East Central University, one of its members conspicuously absent. The lilacs and hollyhocks and roses took turns blooming on the small lawns that front most of Ada's one-family houses. The pecan trees sprouted green husks. Reward money offered in the case reached $10,000. Still, no progress was made.

It wasn't for lack of trying. Searches through the countryside were a constant preoccupation. One day a woman relayed, through her lawyer, a dream she'd had which told where the body was. Police dutifully searched the spot. They found nothing. Detectives lay awake at night, trying to think of someplace they hadn't looked. By day they sometimes bolted from their desks to check out a new hunch. Slowly the case was eating away at the belly of the law.

Then, in early October, came the break police say solved the case. Trying to substantiate a tip connecting Tommy Ward with Denice Haraway's disappearance, Smith and Baskin drove to Norman, eighty miles away. Their hearsay information did not check out, but the detectives were surprised to discover that Tommy Ward himself was now living in Norman, working for an aluminum-siding company. When Ward got off work, they questioned him for nearly two hours on videotape, after advising him of his rights. He denied repeatedly that he had had anything to do with the disappearance. But when asked where he'd been that night, he said he'd been with his brother-in-law—a different alibi from the fishing story he had given at first. The police asked if he would take a voluntary lie-detector test in a few days. Ward said he would. He had nothing to hide, he said.

When Smith and Baskin drove home that night, they were already convinced that Ward had killed Denice Haraway.

Tommy Ward grew up at the edge of Ada, seventh of the eight children of Jesse and Susie Ward. Jesse Ward worked at the glass plant for thirty-two years before his death from cancer in 1979, but his wages were always spread thin. Tommy and his brothers and sisters lived in a house without plumbing, wore hand-me-downs, were alternately laughed at and pitied by the other kids at school. Tommy was a slow learner but a good kid, nice, polite.

When he was eight years old, he was playing at a power plant near the family house and got his hand caught in the moving gears of a machine. Some bones in his hand were crushed before he was pulled free, narrowly escaping a more serious injury. When he was ten, he fell into a large concrete bunker filled with mud, and was sinking quickly until rescuers threw him a rope and saved his life. At twelve, he climbed a tree and fell about forty feet to the ground; he was taken to the hospital, dazed and choking, but soon recovered.

"He was always getting into situations where he was about to die, and then getting out of them," his sister Tricia recalled.

After his father died, he began waking up from nightmares. He told his mother they were too horrible to talk about. He would draw pictures instead—of fantastic animals that no one had ever seen. He started using drugs, got in with a bad crowd. He was arrested several times for misdemeanors, like being drunk and disorderly, but never for anything violent.

Before he went for the lie-detector test, Tommy phoned his mother. He told her he was frightened. "Just tell the truth and you'll be O.K.," Miz Ward, as she is known, advised her youngest son.

On Thursday, October 18, 1984, Tommy Ward went to Oklahoma City and took a polygraph. It was administered by Agent Rusty Featherstone of the O.S.B.I. Throughout the examination, Ward said he had no involvement in the Haraway case. When it was over, the agent told him he was lying, that he had failed the test, that he was holding something back.

Ward insisted that it wasn't so. Then, by his account, he remembered a dream he had had the night he was first questioned. And, he says, he told the police the following dream:

I had a dream that I was at a keg party and then, poof, that I was sitting in a pickup with two guys and a girl. Then this one guy started kissing this girl, and she told him to leave her alone. Then I told him to leave her alone. Then he said, If you don't like it you can go home. Then I looked out the window and we was at the power plant. Then I looked back at him and one of the guys was gone. Then I told him to take me home. Then he said, You are home. Then I looked out the window and I was home. Then, poof, I was at the sink trying to get something black off my arm and I couldn't get it off. Then I woke up.

When he finished, the police told him that it wasn't a dream, that what Tommy was saying had really happened. Tommy denied this. Then, he says, they asked him who the two men in the truck had been, and he said he didn't know, it was only a dream; and Detective Smith said it was Karl Fontenot and Odell Titsworth, wasn't it; and Tommy said no, but if that's who you want it to be, then that's who it was. It went on that way all afternoon, according to Ward. Police would suggest details of the crime. Tommy would at first deny them and then go along, figuring, as he later said, If I tell them lies and they find out they ain't true, they'll let me go.

By early evening, after more than five hours of questioning, the police made a videotape of Tommy Ward. In the tape he is slouched in a chair, drinking a Coke, puffing on a cigarette, telling in grisly detail, his voice flat, almost bored, how he and Karl Fontenot and an ex-con named Odell Titsworth had kidnapped Denice Haraway, driven to a power plant on the outskirts of town, and raped her and cut her; and how he, Tommy, had then left and the others had killed her and tossed her "off the bunker on Sandy Creek."

Most of his statements were in answer to police questions. "She was screaming and everything, and he [Titsworth] was telling her to keep her mouth shut. And he started slapping around on her. And then he pulled his knife out and cut her on the side a little bit, and told her that if she kept on struggling, that he was going to kill her. . . . I was holding her head down. I was holding her by her hair of her head. . . . He [Fontenot] was standing beside the pickup, laughing. . . . [Later] Karl was still raping her, and she had tremendous cuts all over her."

The only reference to a dream on the thirty-minute tape was in a final statement: "I knew I wouldn't have done it if I wasn't drunk, because I thought it was just a dream. And I know me, and I know I wouldn't do anything like that at all. It wasn't me."

Ward was arrested and handcuffed and taken back to Ada, and placed in the one-story windowless cement fortress that is the Pontotoc County jail. The next day Karl Fontenot was arrested. In short order, after first denying any involvement, he, too, made a videotaped confession, in which he said he and Ward and Titsworth, a well-known local tough with four felony convictions, had raped and killed Denice Haraway.

The Ward tape and the Fontenot tape were in agreement that Odell Titsworth had been the ringleader, had had the truck, had done the actual killing. But there were many discrepancies between the two tapes as to how the crime had been committed. The biggest discrepancy concerned the disposal of the body. Fontenot's tape, unlike Ward's, said they had burned the body in an abandoned house near the power plant and then had burned down the house.

"What portion of the house was this in, Karl?"

"It was in one of the bedrooms."

". . . Did you go through the front door portion of the house?"

"Yes."

". . . And then what did you do after you poured the gas on her?"

"We lit the house. We lit the gas and burned the house and her."

"Did the whole house catch on fire or just part of it?"

"It just more or less built itself up, flames built up."

". . . Who lit the match to start it?"

"Odell."

Police arrested Odell Titsworth, who maintained his innocence. The police went public. They said Tommy Ward and Karl Fontenot had confessed, and both had implicated Titsworth. And they summarized the stories on the tapes.

The next morning Tommy Ward called his sister Tricia from the jail. He told her the police said he had killed the Haraway woman, and that he would get the death penalty for it. But he didn't do it, he said, crying. All he had done, he told Tricia, was tell them a dream he'd had. She'd better get him a lawyer.

If the case indeed was solved, the problem of proving it had only begun. Because within a few days the embarrassed police had cleared Odell Titsworth of any involvement. It had come to their attention that two days before Denice Haraway was abducted the police themselves had broken Titsworth's arm, between his elbow and his shoulder, allegedly while he was resisting arrest during a domestic disturbance. There were hospital records to prove his arm had been in a cast the night of Denice's disappearance; doctors said he could not possibly have done what was described on the tapes. He also had alibi witnesses. And when police asked Fontenot to pick out Titsworth's photograph, Fontenot couldn't. He didn't know what Titsworth looked like. The police explanation for all this was that Ward and Fontenot were guilty and had agreed to place most of the blame on Titsworth.

Then came another setback for the police. The burned-out house that Fontenot had described was searched minutely for evidence of bone fragments, teeth, fillings. Not a speck was found to indicate that a human body had been destroyed there. During the search the owner of the house came forward. He informed the police he had burned it down himself, ten months before the night in question. Nothing but a six-inch-high foundation was there the night Denice Haraway disappeared.

Little by little the story on the tapes was turning out to be fantasy. And yet there they were: Ward and Fontenot, on separate tapes, saying they had done it, laconic as they described the torture.

For twenty days the two young men were held in jail, without being formally charged with anything, while police sought further evidence.

Tricia Ward Wolf is a sturdy, pleasant, churchgoing young woman who has been the backbone of the Ward clan ever since their father died. When any of the kids were in trouble, they turned to her—as Tommy was doing now. She had a husband, Bud, who worked at the feed mill, three young children, two foster kids she was helping to raise—and very little money. When she recovered from the first shock of Tommy's arrest—she believed he could not possibly have done such a thing—she and her brother Joel sought a lawyer. Friends told her that settling for a court-appointed attorney would be signing her brother's death warrant. But several local attorneys refused to take the case. Then the family heard about Don Wyatt, whose new office building, not far from McAnally's, looked almost like a church.

Don Wyatt—a maverick among the town's attorneys, a former assistant D.A. who now specialized in accident and injury suits—had read the papers, had heard about the confessions. He didn't want to take these people's money merely to file a guilty plea. But he went to see Tommy Ward, several times. He came away believing there was a strong possibility that Ward and Fontenot were innocent. He took the case. Joel, an auto mechanic, scraped together $3,000 as a retainer. The rest of Wyatt's substantial fee was to be paid within a year—or the lawyer would get title to the ramshackle house in which all the Wards had grown up.

Wyatt filed a writ of habeas corpus. The suspects had to be charged or set free. On November 7, 1984, after nearly three weeks in jail, Tommy Ward and Karl Fontenot were formally charged with robbery, kidnapping, rape, and murder. They were ordered held without bail.

There was still no body.

In early November it would have been difficult to find a dozen people in Ada who did not believe that Tommy Ward and Karl Fontenot had abducted, raped, and brutally murdered Denice Haraway. Down at the mill some of the workers were saying things like: "Those Wards. They're all no good. They ought to kill them all."

In its wild-West days, Ada was renowned as an open city, a haven for outlaws. The proudest moment in its past was the day in 1909 when angry citizens lynched four itinerant thugs accused of killing a local man. It was, in the words of a history book published by an Ada bank, "one mob action in America entirely justified in the eyes of God and man." Now the town was in a lynch mood again. Call after call came into police headquarters threatening that Ward and Fontenot would be killed. It is only forty-three steps across a neat green lawn under a pecan tree from the county jail to the courthouse, but a hearing was held in the jail for Ward's own protection.

The terrible anguish of Denice Haraway's family slowly metamorphosed into the painful acceptance, perhaps in all but the deepest places within, of what now seemed to be fact: that they would never see her again.

Karl Fontenot, his mother dead and his father long gone, heard that his two sisters in Ada had moved to the West Coast, without having come to see him.

For the Ward family, the shadows lengthened. In Tulsa, Joel got middle-of-the-night phone calls on three successive Saturdays, threatening that the entire Ward family would be wiped out. In school, Tricia's ten-year-old daughter was taunted repeatedly about her "killer" uncle. Her grades plummeted; day after day she came home crying.

And Tommy Ward's "dream"—if that's what it had been—was triggering other dreams.

Tricia dreamed she saw Tommy strapped into a chair, being injected with a lethal poison—the prescribed method of execution in Oklahoma—then slumping over, dead. She woke up trembling. Two nights later she had the same dream.

A schoolteacher named Arlene Cameron, in a nearby village called Happyland, dreamed she saw Denice Haraway's body on wooded land a few acres from her house. She told a friend. The two women spent an autumn afternoon trekking through the underbrush. They did not find a corpse in Happyland.

One day Detectives Smith and Baskin went into the jail carrying a paper sack. They approached Tommy Ward. From the sack they pulled a skull, and said, or implied, it was Denice Haraway's. They urged him to explain what he had done with the body.

The skull had been borrowed from the biology lab of East Central University.

Joel remembered a different dream of Tommy's, several months before Denice Haraway disappeared. Tommy had been riding his motorcycle near Tulsa when it broke down. Joel went to pick him up. They went to Joel's house, watched television. On the news was a story of a young woman who had been hit by a car and killed. Her mutilated body had been dragged for a quarter of a mile by the car before it came loose.

In the middle of the night, Joel heard Tommy screaming from the living-room sofa. Tommy told Joel he'd just had a terrible dream. He'd dreamed he was the one driving the car that killed the woman.

Christmas passed, and New Year's Day. At the county jail, awaiting a preliminary hearing, Ward entered his third month of virtual solitary confinement. He had no television, no books except a Bible, no magazines, visitors for no more than ten minutes on Sundays, seen through a small glass window. A churchgoer in his youth, he began to write religious poems to pass the time. Karl Fontenot had not had a single visitor since he was arrested. Alone in the city jail, he drew pictures and tried to strike up conversations with the police.

Ward had told his family he'd been using a lot of drugs in the spring and hadn't remembered what he was doing on the night in question. Now, cold turkey, he remembered, he said. The fishing trip had been another day. The party he'd talked about had been Friday night, not Saturday. On Saturday night he had been at home. That was God's honest truth, he said, and from now on he would stick to the truth. The lies he'd told on the videotape had gotten him into trouble, he realized, instead of clearing him.

The person charged with prosecuting the Haraway case was District Attorney Bill Peterson, scion of a wealthy Ada family, whose grandfather had donated the land for the college football stadium, whose father was a prominent local physician for half a century till he was killed at seventy-two when a tree he was cutting down fell on him. Researching the case, Peterson found two previous cases in Oklahoma law that might be called "no body" cases. One dated to 1909, when a pioneer woman was accused of murdering her husband while they were crossing the state in a covered wagon. Months later, a charred pile of bones was found where the murder allegedly had occurred. Technology at the time was not advanced enough to prove that the bones were her husband's, but the woman was convicted. In the second case, in Oklahoma County in 1983, a man was convicted of killing his wife and throwing her body into the sea from an airplane. The body was never found. But in that case, too, there was some physical evidence: traces of blood were found in the plane and in the trunk of the man's car. In the Haraway case there was no physical evidence whatever.

These two convictions, as well as the notion of corpus delicti, were the legal underpinnings of Peterson's case. Despite a common misconception, the principle of corpus delicti in a murder case does not require the presence of a corpse. The phrase means "the body of the crime" ("body" referring to the act itself and the people involved in the act); it was Peterson's contention that the fact that Denice Haraway had disappeared from all her normal routines, had not been seen or heard from by anyone she knew, and was not the kind of person who would run off was ample circumstantial evidence, beyond a reasonable doubt, that she had been killed. About the theoretical possibility that she had faked an abduction and was still alive, he said, "Elephants could fly. But they don't."

The preliminary hearing to determine whether there was enough evidence to bring the suspects to trial was held in January 1985. Normally such hearings take a few hours, sometimes only a few minutes. In the Haraway case it took five full days of testimony, spread out over a month. When Peterson emphasized that no one had seen or heard from the woman since April 28, George Butner, Karl Fontenot's court-appointed attorney, responded, "Amelia Earhart, too, but that doesn't make her dead."

Two witnesses testified they were sure Tommy Ward was one of the two men they'd seen "acting weird" at J.P.'s, the store up the road from McAnally's. The three witnesses at McAnally's itself were less certain. Lenny Timmons, who had passed in the doorway about two feet away as Denice Haraway and a man left, said his certainty the man was Ward, on a scale of one to ten, was about a six.

No one could place Karl Fontenot at either scene.

Then, without warning, Tommy Ward changed his story, as though he were trying to conform to what the witnesses had said. He said he *had* been at McAnally's that night, but with another man he named, who, he said, had kissed Denice Haraway and asked her to run away with him. And she had.

The hearing was recessed for several days while police checked the story. It wasn't true.

To the angry frustration of his lawyer and his family, Ward admitted he was making up stories again.

Tricia Wolf sat in the crowded courtroom day after day, hoping—almost expecting—Denice Haraway to walk in. It didn't happen. When the videotapes of the confessions were played, spectators wept.

At the conclusion of the hearing, Special District Judge John D. Miller threw out the rape charges for lack of evidence. But he ordered Ward and Fontenot to stand trial on charges of robbery, kidnapping, and murder.

Winter became spring in Ada. Judge Ronald Jones, assigned to try the case, suddenly withdrew from it in the midst of hearing assorted legal motions. He gave no reason. The view of the town was that with no body, and with Tommy Ward and Karl Fontenot already in jail for six months without a trial, it was becoming a political hot potato.

It took the state supreme court two weeks to name a replacement. Donald Powers, a retired judge from several counties away, would come to Ada to hear the case. He had a reputation for running a no-nonsense courtroom.

A friend of Tricia's who had worked at a different convenience store with Denice Haraway years ago told her about how Denice used to be in love with a man from Texas. "Maybe he came back for her and they ran off." Tricia, pregnant with her fourth child, clung to the theory hopefully. "I know I'm clutching at straws," she said, "but when your brother's in jail accused of murder, you clutch at straws."

Unknown to Tricia, the police had had that fellow checked out by the Texas Rangers months before. The man worked on oil rigs. He had been working offshore the night Denice Haraway disappeared.

In late April, a week before the anniversary of his wife's disappearance, Steve Haraway, now a pharmaceutical salesman, went to a party at the home of a friend. A college fraternity brother invited him to a big bash the following week, which many alumni would attend. "I won't have a date," he recalls Steve saying. "I guess I can't have a date for six more years."

The name of the frat bash was "Dream Girl."

In June, with attorneys on both sides asking for more time—and with summer vacations scheduled—Judge Powers set a September trial date. The suspects remained in jail. The summer in Ada was hot, humid. Defense attorney Wyatt sent a private investigator from Yukon, Oklahoma, into the field to seek evidence that might clear Tommy Ward.

People who had known Ward and Fontenot growing up found it difficult to believe they could have done what they had described on the tapes. Tommy had always been the baby of his family. Fontenot was known on the street as an abandoned soul who would tell any tall tale to get attention. He idolized Tommy and was proud to have him as a friend. They weren't well educated, and they certainly had problems, but they did not seem capable of such a vicious crime. For some people, the joker in the deck was drugs. Perhaps, they felt, Tommy's "dream" was a repressed memory of a violent act committed while stoned. But others found flaws in this explanation. If the two men were that stoned, how could they have disposed of a body and a pickup truck so efficiently that no trace of either could be found? But most who did not know them, especially in the more affluent sections of town, were convinced they were guilty. If they weren't guilty, why had they made the tapes? If they weren't guilty, who was?

"Twenty thousand eyes will be watching that trial," a college friend of Steve Haraway's said. "If they convict them [without a body], it will go down in the textbooks. . . . If they ever get out of jail, I don't think they'll live."

The trial of Thomas Jesse Ward and Karl Allen Fontenot, case CRF-84-183, began in the Pontotoc County courthouse, a three-story stone building in downtown Ada, on September 9. Defense motions for a change of venue, on the ground that a fair trial could not be held in Ada, had been denied.

The state's case was much the same as it had been at the preliminary hearing eight months before. There was no new physical evidence. More than twenty relatives of Denice Haraway's, from her mother and her husband to great-aunts and second cousins, testified that they had not seen or heard from her since the day she disappeared. An O.S.B.I. criminal analyst testified that extensive, continuing computerized checks had shown that Denice Haraway had not obtained a driver's license in any of the fifty states, or been arrested, or been hospitalized, and that no unidentified body found anywhere in America was hers. Three witnesses placed Tommy Ward in the vicinity of McAnally's that night. No one could identify Karl Fontenot. The three men who had seen Denice leaving McAnally's with a man repeated their story. Two could make no identifications. Lenny Timmons, who had passed within two feet of them in the doorway, said the man resembled Tommy Ward. On a scale of one to ten, his certainty was still a six.

Ironically, much of the state's case had to be spent disproving major parts of the taped confessions—for instance, that Odell Titsworth had done the actual killing. The state proved that Odell Titsworth could not have been involved. It proved the house allegedly involved had burned to the ground ten months before the disappearance. It concluded its case by showing the jury the tapes: a horrible tale of rape, stabbing, murder.

"Was it a dream to Denice," Bill Peterson asked, "or a living nightmare?"

The defense focused on three main contentions:

● That the police had manipulated the not-too-bright defendants into turning Tommy's dream into confessions. To support this, they called Odell Titsworth to the stand. He said his interrogation had been so fierce and accusatory that, back in his cell, he almost believed he had done it—till he remembered he'd been at home with a broken arm.

"The tapes are gruesome," Don Wyatt told the jury. "But they aren't true."

When the tape of the October 12 questioning of Ward was played, in which for two hours he claimed he was innocent, the defense attorneys repeatedly pointed out that most of the elements in the later confessions were contained in the police questions during this earlier interview. Part of that tape went like this:

Dennis Smith: "What do you think happened to this girl?"

Tommy Ward: "I don't know."

Dennis Smith: "Use your imagination. Two guys took her, got her in a pickup, took her away. What do you think they did with the body?"

Tommy Ward: "No telling."

Dennis Smith: "Use your imagination. What do you think? . . ."

Mike Baskin: "Do you think she screamed? I bet whoever did it can still hear her screaming. What do you think?"

Tommy Ward: "I didn't do it."

Defense attorney Butner hammered away at the idea that all the actions in the later confession had been planted during this interview. Punching his fist into his hand, he enumerated them: "Two men, pickup, kidnapping, raped, murdered, screamed, ran away, slipped and fell, cried."

Under cross-examination, the police admitted they had lied to Ward during this interview, telling him they had witnesses who in fact did not exist. They said this is standard procedure in obtaining confessions.

• That Tommy Ward could not have done it. One of his sisters, Joice, testified he had been at home with her and her children all that evening. And three persons said Tommy's normally long hair, similar to that in the composite drawings, had been cut short the week before Denice Haraway disappeared. His nineteen-year-old sister, Kay, swore under oath she had cut his hair above his ears on April 20. His brother-in-law Bud, a devout churchgoer, swore he had seen and joked with Tommy about his short haircut on April 21. A friend of Ward's produced Polaroid pictures of Tommy with short hair, hand-dated "4-22-84": Easter Sunday, a week before the disappearance. But the friend had two drug convictions, and Assistant District Attorney Chris Ross, in his summation, said, "Her credibility stinks." A picture of the woman's little girl, taken with the same film, had an unopened Easter basket in it. For a time it seemed that this basket might prove Tommy Ward's innocence. But the state, in closing, suggested the picture could have been taken during Easter of '83.

• That other suspects were more likely culprits. The defense called its private investigator, Richard Kerner, to the stand, a man with twenty years' experience as an air-force intelligence officer. Kerner testified about his own investigation, which had led to several gray-primered pickups connected to unsavory characters whose descriptions matched the composite drawings. He named from the witness stand his primary suspect: a man who had been present in the courtroom, seated in the last row, during each of the five scattered days of the preliminary hearing—suggesting an inordinate interest in the case. The investigator discovered that the man had a nephew who lived near the store, who resembled Tommy Ward, and who had a light-colored pickup truck. Two witnesses who had placed Tommy Ward in the area that night said that the man in the courtroom looked much more like Ward's companion than Karl Fontenot did. The man had first told the defense attorneys that he had been in Ada at the time, and then later denied it. Through Kerner's testimony, the defense hoped that the state would feel compelled to put this so-called mystery man on the stand, so that they could, during cross-examination, suggest to the jury that the wrong men were on trial. In the end, the jury never saw him. He was not called by either side. His conflicting statements offstage went unexplained.

After nine days of testimony, the jury of eight women and four men deliberated for one day while the Haraways and the Wards sat a row apart in the crowded courtroom, waiting. An hour into the second day, the jury came in with its verdicts:

Thomas Jesse Ward: Guilty of robbery with a dangerous weapon. Guilty of kidnapping. Guilty of murder in the first degree.

Karl Allen Fontenot: Guilty of robbery with a dangerous weapon. Guilty of kidnapping. Guilty of murder in the first degree.

Tommy Ward broke down crying in the courtroom. Karl Fontenot showed no reaction.

Following the verdicts, a sentencing hearing was held, in which the jury would set the penalty on the murder charge: either life imprisonment or death. The state called one witness: a woman who claimed that on July 30, 1984, Ward and another man had run her car off the road with a pickup and smashed her windshield with a board. Ward's family maintained that he had no pickup, and had been living and working in Norman that summer. But the charge went unanswered from the witness stand. Instead the defense called only Tommy's mother. Miz Ward, barely audible, told the jury her son had not committed these crimes. She asked the jurors to spare his life. One juror cried.

"It may be that somewhere Denice Haraway walks this land," a defense attorney warned. "Don't commit the ultimate mistake."

Three hours later, the jury handed down its unanimous sentences: For Tommy Ward—death. For Karl Fontenot—death.

Ward was sobbing as deputies led him from the courtroom. "Why are they doing this to me?" he asked his sister. "I didn't do it!"

Steve Haraway's father, the dentist, shook hands with the district attorney, and thanked him. "I feel better now," he said.

The most important legal issue in the case was whether the state had, in fact, proved the corpus delicti—that a crime had been committed, and that the defendants were linked to it. Under Oklahoma law, the corpus delicti must be proved independently before any confession can be entered into evidence. In the privacy of his chambers, minutes after the trial ended, Judge Powers volunteered that his ruling in favor of the state on the corpus delicti issue had been "a close call." Had he ruled otherwise, the tapes could not have been shown, and the men would probably have been acquitted.

"I welcome a review by the court of appeals," the judge said. "I think I made the right decision. But I certainly don't want anyone to die for the wrong reason."

Throughout the case there had been discussion about the possibility of a sentence of life imprisonment in return for the body. Tommy Ward and Karl Fontenot, now under sentence of death, still insisted they didn't know where the body was, because they hadn't done it.

The two suspects originally described in the case both had light hair. Karl Fontenot's hair is black as coal. All such exculpatory facts had been swept away by the confessions. As Fontenot's attorney had feared, "the tapes married them together."

In the town, those who had believed from the beginning that the suspects were guilty were confirmed in their beliefs. But many remained unpersuaded. One of these was the most respected criminal lawyer in the region, Barney Ward (no kin to Tommy Ward), an attorney in Ada for thirty-three years. "I don't think they did it," Barney Ward said. "Or if they did, they weren't alone. I don't know these boys, but they're not what you'd call Rhodes scholars. I'm sure they've been offered a deal: turn in who did it or tell where the body is and we'll go easy. But they haven't done that. I don't think they're that loyal. Or that smart. I don't think they know where the body is. Of course, the terrible thing is, if they didn't do it, whoever did is still out there."

The formal sentence of death was pronounced by Judge Powers on October 25, setting in motion an automatic appeal that could take years, that might someday bring the case to the Supreme Court. As the young men were taken away to the state penitentiary, the pecans were ripening on the trees in front of the courthouse, and in front of the jail, and on the old Ward property that had been sold to pay the lawyers, and in the grassy yards of Ada. As they ripened they were taken to a garagelike building near Main Street, filled with machinery, with a sign out front that says: PECAN CRACKER.

The way the machinery works is this. For seventeen cents a pound, the pecans are poured into the funnel-like top of a set of meshing gears. As they pass through the gears the pecans are cracked, crushed. But some small ones slip through. They drop into another set of gears, which mesh closer. Those that survive again fall to a lower level, to gears that crunch tighter still. In the end, no pecans are too small to be cracked and broken, and to tumble in pieces into unmarked paper sacks.

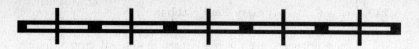

GARY PAUL NABHAN

Harvest
Time

From ENDURING SEEDS

I t is harvest weather. The sky at sunrise is pouring mauve and burnt-orange light out over the undulating land. Farmers' windbreaks, rising between grain fields and wheatgrass pastures, are stained with these same tones: burnt orange and mauve leaves are showering the ground. Only a sprinkle of rain mixes with this morning's wind, but rolling fog threatens to mask the terrain. The weather is pressing humankind to gather what is still left standing in the fields, for soon all will change.

I rose early to begin the drive from Bismarck and Mandan, northeastward toward the geographic center of North America. But before reaching the continental midpoint, I veered westward from the Missouri River at Lake Sakakawea. Following the waters of the reservoir upstream I arrived at New Town, North Dakota, tribal headquarters of the Hidatsa, Arikara (Ree), and Mandan. Along the Upper Missouri, this time of year was once called "the moon of ripe maize." In weather so uncertain, the Indian farmers of the Missouri floodplain would work tirelessly to pull all the maize and squash out of the fields.

Now their former fields lie beneath yards of water behind Garrison Dam. These fields of native maize were at one time so elegant that they deeply impressed botanist John Bradbury, who had encountered corn before in the eastern United States and in tropical Latin America, but none that could compare with the fields on the Upper Missouri in

1811: "I have not seen, even in the United States, any crop of Indian corn in finer order or better managed than the corn about the three villages." He added, "The women . . . are excellent cultivators."

Having read such reports of the historic richness of Mandan, Hidatsa, and Arikara agriculture, I had always admired them. Now, visiting the honey-colored shortgrassed plains and badlands where these tribes live, I admired the beauty of their country as well. At the same time, I realized that 155,000 acres of the Three Affiliated Tribes' holdings—including nearly all of their Class I and Class II farmlands on the fertile bottomlands—were drowned in the 1950s by the filling of Lake Sakakawea, a flood control and irrigation development that serves relatively few non-Indians downstream. The "Village Indians" were forced to move their farmlands away from the river, onto the shortgrass prairies, mesas, and badlands that their ancestors chose not to cultivate.

I was curious about the effects of the move. Like many other ethnic groups around the world, each of these three cultures has within its oral history the memory of being forced out of other regions before settling in the Upper Missouri Valley. Tradition recalls that the Mandan first crossed the Mississippi River at the Falls of Saint Anthony, and archaeologists set the date of Mandan arrival in Dakota country around 1100 A.D. Perhaps by 1300 A.D., the Archaic Mandan became the first village agriculturists of the Upper Missouri. Around 1650, all the Mandan groups that had previously been scattered along the Missouri floodplain were pushed out of South Dakota and southern North Dakota, to become concentrated around the Heart River, a Missouri tributary. This is where the first European visitors to the area found them farming, roughly two hundred and fifty years after Columbus.

The Arikara and Hidatsa have inhabited this stretch of the Missouri for a shorter period of time, but they too have become "native" to the region in terms of the profound way they have adapted to the environment there. The proto-Arikara moved into the Upper Missouri after 1400, after being driven out of the central, semi-arid plains, perhaps by warfare or by an extended drought.

Hidatsa legend maintains that the tribe emerged into its present existence after climbing up a vine from beneath Devil's Lake in northeastern North Dakota. Archaeologists speculate that the linguistically-related, allied groups pushed their way up from northern Illinois into the Red River Valley around 1500, but did not become the unified Hidatsa tribe within North Dakota lands until about 1700. Other scholars suggest that the proto-Hidatsa were a subtribe of the Crow, which split away from the parent tribe around 1650. Sometime before 1700, they obtained corn and other seed from the Mandans, and "relearned" or adapted their agricultural knowledge to fit to their new homeland. Smallpox epidemics beginning in the 1780s, and later threats from the Sioux, encouraged these three tribes to cooperate with one another whenever times got hard.

I felt disturbed and a bit saddened when I arrived in New Town, for I knew that hard times had hit these tribes often, despite a history of them sharing their resources with various neighbors. Given the severity of disruptions that they had suffered since 1790—smallpox, droughts, land grabs, grasshopper infestations, and inundations—it is amazing that they have made their way through to the "New Town" era at all.

When the earlier towns of Van Hook and Sanish were being evacuated as the waters behind the dam rose in the 1950s, the tribes had a contest to decide what they should name their newly combined, relocated community. One suggestion—turned down in favor of the more upbeat name of New Town—was that the names of the old villages should also be combined, so that the community could be known as "Vanish."

The fact remains that the three tribes have not vanished, despite the thirty years their riverbottom farmlands have now been inundated. I wondered if their seeds and agricultural customs had vanished regardless of the persistence of the people themselves. More than anything else, I wanted to hear what these people had to say about any agrarian traditions that might remain.

What was left of the nineteen maize variants that had been described at their villages by various visitors between 1830 and 1920? Did the women still sow any of the kinds of squash that many American gardeners have grown this century? And what became of their handful of bean varieties, among them the progenitor of the Great Northern, at one time the most popular soup bean in America?

My concerns were not limited to the kinds of seeds that had survived, for good farming depends just as much on the survival of appropriate agricultural practices. Did any families continue to save and

select seed stocks, using the sophisticated techniques that their forebears had developed? Did the women still cook foods based on these
native plants, and had such ethnic specialties reinforced their sense
of cultural identity? Had their ways of farming changed when they
moved up to the exposed prairie mesas and plains?

The morning clouds began to dissipate. Sunshine broke through,
and I too lightened up, a little amused that I had arrived in an unfamiliar community carrying such a storm of questions in my head.
Admittedly, I also carried with me something more valuable than
curiosity, something I hoped to share with these people even if I never
got around to asking a single question.

I had brought along some seeds, long ago collected from these
tribes, seeds that deserved to grow in this watershed again, among
these people. I had small red Hidatsa beans, glossy and lovely in the
palm of my hand. And Arikara winter squash, an early Hubbard type,
with blue-green stripes on salmon skin, and puffy, pale, oval seeds.
These seeds were given to me by heirloom seedsaver Glenn Drowns.
I also carried seeds of a Mandan yellow pumpkin, last grown by Dan
Zwiener, and similar in seed size and shape to the early *Cucurbita pepo*
gourds raised in the Mississippi watershed thousands of years ago. And
the fine-tasting Arikara "yellow" beans, long and kidney-shaped, ranging in color from beige to yellow-orange.

These seeds had been donated by members of the Seed Savers
Exchange, but were progeny of seeds collected at Fort Berthold almost
a century ago. The varieties I had with me are mentioned in Oscar
H. Will & Co. seed catalogs at least as far back as 1913, but that
seedhouse continued to feature them until the late 1950s. Sometime
along the way, they had gotten into the hands of an heirloom seed
collector intent on seeing them survive even if they were never portrayed in a commercial catalog again. And so, they had been passed,
season to season, hand to hand, until they had landed in my luggage,
bound for their homeland once more.

The flaw in my plan was that I needed to find gardens in order to find
gardeners, and in New Town there were few to be seen. Gardens were
not common in the other large communities on the reservation, either.
On the drive in toward New Town, I had cruised White Shield on

the eastern Arikara side of the reservation to ask about a family that had once farmed quite a bit.

One of the men of this White Shield family talked with me at their newer tract house, miles away from where their fields once were. His response was polite, perfunctory, and the same that I heard elsewhere the next two days.

"No, we don't garden anymore," he said in an oddly cheerful tone. "Since we moved from out there in the country, we don't grow any corn anymore. It's been years since we moved away from it all."

I searched for gardens and fields of mixed crops as I passed homesteads that still remained "out in the country," but the few that I did see were of non-Indian families. About 45 percent of the remaining agricultural lands on the Fort Berthold Reservation has either been owned or leased by whites, who now plow large tracts of the shortgrass prairie for barley, wheat, oilseed sunflower, and safflower. The gardens they keep are filled mostly with zucchinis, hybrid sweet corn, and short-season tomatoes. In contrast, members of the three tribes have never become accustomed to tilling the upland soils in their new backyards for similar fields or gardens. Perceived as major limiting factors are the marauding gangs of dogs, children, and urban birds that might do considerable damage. Women repeatedly told me, "You just can't garden in town."

I remembered that 69 percent of the families had successful gardens back in 1948 when they were still in the bottomlands. And every year, the same women who tended those gardens with the help of their children canned or dried 23,000 quarts of wild fruit, gathered mostly from the floodplain and the wooded draws beneath the mesa tops. Wild plums, juneberries, chokecherries, and a ground bean were plants that proliferated along river banks or moist slopes above side streams.

I soon gained a sense of where the remaining "country people" lived, and how to tell a non-Indian lessee's farm operation or in-town house from those of tribal members. After roaming a while, I came upon the gardens of the Lone Fight brothers and sisters. They clustered around the old country house of their aunt, Mary White Body, on the edge of New Sanish, overlooking the lake.

A couple of frolicking boys chased each other around, through the three small gardens, and over to where my car was parked. "My aunt—she's not home. We'll go get my mother." The boys scurried indoors.

When they bolted back out of the door, soon followed by their mother, their cheeks were full, and they were chewing on a sugary brown chunk of some homemade sweet.

"Cornballs!" I exclaimed to myself, thinking of traveler Henry the Younger's first taste of them in 1806. He was presented with "a dish containing several balls, about the size of a hen's egg, made of pears [juneberries], dried meat, and parched corn, beaten together in a mortar. . . . Boiled for a short time . . . we found them most wholesome."

"Slow down on those cornballs, you boys!" Donna Lone Fight sighed. "Save some for later on!" After introductions, Donna and I wandered over to a garden planted by her twin brother, Donald. There, beets, watermelons, sweet corn, carrots, and honeydew plants were coming to the end of their season, but had produced amply. Donna pointed across the grass to a blue corn crop another brother had planted, and in a different direction to a third plot. I felt some relief—at least there was one native crop maturing in the garden.

"Did your family plant more before?" I asked.

"They did, but it all came to a stop around 1952 or 1953. They were from Old Sanish, and it's all underwater now. Trees, fields, schoolhouse, home. They say you can see a lot of it, standing there beneath the water. So many of them moved to New Town then. . . ." They haven't grown any of the old things over there, she explained. As another community member said when he saw the kinds of seeds I gave Donna, "There is so much that we forgot to take with us before the flood."

The boys ran past, still taking bites out of their cornballs. Donna had them run and get me one.

"That's an old kind of food here. Not many people make it anymore. An Indian woman over in Parshall comes around selling them now and then. Maybe she grows a lot of corn, or knows someone who does. She must use an awful lot of it."

I thanked Donna and the kids, gave them some seeds to try for the following year, and headed over to Parshall, fifteen miles away.

Vera Bracklin sat on a living room chair, exhausted, holding her granddaughter in her lap. She had just fed ten families who were mourning loved ones who had gone on.

No doubt Vera was used to large-scale cooking. Sometimes in one batch she would cook up thirty quarts of flour corn, juneberries or blueberries, kidney tallow, and sugar into 120 to 140 cornballs.

"What we call it . . . in Hidatsa, is *mah-pi*. For cornballs, you need soft corn, flour corn, to make it. Mine is corn from my mother-in-law. I can't raise it here, but there's a white lady who gives me room to plant out at her place." Vera Bracklin processed as much corn as she could get her hands on, for the door-to-door sales of cornballs helped to keep her family afloat.

It was the kind of work women in her family had done for a long time. She remembered the effort her grandmother made to cleanly thresh all their Great Northern Beans: "My grandmother used to raise a lot of beans. On a windy day, she'd put a tarp down. She'd take a panful of uncleaned beans, and let the wind blow the leaves away."

Vera glanced down, and looked tired again. "But then we lost everything," she recalled. "It seems like they lost the Indian way of living when the dam forced their relocation."

Vera's sentiments echoed those of Austin Engel immediately after the reservoir had flooded out the villages. The tribes had been paid a sum of five million dollars, to relocate 90 percent of their people, rebuild houses and roads, and develop new lands. And yet, village communities became dispersed in a way that made Engel feel that their "traditional source of stability is gone."

"Farming became more difficult," Engel explained. "We were far from the neighbors with whom we used to exchange work. The big farmer was taking over the West, and we didn't know how to compete, except to lease our land to him."

I recalled that earlier, others too had feared that the native ways might end, particularly after the smallpox epidemic of 1837. There had been epidemics prior to 1804, when Lewis and Clark wintered among these people, but the tribes had recovered in the years that followed. By the 1830s, when such notables as German Prince Alexander Philip Maximilian, Carl Bodmer, and George Catlin stayed with these tribes and recorded their customs, they were prosperous farmers, hunters, gatherers, and traders.

Prince Maximilian noted that they "cultivate . . . without ever manuring the ground, but their fields are on the low banks of the river . . . where the soil is particularly fruitful. . . . They have extremely fine maize of different species."

He was so impressed by their maize, beans, gourds, sunflowers, and tobacco, that he took seeds of these crops back to botanical gardens in Europe, where they flowered and presumably set seed. The transatlantic introduction of New World crops such as these did much to enrich Europe's royal gardens and peasant fields.

Catlin, with his eye for the landscape as a whole, gives us the feel of the extent and density of crops around their settlements: "We trudged back to the little village of earth covered lodges, which were hemmed in, and almost obscured to the eye, by the fields of corn and luxuriant growth of wild sunflowers, and other vegetable productions of the soil."

The Mandan tribal population had grown up to sixteen hundred by 1837. Then smallpox hit them like a tidal wave. A total of fifteen thousand people, native and immigrant, were killed by the disease on the Upper Missouri that year. Only one hundred and fifty Mandans survived, less than a tenth of their population. The Hidatsas were reduced to five hundred.

When John James Audubon came through their villages in 1843, the survivors' lives were in ruins. They were so distraught and weakened that their usually orderly villages had fallen into disrepair, and the stench of garbage and rotting animal remains was everywhere. Low mounds of dirt, under which smallpox victims were buried, dominated the surroundings instead of the fields of corn that Catlin had seen. After five or six years, these mounds were still barren of all vegetation. Audubon's traveling companion Edward Harris wrote that "the mortality was too great for them to give the usual burial rites of their people by elevating the bodies on a scaffold as described by Catlin."

Overall, Audubon could hardly believe that these were the same places that Catlin had portrayed as active ceremonial centers, with lovely earthen lodges laid out in regular rows. He wrote that "the sights daily seen will not bear recording; they have dispelled all the romance of Indian life I ever had."

The remnants of the two Sioux-speaking tribes, the Mandan and Hidatsa, abandoned their disease-torn villages to move together to a new location in 1845. There, they began to build another life at Like-A-Fishhook, a bend in the Missouri, where Fort Berthold soon became established. The Arikara families joined them in 1862, and considerable intertribal marriage began, perhaps out of necessity. Nevertheless, the Arikara tongue, a Caddoan—not a Siouxan—language, has persisted to this day, in the midst of the numerically dominant Mandan and Hidatsa.

Their agriculture was not intensively studied until a half century later, yet their ancient folk sciences of bottomland cultivation and seed selection had remained intact. Horticulturist-anthropologist George Will, Sr., wrote in 1930 that "through the terrible catastrophes of the 1830s . . . [and] continual harassing by the Sioux, the three tribes, the Mandan, Arikara, and Hidatsa, preserved their agricultural crops and varieties and carried them down even to the present."

Will's farming ethnographies were complemented by those of ethnobotanist Melvin Gilmore and oral historian Gilbert Wilson. Between the three of them, they documented many aspects of the remarkable folk science that still guided the agriculture of the three tribes after the turn of the century. In some ways, Wilson's recording of the farming knowledge shared by Buffalobird-Woman is the greatest testament to the intelligence of an individual native farmer that we have from this continent.

Buffalobird-Woman, or Maxidiwiac, told Gilbert Wilson how Hidatsa families began to develop new fields on bottomland soils, how they fallowed old ones, and why they chose not to plow up the sod on the shortgrass prairie ground in the hills to farm as the government wanted them to do: "The prairie fields get dry easily and the soil is harder and more difficult to work. Then I think our old way of raising corn is better than the new way taught to us by white men." To prove her point, the seventy-three-year-old woman referred to the quality of maize that she herself had raised in this manner. "Last year, 1911, our agent held an agricultural fair on this reservation. The corn which I sent to the fair took first prize. . . . I cultivated the corn exactly as in old times, with a hoe."

Maxidiwiac was aware that "corn could travel," and that strains planted within "traveling distance" of one another could be contaminated. To keep each of them pure, she planted different maize varieties some distance apart from one another, perhaps farther apart than corn pollen would normally travel. This was important, "for varieties had not all the same uses with us." Indiscriminate varietal intermixing would be costly. At the same time, "we Hidatsas knew that slightly different varieties could be produced by planting seeds that varied somewhat from the main stock." Her people selected these variants, not only for color, but for other qualities as well.

In view of their sophisticated practices of seed selection and isolation, is it any wonder that George Will gathered from the three tribes six kinds of flint corns, nine to ten kinds of flour corns, and a sweet corn? These maize variants differed not only in color, but in taste and texture, ear size, number of days to maturity, and bushiness of the foliage.

Most of these strains excelled in their hardiness, for they could survive the harshness of Dakota weather. They were, for the most part, short, heavily suckering plants, with ears developing at or near ground level, within a protective cover of foliage and heavy husks that shielded developing ears from frosts and hailstorms. The seeds could "sprout in spring weather that would rot most varieties of corn," Will claimed, and could produce harvestable ears after "about 60 days in a favorable year . . . rarely more than 70 days."

Such adaptations paid off, not only for the three tribes, but for thousands of white settlers on the Northern Plains who later adopted the native corn and beans. Before Will and others passed the three tribes' native strains on to the Montana Agricultural Experiment Station for evaluation, the European-American farmers in that state hardly grew any corn—they grew less than ten thousand acres in 1909. The dent corns accessible through catalogs from the East and Midwest simply did not have sufficient tolerance of the growing conditions found in the semi-arid West.

The Three Tribes' corns gained regional acceptance following widely publicized experiments by Atkinson and M. L. Wilson at the Montana station, which demonstrated the superiority of the northern flints. Will devoted a decade to promoting them through his family's mail-order seed business and his own writings. By 1924, Montana's corn acreage had increased to 420,000 acres. In fifteen years' time, the three tribes' flint corns had allowed nearly a fiftyfold increase in Montana maize production.

To be sure, these native corn varieties have made a tremendous contribution to Northern Plains agriculture. The fact remained that I had yet to see even a single mature plant of native maize on the Fort Berthold Reservation. And while Vera Bracklin had some corn planted in the garden of a non-Indian friend, she deferred to an older, more knowledgeable woman on the other side of the reservoir. "You should go see Cora Baker near Mandaree," she suggested. The Bakers, she explained, not only grew a variety of crops, but kept other traditions alive as well.

And so, on a rainy Sunday morning, I drove out from Mandaree through the rolling hills that spilled into Bear Den Creek. Fields are fewer on this far western side of the reservation, which gradually climbs into the badlands. The area had once been dismissed as "good country for rattlesnakes and horned toads," but that did not keep some families from the old Lucky Mound village from finding solace there after relocation. Bear Den Creek is perhaps more sinuous and wooded than the now-flooded Lucky Mound Creek, yet it may have been enough like it to have attracted the exiles from the lake floor.

As I came into the Baker homestead from the dirt road that ends at their driveway, I could see their garden. I walked to their door, hearing cornstalks rustling in the wind. Cora, a soft-spoken, intelligent-looking woman with neatly pulled-back gray hair, welcomed me in.

"Some people I've met around here the last few days thought that you would be one who might like to have some of these old seeds," I offered. "They say that you still grow others like these."

"Old seeds?" Cora asked, showing a subdued interest. "Could I see what you mean?"

I pulled out my now-crumpled envelopes from the Seed Savers Exchange, and poured Hidatsa red beans into Cora's hand. She just looked at them, saying nothing, as if seeing an old friend for the first time in years. She sat down, then looked at the other kinds of seed, identifying them and commenting on how they were used.

"May I keep them? May I grow these? Here, put some in envelopes for me. I'll go get you some of our family's Indian corn to try."

Cora came back with two ears of flour corn from her garden and a gallon jar full of seeds from her sister's field. She gave me a small bag filled with seeds from the jar, and also the two ears.

"Keep them separate," she warned me, "because corn can travel." She said that she was trying to sort the blue out of some of her white corn that had become mixed. By recurrent selection and roguing, she was working toward her goal, much as Buffalobird-Woman would have done seventy-five years ago.

And much as George Catlin's companions would have done 150 years ago, during the final harvest prior to the smallpox epidemic.

The continuity was there. Cora's daughter Mary talked with us, expressing the concerns of one who would not let these seeds escape again. "We had so much going for us down at Lucky Mound, it was hard to believe that we could have lost everything."

But everything had not been lost, neither Cora's family's seeds, nor the skills that they passed on to her. She told me how her family separated out the seed corn from that which they would eat, and braided the husks of the seed ears together, in an arc an arm's length in size.

While Mary and Cora spoke about their Hidatsa agricultural customs, I listened to their fine voices and to the falling leaves rustling against the windows and roof. My mind drifted off and settled on George Will's words about the harvest season of 1947: "The season of the year when the Indians of our Northern Plains used to harvest their main crop is here. The soft, hazy autumn days with hot noons and cool nights heralded the full ripening of the crops in the Indian fields. . . . All was bustle and confusion as the women and girls hastened to breakfast early from the always simmering pot of boiled corn, beans and meat which . . . hung over the fire. . . . As the women sat about the pile of corn for husking, the wise old grandmother kept her eyes open for plump, large and straight-rowed ears of pure color. These she took and put aside . . . for braiding."

Listening to Cora Baker speak, and hearing the wind scattering the leaves outside, I knew it was the time for braiding seedstocks together again.

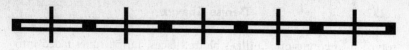

DENISE CHÁVEZ

The Last of the Menu Girls

NAME: Rocío Esquibel
AGE: Seventeen
PREVIOUS EXPERIENCE WITH THE SICK AND DYING: My Great Aunt Eutilia
PRESENT EMPLOYMENT: Work-study aide at Altavista Memorial

I never wanted to be a nurse. My mother's aunt died in our house, seventy-seven years old and crying in her metal crib: "Put a pillow on the floor. I can jump," she cried. "Go on, let me jump. I want to get away from here, far away."

Eutilia's mattress was covered with chipped clothlike sheaves of yellowed plastic. She wet herself, was a small child, undependable, helpless. She was an old lady with a broken hip, dying without having gotten down from that rented bed. Her blankets were sewn by my mother: corduroy patches, bright yellows, blues and greens, and still she wanted to jump!

"Turn her over, turn her over, turn her, wait a minute, wait— turn . . ."

Eutilia faced the wall. It was plastered white. The foamed, concrete turnings of some workman's trowel revealed daydreams: people's faces, white clouds, phantom pianos slowly playing half lost melodies, "Las Mañanitas," "Cielito Lindo," songs formulated in expectation, dis-

231

solved into confusion. Eutilia's blurred faces, far off tunes faded into the white walls, into jagged, broken waves.

I never wanted to be a nurse, ever. All that gore and blood and grief. I was not as squeamish as my sister Mercy, who could not stand to put her hands into a sinkful of dirty dishes filled with floating food—wet bread, stringy vegetables and bits of softened meat. Still, I didn't like the touch, the smells. How could I? When I touched my mother's feet, I looked away, held my nose with one hand, the other with finger laced along her toes, pulling and popping them into place. "It really helps my arthritis, baby—you don't know. Pull my toes, I'll give you a dollar, find my girdle, and I'll give you two. Ouch. Ouch. Not so hard. There, that's good. Look at my feet. You see the veins? Look at them. Aren't they ugly? And up here, look where I had the operations . . . ugly, they stripped them and still they hurt me."

She rubbed her battered flesh wistfully, placed a delicate and lovely hand on her right thigh. Mother said proudly, truthfully, "I still have lovely thighs."

PREVIOUS EXPERIENCE WITH THE SICK AND DYING: Let me think . . .

Great Aunt Eutilia came to live with us one summer and seven months later she died in my father's old study, the walls lined with books, whatever answers were there—unread.

Great Aunt Eutilia smelled like the mercilessly sick. At first, a vague, softened aroma of tiredness and spilled food. And later, the full-blown emptyings of the dying: gas, putrefaction and fetid lucidity. Her body poured out long, held-back odors. She wet her diapers and sheets and knocked over medicines and glasses of tepid water, leaving in the air an unpleasant smell.

I danced around her bed in my dreams, naked, smiling, jubilant. It was an exultant adolescent dance for my dying aunt. It was necessary, compulsive. It was a primitive dance, a full moon offering that led me slithering into her room with breasts naked and oily at thirteen . . .

No one home but me.

Led me to her room, my father's refuge, those halcyon days now that he was gone—and all that remained were dusty books, cast iron bookends, reminders of the spaces he filled. Down the steps I leaped into Eutilia's faded and foggy consciousness where I whirled and danced and sang: I am your flesh and my mother's flesh and you are . . . are . . . Eutilia stared at me. I turned away.

I danced around Eutilia's bed. I hugged the screen door, my breasts indented in the meshed wire. In the darkness Eutilia moaned, my body wet, her body dry. Steamy we were, and full of prayers.

Could I have absolved your dying by my life? Could I have lessened your agony with my spirit-filled dance in the deep darkness? The blue fan stirred, then whipped nonstop the solid air; little razors sliced through consciousness and prodded the sick and dying woman, whose whitened eyes screeched: Ay! Ay! Let me jump, put a pillow, I want to go away . . . let me . . . let me . . .

One day while playing "Cielito Lindo" on the piano in the living room, Eutilia got up and fell to the side of the piano stool. Her foot caught on the rug, "¡Ay! ¡Ay! ¡Ay! ¡Ay! Canta y no llores . . ."

All requests were silenced. Eutilia rested in her tattered hospital gown, having shredded it to pieces. She was surrounded by little white strips of raveled cloth. Uncle Toño, her babysitter, after watching the evening news, found her naked and in a bed of cloth. She stared at the ceiling, having played the piano far into the night. She listened to sounds coming from around the back of her head. Just listened. Just looked. Just shredded. Shredded the rented gown, shredded it. When the lady of the house returned and asked how was she, meaning, does she breathe, Toño answered, "Fine."

Christ on his crucifix! He'd never gone into the room to check on her. Later, when they found her, Toño cried, his cousin laughed. They hugged each other, then cried, then laughed, then cried. Eutilia's fingers never rested. They played beautiful tunes. She was a little girl in tatters in her metal bed with sideboards that went up and down, up and down . . .

The young girls danced they played they danced they filled out forms.

PREVIOUS EMPLOYMENT: None.

There was always a first job, as there was the first summer of the very first boyfriend. That was the summer of our first swamp cooler. The heat bore down and congealed sweat. It made rivulets trace the body's meridian and, before it stopped, was wiped away, never quite dismissed.

On the tops of the neighbors' houses old swamp coolers, with their jerky grating and droning moans, strained to ease the southern implacabilities. Whrr whrr cough whrr.

Regino Suárez climbed up and down the roof, first forgetting his hammer and then the cooler filter. His boy, Eliterio, stood at the bottom of the steps that led to the sun deck and squinted dumbly at the blazing sun. For several days Regino tramped over my dark purple bedroom. I had shut the curtains to both father and son and rested in violet contemplation of my first boyfriend.

Regino stomped his way to the other side of the house where Eutilia lay in her metal crib, trying to sleep, her weary eyes uncomprehending. The noise was upsetting, she could not play. The small blue fan wheezed freshness. Regino hammered and paced then climbed down. When lunchtime came, a carload of fat daughters drove Regino and the handsome son away.

If Eutilia could have read a book, it would have been the Bible, or maybe her novena to the Santo Niño de Atocha, he was her boy . . .

PREVIOUS EXPERIENCE WITH THE SICK AND DYING:

This question reminds me of a story my mother told me about a very old woman, Doña Mercedes, who was dying of cancer. Doña Mercedes lived with her daughter, Corina, who was my mother's friend. The old woman lay in bed, day after day, moaning and crying softly, not actually crying out, but whimpering in a sad, hopeless way. "Don't move me," she begged when her daughter tried to change the sheets or bathe her. Every day this ordeal of maintenance became worse. It was a painful thing and full of dread for the old woman, the once fastidious and upright Doña Mercedes. She had been a lady, straight and imposing, and with a headful of rich dark hair. Her ancestors were from Spain. "You mustn't move me, Corina," Doña Mercedes pleaded, "never, please. Leave me alone, mi'jita," and so the daughter acquiesced. Cleaning around her tortured flesh and delicately wiping where they could, the two women attended to Doña Mercedes. She died in the daytime, as she had wanted.

When the young women went to lift the old lady from her death bed, they struggled to pull her from the sheets; and, when finally they turned her on her side, they saw huge gaping holes in her back where the cancer had eaten through the flesh. The sheets were stained, the bedsores lost in a red wash of bloody pus. Doña Mercedes' cancer had eaten its way through her back and onto those sheets. "Don't move me, please don't move me," she had cried.

The two young women stuffed piles of shredded disinfected rags soaked in Lysol into Doña Mercedes' chest cavity, filling it, and horrified, with cloths over their mouths, said the prayers for the dead. Everyone remembered her as tall and straight and very Spanish.

PRESENT EMPLOYMENT: Work-study aide at Altavista Memorial Hospital

I never wanted to be a nurse. Never. The smells. The pain. What was I to do then, working in a hospital, in that place of white women, whiter men with square faces? I had no skills. Once in the seventh grade I'd gotten a penmanship award. Swirling R's in boredom, the ABC's ad infinitum. Instead of dipping chocolate cones at the Dairy Queen next door to the hospital, I found myself a frightened girl in a black skirt and white blouse standing near the stairwell to the cafeteria.

I stared up at a painting of a dark-haired woman in a stiff nurse's cap and gray tunic, tending to men in old-fashioned service uniforms. There was a beauty in that woman's face whoever she was. I saw myself in her, helping all of mankind, forgetting and absolving all my own sick, my own dying, especially relatives, all of them so far away, removed. I never wanted to be like Great Aunt Eutilia, or Doña Mercedes with the holes in her back, or my mother, her scarred legs, her whitened thighs.

MR. SMITH

Mr. Smith sat at his desk surrounded by requisition forms. He looked up to me with glassy eyes like filmy paperweights.

MOTHER OF GOD, MR. SMITH WAS A WALL-EYED HUNCHBACK!

"Mr. Smith, I'm Rocío Esquibel, the work-study student from the university and I was sent down here to talk to you about my job."

"Down here, down here," he laughed, as if it were a private joke.

"Oh, yes, you must be the new girl. Menus," he mumbled. "Now just have a seat and we'll see what we can do. Would you like some iced tea?"

It was nine o'clock in the morning, too early for tea. "No, well, yes, that would be nice."

"It's good tea, everyone likes it. Here, I'll get you some." Mr. Smith got up, more hunchbacked than I'd imagined. He tiptoed out of the room whispering, "Tea, got to get this girl some tea."

There was a bit of the gruesome Golom in him, a bit of the twisted spider in the dark. Was I to work for this gnome? I wanted to rescue souls, not play attendant to this crippled, dried-up specimen, this cartilaginous insect with his misshapen head and eyes that peered out to me like the marbled eyes of statues one sees in museums. History preserves its freaks. God, was my job to do the same? No, never!

I faced Dietary Awards, Degrees in Food Management, menus for Low Salt and Fluids; the word Jello leaped out at every turn. I touched the walls. They were moist, never having seen the light.

In my dreams, Mr. Smith was encased in green Jello; his formaldehyde breath reminded me of other smells—decaying, saddened dead things; my great aunt, biology class in high school, my friend Dolores Casaus. Each of us held a tray with a dead frog pinned in place, served to us by a tall stoop-shouldered Viking turned farmer, our biology teacher Mr. Franke, pink-eyed, half blind. Dolores and I cut into the chest cavity and explored that small universe of dead cold fibers. Dolores stopped at the frog's stomach, then squeezed out its last meal, a green mash, spinach-colored, a viscous fluid—that was all that remained in that miniaturized, unresponding organ, all that was left of potential life.

Before Eutilia died she ate a little, mostly drank juice through bent and dripping hospital straws. The straws littered the floor where she'd knocked them over in her wild frenzy to escape. "Dioooooooos," she cried in that shrill voice. "Dios mío, Diosito, por favor. Ay, I won't tell your mamá, just help me get away . . . Diosito de mi vida . . . Diosito de mi corazón . . . agua, agua . . . por favor, por favor . . ."

Mr. Smith returned with my iced tea.

"Sugar?"

Sugar, yes, sugar. Lots of it. Was I to spend all summer in this smelly cage? What was I to do? What? And for whom? I had no business here. It was summertime and my life stretched out magically in front of me: there was my boyfriend, my freedom. Senior year had been the happiest of my life; was it to change?

"Anytime you want to come down and get a glass of tea, you go right ahead. We always have it on hand. Everyone likes my tea," he said with pride.

"About the job?" I asked.

Mr. Smith handed me a pile of green forms. They were menus.

In the center of the menu was listed the day of the week, and to the left and coming down in a neat order were the three meals, breakfast, lunch and dinner. Each menu had various choices for each meal.

LUNCH

☐ Salisbury Steak	☐ Mashed potatoes and gravy
☐ Fish sticks	☐ Macaroni and cheese
☐ Enchiladas	☐ Broccoli and onions
☐ Rice almondine	

Drinks	*Dessert*
☐ Coffee	☐ Jello
☐ Tea	☐ Carrot cake
☐ 7-Up	☐ Ice Cream, vanilla
☐ Other	

"Here you see a menu for Friday, listing the three meals. Let's take lunch. You have a choice of Salisbury steak, enchiladas, they're really good, Trini makes them, she's been working for me for twenty years. Her son George Jr. works for me, too, probably his kids one day." At this possibility, Mr. Smith laughed at himself. "Oh, and fish sticks. You a . . . ?"

"Our Lady of the Holy Scapular."

"Sometimes I'll get a menu back with a thank you written on the side. 'Thanks for the liver, it was real good,' or 'I haven't had rice pudding since I was a boy.' Makes me feel good to know we've made our patients happy."

Mr. Smith paused, reflecting on the positive aspects of his job.

"Mind you, these menus are only for people on regular diets, not everybody, but a lot of people. I take care of the other special diets, that doesn't concern you. I have a girl working for me now, Arlene Rutschman. You know . . ."

My mind raced forward, backward. Arlene Rutschman, the Arlene from Holy Scapular, Arlene of the soft voice, the limp mannerisms, the plain, too goodly face, Arlene, president of Our Lady's Sodality, in her white and navy blue beanie, her bobby socks and horn-rimmed glasses, the Arlene of the school dances with her perpetual escort, Bennie Lara, the toothy better-than-no-date date, the Arlene of the high grades, the muscular, yet turned-in legs, the curly unattractive hair, *that* Arlene, the dud?

"Yes, I know her."

"Good!"

"We went to school together."

"Wonderful!"

"She works here?"

"Oh, she's a nice girl. She'll help you, show you what to do, how to distribute the menus."

"Distribute the menus?"

"Now you just sit there, drink your tea and tell me about yourself."

This was the first of many conversations with Mr. Smith, the hunchbacked dietician, a man who was never anything but kind to me.

"Hey," he said proudly, "these are my kids. Norma and Bardwell. Norma's in Junior High, majoring in boys, and Bardwell is graduating from the Military Institute."

"Bardwell. That's an unusual name," I said as I stared at a series of 5 × 7's on Mr. Smith's desk.

"Bardwell, well, that was my father's name. Bardwell B. Smith. The Bard, they called him!" At this he chuckled to himself, myopically recalling his father, tracing with his strange eyes patterns of living flesh and bone.

"He used to recite."

The children looked fairly normal. Norma was slight, with a broad toothy smile. Bardwell, or Bobby, as he was called, was not unhandsome in his uniform, if it weren't for one ragged, splayed ear that slightly cupped forward, as if listening to something.

Mr. Smith's image was nowhere in sight. "Camera shy," he said. To the right of Mr. Smith's desk hung a plastic gold framed prayer beginning with the words: "Oh Lord of Pots and Pans." To the left, near a dried-out water-cooler was a sign, "Bless This Mess."

Over the weeks I began to know something of Mr. Smith's convoluted life, its anchorings. His wife and children came to life, and Mr. Smith acquired a name—Marion—and a vague disconcerting sexuality. It was upsetting for me to imagine him fathering Norma and Bardwell. I stared into the framed glossies full of disbelief. Who was Mrs. Smith? What was she like?

Eutilia never had any children. She'd been married to José Esparza, a good man, a handsome man. They ran a store in Agua Tibia. They prospered, until one day, early in the morning, about three A.M., several men from El Otro Lado called out to them in the house. "Don José, wake up! We need to buy supplies." Eutilia was afraid, said, "No, José, don't let them in." He told her, "Woman, what are we here for?" And she said, "But at this hour, José? At this hour?" Don José let them into the store. The two men came in carrying two sacks, one that was empty, and another that they said was full of money. They went through the store, picking out hats, clothing, tins of corned beef, and stuffing them into the empty sack. "So many things, José," Eutilia whispered, "*too* many things!" "Oh no," one man replied, "we have the money, don't you trust us, José?" "Cómo no, compadre," he replied easily. "We need the goods, don't be afraid, compadre." "Too many things, too many things," Eutilia sighed, huddled in the darkness in her robe. She was a small woman, with the body of a little girl. Eutilia looked at José, and it was then that they both knew. When the two men had loaded up, they turned to Don José, took out a gun, which was hidden in a sack, and said, "So sorry, compadre, but you know . . . stay there, don't follow us." Eutilia hugged the darkness, saying nothing for the longest time. José was a handsome man, but dumb.

The village children made fun of José Esparza, laughed at him and pinned notes and pieces of paper to his pants. "Tonto, tonto" and "I am a fool." He never saw these notes, wondered why they laughed.

"I've brought you a gift, a bag of rocks"; all fathers have said that to their children. Except Don José Esparza. He had no children, despite

his looks. "At times a monkey can do better than a prince," la comadre
Lucaya used to say to anyone who would listen.

The bodies of patients twisted and moaned and cried out, and cursed,
but for the two of us in that basement world, all was quiet save for
the occasional clinking of an iced tea glass and the sporadic sound of
Mr. Smith clearing his throat.

"There's no hurry," Mr. Smith always said. "Now you just take
your time. Always in a hurry. A young person like you."

ARLENE RUTSCHMAN

"You're so lucky that you can speak Spanish," Arlene intoned. She
stood tiptoes, helf her breath, then knocked gently on the patient's
door. No sound. A swifter knock. "I could never remember what a
turnip was," she said.

"Whatjawant?" a voice bellowed.

"I'm the menu girl; can I take your order?"

Arlene's high tremulous little girl's voice trailed off, "Good morning, Mr. Samaniego! What'll it be? No, it's not today you leave,
tomorrow, after lunch. Your wife is coming to get you. So, what'll it
be for your third-to-the-last meal? Now we got poached or fried eggs.
Poached. P-o-a-c-h-e-d. That's like a little hard in the middle, but a
little soft on the outside. Firm. No, not like scrambled. Different.
Okay, you want scrambled. Juice? We got grape or orange. You like
grape? Two grape. And some coffee, black."

A tall Anglo man, gaunt and yellowed like an old newspaper, his
eyes rubbed black like an old raccoon's, ranged the hallway. The man
talked quietly to himself and smoked numbers of cigarettes as he weaved
between attendants with half-filled urinals and lugubrious I.V.'s. He
reminded me of my father's friends, angular Anglos in their late fifties,
men with names like Bud or Earl, men who owned garages or steak
houses, men with firm hairy arms, clear blue eyes and tattoos from
the war.

"That's Mr. Ellis, 206." Arlene whispered, "jaundice."

"Oh," I said, curiously contemptuous and nervous at the same time,
unhappy and reeling from the phrase, "I'm the menu girl!" How'd I
ever manage to get such a dumb job? At least the Candy Stripers wore

a cute uniform, and they got to do fun things like deliver flowers and candy.

"Here comes Mrs. Samaniego. The wife."

"Mr. Ellis's wife?" I said, with concern.

"No, Mr. Samaniego's wife, Donelda." Arlene pointed to a wizened and giggly old woman who was sneaking by the information desk, past the silver-haired volunteer, several squirmy grandchildren in tow. Visiting hours began at two P.M., but Donelda Samaniego had come early to beat the rush. From the hallway, Arlene and I heard loud smacks, much kidding and general merriment. The room smelled of tamales.

"Old Mr. Phillips in 304, that's the Medical Floor, he gets his cath at eleven, so don't go ask him about his menu then. It upsets his stomach."

Mrs. Daniels in 210 told Arlene weakly, "Honey, yes, you, honey, who's the other girl? Who is she? You'll just have to come back later, I don't feel good. I'm a dying woman, can't you see that?" When we came back an hour later, Mrs. Daniels was asleep, snoring loudly.

Mrs. Gustafson, a sad wet-eyed, well-dressed woman in her late sixties, dismissed us from the shade of drawn curtains as her husband, G.P. "Gus" Gustafson, the judge, took long and fitful naps only to wake up again, then go back to sleep, beginning once more his inexorable round of disappearances.

"Yesterday I weighed myself in the hall and I'm getting fat. Oh, and you're so thin."

"The hips," I said, "the hips."

"You know, you remind me of that painting," Arlene said, thoughtfully.

"Which?"

"Not which, who. The one in the stairwell. Florence Nightingale, she looks like you."

"That's who that is!"

"The eyes."

"She does?"

"The eyes."

"The eyes?"

"And the hair."

"The eyes and the hair? Maybe the hair, but not the eyes."

"Yes."

"I don't think so."

"Oh yes! Every time I look at it."

"Me?"

Arlene and I sat talking at our table in the cafeteria, that later was to become *my* table. It faced the dining room. From that vantage point I could see everything and not be seen.

We talked, two friends almost, if only she weren't so, so, little girlish with ribbons. Arlene was still dating Bennie and was majoring in either home ec or biology. They seemed the same in my mind: babies, menus and frogs. Loathsome, unpleasant things.

It was there, in the coolness of the cafeteria, in that respite from the green forms, at our special table, drinking tea, laughing with Arlene, that I, still shy, still judgmental, still wondering and still afraid, under the influence of caffeine, decided to stick it out. I would not quit the job.

"How's Mr. Prieto in 200?"

"He left yesterday, but he'll be coming back. He's dying."

"Did you see old Mr. Carter? They strapped him to the wheelchair finally."

"It was about time. He kept falling over."

"Mrs. Domínguez went to bland."

"She was doing so well."

"You think so? She couldn't hardly chew. She kept choking."

"And that grouch, what's her name, the head nurse, Stevens in 214 . . ."

"She's the head nurse? I didn't know that—god, I filled out her menu for her . . . she was sleeping and I . . . no wonder she was mad . . . how did I know she was the head nurse?"

"It's okay. She's going home or coming back, I can't remember which. Esperanza González is gonna be in charge."

"She was real mad."

"Forget it, it's okay."

"The woman will never forgive me, I'll lose my job," I sighed.

I walked home past the Dairy Queen. It took five minutes at the most. I stopped midway at the ditch's edge, where the earth rose and where there was a concrete embankment on which to sit. To some this was the quiet place, where neighborhood lovers met on summer nights to kiss, and where older couples paused between their evening walks to rest. It was also the talking place, where all the neighbor kids discussed life while eating hot fudge sundae with nuts. The bench was large; four could sit on it comfortably. It faced an open field in the middle of which stood a huge apricot tree. Lastly, the bench was a stopping place, the "throne," we called it. We took off hot shoes and dipped our cramped feet into the cool ditch water, as we sat facing the southern sun at the quiet talking place, at our thrones, not thinking anything, eyes closed, but sun. The great red velvet sun.

One night I dreamt of food, wading through hallways of food, inside some dark evil stomach. My boyfriend waved to me from the ditch's bank. I sat on the throne, ran alongside his car, a blue Ford, in which he sat, on clear plastic seat covers, with that hungry Church-of-Christ smile of his. He drove away, and when he returned, the car was small and I was too big to get inside.

Eutilia stirred. She was tired. She did not recognize anyone. I danced around the bed, crossed myself, en el nombre del padre, del hijo y del espíritu santo, crossed forehead, chin and breast, begged for forgiveness even as I danced.

And on waking, I remembered. *Nabos. Turnips.* But of course.

It seemed right to me to be working in a hospital, to be helping people, and yet: why was I only a menu girl? Once a menu was completed, another would take its place and the next day another. It was a never ending round of food and more food. I thought of Judge Gustafson.

When Arlene took a short vacation to the Luray Caverns, I became the official menu girl. That week was the happiest of my entire summer.

That week I fell in love.

ELIZABETH RAINEY

Elizabeth Rainey, Room 240, was in for a D and C. I didn't know what a D and C was, but I knew it was mysterious and to me, of course, this meant it had to do with sex. Elizabeth Rainey was propped up in bed with many pillows, a soft blue, homemade quilt at the foot of her bed. Her cheeks were flushed, her red lips quivering. She looked fragile, and yet her face betrayed a harsh indelicate bitterness. She wore a creme-colored gown on which her loose hair fell about her like a cape. She was a beautiful woman, full-bodied, with the translucent beauty certain women have in the midst of sorrow—clear and unadorned, her eyes bright with inexplicable and self-contained suffering.

She cried out to me rudely, as if I personally had offended her. "What do you want? Can't you see I want to be alone. Now close the door and go away! Go away!"

"I'm here to get your menu." I could not bring myself to say, I'm the menu girl.

"Go away, go away, I don't want anything. I don't want to eat. Close the door!"

Elizabeth Rainey pulled her face away from me and turned to the wall, and, with deep and self-punishing exasperation, grit her teeth, and from the depths of her self-loathing a small inarticulate cry escaped—"Oooooh."

I ran out, frightened by her pain, yet excited somehow. She was so beautiful and so alone. I wanted in my little girl's way to hold her, hold her tight and in my woman's way never to feel her pain, ever, whatever it was.

"Go away, go away," she said, her trembling mouth rimmed with pain, "go away!"

She didn't want to eat, told me to go away. How many people yelled to me to go away that summer, have yelled since then, countless people, of all ages, sick people, really sick people, dying people, people who were well and still rudely tied into their needs for privacy and space, affronted by these constant impositions from, of all people, the menu girl!

"Move over and move out, would you? Go away! Leave me alone!"

And yet, of everyone who told me to go away, it was this woman in her solitary anguish who touched me the most deeply. How could I, age seventeen, not knowing love, how could I presume to reach out to this young woman in her sorrow, touch her and say, "I know, I understand."

Instead, I shrank back into myself and trembled behind the door. I never went back into her room. How could I? It was too terrible a vision, for in her I saw myself, all life, all suffering. What I saw both chilled and burned me. I stood long in that darkened doorway, confused in the presence of human pain. I wanted to reach out . . . I wanted to . . . I wanted to . . . But *how?*

As long as I live I will carry Elizabeth Rainey's image with me: in a creme-colored gown she is propped up, her hair fanning pillows in a room full of deep sweet acrid and overspent flowers. Oh, I may have been that summer girl, but yes, I knew, I understood. I would have danced for her, Eutilia, had I but dared.

DOLORES CASAUS

Dolores of the frog entrails episode, who'd played my sister Ismene in the world literature class play, was now a nurse's aide on the surgical floor, changing sheets, giving enemas and taking rectal temperatures.

It was she who taught me how to take blood pressure, wrapping the cuff around the arm, counting the seconds and then multiplying beats. As a friend, she was rude, impudent, delightful; as an aide, most dedicated. One day for an experiment, with me as a guinea pig, she took the blood pressure of my right leg. That day I hobbled around the hospital, the leg cramped and weak. In high school Dolores had been my double, my confidante and the best Ouija board partner I ever had. When we set our fingers to the board, the dial raced and spun, flinging out letters—notes from the long dead, the crying out. Together we contacted la Llorona and would have unraveled *that* mystery if Sister Esperidiana hadn't caught us in the religion room during lunchtime communing with that distressed spirit who had so much to tell!

Dolores was engaged. She had a hope chest. She wasn't going to college because she had to work, and her two sisters-in-law, the Nurses González and González—Esperanza, male, and Bertha, female—were her supervisors.

As a favor to Dolores, González the Elder, Esperanza would often give her a left-over tray of "regular" food, the patient having checked out or on to other resting grounds. Usually I'd have gone home after the ritualistic glass of tea but one day, out of boredom perhaps, most likely out of curiosity, I hung around the surgical floor talking to Dolores, my only friend in all the hospital. I clung to her sense of wonder, her sense of the ludicrous, to her humor in the face of order, for even in that environment of restriction, I felt her still probing the whys and wherefores of science, looking for vestiges of irregularity with immense childlike curiosity.

The day of the left-over meal found Dolores and me in the laundry room, sandwiched between bins of feces- and urine-stained sheets to be laundered. There were also dripping urinals waiting to be washed. Hunched over a tray of fried chicken, mashed potatoes and gravy, lima beans and vanilla ice cream, we devoured crusty morsels of Mr. Smith's fried chicken breasts. The food was good. We fought over the ice cream. I resolved to try a few more meals before the summer ended, perhaps in a more pleasant atmosphere.

That day, I lingered at the hospital longer than usual. I helped Dolores with Francisca Pacheco, turning the old woman on her side as we fitted the sheet on the mattress. "Cuidado, no me toquen," she cried. When Dolores took her temperature rectally, I left the room, but returned just as quickly, ashamed of my timidity. I was always the passing menu girl, too afraid to linger, too unwilling to see, too busy with summer illusions. Every day I raced to finish the daily menus, punching in my time card, greeting the beginning of what I considered to be my *real* day outside those long and smelly corridors where food and illness intermingled, leaving a sweet thick air of exasperation in my lungs. The "ooooh" of Elizabeth Rainey's anxious flesh.

The "ay ay ay" of Great Aunt Eutilia's phantom cries awaited me in my father's room. On the wall the portrait of his hero Napoleon hung, shielded by white sheets. The sun was too bright that summer for delicate fading eyes, the heat too oppressive. The blue fan raced to bring freshness to that acrid tomb full of ghosts.

I walked home slowly, not stopping at the quiet place. Compadre Regino Suárez was on the roof. The cooler leaked. Impatient with Regino and his hearty wave, his habit of never doing any job thoroughly, I remembered that I'd forgotten my daily iced tea. The sun was hot. All I wanted was to rest in the cool darkness of my purple room.

The inside of the house smelled of burnt food and lemons. My mother had left something on the stove again. To counteract the burnt smell she'd placed lemons all over the house. Lemons filled ashtrays and bowls, they lay solidly on tables and rested in hot corners. I looked in the direction of Eutilia's room. Quiet. She was sleeping. She'd been dead five years but, still, the room was hers. She was sleeping peacefully. I smelled the cleansing bitterness of lemons.

MRS. DANIELS

When I entered rooms and saw sick, dying women in their forties, I always remembered room 210, Mrs. Daniels, the mother of my cousin's future wife.

Mrs. Daniels usually lay in bed, whimpering like a little dog, moaning to her husband, who always stood nearby, holding her hand, saying softly, "Now, Martha, Martha. The little girl only wants to get your order."

"Send her away, goddammit!"

On those days that Mr. Daniels was absent, Mrs. Daniels whined for me to go away. "Leave me alone, can't you see I'm dying?" she said and looked toward the wall. She looked so pale, sick, near death to me, but somehow I knew, not really having imagined death without the dying, not having felt the outrage and loathing, I knew and saw her outbursts for what they really were: deep hurts, deep distresses. I saw her need to release them, to fling them at others, dribbling pain/anguish/abuse, trickling away those vast torrential feelings of sorrow and hate and fear, letting them fall wherever they would, on whomever they might. I was her white wall. I was her whipping girl upon whom she spilled her darkened ashes. She cried out obscenely to me, sending me reeling from her room, that room of loathing and dread. That room anxious with worms.

Who of us has not heard the angry choked words of crying people, listened, not wanting to hear, then shut our ears, said enough, I don't want to. Who has not seen the fearful tear-streamed faces, known the blank eyes and felt the holding back, and, like smiling thoughtless children, said: "I was in the next room, I couldn't help hearing, I heard, I saw, you didn't know, did you? I know."

We rolled up the pain, assigned it a shelf, placed it in the hardened place, along with a certain self-congratulatory sense of wonder at the world's unfortunates like Mrs. Daniels. We were embarrassed to be alive.

JUAN MARIA/THE NOSE

"Cómo se dice when was the last time you had a bowel movement?" Nurse Luciano asked. She was from Yonkers, a bright newlywed. Er-

minia, the ward secretary, a tall thin horsey woman with a postured
Juárez hairdo of exaggerated sausage ringlets, replied through chapped
lips, "Oh, who cares, he's sleeping."

"He's from México, huh?" Luciano said with interest.

"An illegal alien," Rosario retorted. She was Erminia's sister, the
superintendent's secretary, with the look of a badly scarred bulldog.
She'd stopped by to invite Erminia to join her for lunch.

"So where'd it happen?" Luciano asked.

"At the Guadalajara Bar on Main Street," Erminia answered, mois-
tening her purple lips nervously. It was a habit of hers.

"Hey, I remember when we used to walk home from school. You
remember, Rocío?" Dolores asked. "We'd try to throw each other
through the swinging doors. It was real noisy in there."

"Father O'Kelley said drink was the defilement of men, the undoing
of staunch, god-fearing women," I said.

"Our father has one now and then," Rosario replied, "that doesn't
mean anything. It's because he was one of those aliens."

"Those kind of problems are bad around here I heard," Luciano
said, "people sneaking across the border and all."

"Hell, you don't know the half of it," Nurse González said as she
came up to the desk where we all stood facing the hallway. "It's an
epidemic."

"I don't know, my mother always had maids, and they were all
real nice except the one who stole her wedding rings. We had to track
her all the way to Piedras Negras and even then she wouldn't give
them up," Erminia interjected.

"Still, it doesn't seem human the way they're treated at times."

"Some of them, they ain't human."

"Still, he was drunk, he wasn't full aware."

"Full aware, my ass," retorted Esperanza angrily, "he had enough
money to buy booze. If that's not aware, I don't know what aware is.
Ain't my goddam fault the bastard got into a fight and someone bit
his nose off. Ain't *my* fault he's here and *we* gotta take care of him.
Christ! If *that* isn't aware, I don't know what aware is!"

Esperanza González, head surgical floor nurse, the short but highly
respected Esperanza of no esperanzas, the Esperanza of the short-bobbed
hair, the husky deferential voice, the commands, the no-nonsense
orders and briskness, Esperanza the future sister-in-law of Dolores, my

only friend, Esperanza the dyke, who was later killed in a car accident on the way to somewhere, said: "Now get back to work all of you, we're just here to clean up the mess."

Later when Esperanza was killed my aunt said, "How nice. In the paper they called her lover her sister. How nice!"

"Hey, Erminia, lunch?" asked Rosario, almost sheepishly. "You hungry?"

"Coming, Rosario," yelled Erminia from the back office where she was getting her purse. "Coming!"

"God, I'm starving," Rosario said, "can you hear my stomach?"

"Go check Mr. Carter's cath, Dolores, will you?" said Esperanza in a softer tone.

"Well, I don't know, I just don't know," Luciano pondered. "It doesn't seem human, does it? I mean how in the world could anyone in their right mind bite off another person's nose? How? You know it, González, you're a tough rooster. If I didn't know you so well already, you'd scare the hell out of me. How long you been a nurse?"

"Too long, Luciano. Look, I ain't a new bride, that's liable to make a person soft. Me, I just clean up the mess."

"Luciano, what you know about people could be put on the head of a pin. You just leave these alien problems to those of us who were brought up around here and know what's going on. Me, I don't feel one bit sorry for that bastard," Esperanza said firmly. "Christ, Luciano, what do you expect, he don't speak no Engleesh!"

"His name is Juan María Mejía," I ventured.

Luciano laughed. Esperanza laughed. Dolores went off to Mrs. Carter's room, and Rosario chatted noisily with Erminia as they walked toward the cafeteria.

"Hey, Rosario," Luciano called out, "what happened to the rings?"

It was enchilada day. Trini was very busy.

Juan María the Nose was sleeping in the hallway; all the other beds were filled. His hospital gown was awry, the grey sheet folded through sleep-deadened limbs. His hands were tightly clenched. The hospital screen barely concealed his twisted private sleep of legs akimbo, moist armpits and groin. It was a sleep of sleeping off, of hard drunken wanderings, with dreams of a bar, dreams of a fight. He slept the way little boys sleep, carelessly half exposed. I stared at him.

Esperanza complained and muttered under her breath, railing at the Anglo sons of bitches and at all the lousy wetbacks, at everyone, male and female, goddamn them and their messes. Esperanza was dark and squat, pura india, tortured by her very face. Briskly, she ordered Dolores and now me about. I had graduated overnight, as if in a hazy dream, to assistant, but unofficial, ward secretary.

I stared across the hallway to Juan María the Nose. He faced the wall, a dangling I.V. at the foot of the bed. Esperanza González, R.N., looked at me.

"Well, and who are you?"

"I'm the menu, I mean, I was the menu . . ." I stammered. "I'm helping Erminia."

"So get me some cigarettes. Camels. I'll pay you tomorrow when I get paid."

Yes, it was really González, male, who ran the hospital.

Arlene returned from the Luray Caverns with a stalactite charm bracelet for me. She announced to Mr. Smith and me that she'd gotten a job with an insurance company.

"I'll miss you, Rocío."

"Me, too, Arlene." God knows it was the truth. I'd come to depend on her, our talks over tea. No one ever complimented me like she did.

"You never get angry, do you?" she said admiringly.

"Rarely," I said. But inside, I was always angry.

"What do you want to do?"

"Want to do?"

"Yeah."

I want to be someone else, somewhere else, someone important and responsible and sexy. I want to be sexy.

"I don't know. I'm going to major in drama."

"You're sweet," she said. "Everyone likes you. It's in your nature. You're the Florence Nightingale of Altavista Memorial, that's it!"

"Oh God, Arlene, I don't want to be a nurse, ever! I can't take the smells. No one in our family can stand smells."

"You look like that painting. I always did think it looked like you . . ."

"You did?"

"Yeah."

"Come on, you're making me sick, Arlene."

"Everyone likes you."

"Well . . ."

"So keep in touch. I'll see you at the University."

"Home Ec?"

"Biology."

We hugged.

The weeks progressed. My hours at the hospital grew. I was allowed to check in patients, to take their blood pressures and temperatures. I flipped through the patients' charts, memorizing names, room numbers, types of diet. I fingered the doctors' reports with reverence. Perhaps someday I would begin to write in them as Erminia did: "2:15 P.M., Mrs. Daniels, pulse normal, temp normal, Dr. Blasse checked patient, treatment on schedule, medication given to quiet patient."

One day I received a call at the ward desk. It was Mr. Smith.

"Ms. Esquibel? Rocío? This is Mr. Smith, you know, down in the cafeteria."

"Yes, Mr. Smith! How are you? Is there anything I can do? Are you getting the menus okay? I'm leaving them on top of your desk."

"I've been talking to Nurse González, surgical; she says they need you there full time to fill in and could I do without you?"

"Oh, I can do both jobs; it doesn't take that long, Mr. Smith."

"No, we're going by a new system. Rather, it's the old system. The aides will take the menu orders like they used to before Arlene came. So, you come down and see me, Rocío, have a glass of iced tea. I never see you any more since you moved up in the world. Yeah, I guess you're the last of the menu girls."

The summer passed. June, July, August, my birth month. There were serious days, hurried admissions, feverish errands, quick notes jotted in the doctor's charts. I began to work Saturdays. In my eagerness to "advance," I unwittingly had created more work for myself, work I really wasn't skilled to do.

My heart reached out to every person, dragged itself through the hallways with the patients, cried when they did, laughed when they did. I had no business in the job. I was too emotional.

Now when I walked into a room I knew the patient's history, the cause of illness. I began to study individual cases with great attention, turning to a copy of *The Family Physician*, which had its place among my father's old books in his abandoned study.

Gone were the idle hours of sitting in the cafeteria, leisurely drinking iced tea, gone were the removed reflections of the outsider.

My walks home were measured, pensive. I hid in my room those long hot nights, nights full of wrestling, injured dreams. Nothing seemed enough.

Before I knew it, it was the end of August, close to that autumnal time of setting out. My new life was about to begin. I had made that awesome leap into myself that steamy summer of illness and dread— confronting at every turn, the flesh, its lingering cries.

"Ay, Ay, Ay, Ay, Canta y no llores! Porque cantando se alegran, Cielito Lindo, los corazones . . ." The little thin voice of an old woman sang from one of the back rooms. She pumped the gold pedals with fast furious and fervent feet, she smiled to the wall, its faces, she danced on the ceiling.

Let me jump.

"Goodbye, Dolores, it was fun."

"I'll miss you, Rocío! But you know, gotta save some money. I'll get back to school someday, maybe."

"What's wrong, Erminia? You mad?" I asked.

"I thought you were gonna stay and help me out here on the floor."

"Goddamn right!" complained Esperanza. "Someone told me this was your last day, so why didn't you tell me? Why'd I train you for, so you could leave us? To go to school? What for? So you can get those damned food stamps? It's a disgrace all those wetbacks and healthy college students getting our hard-earned tax money. Makes me sick. Christ!" Esperanza shook her head with disgust.

"Hey, Erminia, you tell Rosario goodbye for me and Mrs. Luciano, too," I said sadly.

"Yeah, okay. They'll be here tomorrow," she answered tonelessly. I wanted to believe she was sad.

"I gotta say goodbye to Mr. Smith," I said, as I moved away.

"Make him come up and get some sun," González snickered. "Hell no, better not, he might get sunstroke and who'd fix my fried chicken?"

I climbed down the steps to the basement, past the cafeteria, past my special table, and into Mr. Smith's office, where he sat, adding numbers.

"Miss Esquibel, Rocío!"

"This is my last day, Mr. Smith. I wanted to come down and thank you."

"I'm sorry about . . ."

"Oh no, it worked out all right. It's nothing."

Did I see, from the corner of my eye, a set of Friday's menus he himself was tabulating—salisbury steak, macaroni and cheese . . .

"We'll miss you, Rocío. You were an excellent menu girl."

"It's been a wonderful summer."

"Do you want some tea?"

"No, I really don't have the time."

"I'll get . . ."

"No, thank you, Mr. Smith, I *really* have to go, but thanks. It's really good tea."

I extended my hand, and for the first time, we touched. Mr. Smith's eyes seemed fogged, distracted. He stood up and hobbled closer to my side. I took his grave cold hand, shook it softly, and turned to the moist walls. When I closed the door, I saw him in front of me, framed in paper, the darkness of that quiet room. Bless this mess.

Eutilia's voice echoed in the small room. Goodbye. Goodbye. And let me jump.

I turned away from the faces, the voices, now gone: Father O'Kelley, Elizabeth Rainey, Mrs. Luciano, Arlene Rutschman, Mrs. Daniels, Juan María the Nose, Mr. Samaniego and Donelda, his wife, their grandchildren, Mr. Carter, Earl Ellis, Dolores Casaus, Erminia and her sister, the bulldog. Esperanza González, Francisca Pacheco, Elweena Twinbaum, the silver-haired volunteer whose name I'd learned the week before I left Altavista Memorial. I'd made a list on a menu of all the people I'd worked with. To remember. It seemed right.

From the distance I heard Marion Smith's high voice: "Now you come back and see us!"

Above the stairs the painting of Florence Nightingale stared solidly into weary soldiers' eyes. Her look encompassed all the great unspeakable sufferings of every war. I thought of Arlene typing insurance premiums.

Farther away, from behind and around my head, I heard the irregular but joyful strains of "Cielito Lindo" played on a phantom piano by a disembodied but now peaceful voice that sang with great quivering emotion: De la sierra morena. Cielito Lindo . . . viene bajando . . .

Regino fixed the cooler. I started school. Later that year I was in a car accident. I crashed into a brick wall at the cemetery. I walked to Dolores' house, holding my bleeding face in my hands. Dolores and her father argued all the way to the hospital. I sat quietly in the back seat. It was a lovely morning. So clear. When I woke up I was on the surgical floor. Everyone knew me. I had so many flowers in the room I could hardly breathe. My older sister, Ronelia, thought I'd lost part of my nose in the accident and she returned to the cemetery to look for it. It wasn't there.

Mr. Smith came to see me once. I started to cry.

"Oh no, no, no, now don't you do that, Rocío. You want some tea?"

No one took my menu order. I guess that system had finally died out. I ate the food, whatever it was, walked the hallways in my gray hospital gown slit in the back, railed at the well-being of others, cursed myself for being so stupid. I only wanted to be taken home, down the street, past the quiet-talking place, a block away, near the Dairy Queen, to the darkness of my purple room.

It was time.

PREVIOUS EMPLOYMENT: Altavista Memorial Hospital

SUPERVISORS: Mr. Marion Smith, Dietician, and Miss Esperanza González, R.N., Surgical Floor.

DATES: June 1966 to August 1966

IN A FEW SENTENCES GIVE A BRIEF DESCRIPTION OF YOUR JOB: As Ward Secretary, I was responsible for . . . let me think . . .

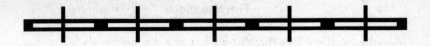

TIM SANDLIN

FROM

Skipped Parts

aspar looked like a short Mark Twain, which is maybe why I don't care for *Huckleberry Finn*. He did a lot of things I hated to Lydia on purpose and a lot of things I hated to me accidentally, but his one unforgivable sin was being short. That stuff is hereditary as hell.

Caspar had a gray hearing aid that he kept turned down except for when he was talking, and he wore a white suit year round, Southern as all get out. Every day, he stuck a fresh yellow mum in his lapel. I used to think the mum had something to do with Me Maw and he'd once had a heart, but Lydia said it was part of some spiffy self-image thing, and if Caspar ever had a heart, he sure wouldn't advertise the fact.

The day we left Greensboro, after these apemen-redneck movers piled all our stuff in a truck and went away, Caspar came out on the porch to deliver some sort of farewell to the family. Lydia was sitting sideways in the porch swing, reading *Reflections in a Golden Eye* by Carson McCullers, and painting her fingernails black. I read the book on the drive west and decided not to ride any horses. The black fingernail polish was a Lydia statement to Caspar, but he missed it.

I was on the plank floor sorting baseball cards. It was late in the summer and there'd been a rash of trades before the final pennant drive, which meant I had all kinds of guys in the wrong place. Willie

Mays had collapsed in the batter's box the day before we left so his card was out on top.

Caspar drew himself up into what passed for posture. He fingered his hearing aid and gave out a little snort. "The purest treasure mortal times afford is spotless reputation."

I looked at Lydia, who shrugged. "You been in the library again, Daddy?"

He hovered over me, looking like an old man pretending to be an even older man. "Do you know why I'm sending you to northwest Wyoming?"

I stared up into his permanently black fingernails. No matter how much Caspar played at Southern gentility, carbon in the cuticles would forever show his roots. "Because Lydia messed up again."

Lydia coughed real ladylike into her hand. Caspar wasted a glare on her before going on. "Because I measured in the Rand Atlas and Jackson Hole is farther from a major league baseball team than any other spot in the country."

"Oh."

"And you are leaving those cards here."

"Caspar."

"There will be no discussion. In Wyoming you are to mature into a gentleman. You will think carbon paper, not baseball."

Lydia almost stood up to him. "Daddy, don't take it out on Sam. He's innocent."

The old goat actually hooked his thumbs under his suspenders. "Nothing you touch is innocent. One mistake out there and he goes to Culver Military Academy. Are the implications clear?"

"Yes, your daddyship."

Caspar stared down at me. "Carbon paper, Sam. The country turns on carbon paper. Nothing else matters to you."

"Yes, sir."

"Bring your cards to the basement."

When Caspar opened the screen door, I snuck Willie Mays and Gil Hodges into my socks. They're the only two I saved. Caspar incinerated every other player from 1958 through 1963 in the basement coal stove. And he made me watch.

"Gentlemen, on punts we have two men we pop free for the block. First one's the outside rusher, that's you, Callahan. Line up on the side of the line that the kicker's kicking foot is on. Got that?"

I nodded. No reason to go into the Yes Sir mentality until I had to.

"You have a second and a half to move from here to a spot two feet in front of the kicker, and you're being blocked one-on-one so there's no time for anything fancy. Just get around the guy and fly."

Practice hadn't been the irritating grunt I'd expected, mainly due to the pleasant temp. My one shot at September football in Carolina came to drippy sweat and stomach cramps followed by heat prostration and first aid from the student trainer. Here, I did the jumping jacks, touch the toes, ran through a few old tires, and did okay.

Thank God nobody had loads of gung-hohood. I figure Stebbins recruited the whole team the way he got me. We were hundreds of miles from a decent college team and, what with limited TV exposure, there was little instilled pigskin fanaticism. A couple guys tried rolling blocks, but I stepped aside and they ate dirt. Neither one seemed to take it personally.

"Our other punt blocker will be Schmidt here. You line up at middle linebacker. Talbot, you cross-block their guard, blow his ass down the line. Then Schmidt comes through the hole."

Why is it coaches use first names in class like normal teachers and last names on the field? And who started this gentlemen jive? Coaches and cops love to call people they don't like gentlemen.

We lined up and shuffled through four or five punts without using the ball. A kid named Skipper O'Brien stood across the line with his elbows up. I let him bump me a time or two, figuring the poor schlock's ego needed a buildup. He had red hair and an overbite you could open a can with. Red-headed children tend to feel inferior.

When it came to the real drill, our punter was so awful that Stebbins did the kicking himself. He said, "Yup, yup, yup," and everybody took off. I faked O'Brien's jock to the outside and zipped right up the middle. The punt boomed off Stebbins's left foot, traveled maybe nine inches and caught me dead in the lungs.

I rolled over and over, wound up armadilloed on my back. Try breathing when you can't. It's a panic deal. I couldn't see squat, but

I could hear, and I felt someone pull me off the ground an inch by a belt loop, then lower me again. God knows why.

Stebbins's voice floated in. "Nice block, Callahan. Get up, we'll try it again."

My mouth and nose felt sealed in Saran Wrap. The thing lasted forever.

More voices. "Think he'll die?"

"Doubt it."

"He don't look like a nigger."

"His mom tried to pick up Ft. Worth at the White Deck last night."

"I heard it other way around."

A toe poked me in the ribs. "He's turning blue."

"Maybe the nigger comes out when he's hurt."

Stebbins's voice again: "He's no nigger, he's not fast enough."

I pretended to pass out.

I got the wind knocked out of me one other time. In North Carolina, I was little, six or seven, and Lydia and I were playing seesaw. She had to scoot way up near the middle so our weights sort of balanced out. It was fun because the air was nice that day and Lydia didn't play outdoors stuff with me too often. About all I could ever get out of her was an occasional game of crazy 8s.

So I'm going up and down, up and down, admiring to myself how pretty Lydia is down the board from me. She had on a gray, sleeveless shirt and white shorts. She'd spread a magazine out on the board in front of her so she could amuse herself and me at the same time. Every now and then she'd raise her face to swipe the bangs off her forehead, and she smiled at me kind of absentmindedly, as if she'd forgotten I was there.

Then, while I'm way up a mile high on top of the world, the damn coach of some swim team walks up in his stretchy trunks and rubber thongs. Had a blue whistle on a cord around his neck. I hate coaches.

He cocked his head to one side and banged on the skull bone over his right ear. "Does your little brother know how to swim?"

Lydia marked her spot in the magazine with her finger and turned to stare at the bare-chested coach.

He switched sides of the head and banged some more. "Every young

man should know how to swim. It is vital to his safety and the safety
of his loved ones."

Lydia looked up the board at me. "Sam, do you know how to
swim?"

"No." I wasn't happy about being passed off as a little brother.

She turned to the coach. "No."

"I could teach the little snapper. Maybe you and me should walk
over to the ice cream stand and discuss it. My treat, I'll even stand
the boy a single cone."

Lydia stared at him a few seconds more, just enough to cause him
to stop banging on the sides of his head, then she said, "I do not
receive gentlemen without the decency to cover their repellent chest
mange," and dignified as all get out, she swung her right leg across
the board and *got off the seesaw*. I couldn't believe it. I didn't breathe
for five minutes or stop crying for an hour, not until the stupid swimmer
went away.

I was depressed that fall. I'd never been depressed to the point where
I knew it before. Depression is like a headache or true love or any of
those indefinable concepts. If you've never been there, you don't know
what it's like until you're too far in to stop the process.

But I remember coming home from football practice to entire evenings on the couch next to Lydia, neither of us talking or reading or
anything. We'd just sit with our eyes glazed, waiting for 10:30.

I figured out the stove deal so we ate frozen pizzas three nights a
week and at the White Deck the other four. That's something of an
exaggeration. Lydia bought rib eyes every now and then, and I got
good with Kraft Macaroni and Cheese in a box. Some Sundays we
drove to Jackson for late breakfast at the Wort Hotel.

So far as I can tell, Lydia made good on the emotional catatonia
threat. She went a good month without speaking to a human other
than me and Dot. Even with Dot, Lydia took to pointing at things on
the menu or going through me.

"Tell her this hamburger is overcooked. Your sneakers have more
flavor."

I turned to Dot and shrugged.

Dot laughed like we were perfectly pleasant folks making a joke.

She had nifty dimples. I had a crush on her that wouldn't let go, and Lydia's attitude caused me some embarrassment.

Once when Lydia left me the money to pay and fluffed out the door, I explained things to Dot at the cash register.

"My mom's kind of high-strung. She doesn't mean anything personal."

Dot looked sad for the first time. "No one should apologize for their mother," she said. "All moms are doing the best they can."

"Are you sure?"

A guy did try to talk to us once. Big, wide fella with a grin, he came slamming through the door and walked straight toward our table, pulled a chair over and straddled it backward with his hands across the top slat. The middle finger on his right hand was missing two joints.

He held the stub out to me. "Look."

I looked but didn't see anything other than a short finger. Lydia didn't look. "It's short," I said.

"Look at the tip."

I shrugged. Seemed like a fingertip to me.

"I lost it in a chainsaw and at the hospital they took a skin graft off this arm," he showed me a scar on his left arm, "and stuck it over the tip."

"Why are you telling me this?"

"Look close and see."

I finally figured out that he meant he didn't have a fingerprint so he could commit crimes. I looked so I could say, "Gee, no fingerprint," but then I saw all this wiry hair.

"Your fingertip's hairy."

The big lug's grin showed a flashy gold tooth. "Never seen anything like it, huh? Look, ma'am." He stuck the finger between Lydia's face and her food. I couldn't believe it, the guy had his hand in a pornographic position three inches from her nose, and she was speechless. Normally, Lydia practically spit at anyone who called her "ma'am."

"They shaved the skin off my arm before grafting it, but the hair all grew back. Ever see anything like that?"

He turned his hand sideways into the handshake position. "Ft. Worth Jones, ma'am. I'm more than pleased to meet you."

Lydia stared at the hand a moment, then up at the guy's expansive face.

I said, "I heard your name at football practice."

The gold tooth flashed in the fluorescent light. "Hope they said something good."

"How do you spell *Fort?*"

He looked perplexed by the question. "F-t-period. Like the town."

"Oh."

He still had his hand out. "Saturday night's movie night at the VFW, little lady. *The Inspector General.* I'd be pleased if you'd accompany me."

I was sure "little lady" would spark a Lydia volcano, but nothing happened. She just sat there. My theory is Ft. Worth was so far from her frame of reference that Lydia couldn't see him.

Ft. Worth looked at me. "Is she okay?"

"Medication."

He stared intently at Lydia's eyes. "Yeah. Would you tell her I dropped by."

I nodded.

The tall stranger stepped through the White Deck screen door and strode to the counter. "Black coffee and rare beefsteak."

When Dot brought out the stranger's supper, she refilled his coffee cup. "What brings you to town, stranger?"

"Passing through."

Dot was amazed at his calmness. "Honey, nobody passes through GroVont. Where you headed?"

"Paris, France." The stranger paused to light a Cuban cigar. "Want to come along?"

Dot looked around to see to whom the stranger was speaking. "You want me to run away to Paris, France?"

"Your considerable beauty and charm are wasted in this king-hell hole. I want to uncover your light and let it shine on the world."

"But I'm overweight."

The stranger studied Dot from her white sneakers to her teased hair. "I like 'em with meat."

As Dot took off her apron and threw her order book in the trash, she asked, "What's your line, mister?"

"I'm God's gift to waitresses."
"And what's your name?"
"Callahan, ma'am. Sam Callahan."

I actually dragged Lydia to a football game. We were playing Victor, Idaho, and I started at split end—even caught a pass, a first for me and the team.

The rodeo grounds east of town had bleachers, but the football field didn't—says something about local priorities. The football field was a flat spot on the valley floor cleared of sagebrush and marked off with lime. Probably the only playing field in America completely surrounded by national park. Spectators backed their trucks up to the sidelines and sat on tailgates, a few even had strap-back lawn chairs. Almost everyone had access to a cooler.

Maurey Pierce was one of the cheerleaders. They wore these really short, considering the temperature, pleated white skirts and red turtleneck sweaters with GV over what would have been the right breast if any of them had had breasts. I took the color scheme as a joke because our football uniforms were tan and brown, like the hills behind the school. We were in camouflage.

As the team ran onto the field, the cheerleaders jumped up and bent their knees and yelled "Go Badgers," our nickname, and threw their pom-poms in the air. Maurey's pom-pom landed right in front of me and I stepped on it on purpose.

At the bench, as the guys milled around, hitting each other in the shoulder pads and growling, I checked back to see Maurey standing there with a muddy pom-pom in her right hand and a godawful look on her face. Ugly, mean. I guess nobody'd ever stepped on anything of hers before. Her legs were pretty, but the knees stuck in a little.

Lydia parked Caspar's '62 Olds on the south 10-yard marker, way off from everyone else, and kept the engine running and the heater on. I knew that was a mistake, but I was so psyched about my mom being out in front of the whole town, I forgot. You see, this big cottonwood tree stood off that end zone, the only decent-sized tree anywhere near school.

Toward the end of the first quarter, a steady stream of men and boys started drifting up to the cottonwood, then back past the Olds and onto their trucks, lawn chairs, and coolers. Practically every guy waved to Lydia, coming and going.

I caught my pass on the last play of the first half. We were behind, 24-zip with nothing to lose, so Stebbins called for the Hail Mary bomb. Jimmy Crandall, the quarterback, figured out what he meant and showed the rest of us with a stick in the dirt.

The play involves both receivers and all three running backs splitting off to the right side of the line and when Jimmy goes "Yup, yup," we take off hell-bent for downfield, he throws the ball as far as he can, and we see what happens from there.

Jimmy "yupped" and everybody took off but me. I'd watched the Crandall kid throw in practice. Had an arm like a broomstick. So our receivers and all their defenders charge off forty yards downfield and Jimmy launches this wounded duck that wobbles about twelve yards to where I'm waiting—hits me in both hands and the chest, I hang on, the crowd goes wild. About ten potato heads jumped on me, but I didn't fumble and we got our first first down of the half, what would prove to be the only first down of the game.

Ft. Worth and a bunch of those White Deck hoodlums leaped in their trucks and honked horns. Maybe it was sarcasm, hell, I don't know. But I was proud. None of those kids who ate at home every night had caught a pass.

I played it superior when I left the field and passed the cheerleaders, but I snuck a quick glance and a couple of them were watching me. Women always love a football star. Maurey wasn't one of the couple, she was deep in her own superior routine.

I jogged over to the Olds and knocked on the window until Lydia rolled it down. She had the rearview mirror cocked off sideways.

"You see me catch that pass?" I asked.

"What?" Her eyes were stuck on the mirror. A bunch of high school boys waved at her as they walked behind the car toward the cottonwood. "You know what that tree is?" Lydia asked me.

I glanced over and got embarrassed. "It's the pee tree."

"Have you ever used it?"

"A few times during practice."

Lydia's eyes finally came back to look at me. They held that reckless Carolina glitter that I'd both loved and feared before our drive west, before the post-10:30 doldrums set in all day. "Sam, honey bunny, I believe I've seen every penis in GroVont."

I stood up straight and looked across the top of the Olds to the pee tree. It was disgusting. Nobody tried to cup with their hands or anything. And they knew too. The high school boys were nudging each other and giggling and sneaking leers our way.

I said, "I call that sick."

Lydia smiled as she gazed back into the crooked mirror. "I call that hospitality."

The next day, Saturday, it started snowing. I wasn't total hick enough to run into the street hollering, *"Jeeze Louise, what's this white stuff?"* I'd seen snow in Carolina, just not a whole lot. It was still a cold novelty. We both kept it casual—"Look outside, honey bunny, Jack Frost came last night"—but, underneath, Lydia and I were pretty excited.

She stared out the window the same old way, right foot on the sill, Dr Pepper in one hand, cigarette in the other, but something had changed. She wasn't staring into the void or herself or wherever Lydia went when she did her lost-in-space number. She was looking out the window.

"What're those bushes over there?" She pointed with her cigarette across the street behind old Soapley's trailer.

"That's sagebrush."

"Kind of pretty with the snow on it."

We'd been living in a sagebrush ocean for two months. Something, either the snow or the penis parade, had opened the connection between Lydia's eyes and her brain.

"You ever notice those mountains the other side of town?"

"It's the Tetons, Lydia. We live smack in the middle of Grand Teton Park."

"I knew that." Her lips had a near smile, as if she remembered something. Which made me nervous. I wanted Mom to wake up, sure; it's no fun coming home to an emotional slug, but Lydia awake could be a powerful thing. The difference between a passive and an aggressive Lydia was like the difference between mononucleosis and a hurricane.

I ripped off Lydia's new book, *Catch-22*, and rode my bike down to the White Deck. The snow was only an inch or so deep, but I still hit a slush spot and crashed the bike. Right out in front of Dupree's Art Gallery, I slid sideways under a parked GMC. Afforded Dougie Dupree no end of entertainment. I got an earful of cold mud and the right half of my clothes wet. Bent my handlebars.

Added to all that indignity, Dot wasn't even working. Some prissy little bopper hardly older than me bounced over and took my order for peach cobbler and coffee. Only other customers in the joint were two slack-cheeked retirees, named Bill and Oly, arguing over a fish they didn't catch in 1943.

"It was a brown, didn't you see the jump it made."

"Brookie. Biggest damn brookie anyone around here ever saw. Fought like hell when she hit my gray ghost, but she didn't jump. Brookies don't jump."

"Weren't a ghost. Was renegade you rubbed worm all over."

I'd hoped Dot would see me reading this fabulously sophisticated novel full of sex and rebellion and think I was interesting. Instead, I dumped four spoons of sugar and a load of cream in the coffee and sat there with *Catch-22* propped open by the napkin box, staring out the window.

Not that the book wasn't a kick. It was the first time I realized death and despair can be funny, depending on how you look at it. All comedy, from "I Love Lucy" to *The Taming of the Shrew*, would be sad if it were true. This idea would eventually grow into my philosophical outlook on life.

But snow was more important than outlooks that day. Since then, an incredible amount of my time has been spent looking at snow, playing in snow, fighting with snow. Like true love, it has caused me hordes of pleasure, pain, and anxiety. From the White Deck window, it appeared soft and harmless. Lydia might seem soft and harmless, seen through a window. Goes to show you.

Two yards either way and Sam Callahan would have missed the dying trapper. As it was, Sam heard the low moan, "Diphtheria," just before he stumbled over a frozen lump in the blizzard.

"Diphtheria," it said again.

Sam brushed snow crystals off the old man's face and held the frozen body in his arms without doing anything that might be misconstrued as latent homosexuality. "What's that, old-timer?"

The man coughed for several minutes, then spoke. "There's diphtheria in Yellowknife."

"I'm not afraid of sickness."

The dying man's eyes were frozen open so he couldn't blink. "The serum. I have the serum in my pack. Those settlers won't die if they get the serum."

Sam made his decision. "I will take the serum to Yellowknife."

"But the blizzard. No one could make it through this blizzard."

"I'll make it, or I'll die trying."

The old man's lower lip quivered. "I did," he whispered, then he was dead.

Maurey Pierce banged through the door followed by LaNell and LaDell Smith, the twins all giggles and flouncing curly hair. Maurey stopped when she saw me and did a narrowing-of-the-eyes number. I narrowed mine right back. Overt hostility hadn't erupted in the first two and a half months of our relationship. I'd call it extreme wariness, at least on my part. Maurey seemed to regard me as a very large, but non-threatening bug.

She dropped into the next booth with her back to me. LaNell and LaDell made a minor scene on who had to sit on the inside. LaNell and LaDell are the kind of twins whose clothes will match their entire lives. From the back, they're kind of cute in a narrow-shoulders, big-hips fashion, but they both squint up their eyes like they just put in new contact lenses and haven't gotten used to them yet.

I'm afraid God only passed out one brain between them.

At first, they made a major point of ignoring me. They all ordered hamburgers with Pepsi and went into this drawn-out debate on Liz Taylor's treatment of Eddie Fisher. Maurey defended Liz. "Maybe she and Richard are in love," which outraged the twins no end.

They cited Debbie Reynolds and Eddie's mother and Burton's wife Sybil or Sydney or something. I didn't give a hoot and I don't think Maurey did either. Nothing that happened to anyone more than fifty miles away could possibly affect GroVont, Wyoming, so it seemed stupid to worry about Liz and Eddie.

Then the bopper waitress, whose name was Laurie, brought me a coffee heater. "Anything else?"

"I'm fine, thanks."

I should never have spoken. Or maybe they'd exhausted Liz talk and they'd have turned on me anyway. LaNell's voice was comparable to cutting a cardboard box with a butter knife. "Hey, Sam, don't you know you're too young to drink coffee."

I gave her the mystery smile I'd been working on just in case I ever found myself in a Western poker parlor.

LaDell came in next. "Your mother should tell you not to button the top button on that kind of shirt. You look like a squirrel." The pair stared at me with their upper lips warped so I could see watermelon-colored gums over their incisors.

I defended my button. "It's cold outside."

"It's cold outside," LaDell mimicked. "Wait'll January."

I wished I could see Maurey's face. Her back hadn't moved so at least she wasn't laughing at me like the retard twins. Maybe she felt an empathetic connection.

LaDell continued. "Hey, Maurey, he's reading a book on a Saturday. Trying to show off and study in public."

"It's not a school book. It's literature."

"Litter tour. Litter tour." What makes people between the ages of eleven and fifteen such mean jerks? I'd rather be ninety-five than thirteen again.

Maurey swung her arm onto the back of the booth and turned her head to look at me. "What literature?"

I showed her the cover of *Catch-22*. "It's new. This book will change the way we look at both the novel and war forever." I stole that from a blurb off the back cover. Then, I added my own, "And sex."

The twins oohed harmoniously. Maurey's eyes never left the book. "What do you know about sex?"

Actually, *Catch-22* had a ridiculously small amount of sex in it. "After I finish this book I'll know a lot more about it than you."

Bill picked up the napkin dispenser and slammed it into Oly's temple. Oly fell sideways out of the booth, his upper plate skittered across the cafe floor and stopped under a stool. After a few moments' disorientation, Oly made it to his knees and began to crawl after his teeth.

Us kids, even Laurie, all pretended we hadn't seen a thing. Young people aren't allowed to notice grown-ups conking each other.

Bill sat there with the napkin dispenser in his hand, watching his friend crawl away. He had the blankest look on his face. He blinked twice and swallowed, then he called to Oly, "Was a brookie."

Joseph Heller knocked on the cabin door. It was opened by a weathered-looking boy of thirteen. "May I see your father?" Joseph Heller asked.

"I have no father."

"Is this not the home of Sam Callahan?"

"I'm Sam Callahan."

Joseph Heller stared at the boy in amazement. "Surely you can't be the Sam Callahan who wrote White Deck Madness, the greatest American novel since Moby Dick."

The boy smiled mysteriously. "The New York Times Book Review rated it higher."

Joseph Heller could not believe this young man was the same writer who had wrenched his heart out and made it bleed. Yet, as he looked closer, Joseph Heller saw the sadness and depth behind the boy's deep blue eyes.

"Yes," Joseph Heller said. "I believe you are a novelist."

"Thank you, sir."

"May I have your autograph?"

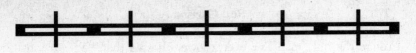

RON CARLSON

The H Street Sledding Record

The last thing I do every Christmas Eve is go out in the yard and throw the horse manure onto the roof. It is a ritual. After we return from making our attempt at the H Street Sledding Record, and we sit in the kitchen sipping Egg Nog and listening to Elise recount the sled ride, and Elise then finally goes to bed happily, reluctantly, and we finish placing Elise's presents under the tree and we pin her stocking to the mantel—with care—and Drew brings out two other wrapped boxes which anyone could see are for me, and I slap my forehead having forgotten to get her anything at all for Christmas (except the prizes hidden behind the glider on the front porch), I go into the garage and put on the gloves and then into the yard where I throw the horse manure on the roof.

Drew always uses this occasion to call my mother. They exchange all the Christmas news, but the main purpose of the calls the last few years has been for Drew to stand in the window where she can see me out there lobbing the great turds up into the snow on the roof, and describe what I am doing to my mother. The two women take amusement from this. They say things like: "You married him" and "He's your son." I take their responses to my rituals as a kind of fond, subtle support, which it is. Drew had said when she first discovered me throwing the manure on the roof, the Christmas that Elise was four,

269

"You're the only man I've ever known who did that." See: a compliment.

But, now that Elise is eight, Drew has become cautious: "You're fostering her fantasies." I answer: "Kids grow up too soon these days." And then Drew has this: "What do you want her to do, come home from school in tears when she's fifteen? Some kid in her class will have said—*Oh, sure, Santa's reindeer shit on your roof, eh?*" All I can say to Drew then is: "Some kid in her class! Fine! I don't care what he says. I'm her father!"

I have thrown horse manure on our roof for four years now, and I plan to do it every Christmas Eve until my arm gives out. It satisfies me as a homeowner to do so, for the wonderful amber stain that is developing between the swamp cooler and the chimney and is visible all spring-summer-fall as you drive down the hill by our house, and for the way the two rosebushes by the gutterspout have raged into new and profound growth during the milder months. And as a father, it satisfies me as a ritual that keeps my family together.

Drew has said, "You want to create evidence? Let's put out milk and a cookie and then drink the milk and eat a bite out of the cookie."

I looked at her. "Drew," I had said, "I don't like cookies. I never ate a dessert in my life."

And like I said, Drew has been a good sport, even the year I threw one gob short and ran a hideous smear down the kitchen window screen that hovered over all us until March when I was able to take it down and go to the carwash.

I obtain the manure from my friend Bob, more specifically from his horse, Power, who lives just west of Heber. I drive out there the week before Christmas and retrieve about a bushel. I throw it on the roof a lump at a time, wearing a pair of welding gloves my father gave me.

I put the brake on the sled in 1975 when Drew was pregnant with Elise so we could still make our annual attempt on the H Street Record on Christmas Eve. It was the handle of a broken Louisville Slugger baseball bat, and still had the precise "34" stamped into the bottom. I sawed it off square and drilled and bolted it to the rear of the sled, so that when I pulled back on it, the stump would drag us to a stop.

As it turned out, it was one of the two years when there was no snow, so we walked up to Eleventh Avenue and H Street (as we promised: rain or shine), sat on the Flexible Flyer in the middle of the dry street on a starry Christmas Eve, and I held her in my lap. We sat on the sled like two basketball players contesting possession of her belly. We talked a little about what it would be like when she took her leave from the firm and I had her home all day with the baby, and we talked remotely about whether we wanted any more babies, and we talked about the Record, which was set on December 24, 1969, the first Christmas of our marriage, when we lived in the neighborhood, on Fifth Avenue in an old barn of a house the total rent on which was seventy-two fifty, honest, and Drew had given me the sled that very night and we had walked out about midnight and been surprised by the blizzard. No wonder we took the sled and walked around the corner up H Street, up, up, up to Eleventh Avenue, and without speaking or knowing what we were doing, opening the door on the second ritual of our marriage, the annual sled ride (the first ritual was the word "condition" and the activities it engendered in our droopy old bed).

At the top we scanned the city blurred in snow, sat on my brand new Christmas sled, and set off. The sled rode high and effortlessly through the deep snow, and suddenly, as our hearts started and our eyes began to burn against the snowy air, we were going faster than we'd planned. We crossed Tenth Avenue, nearly taking flight in the dip, and then descended in a dark rush: Ninth, Eighth, Seventh, soaring across each avenue, my arms wrapped around Drew like a straitjacket to drag her off with me if a car should cross in front of us on Sixth, Fifth Avenue, Fourth (this all took seconds, do you see?) until a car did turn onto H Street, headed our way, and we veered the new sled sharply, up over the curb, dousing our speed in the snowy yard one house from the corner of Third Avenue. Drew took a real faceful of snow, which she squirmed around and pressed into my neck, saying the words: "Now, that's a record!"

And it was the Record: Eleventh to Third, and it stood partly because there had been two Christmas Eves with no snow, partly because of assorted spills brought on by too much speed, too much laughter, sometimes too much caution, and by a light blue Mercedes that crossed Sixth Avenue just in front of us in 1973. And though some years were flops, there was nothing about Christmas that Elise looked forward to as much as our one annual attempt at the H Street Sledding Record.

I think Drew wants another baby. I'm not sure, but I think she wants another child. The signs are so subtle they barely seem to add up, but she says things like, "Remember before Elise went to school?" and "There sure are a lot of women in their mid-thirties having babies." I should ask her. But for some reason, I don't. We talk about everything, *everything*. But I've avoided this topic. I've avoided talking to Drew about this topic because I want another child too badly to have her not want one. I want a little boy to come into the yard on Christmas morning and say: "See, there on the roof! The reindeers were there!" I want another kid to throw horse manure for. I'll wait. It will come up one of these days; I'll find a way to bring it up. Christmas is coming.

Every year on the day after Halloween, I tip the sled out of the rafters in the garage and Elise and I sponge it off, clean the beautiful dark blond wood with furniture polish, enamel the nicked spots on the runner supports with black engine paint, and rub the runners themselves with waxed paper. It is a ritual done on the same plaid blanket in the garage and it takes all afternoon. When we are finished, we lean the sled against the wall, and Elise marches into the house. "Okay now," she says to her mother: "Let it snow."

On the first Friday night in December, every year, Elise and Drew and I go buy our tree. This too is ritual. Like those families that bundle up and head for the wilderness so they can trudge through the deep, pristine snow, chop down their own little tree, and drag it, step by step, all the way home, we venture forth in the same spirit. Only we take the old pickup down to South State and find some joker who has thrown up two strings of colored lights around the corner of the parking lot of a burned-out Safeway and is proffering trees to the general public.

There is something magical and sad about this little forest just sprung up across from City Tacos, and Drew and Elise and I wander the wooded paths, waiting for some lopsided pinon to leap into our hearts.

The winter Drew and I became serious, when I was a senior and she was already in her first year at law school, I sold Christmas trees during vacation. I answered a card on a dorm bulletin board and went to work for a guy named Geer, who had cut two thousand squat pinons from the hills east of Cedar City and was selling them from a dirt lot on Redwood Road. Drew's mother invited me to stay with them for the holidays, and it gave me the chance to help Drew make up her mind about me. I would sell trees until midnight with Geer, and then drive back to Drew's and watch every old movie in the world and wrestle with Drew until our faces were mashed blue. I wanted to complicate things wonderfully by having her sleep with me. She wanted to keep the couch cushions between us and think it over. It was a crazy Christmas; we'd steam up the windows in the entire living room, but she never gave in. We did develop the joke about "condition," which we still use as a code word for desire. And later, I won't say if it was spring or fall, when Drew said to me, "I'd like to see you about this condition," I knew everything was going to be all right, and that we'd spend every Christmas together for the rest of our lives.

One night during that period, I delivered a tree to University Village, the married students' housing off Sunnyside. The woman was waiting for me with the door open as I dragged the pine up the steps to the second floor. She was a girl, really, about twenty, and her son, about three, watched the arrival from behind her. When I had the tree squeezed into the apartment, she asked if I could just hold it for a minute while she found her tree stand. If you ever need to stall for a couple of hours, just say you're looking for your tree stand; I mean the girl was gone for about twenty minutes. I stood and exchanged stares with the kid, who was scared; he didn't understand why some strange man had brought a tree into his home. "Christmas," I told him. "Christmas. Can you say 'Merry Christmas'?" I was an idiot.

When the girl returned with her tree stand, she didn't seem in any hurry to set it up. She came over to me and showed me the tree stand, holding it up for an explanation as to how it worked. Close up the girl's large eyes had an odd look in them, and then I understood it when she leaned through the boughs and kissed me. It was a great move; I had to hand it to her. There I was holding the tree; I couldn't make a move either way. It has never been among my policies to kiss strangers, but I held the kiss and the tree. Something about her eyes.

She stepped back with the sweetest look of embarrassment and hope on her pretty face that I'd ever seen. "Just loosen the turn-screws in the side of that stand," I said, finally. "And we can put this tree up."

By the time I had the tree secured, she had returned again with a box of ornaments, lights, junk like that, and I headed for the door. "Thanks," I said. "Merry Christmas."

Her son had caught on by now and was fully involved in unloading the ornaments. The girl looked up at me, and this time I saw it all: her husband coming home in his cap and gown last June, saying, "Thanks for law school, honey, but I met Doris at the Juris-Prudence Ball and I gotta be me. Keep the kid."

The girl said to me, "You could stay and help."

It seemed like two statements to me, and so I answered them separately: "Thank you. But I can't stay; that's the best help. Have a good Christmas."

And I left them there together, decorating that tree; a ritual against the cold.

"How do you like it?" Elise says to me. She has selected a short broad bush which seems to have grown in two directions at once and then given up. She sees the look on my face and says, "If you can't say anything nice, don't say anything at all. Besides, I've already decided: this is the tree for us."

"It's a beautiful tree," Drew says.

"Quasimodo," I whisper to Drew. "This tree's name is Quasimodo."

"No whispering," Elise says from behind us. "What's he saying now, Mom?"

"He said he likes the tree, too."

Elise is not convinced and after a pause she says, "Dad. It's Christmas. Behave yourself."

When we go to pay for the tree, the master of ceremonies is busy negotiating a deal with two kids, a punk couple. The tree man stands with his hands in his change apron and says, "I gotta get thirty-five bucks for that tree." The boy, a skinny kid in a leather jacket, shrugs and says he's only got twenty-eight bucks. His girlfriend, a large person with a bowl haircut and a monstrous black overcoat festooned with buttons, is wailing, "Please! Oh no! Jimmy! Jimmy! I love that tree! I want that tree!" The tree itself stands aside, a noble pine of about twelve feet. Unless these kids live in a gymnasium, they're buying a tree bigger than their needs.

Jimmy retreats to his car, an old Plymouth big as a boat. "Police Rule" is spraypainted across both doors in balloon letters. He returns instantly and opens a hand full of coins. "I'll give you thirty-one bucks, fifty-five cents, and my watch." To our surprise, the wily tree man takes the watch to examine it. When I see that, I give Elise four dollars and tell her to give it to Kid Jimmy and say, "Merry Christmas." His girlfriend is still wailing but now a minor refrain of "Oh Jimmy, that tree! Oh Jimmy, etc." I haven't seen a public display of emotion and longing of this magnitude in Salt Lake City, ever. I watch Elise give the boy the money, but instead of saying, "Merry Christmas," I hear her say instead: "Here, Jimmy. Santa says keep your watch."

Jimmy pays for the tree, and his girl—and this is the truth—jumps on him, wrestles him to the ground in gratitude and smothers him for nearly a minute. There have never been people happier about a Christmas tree. We pay quickly and head out before Jimmy or his girlfriend can think to begin thanking us.

On the way home in the truck, I say to Elise, "Santa says keep your watch, eh?"

"Yes, he does," she smiles.

"How old are you, anyway?"

"Eight."

It's an old joke, and Drew finishes it for me: "When he was your age, he was seven."

We will go home and while the two women begin decorating the tree with the artifacts of our many Christmases together, I will thread popcorn onto a long string. It is a ritual I prefer for its uniqueness; the fact that once a year I get to sit and watch the two girls I am related to move about a tree inside our home, while I sit nearby and sew food.

On the morning of the twenty-fourth of December, Elise comes into our bedroom, already dressed for sledding. "Good news," she says. "We've got a shot at the record."

Drew rises from the pillow and peeks out the blind. "It's snowing," she says.

Christmas Eve, we drive back along the snowy Avenues, and park on Fifth, as always. "I know," Elise says, hopping out of the car. "You two used to live right over there before you had me and it was a swell place and only cost seventy-two fifty a month, honest."

Drew looks at me and smiles.

"How old are you?" I ask Elise, but she is busy towing the sled away, around the corner, up toward Eleventh Avenue. It is still snowing, petal flakes, teeming by the streetlamps, trying to carry the world away. I take Drew's hand and we walk up the middle of H Street behind our daughter. There is no traffic, but the few cars have packed the tender snow perfectly. It *could* be a record. On Ninth Avenue, Drew stops me in the intersection, the world still as snow, and kisses me. "I love you," she says.

"What a planet," I whisper. "To allow such a thing."

By the time we climb to Eleventh Avenue, Elise is seated on the sled, ready to go. "What are you guys waiting for, Christmas?" she says and then laughs at her own joke. Then she becomes all business: "Listen, Dad, I figure if you stay just a little to the left of the tire tracks we could go all the way. And no wobbling!" She's referring to last year's record attempt, which was extinguished in the Eighth Avenue block when we laughed ourselves into a fatal wobble and ended in a slush heap.

We arrange ourselves on the sled, as we have each Christmas Eve for eight years. As I reach my long legs around these two women, I sense their excitement. "It's going to be a record!" Elise whispers into the whispering snow.

"Do you think so?" Drew asks. She also feels this could be the night.

"Oh yeah!" Elise says. "The conditions are perfect!"

"What do you think?" Drew turns to me.

"Well, the conditions are perfect."

When I say *conditions*, Drew leans back and kisses me. So I press: "There's still room on the sled," I say, pointing to the "F" in Flexible Flyer that is visible between Elise's legs. "There's still room for another person."

"Who?" Elise asks.

"Your little brother," Drew says, squeezing my knees.

And that's about all that was said, sitting up there on Eleventh Avenue on Christmas Eve on a sled which is as old as my marriage with a brake that is as old as my daughter. Later tonight I will stand in my yard and throw this year's reindeer droppings on my very own home. I love Christmas.

Now the snow spirals around us softly. I put my arms around my family and lift my feet onto the steering bar. We begin to slip down H Street. We are trying for the record. The conditions, as you know by now, are perfect.

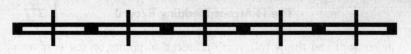

JOANNE GREENBERG

Offering Up

The wind blows all night. It howls down Chinaman's Gap and through Whiskey Gulch and over Victory Pass hell-bent. Our monastery lies supine beneath the beating on its little shoulder of upland under the gray knees and breasts of the mountains. The chapel is protected by the refectory and barn but the chapter house and cloister with the dormitory bear the wind's full force, funneled, aimed, channeled like a fist through the gullies between the mountains. I look at the brothers' faces next day at Mass and see mirrors of my own grainy-eyed sleeplessness. Is the anguish the same? I know two in whom it is.

I'm the brother who does most of the shopping. Today I leave after breakfast and am back at four. When I turn off the highway and take the bumpy road to our gate, I think about its metaphor. The road is savage with mud in winter and spring and there are always washouts and dangerous ice. In summer it bakes and chokes the rider with dust as soft and pervasively gritty as ground glass. After this long, bumpy ride, four miles, the traveler senses a lift in the land and then comes the gate and beyond it, the welcoming spread of the field and the chapel, the guesthouses and chapter house, the harmonious cluster of all of them—the distant view allows no sight of patching, staining, weathering—it all looks rested, quietly breathing, at peace.

There's an electronic system at the gate now, saving us from having to call a brother from his work. I press the button and speak to Brother Herb in the office and the buzzer sounds, the gate opens, and I go through. For discipline's sake, we don't use an automatic closing device. Gravity swings the gate open and we have to get out of the truck to close it. I have learned from Brother Herb's voice that he is not having a peaceful day. Does the wind keep him trying to pull up sleep around him? In this community, where we hope to reach God, there is never, not ever, an escape from man. In the world outside, a friend's loss of faith, selfish impulse, annoying habit, stroke, illness, loss of capacity are misfortunes which usually signal withdrawal. Here there is no release from a tiresome brother or one whose illness renders him wretched. Your narrow-eyed judge is saying his office three steps away from you and will be there at Compline and there again at Lauds and at Matins when patience and love are still sleeping even though you are standing up and uttering the words of praise.

Brother Herb's annoyance has been partly caused by me. "You were supposed to have been back an hour ago."

"They didn't have Matt's prescription ready. I had to wait."

"Dale was ready to do the tune-up."

"Perhaps there's still time." I get back in the truck and drive it over to unload. Herb's officiousness irritates me, and during the evening walk, I will recite the Veni Sancte Spiritus, I'll get to the part that says, "bend what is unbending" and I'll think of him and wish I didn't dislike him so much.

I pick up Brother Peter, whom I still think of as being new even though he's been here five years and is a professed brother, and we go from area to area unloading. Flour to the locker, lumber to the shed, Matt's prescription to the refectory along with all the other personal shopping I've done for the brothers. The Limbate inhaler I got for myself, Tim, and Johnny is in my jacket pocket, a little bulge that makes me nervous. I want to go up to my room and hide it, but there's no time. I'll have to wait until recreation at least before I'm able to get away. It is the fourth inhaler I've gotten. Like booze and cigarettes, Limbate, legal out there, is not legal in here. Like booze and cigarettes, there would be talk about a brother buying some, and they know all of us in Granite. I had to go to Aureole where they don't know me, and I went cursing and came back cursing the thirty extra miles, which was why I was late.

In the secular world, they'll tell you the stuff is not addictive. Considering our experience, I'd have to disagree. Studies in physiology don't cover it. I think we addict to whatever will free us from our paradoxes, from the shock of difference, between what we wish we were and what we know we are. I realize I'm addicted; my hand shook perceptibly when I reached out for the inhaler from a stack of them and took it. I was breathing hard, too, and had to make a conscious effort to calm myself. The stuff is forbidden and I use it anyway, and I watch it beget other wrongs. Rotten meat doesn't summon a single maggot only.

We try to limit the harm. Brothers are forbidden to enter one another's rooms; Tim and Johnny come to my room twice a week when the brothers are supposed to be sleeping. That was my idea, and using was my idea. Johnny found a discarded inhaler cap in my trash and came to me. Tim intuited something, God only knows how, and so we three are changed. The sins multiply. We're what no brothers should be: secretive, frightened, rule-breaking, and the monastery is not what it should be, at least not for us.

Why don't we stop? I don't want to and the others don't either. I swear to myself that I will stop. The inhaler, which I keep in a little sling in the closet, belongs to the three of us. There are nights when I could break it, shatter it under my knees as I pray, but it isn't mine alone, and keeping it is a privilege, a favor to me. Twice I let Johnny keep it and the insecurity and loss of control made me a nervous wreck.

After Pete and I deliver all the shopping, I take the truck over to where Brother Dale is supposed to be waiting. He isn't there and I don't see him until mail call and recreation. I give him the story about

Matt's prescription, which he seems to accept. There are three hundred doses in an inhaler, although the last fifty or so seem weaker. We use it twice a week, except during Lent—I know how ludicrous that sounds. With two breaths in a dose, and the three of us using, we get a new one every five or six months; well beyond what suspicion could attach to for consistent latenesses or especially long trips to town. Today is Wednesday and I want my two breaths—I think of cheating, doing it tonight, lying down on my bed alone. I know if I did that, I'd do it every night as some people on the outside do.

In the moments when we go to clean up before supper, Johnny calls me with a question and I answer it, and his eyes ask and I smile and nod imperceptibly. He'll tell Tim. This is the worst of it, when I bring the new inhaler in and have to get rid of the old one, when we sneak around like kids, signaling over the heads of the brothers, when there are pounding hearts and guilty looks, justification and fear. Tomorrow it will be routine, and for almost half a year we'll be ordinary brothers, working, praying, living monastic life as authentically as we can, considering.

The night chant is my favorite. It's the Salve Regina, haunting even in English. We come out of chapel still singing it and into the night, to the dormitory. The sky over the valley is huge and on moonless nights, so thick with stars that the sight catches and makes us weep, sometimes. Only the oldest brothers use flashlights. I like to hang back and let my feet find the path, past the loom of the outbuildings and refectory all the way to the chapter house and dormitory where we end the day.

We are in Night Silence then. I try to do as much as I can in darkness, going about my preparations by feel. There is neither light nor heat in the dormitory; we use Coleman lamps and heaters which we carry —a little self-denial, that we don't come into a room already warm for us.

There is a crucifix on my whitewashed wall on which Jesus hangs exhausted. In the old days there was a nail below it on which a scourge hung and on certain days, the brothers were required to use it as they recited the penitential psalms. On sleepless nights, windy nights also, they must have had a go at the old Adam: wish, desire, guilt, recrimination. We don't do that any more, or pray kneeling on a rope or on pebbles. Our underwear is bought downtown and not sewn here of rough burlap. We are enjoined to imitate Christ in his virtue, not in his suffering.

I think the whips didn't work. The effects must have lasted no longer than the pain itself at its most intense, and there is always the danger of addiction to pain as to pleasure. The nail and scourge are gone; my back is unscarred but there are the sleepless nights under the scourge of the wind. It drives before it all the wrongs I did great and small, and the recrimination that confession is supposed to silence.

We wake before dawn for Matins. The wind has died; the air is gray and soft, a sweet air for February. In the pre-dawn, our singing has the abstracted quality of the sleep-talker. I love this hour almost as much as the last one of the night. Later I realize that for hours at a time I have forgotten about the inhaler, and that it is Thursday, that at the end of this day, we will use it, all three of us.

Perhaps the others only seem to be untroubled; their faces are serene as they pray. Maybe I seem that way also, although inside I am waiting, alert, eager, but never out of sight of fear. The monastic day leaves no room for private discussion, or any discussion among the three of us. Recreation is time for general talk only. The rest of the day, except for the demands of work, we pass in silence. There are things I need, urgently need, to talk over with my fellow users. It has to be done in typical monastic style, by a combination of luck and planning that will give us time alone.

I work in the bakery. Though it's only February, we have begun to stockpile the tinned rum cakes we sell at Christmas. The work is hard but neither unpleasant nor mindless, and unlike the brothers who are in the laundry or cooking, we are merry. Now and then we sing. I've been happy in this life; its purpose and dedication have uplifted me. Celibacy doesn't bother me much when I consider what married sex was like for my parents and what the abuse of chastity is doing to my sister and brother. When I burn, I remember that.

After recreation, I go to Father Abbot—it's Don Kinear now—and I talk to him about the brochures we send with our cakes. By the time we finish, it's time to make the evening walk, checking everything for the night. We lock up. We have Night Prayer and the Salve again; these motions are to quiet the soul, to still it. My heart is beating with expectation.

In my room, I wait restlessly past lights out. The monastic day allows no waste of time. Even recreation is purposeful. Now I hang in limbo and wish the time away. It's 9:00. It's 9:30. It's 10:00. There is a single soft knock and the door opens and Tim and Johnny slide in silently and go down on their knees. I don't know why we take our Limbate this way. I go to the closet, moving the clothes back, find the fourth hanger, and take the inhaler out of the sling. I bring it over, kneel with them, and give the inhaler to Johnny, who is on my right. I hear him using it: shake, one breath, two. Then Tim, the shake, one, two, and then it comes to me, smoothly in my hand, and I shake it and hold it before my mouth, barrel up. I breathe in, once, twice.

There is the usual anxious moment because Limbate is tasteless and odorless and I always wonder if I'm not breathing a dud. It takes almost three minutes for the drug to reach the limbic area of the brain. We wait with no other thought and then I hear Johnny sigh and then Tim and then the relief moves through me. My memory remains intact, available, but shame, chagrin, regret, self-hate slide off and what I remember is memory only—my spirit is lightened, gentled, unashamed. Tim gets up, touches my arm in leave-taking, and slides silently away. Johnny follows. I go to bed and to the untroubled sleep that Limbate does not initiate, but allows.

Its critics call it chemical lobotomy, but Limbate doesn't change the moral or ethical sense; it only stills the voices of recrimination for thoughts and acts already done. It doesn't help in schizophrenia, except that part which connects to regret. For people fixated in shame and remorse, Limbate is the drug of choice.

When it first came out, Father Abbot—it was Stu Miller then—took me and Andrew and two brothers from the house in North Carolina, to Denver for a day of lectures on it—its pharmacology, side effects, etc. We sat in the back, a line of brown habits looking very medieval, and listened to speakers telling us what Limbate did and couldn't do.

Some people would use Limbate every day, more would use it only after traumatic or tragic events, twenty percent would never use it because they didn't experience gnawing regret for past acts, or not above a momentary pang. It amazed me to learn that so many of us have no night haunts, no long sighs, no tears wept and wept again for a word said amiss or a word not said at all. "Who are those people," I asked the psychologist, "those happy, few?" He looked at me quizzically, I remember.

"Some of them might be doing time," he said. Regret may be a way of teaching lessons learned in no other school.

Then I sat in the line of brothers and ached and wondered if they bore the weight I did. Absolution after confession is supposed to establish the regret and then deal with it. Hard work, prayer, simplicity of life are supposed to thin out the forest in which regret wanders, without purpose. During the day our lives work well. We pray, work, simplify the essentials. At night, it's every brother for himself. Armies of recriminations stream across my undefended borders: the son I was, the brother, the friend.

In the end Limbate was forbidden. I started about four years ago. I had been shopping. I was in the denims and dark shirt we use for ordinary trips outside, this one to Gold Flume for some special hardware. I found myself in the drugstore—the inhalers were on a rack. I lifted one off and read the label and then I just took it, paid for it along with the other things. I was trembling, and like a thief I sat in the truck and used it to banish the guilt of using it. Then I hid it and used it after lights out once a week.

But for Tim and Johnny, I think I would have stayed a Sunday night user—except for Lent. They wanted it twice a week. I caved in. We're

you to a great jazz place.' We went. We both got smashed. She cried some more—I was a wonderful friend, etc., etc. In the boozy bloom, sympathy flowed, we both cried. He had abandoned her. Abandoned. It was dramatic stuff. Those mountain roads are not easy when you're cold sober. When we crashed, I was thrown out first, two feet onto a soft shoulder. She went flying out the passenger side into thin air and off the cliff. They found her six hundred feet down the gully." We waited. The telling hadn't been easy but it had been possible, which I don't think it would have been without the Limbate. "I went home; she went to the morgue. The next day Bill came back to patch things up. There was nothing left of Ginny but my story. He got drunk and stayed drunk for two days. He came to my apartment and called me a murderer and then went to his brother's in Longmont and got his brother's gun and shot himself. They gave me two years probation and suspended my license for six months."

"Is that what you go over?"

He nods. "Detail by detail. I make and remake their lives and my own. I do the drive over and over. I do the drinking again and again, drink by drink."

Johnny and I hear Tim with some surprise. We had known none of this. Monastic life is concentrated in the present. We are still for a while, then Johnny says, "I had no big events. I was in foster homes—six of them. Two were hell. Plain hate might have been better to feel, but I remember what went on with shame. I used to be such a whining, begging kid. I cringe when I think about that and wonder if he's still inside me, that helpless, pleading victim."

"We're telling this to one another," Tim says. "Who else knows it?"

"In my case, there isn't that much to tell," I say. "A hundred ugly, cruel remarks. I deal with them in Confession but they won't be absolved and go away." We ride on in silence.

Then Johnny says quietly, "Lent is coming." We don't speak. After a while he says, "I don't think I can make it without help this year," and we are deadly still.

It's not as easy as I thought it would be, talking in the truck. I'm driving, partly concentrating on the road, and we don't have much time. Here's town already and the wood to get. I had thought the urgency would help, but it doesn't. I head for Krohn's Lumber and Hardware. "Did you make the list?"

"I was supposed to do that on the way," Johnny says.

"We'll stop here and you can do it."

Johnny used to do carpentry and cabinetwork. He figures quickly from the measurements he took and I realize that although I know a good deal about him, having lived with him for eleven years, there are big areas in his life that are closed to me because we don't talk much about personal pasts here. It isn't forbidden; now and then someone will share a letter or memory; I know that Tim gets boils and that Johnny has violent nosebleeds when he is emotionally upset. I never knew about Tim's accident or Johnny's abusive foster fathers, though, and no one knows about my father, piled in his wheelchair, saying ugly things in that soft, oily voice . . . I stop the thought. I'm sweating with a rage Limbate doesn't touch.

Lumber. Hardware. Lots of people are out today. The wind hits hard on the east side of the town and some people from the outskirts are regulars at the lumberyard the morning after a big blow. Our wait is long. On the way home, Johnny says, "I don't think I can do Lent this time; not without help. I don't think I can take forty days."

"We've done it before," Tim says, "and we can work so hard that sleep will sandbag us." His voice is hollow, tough, and sounds studied. He must have been saying this to himself for weeks.

The truth is that we are all afraid. We sit in the truck and tremble, thinking about the forty nights with no Limbate. "We'll have to take what we get," I say, "and the nights only come one by one."

"Let me discipline myself," Johnny says. "I'll keep the Limbate in my room during Lent and I'll use it only when I need it, and . . ."

"NO!" I find I am shouting. "No! It's mine; I buy it. I take the risks getting and keeping it. I carried it through the gate in my pocket . . ." They are staring at me and the truck is on the wrong side of the road. I bring it back and then pull over and turn off the ignition. I am shaking with anger. "Buy your own," I say.

"I can't," he whispers. He puts his hands over his face. We hear his voice between them. "If I did, I'd use it every night."

Tim is quiet. "We're in an Order," I say. "We chose the life. It's a life full of restrictions. No booze, cigarettes, girls, lobster dinners. Limbate. We don't use Limbate."

"But we do."

"Not in Lent. We decided . . ."

"You're so pious, I can hardly stand it," Tim says to me.

I put my head back against the seat and feel weak. "I have to sound this way. Things have been going through my mind, things I haven't thought about since I came in. I wonder about trying to get so tired I can't think, about copping doses when you're not there. It's Lent. We're *supposed* to feel remorse."

"I'm not ready; it starts next week . . ."

"Then we'd better get ready."

We sit in dead silence. There is only the sound of our breathing; no car passes. Then Tim begins to recite the De Profundis and we join him and I turn the key and start up. We go home in true monkish style: pouring our pain into those ancient receiving words.

Lent comes. In the solemnity of the season monastic practice is more rigorous. There's little leisure, no recreation. Many of the brothers have personal penances of total silence. There is a set of fasts and many of us do voluntary ones as well. We have more work, too, cleaning the entire monastery for Easter, building by building, room by room; inventories, repairs. I have a calendar I check off day by day of the forty; unnecessary, since Lenten liturgy does that for us. It reminds me of a space-shot countdown.

On the tenth day the wind wakes up, Lent-hungry, and roars down on us from the west-northwest. I lie in bed reliving a fight with a friend in college, my fault. It led to hard words on both sides, his unremembered, mine vicious and cutting. I said personal things; I stripped him. My father had used our secrets against us—things said in confidence or learned from others about us. I had sworn never to do that and I seldom did, but the cruelty in what I let myself say frightened people about what I knew, and after experiencing what I could do, they were never easy with me again. The words come back in the wind. I hear them over and over, harder to bear because in the closet is a hanger and on the hanger is the Limbate and two breaths of it will still the regret.

It must be two o'clock. I hear a sound. The moon is down. I sit up in bed and try to clear my vision. I get up. It's bone-gnawing cold. Someone is here, in the room. I hear the closet door slide quietly. I go to the figure I now see faintly, a person my size. I touch him on the back and hear his pulled-in breath of surprise. He starts, then sways. It's Johnny. "I have to use the inhaler," he says.

He and Tim have seen me get it, but since it has always been in darkness, neither of them knows exactly where it is. "It's freezing," I say. We are whispering; I don't know why. The rooms are private enough to allow all the coughing, muttering, and groaning that people do at night and still be unheard. "Please, Johnny . . ."

"I need it. I can't stand this."

"Please," I say. "Get in bed; you'll freeze out here. Go on. Now."

My urgency and command get to him. He is in my room; he has been compromised already by coming, and if anyone finds us the result might be expulsion. He goes to the bed and gets in. I plug in the small heater and get under the blankets at the foot of the bed; we are sitting side by side under them.

Johnny laughs, I think at the edge of tears. "Caught in bed together . . ."

"During Lent," I add. He has begun to weep, tiredly. He has wept earlier, I think. "Listen, Johnny; the inhaler's not here. I buried it when Lent began because I didn't think I could take knowing it was here. It's in a little box under the chapel side of the bakery."

There's a long silence and then Johnny says, "No, Marty, it's here. I know because I've used it twice."

I'm shocked. I sit trying to sift thoughts that won't yield reason to me. Then anger comes. I get up and stand in the still chilly room. "If you don't get out of here now, I'm going to smash the inhaler for plain spite. You gluttonous cheat! I've been hanging in what I thought was at least a shared suffering. You were lying . . . you . . ." I bite back the words.

"I need it," he says simply.

I walk over to where he is and whisper into his face. "You gutless, chinless, dribbling wimp. Your foster fathers must have had a hell of a time beating you—who can beat Jell-O? We *decided*; suckfinger—"

"*You* decided," he says, and then gets up and leaves.

Two hours later we are up for Lauds and I am feeling poleaxed, ruined inside. I sing the morning chants and pray the prayers without looking for Johnny, although, of course, I know where he's standing. He has spoken to me in confidence and I've used it in anger. Then, I think he had it coming. He deserved to know what he was doing by breaking faith. Limbate is a luxury, not something we deserve, and he betrayed our trust.

The breakfast table is silent but this morning the silence is anything but peaceful. Anton and Carl are nodding off, Del is yawning. Everyone looks surly or pouting. We have given up tea and coffee as our group penance. As with Limbate, the first few days went by on a sacrifice-high. We were psyched up for our denial and we felt clean and proud. We were happy that our monastic practice was in keeping with the more rigorous practice of the past. But the days are daily and by the ninth or tenth, flesh and spirit begin the long exhaustion of withdrawal. I want coffee, I want Limbate, I want my bread buttered. I want a heater in the chapel. I want sleep. Without these things I am angry and self-pitying. I am a creature I despise. By which the Rule means to teach us on what fragile stalks our pathetic virtues are balanced.

I am still righteously indignant. After morning work, Father Abbot asks me to pick up a big order in town. Many lay people spend Good Friday through Easter with us on retreats, and we are getting the guest houses ready. Toilet paper, towels, soap, sheets. It's cold. Before I leave I go back to the dormitory for a jacket. In my room I go to the closet and take my jacket and turn. The floor. There are drops of blood on the polished wood. One, two, three, four from the bed, five, six, seven to the door. I blew up at Johnny. I lost my temper, but the cause was just, I was severe . . . he bled. He is my friend, brother, accomplice, and he bled with the horror of what I said to him.

As this dawns on me I stand blinking at the unmistakable drops and then move through the door and follow them, one, two, three, four down the hall. They stop suddenly and I have a picture of him in the darkness realizing he was bleeding, pinching his nose, and then guiltily, as I do now, wondering if the blood he has already dropped would accuse him. I get a rag and clean the floor in the hall. The blood in my room I let stay.

It's always something of a jolt to leave the monastery for the outside, even to shop. In the old days, brothers used to go in twos, less to keep an eye on one another than to provide the monastic reality even in the person of one other brother. It's no longer possible; the order has shrunk and while this has its advantages in the sense of fraternity and spirituality, every brother is vital to the running of the house. We can't afford time taken in town.

Lent, with its pinched belly, sleepless eyes; Lent, with no coffee, no tea, no cocoa, no Limbate, is absent in Granite. People look easy and rested. The merchants who know us by name joke with me, and when we talk about the wind they do it from the comfort of Ascension without the suffering that precedes it. For them, Easter is still a month away.

I'm riding back when exhaustion hits. I've been sleeping as I drive and nearly go into the ditch. I pull over and am out before I know it, and an hour later I go sheepishly back to face Brother Herb. The sleep did me good. Going into it I decided what I would do that would allow me to clean up the blood and apologize to God for the whole Limbate mess. I will do a vigil.

There's a list on the bulletin board outside the brothers' entrance to the refectory. Some brothers want their vigils in chapel and yet alone. Now and then there's a note about special intention: for world peace or against hunger, and there'll be many brothers doing it. I pass by the list and look to see if tomorrow night has been checked off. To keep the penance private, there are no names, just check marks. The night is free. I put my check mark opposite the date I want the chapel to myself. To complete the requirements of privacy and modesty, we go to the dorm after late prayer and then come back. We also leave the chapel before Lauds and return to the dorm so as to come in with the brothers at early prayer. Father Abbot is not a believer in holiness one-upmanship.

I feel good about doing this vigil. There's only the problem of the Limbate. We promised we wouldn't take it during Lent. I don't want to add suspicion to the sin of wrath, or temptation to their pain. We live close here and clues are read almost subconsciously in the way it must be for many married people. Tim and Johnny will know when I won't be in my room. I go and get the Limbate, stick it in a plastic sandwich bag, go to the bakery, and bury it in the stored flour we won't be using until after Easter. I'm ready for my night of prayer and penance.

I come into the chapel and quiet myself. I have planned each of the six hours carefully. In each I will offer a different group of prayers and I hope to accomplish a specific as well as general confession and contrition and to receive absolution and healing.

I begin by lighting the candles for my father and mother, hours one and two, and for my brother and sister, hours three and four, for Tim and Johnny and myself, hour five. In hour six I hope to close the vigil and experience the peace for which I am struggling.

I pray for my father, trying to accept his cruelty without consenting to it, to put it in the perspective of his pain, his twisted body. I struggle for this height, achieve it for a moment, and then slip away from it into self-pity. Still, it was there, a moment's freedom from personality and my own pain and into a wider place where forgiveness is possible. I pray for my mother, my confused, cowed mother, who mistook my father's rancorous sarcasm for brilliance. I do the Stations of the Cross. I say some of my favorite portions of the Penitential Liturgy. I pray for Annie, my sister, and Claude, my brother, seeing them as clearly as I can in all their early-blighted possibility. I begin to cry. I see Tim and Johnny, whom I know better than my parents and in some regards not at all. I pray for myself.

Seen in comparison to my parents' life, to Annie's and Claude's, my life seems ordered, decent, productive. Like the monastery in distant prospect, there is simplicity, and peace. It's only when one comes close that the weathering is seen, the stable-muck, the signs of disarray.

I kneel and then lie facedown, cruciform, my head toward the altar, and recite the Miserere. Then I begin to tell God, to speak out of the heart of myself. I tell Him about the Limbate, about how we've fought it and how Johnny has been misusing it and how I hate him for it. Is Tim sneaking into my room, too, to get extra hits on it? Will I draw in a breath three months from now and breathe no ease from the nozzle and feel cuckolded, betrayed?

I am in our traditional posture of utter surrender. It isn't the humility of kneeling; it is complete yet the words coming out of my mouth have no smallest measure of submission in them. All the pain, all the anger, the pent-up remorse and sorrow, helplessness and rage blow through me like the night wind down Whiskey Gulch. I let it come. It howls out of me, nothing like what I planned when I planned this vigil or conceived of doing when I knelt and then went down to full length to mark the hour of the death of selfishness and the rebirth of selfhood.

I cry myself dry. I have accused everyone for whom I have come here to pray. When I stop and am finished at last, I realize there's still an hour before Lauds. I get up on my knees and then stand and turn. There is Father Abbot, still on his knees where he has been since . . . when? There are black flashes and I begin to lose balance and he's up and supporting me.

"I'm sorry, Martin, I didn't check the list and I came . . . you seemed overwhelmed—I thought . . ." and then, "Come on," he says.

I have destroyed myself—destroyed all three of us. Father knows, and what he knows is not under the seal of the confessional. He will call a meeting, chapter, probably all the brothers. They will judge us. We may be sent to other houses. We may be asked to leave the order altogether. I don't want to leave. This is my home. This is Tim's home and Johnny's. I can't beg or protest, I can't speak at all.

I begin to dream; it's the way of people whose exhaustion has left them unguarded, the odd, irrational thought walks in without being stopped and searched. What if rats got into the bakery and found the bag of flour stored there and ate their way in and ate the inhaler. Evidence destroyed and a rat with regrets but no remorse.

The wind has picked up. I can hear it experimenting with some wood that's stacked near the barn. It comes through the passage between barn and chapel, bakery and dairy house. It goes everywhere, inspecting, nosing out sin, and now it's found the dormitory where some brothers are not sleeping and there is its whip—remorse . . . remorse.

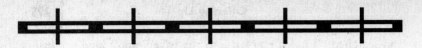

RUSSELL MARTIN

FROM

Beautiful Islands

Seeing Colorado from space was like looking back with new uncertainty on a place you've known forever but have never understood. Late spring snow still draped the high spines of the San Juans and the Sangre de Cristos, and the valleys spread like disheveled rugs between the ranges. Yet I couldn't see the towns that I knew were tucked into the folds of the mountains and that sprawled across the sage-strewn plains. I couldn't see Durango, my hometown, couldn't gauge by a gridwork of streets where the house must be. My father had joked with me over the phone before the launch, promising he would go outside and wave into the sunlit sky; and I bet he actually did wave a time or two. But I never waved back because it was hard to imagine that he was actually somewhere in my field of vision—an indiscernible speck in faded jeans and house slippers standing on the cement slab by the back door. And it was hard to imagine that the entire rumpled and wind-scoured region wasn't just some glorious gas station map that had been wrapped around the sensuous curve of the earth. That canyoned and summited corner of Colorado was profoundly familiar to me, but from the silent vantage of space it looked like someplace that was worlds away, forever inaccessible.

Colorado had seemed plenty far enough away from Houston as well, and I had considered flying up for a visit, but I finally decided to drive. We had spent about ten days in debriefings following the flight, and then NASA sent Bill Grimes, Cathy Cohn, and me out on the promotional circuit for a couple of weeks, so the idea of throwing some quarts of beer into a cooler and heading across the hard, anvil-hot prairies of Texas sounded strangely appealing. I stopped at Pe-Te's for lunch on the day I left, mentioned I was heading north for a few days, then chewed on pork ribs while Pe-Te told me about the time he almost froze to death hunting elk above Pagosa Springs. I laughed, told him I figured Cajuns ought to stay the hell out of the high mountains for the general safety of us all, then had him make me a couple of barbecue sandwiches for the road.

I hadn't seen the kids since the day before the launch and I wanted to stop in Austin to take them out for a hamburger or something, but Peggy had made it clear that I was never to stop by unannounced, and I was afraid that that *Texas Monthly* jerk would be there, so I simply blew the kids a kiss as I drove up 290 into the Hill Country, promising myself that we'd have a real reunion on my way back. I had been a father *in absentia* for only a couple of months, and it was a role I wasn't very good at. When I was away from Matt and Sarah, as I was most of the time now, it was hard not to convince myself that I was a bastard for not being with them. Yet when we were together, I always seemed to be glancing into mirrors, wondering if I appeared to be a good father to the rest of the world, rather than simply paying attention to those two remarkable little people. Peggy and I had at least succeeded with them, hadn't we? At least our children were evidence that our twelve years together had had some meaning, a more precious legacy than simply a couple of fat photo albums too painful now to open. As I drove through Dripping Springs and on through the secure and sultry darkness, eating Pe-Te's sandwiches and listening to a country disc jockey dedicate songs to "all you boys high-ballin' out on I-20," it seemed to me that driving those whining eighteen-wheelers on all-night hauls wouldn't be a bad occupation. But by the time I got to San Angelo I was so road weary that I was already looking for a new line of work, and I stopped at the Holiday and got a room.

The bar, called the Branding Iron as I recall, was still open, but empty except for a guy who looked as if he had roughnecked for ninety years and his girlfriend in vinyl pants. The bartender probably would have been just as lovely even if it weren't after midnight and if I weren't alone and awkwardly lonely. We talked while I drank better scotch than I usually drink and while she began to clean up the bar. I told her I was from Houston and she told me about the time she and her best friend, who lived there now, had gone to a club on Richmond called Cooter's, how they had quickly discovered that every male in the place was rabidly on the make.

"Did you take anyone up on it?" I asked.

She grinned, shook her head, and dipped two glasses into the rinse sink. "It's quite a world out there, isn't it?"

When she asked me what I did for a living I told her I was an engineer, my standard reply, but I was immediately sorry I hadn't tried the truth. It was late; she just wanted to get home, no doubt, and I was just another engineer. I finished my drink, went to my room and fell asleep with what seemed to be the undeniable knowledge that had she known I was an astronaut she would suddenly have found me irresistible and certainly would not have gone home.

In the morning I was glad to be waking up alone, glad to avoid saying a cold and sober good-bye in the unforgiving fluorescent light of a motel room, anxious to drive as fast as I could across the sere sweep of west Texas. I ate breakfast in Big Spring, made Lubbock by eleven, then rolled northwest toward New Mexico among the polled Herefords and Brangus cattle, the stubbled cotton fields, and the scattered, persistent pump jacks sucking oil out of the smooth skin of the plains.

My father would be full of questions, I knew, and I wanted to get to Durango before it got late. He and Mom had gone to Canaveral to watch the launch that Tuesday in May, and I was able to have lunch with them and the kids in the crew quarters the day before, but it was an awkward way to see them. They both seemed surprisingly nervous and I was paying most of my attention to the kids. When I got back to Houston, Dad told me over the phone that Mom had decided she just couldn't watch the liftoff, shutting her eyes and squeezing his hand until that crackling roar of the solid boosters reached them. She opened her eyes, he said, expecting to see the orbiter augering into the alligator marshes. But all she saw was those beautiful sun-bright streams of exhaust as we arced out over the Atlantic.

When I got to Durango, I wanted to tell my parents how glad I was that they got to see that sight—knowing their son was sitting atop those shrieking rockets. I wanted them to know that I owed them a lot and that I really was trying to be a decent adult, but I didn't know how to say it without my words sounding like the maudlin verse in a greeting card. Still, I hoped I would find something I would be brave enough to say.

By the time I got to Albuquerque, the stupefying Texas humidity was gone, the sooty air in the city was hot and powder dry. Just outside Bernalillo I picked up a young Navajo who was standing by the side of the road with one arm outstretched, the other clutching a paper sack. He wore a T-shirt that said KISS ME in red paint that was meant to look like lipstick, blue running shoes, and his long hair, black as space, was folded and wrapped with a cotton ribbon. He said he was going to Nageezi and I told him I could take him that far. When I asked if he was a student, he said no and then was silent.

"Where are you going?" he asked as we passed the turnoff into the Jemez Mountains.

"Home," I said. "Durango."

"What do you do for a job?" he asked, now seeming ready for conversation.

"I'm . . . an astronaut. I work for the government." This time I told the truth.

"Oh," he said, then was silent again. I could see a flannel shirt and the brown spine of a book in his sack but I couldn't read its title. The red hills were spotted with squat piñon trees, and the dark layers of the distant mesas were distinct in the evening light.

"Do you go to the moon?" the young man asked after a while.

"No. No, we only go into earth orbit these days."

"Why do the other astronauts go to the moon?"

"Well. I think the main reason they went was to see if they could get there. It was exploring."

"Oh," he said. "Do they like the moon very much?"

"I think they were glad to get back."

"I bet," he said.

When I stopped on the shoulder of the road across from the trading post at Nageezi, I asked him if he lived nearby.

"Over behind that round hill," he said. The spare ground, covered with small sage and saltbush and dry chamisa, stretched away in a series of shallow depressions and stunted hills. I held out my hand and told him my name was Jack. We shook hands and he said, "Good luck if you go to the moon," before he shut the door.

As I drove on in the advancing darkness, I couldn't help but wonder what the moon means to a Navajo teenager who lives in the barren, lunar landscape of the San Juan basin. I wondered whether he was the sort who would figure all we got out of Apollo was the boxes of rocks, or whether flying out to another world would seem as reasonable to him as hitchhiking to Albuquerque and back. I looked out the window for the moon and found a pale crescent in the western sky—not a cratered sphere caught in the empty sea of the solar system, just a new moon, small and intangible, suspended above the Carrizos.

I was tempted by the Lottaburger in Bloomfield but realized I could get to Durango in less than an hour, so I stayed on the road, anxious and wide awake, glad to be arriving in the enveloping and quiet night. I stopped on the bridge at the base of Cedar Hill and peed between the rusted tangle of trusses into the river, the same river I'd grown up beside, then crossed the state line and headed for town. Yard lights like the pinpoints of stars spread across the flat farm country, and the bright streetlights at the southern edge of town lit the new shopping mall and the five acres of asphalt that surrounded it, its empty parking lot making the whole enterprise appear out of place, unneeded. The sight of it also made me realize that this wasn't a town I knew well anymore. It would always be home; it would always belong to me in a strange, emotive sense. It was probably a possession I would never really know again, yet I could never sell it or give it away.

It looked as if every light in the house was on when I turned off Seventh Avenue into the steep driveway. The sagging basketball hoop and the backboard with a rectangle outlined in electrician's tape had been gone for fifteen years, but it still surprised me to find them missing. And there was a new Subaru they hadn't told me about. But just as I was about to get in to investigate the new car, Dad opened the back door.

"Don't leave," he hollered. "You just got here."

I closed the door of the car and walked over to give him a hug. He had taken his collar off and his white T-shirt was visible through the open front of his black shirt. His eyes were bright in the dim light, but it was obvious that he had tempered the wait with a tall highball or two.

"Hi, Dad," I said while he held me. "Nice car."

"Wonderful to have you," he said, and when we pulled apart his eyes were wet. "Come on. Your mother's anxious to see you. Yes, we're really going to enjoy it. I'll take you for a ride tomorrow."

My mother met us in the laundry room. I gave her a kiss, assured her that I had done nothing but eat all day, then wandered through the house, sizing it up like some sort of prospective buyer. Dad handed me a drink in the living room, and there was one for himself in his other hand.

"Sit. Sit," he said. "How was the drive?"

"Good. Just what I needed. But it's a big trip."

"You've had your share of those lately," Mom said, her voice and her smile betraying a pride in me I didn't think I deserved. "Did you stop in Austin?"

"No. They weren't expecting me. Peggy's pretty firm about me scheduling my visits."

"But they're your children as well," she said. "Sometimes I don't think she's as aware of that as she should be." She seemed startled by what she had said, a little embarrassed, then quickly added, "—but the kids were thrilled with the launch. Matthew tried to be the picture of nonchalance about it all, but by the time they got us up on the roof of that building to watch he could hardly stand still. I think he was really kind of afraid."

"Sure he was," Dad said. "We all were. But then you were off and it looked like everything was going to be all right. It was hard to believe you were really inside it."

"How did Sarah react?" I asked.

"She was a real trouper," Mom said. "I don't think she expected all the noise and so much steam and smoke. She asked me if it hurt you, and I told her it didn't hurt a bit, which was probably something of a white lie, wasn't it?"

"Not really. You are pretty well crunched into your seat for a bit, but it's all so quick. I hope neither of them got too upset. I probably should have been more careful to explain to them what to expect."

"They were fine," Dad said. "Just fine." He paused to sip his drink. "You and their mother have put them through all kinds of new experiences in the last six months, and that launch was undoubtedly one of the better ones."

"It didn't take you long to bring that up," I said. "You're welcome to give me your usual pastoral line about how these things are so hard on the children, Dad, but you ought to give us a little more credit."

"Don't you two start in," Mom said. "Let's leave that alone, Richard. Jack's barely in the door."

Dad stared at the print of the Georgia O'Keeffe painting of the church at Ranchos de Taos, a Christmas gift from his parishioners a few years before, then took a long drink of his scotch. He had always played silence to great effect, its tension his reliable ally. I had learned long ago to give him as much of it as he wanted, so I said nothing, but I winked at Mom as she went out to the kitchen.

When he was ready to speak again, he cupped his glass in his hands, leaned forward in his chair, and spoke quietly, his words coming as if they had been rehearsed: "Your mother and I went through some very difficult times during the years I was in seminary. You and Mary were barely out of diapers; she was still nursing Michael. We had to live on next to nothing. But the worst of it probably was that I felt that if I was going to be a priest I had to somehow prove my sainthood. I was going to be wearing a collar and that was going to change everything. When we fought, I tried to make her feel guilty for fighting with a holy man." He smiled. "I'm sure I was a real joy to live with. I've kind of assumed that something similar happened last year with you two. You being too busy getting ready for the flight. Peggy feeling that you had abandoned her for a spaceship."

"She was the one that did the abandoning, Dad. I didn't run off with some asshole from Austin."

"No, I don't think you abandoned her, Jack, and I doubt she really meant to abandon you. But now that your flight's over, things might seem rather different to both of you."

"You are a nosy bastard, aren't you?" I said, grinning when I said it. I knew I wasn't prepared to have him solve my marital problems so early in my visit.

"I'm in the nosy business. We clerics begin with the presumption that absolutely everything is our vital concern. That's probably why we seem so damn overbearing."

"What about that?" I asked, obviously changing the subject. "Are you really going to retire?"

"I've decided not to decide. If the Holy Spirit wants me to stay at St. Mark's after I'm sixty-five, he'll just have to let me know by keeping me alive. I guess Mom told you we buried Hal yesterday?"

"No . . ." I didn't know what to say. "The cancer?"

He nodded, his eyes got wet again, and he pulled on his nose. "They thought they had it licked. Then about a month ago they did a biopsy of a little spot in his stomach—positive—and they sent him to Denver for more tests. It had spread all through his lungs and liver. He was in the hospital here for about three weeks." Dad ran his fingers through the thick hair at his temples. The skin on the top of his head was taut and pink. "When I went to see him on Saturday, he asked me whether I would rather see him die in a hospital bed or die catching trout. So Sunday afternoon I got him dressed and snuck him out a service entrance. We drove up to Rockwood and I put him in a lawn chair next to the bank. He fished for almost an hour before he got too weak. The river seemed like such a tonic."

"Did he catch anything?"

"No," Dad said, "but he didn't mind. He died back at the hospital that night. Asked all about your flight, Jack. He was looking forward to seeing you. He said he sure would put that on his list of things to do before he died."

"It ought to be on everyone's list," I told him, wishing I could say something about Hal and how I was so sorry.

"I told Hal they ought to send burned-out priests on space missions. I bet one weightless orbit would be better than all the retreats you could ever stand. Say. I was kind of hoping that at coffee on Sunday maybe you'd talk about it a little. Everyone is very interested."

"And that way you'd cleverly get me to church."

"You can't blame a fellow for scheming a little."

"I guess it wouldn't hurt me," I said. "You sure you don't mind having a heathen address your flock?"

"Oh, I'll be keeping my eye on you," he said, then smiled as Mom came back into the room. "He said yes to my proposition, Dorothy. I only had to agree to a five-figure sum."

"Perfectly reasonable," she said, "if you'll really let him talk. No annoying interruptions."

"Dorothy!" Dad said. "You've got me confused with one of your other men of the cloth. I—"

"You be still," she said. "That kind of talk doesn't become you. And I think I'll call it a night."

"We haven't even heard about the flight yet. Come sit down. Your son has grand things to tell us."

"I'll hear everything in the morning. Good night, Jack," she said, bending over to kiss the top of my head. "And good night to you, Father Healy."

Dad blew her a kiss, then watched her disappear down the hall. I refused his offer of another drink, then changed my mind when he got up to help himself to another. He had always preferred to let my mother go to bed without him, it seemed, staying awake, drinking and reading until his head collapsed into the corner of the recliner and he slept. I remember that when I was still home I would often get up in the middle of the night and find him slumped in his chair and snoring, a book by Teilhard de Chardin lying in his lap. I always wanted to close his book, to take his watery drink to the kitchen, to nudge him and send him off to bed, but I never did. Time after time, I just turned off the lamp that stood beside the chair, then slowly made my way across the carpet, leaving him alone in the darkness.

But that night there was my mission to discuss, and his book stayed shut, and I drank with him into the early morning. He wanted to hear about the reason for the countdown delay, wondered whether we were aware of how much media attention we were getting, asked me all about the EVA, how the backpack worked, and what it felt like as I flew away from the orbiter. I remember that when I was in high school kids used to tell me what a good listener he was, but that ability to listen always seemed limited to the hours he wore the collar. I don't think Mike or Mary or I ever thought he paid any sort of rapt attention to us. But that night, he was undeniably entranced by my descriptions of the flight. Space seemed to be a subject that tapped the inveterate tinkerer in him as well as the starry-eyed theologian. He was enthralled with the thought that humans could go to inhuman realms, and the idea of seeing the earth spin in the blackness seemed almost sacramental to him.

"When we saw those first pictures on TV of you and Bill Grimes out there, completely away from the shuttle, I couldn't believe it. Your mother and I both had big tears streaming down our faces. I mean, good heavens, there you were in absolute space. I thought, what a very lucky man he is."

"I know I am," I said. "Whenever I had a second just to drink it all in, that was what crossed my mind. Why do I get to do this? I felt so damn . . . fortunate. Why not Mary or Matt . . . or Hal McGinnis?"

"Matthew's time will come. He'll have a hell of a life. And Hal . . . I'm going out to see Jane tomorrow, by the way. Losing her dad on top of everything else has been quite a blow. Hal's brother and his wife were going to leave today. Come with me. I told her I'd try to drag you along."

"Sure. I'd like to," I said. I told him about how we had finally snared the satellite, and then I demanded a bed.

"Off you go," he said. "I'll be along in a bit."

The next morning, I asked my father if he had heard from Mike recently as we drove west out of town, crossing the run-off swollen river, then twisting through the bare canyon that was still and shadowed in the morning light. Mike had called from Denver on Tuesday, he said, and he seemed to be doing better. He was working at a bakery in the mornings and spending his afternoons at St. Andrew's, helping in the kitchen and cleaning the room where the street people slept, their canvas pads strewn across the checkered linoleum floor.

"As long as he stays on the Thorazine, he seems to do just fine," Dad said. "But then for no reason he'll stop taking it, and I'll get a call that he's threatening Father Long with a Buck knife because John takes his mind away while he sleeps. John Long has been tremendous with Michael. You remember John, don't you? We wanted to bring Michael to the Cape with us, but since he finally seems to be getting settled, we decided we'd better not. And I'm sure Mary was sick about not being able to come."

"She called a couple of days after I got back to Houston," I said. "Vintage Mary. She was certainly not going to be overly impressed by some expensive federal enterprise that smacks of militarism, but she did say she wished she could have seen the launch. I told her I hoped there'd be another one sometime. The next time, she said, she could guarantee she wouldn't be strapped with a ten-month-old."

It was still hard to imagine Mary as a mother. She had not married

Robert until she was thirty-three, and the daughter, named Adrian, had not arrived until a few days following Mary's thirty-ninth birthday. She would be devoted to her child, I was sure of that—she would be patient and endlessly understanding, and her fascination with Adrian's progress would smother other, less captivating concerns. Yet Mary was utterly independent, and it was hard to imagine her surrendering to the mundane commitments of motherhood.

The eldest of the three of us, Mary had very decidedly emancipated herself at seventeen when she went to college in California. She seldom wrote or telephoned our parents, and her Christmas visits were always short, plagued by a kind of unspoken argument about her responsibility to her family. When Mary had her first one-person show in Berkeley a couple of years after she graduated, she didn't tell any of us about it until the show had already come down. Mom and Dad were crushed that she had not wanted them to see it, or to come to the opening, but she professed shock at why they would have even considered it, telling them her work was tentative and unfocused, missing the point entirely.

I had always struggled with the question of what I wanted to do with myself, with what would ever be worth doing for dozens of years; Michael had struggled with the neurochemical chaos inside his brain; but Mary had always been resolute. Painting was, for her, not so much a decision as an obligation. She was very critical of her talent, never satisfied with a specific piece, yet she painted, year after year, as if she were meeting the terms of a demanding personal contract.

I had never understood what she and Robert shared, nor did I know how this zoology professor and the abstract painter had ever managed to meet. When she spoke of him—on the few occasions when we talked on the telephone—she would only refer to him in the most cursory way, always saying how busy he was, how his job at Cal was all-consuming. About young Adrian, however, I was happy to discover that Mary was willing to talk at length. Adrian, it seemed, was her first creation in which she was willing to take some pride.

My father said he was sure Mary was still painting, but that since she had stopped teaching when Adrian was born, he was worried that their financial situation was getting rather pinched. Yet he was gratified and a little relieved to hear from Mary that a gallery in San Francisco had recently sold two of her large paintings.

The highway met Cherry Creek and followed its twisting course beneath the snow-shrouded peaks of the La Platas. The aspen were in leaf; the trees swayed in the warm breeze of early summer, their white trunks straight and thick and knotted. Dad turned onto the dirt road in Thompson Park, the tires of his new blue car churning a column of dust behind us. He waved at a rancher in a straw hat and tall rubber boots who was irrigating a green hay field, then drove another mile before turning into the lane that led past the barn and the hay shed to the house. Jane, dressed in jeans and a snap-button shirt, her dark, gray-streaked hair held up with a silver clip, was tossing scratch to red chickens when she saw us. She emptied the grain from her bucket and came over to the car, hugging Dad first, then holding her arms out to me.

"Hello, spaceman," she said, "You don't look like it's harmed you." Her broad face was tan and smooth, her smile as disarming as ever. "Welcome back to solid ground."

I told her it felt good to be back. Her shirt was rolled up to her elbows and she saw me glance at the smooth stump at her right wrist. I had heard about the accident, of course, and I knew that her hand was gone, but the visual evidence was nonetheless an unsettling surprise.

"Oh yes, you haven't seen this," she said, lifting the stump up to my eyes. "What do you think? Some people pierce their ears. I chop off my hand." Always brash and uninhibited, Jane had no doubt thrust the evidence of her misfortune into dozens of people's faces in the months since she had lost her hand and her husband.

"Very becoming," I said. "I like it. How are you getting along?"

"Well, if it wasn't my goddamned right one it wouldn't have been so bad, but I swear it's like trying to work with five toes and an ax handle this way. But . . . all things considered, I—"

"She's doing beautifully," Dad said. "I saw her saddle a horse when I was out the other day and she didn't seem to have any trouble."

"But you didn't see it roll off his back when I stepped in the stirrup, did you?" She grinned, told us to follow her into the house, and I watched her as she turned and marched toward the back door. I had always been attracted to Jane; we had even dated—both of us feeling a weird incestuousness about it—during one summer when I was home from college, but I was surprised to find that as a one-handed widow now pushing forty Jane seemed so strong and so alluring.

Kenny had been dead for almost a year; she had been hospitalized for two months and had worn a back brace for two more. Her hand was severed by the hitch of the horse trailer when it landed beside the overturned truck. Kenny was also thrown out of the pickup and was crushed by the side of the trailer. Both horses lived for over an hour before a state patrolman finally took out his revolver and shot them. The neighbors got the last cutting of hay in, and Jane hired an illegal from Chihuahua to feed for her that winter. Dad said she wanted to sell the cows and half the place. As we sat down at the kitchen table, she told me she planned to keep the horses and to stay out in the park indefinitely.

"I had thought about finding a house in town for Dad and me, but I didn't really want to live in town. Now that he's gone, I'm sure I'll stay put. I saw you on TV, Jack. Couldn't really tell it was you out on your spacewalk, but you looked great floating around inside the shuttle. You guys must have had a terrific time."

"I doubt they got a lick of work done," Dad said.

"Strictly recreational," I told them; then I said something to Jane about her dad. Hal and my father had been friends since Dad first arrived at St. Mark's. But unlike Dad, Hal was always as captivated by the skies as I was. He and I used to spot constellations and watch lunar eclipses in my parents' backyard, and I was fascinated by his stories about the Northern Lights from his years spent in Alberta. I got a telegram from him in Houston years ago on the day the first Viking lander touched down on Mars. It just read, WE MADE IT! BEST, HAL.

"He watched your launch at the hospital," Jane said. "He told all the nurses and technicians that he had a friend flying on the shuttle and that they, by God, couldn't sedate him."

"When we got back," Dad said, "he had to hear every last detail about the launch. I brought him one of those souvenir hats that says NASA, and he wore it in bed while we watched the landing." He paused. "I'm going to miss that man."

"Me too," Jane said; then she got up from the table. "Shoot, it's after eleven. It's not too early for a beer, is it?" She went to the refrigerator. "Come on. We'll take these out to the porch."

"I'll meet you there," I said. "I want to go look at your horses." I took a beer and walked through the corrals by the barn and out into the pasture. Four horses grazed on the bromegrass near the south fence. They picked their heads up and studiously watched me approach. A bay mare finally took a few steps in my direction, then stopped when she noticed I wasn't carrying a grain bucket. When I reached her, I rubbed her neck and let her smell the bottle to prove it was nothing of interest. The other three, still wary of a hatless man in khaki pants, kept their distance. A second mare, surely ready to foal, had a big, bell-shaped belly, and her steps seemed labored as she moved along the fence. I ought to be a horseman, I thought. I ought to trim hooves, attend the births of pinto colts, spend weekday afternoons in smoky sale barns, and tell inquiring strangers that I was a stockman when I hung my hat on the racks in the local cafés. The bay mare, still not convinced, grabbed at the neck of the bottle with her mouth and hit it against her teeth. She stepped away, and I turned back toward the barn. I could see Jane and Dad sitting in a swing on the porch, and I waved but they didn't notice. The sun was high in the cloudless sky, and the sweet aroma of the cottonwoods wafted up from the creek. A magpie scolded me from a fence post, and the horses went back to the grass.

I couldn't hear what Dad was saying as I came around the corner of the house. Jane nodded and said, "Yes, I suppose so," then waved to me to join them.

"That mare looks like she's about ready," I said.

"I hope so, poor thing. She's so uncomfortable, especially now that it's getting hot. She's a sweetheart. This is her first foal. I'm a little nervous about it. Knowing me, I'll probably end up with a huge vet bill for having him come watch a perfectly normal birth. I told your dad I'm going to ride the roan up to the cabin tomorrow to get some of Dad's things. You can have Brenda, that bay that likes you, if you want to come."

"The cabin?"

"That hunting shack of Dad's up in Echo Basin. Want to?"

"Yes. I do. But you have to promise not to laugh at me when she makes me look ridiculous. I haven't been on a horse in ages."

"I thought all you Texans could cowboy," Dad said.

"Maybe all those Texans can," I said. "I just use their license plates.

What time?" On the way to the car, Jane suggested I come out about noon; she said she'd have the horses trailered and the whiskey packed in the saddlebags.

"Don't get him too relaxed," Dad told her. "I've got him reserved for Sunday morning."

"I'll take care of him," she said. "And thanks, Dick. You've been awfully sweet to us, to me," She pushed the door of the car shut, and the way she looked at my father in that instant made me aware of how close the two of them had become. Something in her face, too—perhaps it was the sorrow it still reflected, perhaps it was a nascent hint of happiness—made my feelings for her seem like a sudden infatuation.

At dinner that night, my mother was worried about Mike, about whether he would end up in the hospital again, and I told her I had thought about going up to Denver before heading back to Houston. I hadn't seen Michael in almost two years, and I wasn't particularly anxious to see him again and to hear his incoherent stories. But Mike was doing very well, they said, and I admitted that it would be good for the two of us to be back in touch.

Mike was only two years behind me in school and we had been close until I was a junior or senior in high school. I was student body president and was, no doubt, rather impressed with myself, and I began to be horribly embarrassed by a brother who would lean for hours against the tiled walls of the science-wing restroom because, he said, the kids in the hallways wanted to steal his clothes. Mom remained Michael's great ally during the two years he tried to go to college, and although Dad had read a seemingly endless series of articles and books about schizophrenia, he, like me, responded to Mike with a certain exasperation.

"It would mean a lot to Michael if you could stop for a day or so," Mom said. "He really needs to know he has a family who cares about him." My mother's voice always assumed a terrible sadness when she talked about Michael, the child to whom, for reasons I doubt even she knew, she had always been closest, the son whose private anguish had deepened her love and protection. When she spoke with concern about Michael, I always wanted to give her a kind of comic hug and to tell her with unfounded optimism that he was going to be just fine.

But I never did, perhaps because I somehow sensed that she knew a contradictory truth.

"I'll call and find out when I have to be back. I'd enjoy the drive through the mountains. Mike and I could catch up on a lot of things. And doesn't Jane's offer to ride up to Hal's cabin sound great?" I asked, getting away from the subject I knew they were desperate to talk about, but the one that I somehow couldn't address.

I borrowed a pair of boots from Dad on Saturday and he insisted that I take his straw hat as well. I told him I'd feel a little stupid in a cowboy hat, but he convinced me that without it the sun would burn me up. When I got to Jane's, the horses, as promised, were in the trailer, and she had sandwiches for us to eat in the truck. She asked me to drive, and I'm sure she noticed how timidly I negotiated Mancos Hill. I was more at ease on the Forest Service road that led into the basin, but pulling the heavy trailer was unsettling and the conversation was often cut by my silent attention to the road.

"I could see the La Platas from orbit," I said to break the silence. "They were just a minuscule white group of ridges, but they were easy to spot. It's funny. I felt so proprietary about this place, seeing it from two hundred miles up."

"Do you want to go again?"

"I'd love to. But working for the government gets pretty gruesome. You never know what in the hell they've got planned for you. And ass kissing is the only real talent you're required to have. If Peggy and the kids moved farther away, I'd have some real second thoughts. There was a time when all I ever imagined doing was teaching astronomy at some little college somewhere. Now that possibility seems so remote I can hardly imagine it. Maybe I'm destined to become a beer distributor, like all the other ex-astronauts."

"I was sorry to hear about you two splitting up, Jack. I always assumed that you two really had made that pact that everybody aims for. But . . . did it have something to do with her finally deciding she had to see if she could walk without a net? Not that it's any of my business."

"What do you mean?"

"I know what it's like to live in somebody's shadow. Kenny was Mr. Wonderful around here, on every committee and invited to every social event, the heartthrob of all the horny young wives whose husbands were getting fat. They all thought I was just this weird complication in his life, an aloof bitch who wouldn't even join the bridge clubs. I was in the hospital, but they told me that at his funeral they had to set up loudspeakers in the parish hall and out in the courtyard so everyone who came could hear the service. Poor Kenny. He would have loved to know he could draw that kind of crowd. He wanted to run for county commissioner. Now that he's gone, people just can't associate me with him anymore. It's the first time I've ever really felt like an individual, I guess."

I pulled the truck to the edge of the road when Jane motioned toward the sign that marked the trail. "You and Peggy probably do have something in common," I said. We backed the horses out of the trailer. Their saddles were already on, so all I had to do was to fumble at getting the curb bit into Brenda's mouth and tie the nylon bags to the saddle skirts. I watched Jane tie a rolled canvas pannier behind the cantle of her saddle, anxious to help but afraid to offer. She mounted the roan gelding, then held the reins in her teeth while she struggled to adjust the stirrups with her left hand.

"Son of a bitch," she said. "I forgot that my irrigator used this saddle last week." She turned to me, her voice softened as if she was telling me something she wouldn't have shared with everyone. "Doctor keeps telling me it's time for a prosthesis, but, God, I don't want to wear some stupid hook or a plastic hand. I don't care how much easier it would be." I didn't know how to respond, so I was silent again.

The trail was wide as it led into the timber, and the horses walked abreast. Brenda was a good walker and seemed relaxed in the trees, but the roan, named Sport, snorted and seemed to hunt for an excuse to spook. Jane held him on a tight rein and slapped his ears with her handless arm a time or two before he abandoned his hopes for chaos. "So," she said, "you want to become a beer distributor."

"Maybe a cowboy," I said. "This seems to suit me."

"I like your hat. Makes you look like Smiley Burnette."

"It's my father's fault. The image would be more like the Lone Ranger if it was my own hat."

"That's the astronaut coming out. You want people to think you're perfect."

"But you don't buy it in my case, right?"

"This whole space business . . . I don't know," she said. "I just have never got it. I'm glad for you, Jack, I don't mean that, but isn't it just a big show? All for the patriotic glory of it?"

"My Rotary Club speech about the space program would put you to sleep," I said. "But no. I think it's pretty important. Even going to the moon made sense if you accept the idea that you ought to go wherever you can get to."

"So now we know the moon is rocky and gray and wouldn't be much of a vacation."

"There's an old book by Oriana Fallaci about the space program in the years before the first moon landing. She began her research as this outrageous skeptic, but by the end she seemed to think space travel was some sort of valiant symbolic quest. She interviewed Wally Schirra, who is your classic right-stuff kind of guy, Spartan and tight-lipped as they come. But old Wally ended up gushing to her that the moon and Mars are ugly islands. Nobody would want to live there, he said. But the reason for going to the ugly islands was to prove you could do it, so you could keep searching for the beautiful islands."

"Assuming there are some."

"Oh, they're there."

"An act of faith?"

"An act of a telescope. I mean, I don't know if we'll ever find one that has oxygen and aspen trees, but that doesn't bother me. We have to look because that's what we're programmed for—I mean, maybe even genetically. Basically what we do as a species is poke around, snoop, isn't it?"

We rode out of the trees into a small meadow, its grass still matted by the weight of the winter's snow. A doe that was drinking in a quiet meander of the creek looked warily at us, then bounded into the stand of spruce that swept up toward the barren rock. The trail narrowed at the far side of the meadow, then made two switchbacks as it climbed through the damp floor of the forest. Sport was winded enough to be steady now, and Brenda followed so obediently that I had nothing to do but sit. The cabin, built out of pine planks that must have been hauled up thirty years before, stood on a small bank of bald rock. Loose tar paper on the roof flapped in the mountain wind, and the one window was covered with cardboard. We tied the horses to a fallen log, then looked inside.

The small room smelled musty but strangely sweet. It was dusty and dark and the mice had made themselves at home; their dry turds were scattered across the table, the long counter, and the plastic sheet that covered the bed. Hal had left four boxes of split wood next to the rusted Ashley, and the dishes were carefully stacked beside the washbasin. Jane looked inside a three-legged chest of drawers for the things she had come for—a deerskin jacket, an old revolver, a thick roll of topographical maps, and a stack of books. She took them outside, sat down on the west side of the shack in the late-afternoon sun, and put them inside the canvas pannier. "I didn't like the idea of these things that were important to him sitting up here where they could be stolen now that he's gone," she said. I sat down beside her and could see Ute Mountain in the west, and off to the southwest, the high plateau of Mesa Verde, cut by its finger canyons. "He only liked to come here alone," she said. "I used to suggest that the two of us ride up here occasionally, but he always had some lame excuse. Then out of the blue one day he'd call and say he was on his way out the door, headed for the cabin. Always a great urgency about it. He kept that little telescope here too. But he brought it down last fall when he discovered some hunters had stayed here." She finished the packing, then took a pint of scotch out of her jacket pocket.

"You'll join me, I trust," she said before she put the bottle to her lips. "This has become quite a habit since the accident. I used to wonder why people drank alone, but I don't wonder anymore. I suppose I count Johnnie Walker among my best friends these days." She grinned, and considered before she spoke again. "What's it been like for you alone, Jack?"

"I've been lucky," I said. "With the mission, I've been busy enough, gone enough that I haven't really had to face it. I'm sure that's part of the reason why I decided to drive up. I still wasn't ready to face the office routine and that god-awful empty house of mine."

Jane stared into the distance. "I haven't washed my windows for nearly a year," she said. "I leave the newspapers in rolls and stack them like kindling in the kitchen closet. Maybe this is what they mean by mourning, but I think it's inertia. It's a sort of weird inertia caused by being left alive. Like I'm numb. Like I just don't give a damn about anything. Even when we knew it was just a matter of days for Dad, I couldn't cry. I couldn't tell him the things I always assumed I would say."

I put my hand on her leg, smoothing the faded fabric of her jeans, and Jane turned to me and kissed me. She smelled wonderful, like my memories of Peggy, and she pressed herself against me. She lifted my hat off when we looked at each other again. "I'm not so inert that I couldn't make love to you," she said, her voice quiet now, its cynical edge evaporating. "I don't think I could have till . . . well . . . ."

We stood and went inside the cabin. I sat on the edge of the table while she pulled the plastic from the bed. She sat on the edge of the bed, kicked off her boots, and unbuttoned her shirt with her single hand. Her breasts were tan and round and lovely, her nipples hard. "You stop wearing bras when you lose a hand," she said with a shy smile. "Come here, for heaven's sake."

I was glad to follow instructions. She must have known how much I wanted her, but for some reason I preferred to pretend I was merely compliant. I went to the bed and undressed before I touched her again. We stared at each other, saying nothing while I stood, then I curled beside her on the cold cotton bedspread. I reached for her head and found her mouth again. It had been nearly two months since I had made love to anyone, too much aching time since that strange weekend in April when Barbara Collingwood, another astronaut, and I had gone to Padre Island for the expressed purpose of coming to each other's carnal rescue. There was something similar happening with Jane and me, but bound up in it too, for both of us, were the accident and her dad and our strange connection to each other shaped by that backwater corner of Colorado. We held each other desperately, shouting and sweating, almost fighting, before we were finished and were again aware of the cold.

I pulled the bedspread over us; Jane dozed with her head on my shoulder. Her handless arm was stretched across my chest and I could see the pale, precise scar that curled around the stump. I kissed her forehead. "Let's stay," I said. "The night. There's lots of wood."

"We'll bother the mice," she said. "Won't be much of a dinner. That . . . was the first time since Kenny. God, it seems like ages ago."

"You think your dad would mind us staying here in his private retreat?"

"If he knew you were here I think he'd arrange some sort of dispensation."

Before we got up, Jane mentioned the accident again, telling me it had been a long time before she realized she was mourning the loss of her hand as well as her husband. "At first, it seemed like such a little thing. Kenny, the horses were dead—gone forever—and my hand, well, it was nothing in comparison. Then, after a few months, I started to get angry, really mad, about being left with this stump. I was alone, and I was damn lonely, I suppose, and to top it all off, now I was some sort of freak."

"No," I said, "you don't—"

"You don't realize what it does to you, Jack. Everything you do is a big procedure, and you're reminded a million times a day of how incompetent you are. Then, finally, the resignation sets in, and that's the paralyzing part."

"But you haven't really had to give anything up, have you?" I asked, as if I had to counter with a feeble optimism.

"I've given up taking my abilities for granted," she said. "That's something more than you'd guess it would be. Before, I basically assumed I could do anything I chose. There weren't any limits. Now, the limits are the first things that cross my mind."

I built a fire in the Ashley when I got up from the bed, and at dusk I built a second fire in a ring of stones that lay off to the side of the cabin. We unsaddled the horses and Jane tied their lead ropes to a snag that looked as if long ago it had been hit by lightning. We sat by the campfire in the thickening darkness, ate two apples and a candy bar, and finished the scotch. I took Hal's deerskin jacket out of the pannier and put it on; Jane wrapped herself in a wool blanket. The crescent moon, looking as if it had leaped above Ute Mountain, had grown to nearly a quarter, and the serpentine stars of Hydra hung above it. I pointed out Betelgeuse and the bears and tried to spot the dim outline of Pegasus, but could not. Before we went inside, I told Jane that from orbit, the only way we could locate the earth at night was to find the arc where the stars stopped. It seemed so strange that that sweep of total darkness, of emptiness, was the familiar earth itself, just a rocket's throw away.

Brenda and Sport began to whinny in the dead of night. When I opened the door nothing seemed to be wrong, but I waited until they were quiet before I went back inside. I don't think I slept again. I remember lying in Hal's bed until it grew light, imagining how improbable it was that I was there in his mountaintop retreat, his daughter asleep beside me.

I didn't realize what I had done—or what I'd forgotten to do—until Jane was awake, kidding me about spending my Sunday morning with an old widow-woman instead of attending my father's church. By then it was too late to make it back to town to give the talk I had promised him I would, but we hurried anyway, closing up the cabin and riding the horses back down to the truck in a flurry of preoccupied and guilty activity. At Jane's ranch, I tried to slow down long enough to thank her for the outing and the night, but she hurried me on my way, knowing better than I did, I suppose, how disappointed my dad would be.

My mother was in the kitchen when I got back to the house; she didn't say anything when she looked up from the letter she was writing at the table. I sat down in a chair across from her and asked her where he was.

"He's in the backyard. Trimming roses. But don't go out. I'm not sure he'd speak to you."

"I completely forgot," I said. "I'm so sorry. We decided to stay up at the cabin. I didn't remember until this morning, and by then it was too late to get down in time."

"He told them you suddenly had been called back to Texas. He was so embarrassed, Jack. That was the worst of it."

"Jesus. That was probably the cruelest thing I could have done to him."

"Well . . . just leave him alone."

"I guess I ought to go ahead and go now that he's told people I have."

"Did you have a good time?"

"Yes . . . very, but I ought to apologize at least."

"Wait till this evening. You two can talk after dinner. Just let him garden for now."

"I better just say something and go," I said, and I got up and went out the back door. Dad was kneeling in the brown soil of the rose bed, his shirt off, his hands in cotton gloves. I sat on the grass beside him and watched him work before I spoke. His back was moist; his belly looked bigger than I had imagined it was.

"I just wanted to say that I'm terribly sorry," I said. "It wasn't intentional. We decided to stay and I forgot. I just forgot."

He turned the soil with a hand spade. "The worst thing about being a parent," he said, "is that it's irreversible." The dark soil was damp; it stuck to his ragged gloves. "I don't want an apology; don't want to accept one. It didn't matter."

"Yes it did. You asked me to do something for you and I let you down."

"You're thirty-six years old, Jack. You're free to let down anyone you want to." He still did not look at me. "That cabin meant a lot to Hal. Now I guess the wind and snow will have it ruined before long. Come back and see us, Jack."

"I guess I ought to go, shouldn't I?"

"We've had a good visit. Find your mother before you go. Give the kids a big hug for us."

"I'll give you a hug."

"Let's wait till next time," he said, patting the soil with his broad hands as I turned back to the house.

My mother was still at the table and I told her I was on my way to Denver. "I'd like to see Mike in good shape," I said.

She got up, embraced me and held me for a moment. "I'm sorry, Jack," she said. "This family is funny, isn't it?" It was something I had heard her say dozens of times before. Whenever one of us fought with my father, whenever Mary's correspondence dwindled to months of silence, whenever the voices began to shout inside Michael's head, my mother would smile sadly and tell us what a funny clan we were. She knew, of course, that our troubles were much like any other family's. In saying we were funny, she meant to tell us how readily we could break her heart.

I got my things, drove through the quiet Sunday streets and out of town to Jane's. No one answered the door. I checked the barn and the outbuildings and walked through the near pasture. God, I wanted to see her again. I left a note taped to the door, and went back through town, drove east into the tall ponderosas and over Wolf Creek Pass. I found a phone at a gas station in Del Norte.

"Come to Texas," I said to Jane when she answered.

"How was he?" she asked.

"Hurt. Furious. Sad that he had to have kids. Will you come?"

"I'll keep you posted," she said. "And thank you."

I was in Pueblo by dusk. The interstate was almost empty and the bare brown plains rolled away in the darkness. The moon at last lifted above the high hump of Pikes Peak, but it couldn't keep me company, couldn't keep my mind off what I had done to my father, or the way he had hurried me out of his garden. Even the recurrent image of Jane—her shirt unbuttoned, her arms opening out to me—couldn't convince me that I had ever done a damn bit of good for anyone.

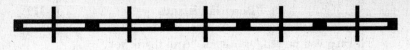

TERRY TEMPEST WILLIAMS

Whimbrels

From REFUGE

Lake Level: 4203.25′

The Bird Refuge has remained a constant. It is a landscape so familiar to me, there have been times I have felt a species long before I saw it. The long-billed curlews that foraged the grasslands seven miles outside the Refuge were trustworthy. I can count on them year after year. And when six whimbrels joined them—whimbrel entered my mind as an idea. Before I ever saw them mingling with curlews, I recognized them as a new thought in familiar country.

The birds and I share a natural history. It is a matter of rootedness, of living inside a place for so long that the mind and imagination fuse.

Maybe it's the expanse of sky above and water below that soothes my soul. Or maybe it's the anticipation of seeing something new. Whatever the magic of Bear River is—I appreciate this corner of northern Utah, where the numbers of ducks and geese I find resemble those found by early explorers.

Of the 208 species of birds who use the Refuge, sixty-two are known to nest here. Such nesting species include eared, western, and pied-billed grebes, great blue herons, snowy egrets, white-faced ibises, American avocets, black-necked stilts, and Wilson's phalaropes. Also nesting at Bear River are Canada geese, mallards, gadwalls, pintails, green-winged, blue-winged, and cinnamon teals, redheads, and ruddy ducks. It is a fertile community where the hope of each day rides on the backs of migrating birds.

These wetlands, emeralds around Great Salt Lake, provide critical habitat for North American waterfowl and shorebirds, supporting hundreds of thousands, even millions of individuals during spring and autumn migrations. The long-legged birds with their eyes focused down transform a seemingly sterile world into a fecund one. It is here in the marshes with the birds that I seal my relationship to Great Salt Lake.

I could never have anticipated its rise.

My mother was aware of a rise on the left side of her abdomen. I was deep in dream. This particular episode found me hiding beneath my grandmother's bed as eight black helicopters flew toward the house. I knew we were in danger.

The phone rang and everything changed.

"Good morning," I answered.

"Good morning, dear," my mother replied.

This is how my days always began. Mother and I checking in—a long extension cord on the telephone lets me talk and eat breakfast at the same time.

"You're back. So how was the river trip?" I asked, pouring myself a glass of orange juice.

"It was wonderful," she answered. "I loved the river and I loved the people. The Grand Canyon is a . . ."

There was a break in her voice. I set my glass on the counter.

She paused. "I didn't want to do this, Terry."

I think I knew what she was going to say before she said it. The same way, twelve years before, I knew something was wrong when I walked into our house after school and Mother was gone. In 1971, it had been breast cancer.

With my back against the kitchen wall, I slowly sank to the floor and stared at the yellow flowered wallpaper I had always intended to change.

"What I was going to say is that the Grand Canyon is a perfect place to heal. I've found a tumor, a fairly large mass in my lower abdomen. I was wondering if you could go with me to the hospital. John has to work. I'm scheduled for an ultrasound this afternoon."

I closed my eyes. "Of course."

Another pause.

"How long have you known about this?"

"I discovered it about a month ago."

I found myself getting angry until she answered the next obvious question.

"I needed time to live with it, to think about it—and more than anything else, I wanted to float down the Colorado River. This was the trip John and I had been dreaming about for years. I knew the days in the canyon would give me peace. And Terry, they did."

I sat on the white linoleum floor in my nightgown with my knees pulled in toward my chest, my head bowed.

"Maybe it's nothing, Mother. Maybe it's only a cyst. It could be benign, you know."

She did not answer.

"How do you feel?" I asked.

"I feel fine," she said. "But I would like to go shopping for a robe before my appointment at one."

We agreed to meet at eleven.

"I'm glad you're home." I said.

"So am I."

She hung up. The dial tone returned. I listened to the line until it became clear I had heard what I heard.

It's strange to feel change coming. It's easy to ignore. An underlying restlessness seems to accompany it like birds flocking before a storm. We go about our business with the usual alacrity, while in the pit of our stomach there is a sense of something tenuous.

These moments of peripheral perceptions are short, sharp flashes of insight we tend to discount like seeing the movement of an animal from the corner of our eye. We turn and there is nothing there. They are the strong and subtle impressions we allow to slip away.

I had been feeling fey for months.

Mother and I drove downtown, parked the car, and walked into Nordstrom's. I recalled the last department store we were in when the only agenda was which lipstick to choose.

We rode the escalator up two floors to sleepwear. Mother appeared to have nothing else on her mind but a beautiful piece of lingerie.

"What do you think about this one?" she asked as she held a navy blue satin robe up to her in the mirror.

"It's stunning," I answered. "I love the tiny white stars—"

"So do I. It's quite dramatic." She turned to the clerk. "I'll take this, please." And handed her the robe.

"Would you like this gift wrapped?" asked the saleswoman.

I started to say no. Mother said yes. "Thank you, that would be very nice."

My mother's flair for drama always caught me off guard. Her love of spontanaety made the most mundane enterprise an occasion. She entered a room, mystery followed her. She left and her presence lingered.

I thought of the last time we were in New York together. We slept late, rising mid-morning to partake of steaming hot blueberry muffins downtown in a sidewalk cafe. It was my mother's sacrament. We shopped in the finest stores and twirled in front of mirrors. We lived in the museums. Having overspent our allotment of time at the Met in the Caravaggio exhibit, we opted for a quick make-over at Bloomingdale's to revive us for the theatre. The brass and glass of the department store's first floor was blinding until we finally bumped into the Lancôme counter.

"It's wonderful to be in a place where no one knows you," Mother said as she sat in the chair reserved for customers. "I would never do this at home."

The salesclerk acquainted her with options. She looked at my mother's hazel eyes, the structure of her face, her dark hair cut short.

"Great bones," the makeup artist said. "For you, less is more."

I watched the woman sweep blush across my mother's cheekbones. A hint of brown eyeshadow deepened her eyes as framboise was painted across her lips.

"How do I look?" she said.

"Dazzling," I answered.

Mother gave me her chair. The Lancôme woman looked at my face and shook her head.

"Do you spend a lot of time in the wind?"

The hospital doors seemed heavy as I pushed them open against the air trapped inside the vestibule. Once inside, it reeked of disease whitewashed with antiseptics. A trip to the hospital is always a descent into the macabre. I have never trusted a place with shiny floors.

We found our way to the lab through the maze of hallways by following the color-coded tape on the floors. Mother was given instructions to change into the hospital's blue and white seersucker robe. They say the gowns are for convenience, so they can do what they have to do fast. But their robes seem more like socialistic wraps that let you know that you belong to the fraternity of the ill waiting patiently in rooms all across America.

"Diane Tempest."

She looked too beautiful to be sick. Wearing their white foam slippers, she disappeared down the hall into a room with closed doors.

I waited.

My eyes studied each person in the room. Why were they there and what were they facing? They all seemed to share an unnatural color. I checked my hands against theirs. I tried to pick up snippets of conversation that pieced together their stories. But voices were soft and words were few.

I could not read the expression on Mother's face when she came out of X ray. She changed into her clothes and we walked out of the hospital to the car.

"It doesn't look good," she said. "It's about the size of a grapefruit, filled with fluid. They are calling in the results to the doctor. We need to go to his office to find out what to do next."

There was little emotion in her face. This was a time for details. Pragmatism replaced sentiment.

At Krehl Smith's office, the future was drawn on an 8½-by-11-inch pad of yellow paper. The doctor (her obstetrician who had delivered two of her four babies) proceeded to draw the tumor in relationship to her ovaries. He stumbled over his own words, not having the adequate vocabulary to tell a patient who was also a friend that she most likely had ovarian cancer.

We got the picture. There was an awkward silence.

"So what are my options?" Mother asked.

"A hysterectomy as soon as you are ready. If it is ovarian cancer then we'll follow it up with chemotherapy and go from there . . ."

"I'll make that decision," she said.

The tears I had wanted to remain hidden splashed down on the notes I was taking, blurring the ink.

Arrangements were made for surgery on Monday morning. Mother wanted to prepare the family over the weekend. Dr. Smith suggested that two oncologists be called in on the case; Gary Smith and Gary Johnson. Mother agreed, requesting that she be able to meet with them before the operation for questions.

There was another awkward silence. Details done. Mother stood up from the straight-back chair.

"Thank you, Krehl."

Their eyes met. She turned to walk out the door, when Krehl Smith put his arm through hers. "I'm so sorry, Diane. I know what you went through before. I wish I had more encouraging news."

"So do I," she said. "So do I."

Mother and I got into the car. It started to rain. In a peculiar sort of way, the weather gave us permission to cry.

Driving home, Mother stared out her window. "You know, I hear the words on the outside, that I might have ovarian cancer, but they don't register on the inside. I keep saying to myself, this isn't happening to me, but then why shouldn't it? I am facing my own mortality—again—something I thought I had already done twelve years ago. Do you know how strange it is to know your days are limited? To have no future?"

Home. The family gathered in the living room. Mother had her legs on Dad's lap. Dad had his left arm around her, his right hand rubbing her knees and thighs. My brothers, Steve, Dan, and Hank, were seated across the room. I sat on the hearth. A fire was burning, so were candles. Twelve years ago, we had been too young to see beyond our own pain; children of four, eight, twelve, and fifteen. Dad was thirty-seven, in shock from the thought of losing his wife. We did not do well. She did. Things were different now. We would do it together. We made promises that we would be here for her this time, that she would not have to carry us.

The conversation shifted to mountain climbing, the men's desire to climb the Grand Teton in the summer, then on to tales of scaling Mount Everest without oxygen—it could be done.

Mother said she would like to work in the garden if the weather cleared. We said we would all help.

"That's funny," she said. "No one has ever offered to help me before."

She then asked that we respect her decisions, that this was her body and her life, not ours, and that if the tumor was malignant, she would choose not to have chemotherapy.

We said nothing.

She went on to explain why she had waited a month before going to the doctor.

"In the long run I didn't think one month would matter. In the short run, it mattered a great deal. The heat of the sandstone penetrated my skin as I laid on the red rocks. Desert light bathed my soul. And traveling through the inner gorge of Vishnu schist, the oldest exposed rock on the planet, gave me a perspective that will carry me through whatever I must face. Those days on the river were a meditation, a renewal. I found my strength in its solitude. It is with me now."

She looked at Dad. "Lava Falls, John. We've got some white water ahead."

I know the solitude my mother speaks of. It is what sustains me and protects me from my mind. It renders me fully present. I am desert. I am mountains. I am Great Salt Lake. There are other languages being spoken by wind, water, and wings. There are other lives to consider; avocets, stilts, and stones. Peace is the perspective found in patterns. When I see ring-billed gulls picking on the flesh of decaying carp, I am less afraid of death. We are no more and no less than the life that surrounds us. My fears surface in my isolation. My serenity surfaces in my solitude.

It is raining. And it seems as though it has always been raining. Every day another quilted sky rolls in and covers us with water. Rain. Rain. More rain. The Great Basin is being filled.

It isn't just the clouds' doing. The depth of snowpack in the Wasatch Mountains is the highest on record. It begins to melt, and streams you could jump over become raging rivers with no place to go. Local canyons are splitting at their seams as saturated hillsides slide.

Great Salt Lake is rising.

Brooke and I opt for marriage maintenance and drive out to Black's Rock on the edge of the lake to watch birds. They'll be there in spite of the weather. And they are.

Avocets and black-necked stilts are knee-deep in water alongside Interstate 80. Flocks of California gulls stand on a disappearing beach. We pull over, get out of the car and begin walking up and over lakeside boulders. I inhale the salty air. It is like ocean, even the lake is steel-blue with whitecaps.

Brooke walks ahead while I sit down with my binoculars and watch grebes. Eared grebes. Their red eyes flash intensely on the water, and I am amazed by such buoyancy in small bodies. Scanning the horizon, all I can see is water. "Lake Bonneville," I think to myself.

It is easy to imagine this lake, born twenty-eight thousand years ago, in the Pleistocene Epoch, just one in the succession of bodies of water to inhabit the Bonneville Basin over the last fifteen million years. It inundated nearly twenty thousand square miles of western Utah, spilling into southern Utah and eastern Nevada—a liquid hand pressing against the landscape that measured 285 miles long and 140 miles wide, with an estimated depth of 1000'.

Across from where I sit, Stansbury Island looms. Distinct bench levels tell a story of old shorelines, a record of where Lake Bonneville paused in its wild fluctuations over the course of fifteen thousand years. Its rise was stalled about twenty-three thousand years ago when the lake's elevation was about 4500' above sea level; over the next three thousand years, it rose very little. The relentless erosion of wave against rock during this stable period cut a broad terrace known to geologists as the Stansbury Shoreline.

The lake began to swell again until it reached the 5090' level sixteen thousand years ago. And then for a millenium and a half, the lake carved the Bonneville Shoreline, the highest of the three main terraces. Great tongues of ice occupied canyons in the Wasatch Mountains to the east, while herds of musk oxen, mammoths, and saber-tooth cats frequented the forested shores of Lake Bonneville. Schools of Bonneville cutthroat trout flashed through these waters (remnants of which still cling to existence in the refuge of small ponds in isolated desert mountains of the Great Basin). Fossil records suggest birds similar to red-tail hawk, sage grouse, mallard, and teal lived here. And packs of dire wolves called up the moon.

About 14,500 years ago, Lake Bonneville spilled over the rim of the Great Basin near Red Rock Pass in southeastern Idaho. Suddenly, the waters broke the Basin breaching the sediments down to bedrock, releasing a flood so spectacular it is estimated the maximum discharge of water was thirty-three million cubic feet per second. This event, known today as the Bonneville Flood, dropped the lake about 350', to 4740'. When the outlet channel was eroded to resistant rock, the lake stabilized once again and the Provo Shoreline was formed.

As the climate warmed drawing moisture from the inland sea, the lake began to shrink, until, eleven thousand years ago, it had fallen to present-day levels of about 4200'. This trend toward warmer and drier conditions signified the end of the Ice Age.

A millenium later, the lake rose slightly to an elevation of about 4250', forming the Gilbert Shoreline, but soon receded. This marked the end of Lake Bonneville and the birth of its successor, Great Salt Lake.

As children, it was easy to accommodate the idea of Lake Bonneville. The Provo Shoreline looks like a huge bathtub ring around the Salt Lake Valley. It is a bench I know well, because we lived on it. It is the ledge that supported my neighborhood above Salt Lake City. Daily hikes in the foothills of the Wasatch yielded vast harvests of shells.

"Lake Bonneville . . ." we would say as we pocketed them. Never mind that they were the dried shells of land snails. We would sit on the benches of this ancient lake, stringing white shells into necklaces. We would look west to Great Salt Lake and imagine.

That was in 1963. I was eight years old. Great Salt Lake was a puddle, having retreated to a record low surface elevation of 4191.35'. Local papers ran headlines that read, GREAT SALT LAKE DISAPPEARING? and INLAND SEA SHRINKS.

My mother decided Great Salt Lake was something we should see before it vanished. And so, my brothers and I, with friends from the neighborhood, boarded our red Ford station wagon and headed west.

It was a long ride past the airport, industrial complexes, and municipal dumps. It was also hot. The backs of our thighs stuck to the

Naugahyde seats. Our towels were wrapped around us. We were ready to swim.

Mother pulled into the Silver Sands Beach. The smell should have been our first clue, noxious hydrogen sulphide gas rising from the brine.

"Phew!" we all complained as we walked toward the beach, brine flies following us. "Smells like rotten eggs."

"You'll get used to it," Mother said. "Now go play. See if you can float."

We were dubious at best. Our second clue should have been the fact that Mother did not bring her bathing suit, but rather chose to sit on the sand in her sunsuit with a thick novel in hand.

The ritual was always the same. Run into the lake, scream, and run back out. The salt seeped into the sores of our scraped knees and lingered. And if the stinging sensation didn't bring you to tears, the brine flies did.

We huddled around Mother, the old Saltair Pavilion was visible behind her, vibrating behind a screen of heatwaves. We begged her to take us home, pleading for dry towels. Total time at the lake: five minutes. She was unsympathetic.

"We're here for the afternoon, kids," she said, and then brought down her sunglasses a bit so we could see her eyes. "I didn't see anyone floating."

She had given us a dare. One by one, we slowly entered Great Salt Lake. Gradually, we would lean backward into the hands of the cool water and find ourselves being held by the very lake that minutes before had betrayed us. For hours we floated on our backs, imprinting on Great Basin skies. It was in these moments of childhood that Great Salt Lake flooded my psyche.

Driving home, Mother asked each one of us what we thought of the lake. None of us said much. We were too preoccupied with our discomfort: sunburned and salty, we looked like red gumdrops. Our hair felt like steel wool, and we smelled. With the lake so low and salinity around 26 percent, one pound of salt to every four pounds of water, another hour or two of floating in Great Salt Lake and we might have risked being pickled and cured.

Brooke brought me back a handful of feathers and sat behind me. I leaned back into his arms. Three more days until Mother's surgery.

The family spontaneously gathered at Mother's and Dad's; children, spouses, grandparents, and cousins. We sat on the lawn, some talked, others played gin rummy, while Mother planted marigolds in her garden.

Mother and I talked.

"I don't want you to be disappointed, Terry."

"I won't be," I said softly. My hands patted the earth around each flower she planted.

"It's funny how the tears finally leave you," she said, turning her trowel in the soil. "I think I've experienced every possible emotion this week."

"And how do you feel now?" I asked.

She looked out at the lake, wiped her forehead with the back of her gardening glove, and removed more marigolds from the flat.

"I'll be glad to have the operation behind me. I'm ready to get on with my life."

Dad mowed the lawn between clumps of relatives. It felt good to be outside, to feel the heat, and to hear the sounds of neighborhoods on Saturdays in the spring.

The sun set behind Antelope Island. Great Salt Lake was a mirror on the valley floor. One had the sense of water being in this country now, as the quality of light was different lending a high gloss to the foothills.

At dusk, we moved inside to the living room and created a family circle. Mother sat on a chair in the center. As the eldest son, Steve annointed Mother with consecrated olive oil to seal the blessing. The men who held the Melchizedek Priesthood, the highest order of authority bestowed upon Mormon males, gathered around her, placing their hands on the crown of her head. My father prayed in a low, humble voice, asking that she might be the receptacle of her family's love, that she might know of her influence in our lives and be blessed with strength and courage and peace of mind.

Kneeling next to my grandmother, Mimi, I felt her strength and the generational history of belief Mormon ritual holds. We can heal ourselves, I thought, and we can heal each other.

"These things we pray for in the name of Jesus Christ, amen."

Mother opened her eyes. "Thank you . . ."

My sister-in-law, Ann, and I slipped into the kitchen to prepare dinner.

Some things don't change. After everyone had eaten, attention shifted to the weather report on the ten o'clock news, a Western ritual, especially when your livelihood depends on it as ours does. A family construction business, now in its fourth generation, has taught me to look up before I look down. You can't lay pipe when the ground is frozen, neither can you have crews digging trenches in mud.

The weatherman not only promised good weather, but announced that most of the planet would be clear tomorrow according to the satellite projection—a powerful omen in itself.

After everyone left, I asked Mother if I could feel the tumor. She lay down on the carpet in the family room and placed my hand on her abdomen. With her help, I found the strange rise on the left side and palpated my fingers around its parimeter.

With my hands on my mother's belly, I prayed.

We wait. Our family is pacing the hall. Other families are pacing other halls. Each tragedy has its own territory. A Tongan family in the room next to Mother's sings mourning songs for the dying. Their melancholy sweeps over us like the shadow of a raven. What songs would we sing, I wonder. Two doors down, a nurse calls for assistance in turning a patient over on a bed of ice. Minutes later, I hear the groaning of the chilled woman.

It has been almost four hours. For most of the time, I have been sitting with my mother's parents. My grandmother, Lettie, is in a wheelchair. She suffers from Parkinson's disease. Her delicate hands tremble as she strokes my hair. I am leaning against the side of her knee. She and my grandfather, Sanky, are heartsick. Mother is their only daughter; one of their two sons is dead. Mother has always cared for her parents. Now that she needs their help, Lettie feels the pain of a mother unable to physically attend to her daughter.

The three doctors appear: Smith, Smith, and Johnson, green-robed and capped. Dad meets them halfway, cowboy boots toe-to-toe with surgical papered shoes. I try to read lips as he receives the bad news followed by the good news.

"Yes, it was malignant. No we didn't get it all, but with the chemotherapy we have to offer, there is reason to be hopeful." The doctors say they will meet with us in a couple of days when they get the pathology report back, then they will go over specific details and options with Mother and the family.

Dad—tall, rugged, and direct—asks one question. "What's the bottom line—how much time do we have?"

The doctors meet his narrow blue eyes. Gary Smith shakes his head. "We can't tell you that. No one can."

The curse and charisma of cancer: the knowledge that from this point forward, all you have is the day at hand.

Dad turned around defeated, frustrated. "I'd like to get some answers." His impatience became his stride as he walked back down the hall.

Bad news is miraculously accommodated. With one hope dashed —the tumor was malignant (an easier word to stomach than cancer) —another hope is adopted: the chemotherapy will cure. Now all we had to do was convince Mother. We made a pact among ourselves that we would not discuss anything with her until the next morning. We wanted her to rest.

Two orderlies wheel Mother back into her room. The tubes, bags, blood, and lines dangling from four directions did not foster the hope we were trying to sustain. Our faith faltered in the presence of her face—white, wan, and weakened. Dad whispered that she looked like a skinned deer.

Mother opened her eyes and faintly chuckled, "That bad, uh?"

No one else laughed. We just looked at one another. We were awkward and ill-prepared.

Dad took Mother's hand and spoke to her reassuringly. He tried stroking her arm but quickly became frustrated and frightened by all the tubing connected to her veins. He sat with her as long as he could maintain his composure and then retreated to the hall where his parents, Mimi and Jack, were standing by.

Steve, Dan, and Hank took over, each one nursing her in his own way.

"Don't worry about fixing dinner for Dad, tonight, Mom, we'll take care of him," said Steve.

Dan walked out of the room and came back with a cup of ice chips. "Would you like to suck on these, Mother? Your mouth looks dry."

Hank, sixteen, stood in the corner and watched. Mother looked at him and extended her hand. He walked toward her and took it.

"Love you, Mom."

"I love you, too, dear," she whispered.

My brothers left the room. I stood at the foot of her bed, "How are you feeling, Mother?"

It was a hollow question, I knew, but words don't count when words don't matter. I moved to her side and stroked her forehead. Her eyes pierced mine.

"Did they get it all?"

I blinked and looked away.

"Did they, Terry? Tell me." She grabbed my hand.

I shook my head. "No, Mother."

She closed her eyes and I watched the muscles in her jaw tighten. "How bad is it?"

Dad walked in and saw the tears streaming down my cheeks. "What happened?"

I shook my head again, left the room and walked down the hall. He followed me and took hold of my shoulder.

"You didn't tell her, did you?"

I turned around, still crying, and faced him. "Yes."

"Why? Why, when we agreed not to say anything until to-morrow? It wasn't your place." His anger flared like the corona of an eclipsed sun.

"I told her because she asked me, and I could not lie."

The pathologist's report defined Mother's tumor as Stage III epithelial ovarian cancer. It had metastasized to the abdominal cavity. Nevertheless, Dr. Gary Smith believes Mother has a very good chance against this type of cancer, given the treatment available. He is recommending one year of chemotherapy using the agents Cytoxan and cisplatin.

Before surgery, Mother said no chemotherapy.

Today, I walked into her room, the blinds were closed.

"Terry," she said through the darkness. "Will you help me? I told myself I would not let them poison me. But now I am afraid not to. I want to live."

I sat down by her bed.

"Perhaps you can help me visualize a river—I can imagine the chemotherapy to be a river running through me, flushing the cancer cells out. Which river, Terry?"

"How about the Colorado?" I said.

It was the first time in weeks I had seen my mother smile.

June 1, 1983. Mayor Ted Wilson has ordered the channeling of three mountain streams, Red Butte, Emigration, and Parley's, into a holding pond at Liberty Park near the center of town. From Liberty Park, the water will be funneled into the Jordan River, which will eventually pour into Great Salt Lake.

Normally, these three Wasatch Front rivers converge underground in an eighty-inch pipe, but when the pipe gets too full, it blows all the manhole covers sky high, causing massive flooding on the streets. It's called "Project Earthworks."

Yesterday's temperature was sixty-two degrees Fahrenheit. Today it is ninety-two. All hell is about to break loose in the mountains. A quick thaw is a quick flood.

Ten days have passed and, between all of us, we have kept vigil. Mother's strength is returning and with typical wit, she hinted that a bit of privacy might be nice. I took her cue and drove out to the Bird Refuge.

It looked like any other spring. Western kingbirds lined the fences, their yellow bellies flashing bright above the barbed wire. Avocets and stilts were still occupying the same shallow ponds they had always inhabited, and the white-faced glossy ibises six miles from the Refuge were meticulously separating the grasses with their decurved bills.

Closer in, the alkaline flats, usually dry, stark, and vacant, were wet. A quarter mile out, they were flooded.

The Bear River Migratory Bird Refuge at an elevation of 4206', was two feet from being inundated. I walked out as far as I could. It had been a long time since I had heard the liquid songs of red-wing blackbirds.

"Konk-la-ree! Konk-la-ree! Konk-la-ree!"

The marsh was flooding. The tips of cattails looked like snorkels jutting a few inches above water. Coots' nests floated. They would fare well. With my binoculars, I could see snowy egrets fishing the small cascades that were breaking over the road's asphalt shoulders.

I could not separate the Bird Refuge from my family. Devastation respects no boundaries. The landscape of my childhood and the landscape of my family, the two things I had always regarded as bedrock, were now subject to change. Quicksand.

Looking out over the water, now an ocean, I felt foolish for standing in the middle of what little road was left. Better to have brought a canoe. But I rolled up my pantlegs over the tops of my rubber boots and continued to walk. I knew my ground.

Up ahead, two dozen white pelicans were creating a spiral staircase as they flew. It looked like a feathered DNA molecule. Their wings reflected the sun. The light shifted, and they disappeared. It shifted again and I found form. Escher's inspiration. The pelicans rose higher and higher on black-tipped wings until they straightened themselves into an arrow pointing west to Gunnison Island.

To my left, long-billed dowitchers, stout and mottled birds, pattered and probed, pattered and probed, perforating the mud in masses. In an instant, they flew, sweeping the sky as one great bird. Flock consciousness.

I turned away from the water and walked east toward the mountains. Foxtails by the roadside gathered light and held it. Dry stalks of rumex, russet from last year's fall, drew hunger pangs—the innocence of those days.

Before leaving, I noticed sago pondweed screening shallow water near the edge of the road. Tiny green circles of cholorophyll were converting sunlight to sugar. I knelt down and scooped up a handful. Microscopic animals and a myriad of larvae drained from my hands. Within seconds, the marsh in microcosm slipped through my fingers.

I was not prepared for the loneliness that followed.

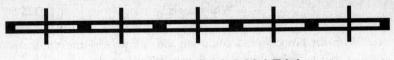

DAVID QUAMMEN

Strawberries under Ice

The Gradient of Net Mass Balance

The center of Greenland lies eleven hundred feet below sea level, giving the great frozen island somewhat the profile of an atoll. The reason for that sunken shape is not chiefly geologic; it's not a matter of tectonic vectors, mountain-building lateral pressures, ramming and grinding slabs of earthen crust. The reason is climate. Greenland is squashed to concavity by the weight of its overlying ice. Antarctica is squashed likewise.

Melt the ice away and Greenland's interior would bounce upward, like a pounded-out dent in the roof of a Chevy. Melt the ice (all seven million cubic miles of it) off Antarctica and the Earth itself would change shape. It would become almost spherical. Thaw the state of Montana back to bedrock and who can say what would happen. The damage would be slightly more subtle.

Ice is lighter than water but still heavy. The stuff answers gravity. Ice is a solid but not an absolute solid. The stuff flows. Slowly but inexorably—at one ten-thousandth the rate of springwater under similar conditions of gravity and slope—it runs downhill. We think of iciness as a synonym for cold, but cold is relative and ice happens to function well as insulation against heat loss: low thermal conductivity. Also it *releases* heat to immediate surroundings in the final stage of becoming frozen itself. Ice warms. On the particular night we will

336

come to presently, it warmed me. What it is, ice, is water transmogrified to the crystalline and paradoxical state.

When a tongue of ice flows down a mountain valley we call it a glacier. When it flows out in all directions from a source point at high elevation, like pancake batter poured on a griddle, we call it a sheet. Much of Antarctica is covered by a vast single sheet, within which the flow pattern is generally centrifugal but complex, with localized streams and eddies of ice moving independently at different rates. Out at the Antarctic circumference are glaciers and seaborne shelves, from which icebergs calve off under their own weight. On Greenland the arrangement is similar. But this is not an essay about Antarctica and Greenland. Both sheets and glaciers are supplied with their substance, their impetus, their ice, by snow and other forms of precipitation back uphill at the source. Since ice has that certain stiffness, that coy but yielding relationship with gravity, a big heavy glacier runs downhill more quickly than a little light one; a thick high-domed sheet flows outward more quickly than a thin one. While old ice is continually lost by calving and melting in the lowlands, new ice is deposited in the highlands, and any glacier or sheet receiving more new ice than it loses old, through the course of a year, is a glacier or sheet that is growing. The scientists would say that its net mass balance is positive.

The Antarctic sheet has a positive balance. Accumulation of new ice runs ahead of ablation, as the scientists would put it, by some hundred cubic miles yearly. Greenland is a much smaller world of ice with a much smaller balance; the scientists don't even agree whether that balance is just above zero or just below. Greenland may be getting either more icy or less. We live in a warmish interlude to an epoch of great freeze-overs, possibly near the end of that interlude, and by some judgments the total amount of ice on our planet is increasing. On the other hand sea levels are rising, which seems to imply a global decrease in ice; and there's the dire boring problem of human impact on temperatures, from all our stoking of the engines of civilization. Do we stand on the threshold of a new Ice Age or a greenhouse? No one knows. But in the short run Montana at least seems to be getting warmer, God help it.

Each point on a great ice body has its own numerical value for mass balance. Is the ice right here thicker or thinner than last year? Measured at any particular point, is the glacier becoming more robust or less? Is it thriving or dying? The collective profile of all those individual soundings—more ice or less? thriving or dying?—is called the gradient of net mass balance. This gradient tells, in broad perspective, what has been lost and what has been gained. On the night in question, I happened to be asking myself exactly the same: What's been lost and what gained? Because snow gathers most heavily in frigid sky-scraping highlands, the gradient of net mass balance correlates steeply with altitude. Robust glaciers come snaking down out of the Alaskan mountains. Places like central Greenland and Antarctica, squashed low by the weight of ice, have grown their own lofty highlands from ice itself: The bedrock of East Antarctica lies roughly at sea level but the ice surface rises to 13,000 feet. Also because snow gathers most heavily in frigid sky-scraping highlands, I had taken myself on the afternoon preceding the night in question to a drifted-over pass in the Bitterroot Mountains, all hell-and-gone up on the state border just west of the town of Tarkio, Montana, and started skiing uphill from there.

I needed as much snow as possible. I carried food and a goosedown bag and a small shovel. The night in question was December 31, 1975.

I hadn't come to measure depths or calculate gradients. I had come to insert myself into a cold white hole. First, of course, I had to dig it. This elaborately uncomfortable enterprise seems to have been part of a long foggy process of escape and purgation, much of which you can be spared. Suffice that my snow cave, to be dug on New Year's Eve into a ten-foot-high cornice on the leeward side of the highest ridge I could ski to, and barely large enough for one person, would be at the aphelion of that long foggy process. At the perihelion was Oxford University.

At Oxford University during one week in late springtime there is a festival of crew races on the river and girls in long dresses and boys in straw hats and champagne and strawberries. This event is called Eights Week, for the fact of eight men to a crew. It is innocent. More precisely: it is no more obnoxious, no more steeped in snobbery and dandified xenophobia and intellectual and social complacence, than any other aspect of Oxford University. The strawberries are served under heavy cream. Sybaritism is mandatory. For these and other reasons, partly personal, partly political, I had fled the place screaming during Eights Week of 1972, almost precisely coincident (by no co-incidence) with Richard Nixon's announcement of the blockade of Haiphong harbor. Nixon's blockade and Oxford's strawberries had nothing logically in common, but they converged to produce in me a drastic reaction to what until then had been just a festering distemper.

It took me another year to arrive in Montana. I had never before set foot in the state. I knew no one there. But I had heard that it was a place where, in the early weeks of September, a person could look up to a looming horizon and see fresh-laid snow. I had noted certain blue lines on a highway map, knew the lines to be rivers, and imagined those rivers to be dark mountain streams flashing with trout. I arrived during the early weeks of September and lo it was all true.

I took a room in an old-fashioned boarding house. I looked for a job. I started work on a recklessly ambitious and doomed novel. I sensed rather soon that I hadn't come to this place temporarily. I began reading the writers—Herodotus, Euripides, Coleridge, Descartes, Rousseau, Thoreau, Raymond Chandler—for whom a conscientious and narrow academic career had left no time. I spent my nest-egg and then sold my Volkswagen bus for another. I learned the clownish mortification of addressing strangers with: "Hi, my name is Invisible and I'll be your waiter tonight." I was twenty-six, just old enough to realize that this period was not some sort of prelude to my life but the thing itself. I knew I was spending real currency, hard and finite, on a speculative venture at an unknowable rate of return: the currency of time, energy, stamina. Two more years passed before I arrived, sweaty and chilled, at that high cold cornice in the Bitterroots.

By then I had made a small handful of precious friends in this new place, and a menagerie of acquaintances, and I had learned also to say: "You want that on the rocks or up?" Time was still plentiful but stamina was low. Around Christmas that year, two of the precious friends announced a New Year's Eve party. Tempting, yet it seemed somehow a better idea to spend the occasion alone in a snow cave.

So here I was. There had been no trail up the face of the ridge and lifting my skis through the heavy snow had drenched and exhausted me. My thighs felt as though the Chicago police had worked on them with truncheons. I dug my hole. That done, I changed out of the soaked freezing clothes. I boiled and ate some noodles, drank some cocoa; if I had been smart enough to encumber my pack with a bottle of wine, I don't remember it. When dark came I felt the nervous exhilaration of utter solitude and, behind that like a metallic aftertaste, loneliness. I gnawed on my thoughts for an hour or two, then retired. The night turned into a clear one and when I crawled out of the cave at three A.M. of the new year, to empty my bladder, I found the sky rolled out in a stunning pageant of scope and dispassion and cold grace.

It was too good to waste. I went back into the cave for my glasses.

The temperature by now had gone into the teens below zero. I stood there beside the cornice in cotton sweatpants, gaping up. "We never know what we have lost, or what we have found," says America's wisest poet, Penn Warren, in the context of a meditation about John James Audubon and the transforming power of landscape. We never know what we have lost, or what we have found. All I did know was that the highway maps called it Montana, and that I was here, and that in the course of a life a person could travel widely but could truly open his veins and his soul to just a limited number of places.

After half an hour I crawled back into the cave, where ten feet of snow and a rime of ice would keep me warm.

Ablation

Trace any glacier or ice sheet downhill from its source and eventually you will come to a boundary where the mass balance of ice is zero. Nothing is lost, over the course of time, and nothing is gained. The ice itself constantly flows past this boundary, molecule by molecule, but if any new ice is added here by precipitation, if any old ice is taken away by melting, those additions and subtractions cancel each other exactly. This boundary is called the equilibrium line. Like other forms of equilibrium, it entails a certain cold imperturbability, a sublime stasis relative to what's going on all around. Above the equilibrium line is the zone of accumulation. Below is the zone of ablation.

Ablation is the scientists' fancy word for loss. Down here the mass balance is negative. Ice is supplied to this zone mainly by flow from above, little or not at all by direct precipitation, and whatever does come as direct precipitation is less than the amount annually lost. The loss results from several different processes: wind erosion, surface melting, evaporation (ice does evaporate), underside melting of an ice shelf where it rests on the warmer seawater. Calving off of icebergs. Calving is the scientists' quaint word for that event when a great hunk of ice —as big as a house or, in some cases, as big as a county—tears away from the leading edge of the sheet or the glacier and falls thunderously into the sea.

Possibly this talk about calving reflects an unspoken sense that the larger ice mass, moving, pulsing, constantly changing its shape, is almost alive. If so the analogy doesn't go far. Icebergs don't suckle or grow. They float away on the sea, melt, break apart, disappear. Wind erosion and evaporation and most of those other ablative processes work on the ice slowly, incrementally. Calving on the other hand is abrupt. A large piece of the whole is there, and then gone.

The occurrence of a calving event depends on a number of factors—flow rate of the whole ice body, thickness at the edge, temperature, fissures in the ice, stresses from gravity or tides—one of which is the strength of the ice itself. That factor, strength, is hard to measure. You might never know until too late. Certain experiments done on strength-testing machines have yielded certain numbers: a strength of thirty-eight bars (a bar is a unit of pressure equal to 100,000 newtons per square meter) for crushing; fourteen bars for bending; nine bars for tensile. But those numbers offer no absolute guide to the performance of different types of ice under different conditions. They only suggest in a relative way that, though ice may flow majestically under its own weight, though it may stretch like caramel, though it may bend like lead, it gives back rocklike resistance to a force coming down on it suddenly. None of this cold information was available to me on the day now in mind, and if it had been I wouldn't have wanted it.

On the day now in mind I had been off skiing, again, with no thought for the physical properties of ice, other than maybe some vague awareness of the knee strain involved in carving a turn across boilerplate. I came home to find a note in my door.

The note said that a young woman I knew, the great love of a friend of mine, was dead. The note didn't say what had happened. I should call a number in Helena for details. It was not only shocking but ominous. Because I knew that the young woman had lately been working through some uneasy and confusing times, I thought of all the various grim possibilities involving despair. Then I called the Helena number, where a houseful of friends were gathered for communal grieving and food and loud music. I learned that the young woman had died from a fall. A freak accident. In the coldest sense of cold consolation, there was in this information some relief.

She had slipped on a patch of sidewalk ice, the night before, and hit her head. A nasty blow, a moment or two of unconsciousness, but she had apparently been all right. She went home alone and was not all right and died before morning. I suppose she was about twenty-seven. This is exactly why head-trauma cases are normally put under close overnight observation, but I wasn't aware of that at the time, and neither evidently were the folks who had helped her up off that icy sidewalk. She had seemed okay. Even after the fall, her death was preventable. Of course most of us will die preventable deaths; hers was only more vividly so, and earlier.

I had known her, not well, through her sweetheart and the network of friends now assembled in that house in Helena. These friends of hers and mine were mostly a group of ecologists who had worked together, during graduate school, as waiters and bartenders and cooks; I met them in that context and they had nurtured my sanity to no small degree when that context began straining it. They read books, they talked about ideas, they knew a spruce from a hemlock, they slept in snow caves: a balm of good company to me. They made the state of Montana into a place that was not only cold, true, hard, and beautiful, but damn near humanly habitable. The young woman, now dead, was not herself a scientist but she was one of them in all other senses. She came from a town up on the High Line.

I had worked with her too, and seen her enliven long afternoons that could otherwise be just a tedious and not very lucrative form of self-demeanment. She was one of those rowdy, robust people—robust in good times, just as robust when she was angry or miserable—who are especially hard to imagine dead. She was a rascal of wit. She could be hilariously crude. We all knew her by her last name, because her first seemed too ladylike and demure. After the phone call to Helena, it took me a long time to make the mental adjustment of tenses: She had been a rascal of wit.

The memorial service was scheduled for such-and-such day, in that town up on the High Line.

We drove up together on winter roads, myself and two of the Helena friends, a husband-and-wife pair of plant ecologists. Others had gone ahead. Places available for sleeping, spare rooms and floors; make contact by phone; meet at the church. We met at the church and sat lumpish while a local pastor discoursed with transcendent irrelevance about what we could hardly recognize as her life and death. It wasn't his fault, he didn't know her. There was a reception with the family, followed by a post-wake on our own at a local bar, a fervent gathering of young survivors determined not only to cling to her memory but to cling to each other more appreciatively now that such a persuasive warning knell of mortality had been rung, and then sometime after dark as the wind came up and the temperature dropped away as though nothing was under it and a new storm raked in across those wheatlands, the three of us started driving back south. It had been my first trip to the High Line.

Aside from the note in the door, this is the part I remember most clearly. The car's defroster wasn't working. I had about four inches of open windshield. It was a little Honda that responded to wind like a shuttlecock, and on slick pavement the rear end flapped like the tail of a trout. We seemed to be rolling down a long dark tube coated inside with ice, jarred back and forth by the crosswinds, nothing else visible except the short tongue of road ahead and the streaming snow and the trucks blasting by too close in the other lane. How ironic, I thought, if we die on the highway while returning from a funeral. I hunched over the wheel, squinting out through that gap of windshield, until certain muscles in my right shoulder and neck shortened themselves into a knot. The two plant ecologists kept me awake with talk. One of them, from the back seat, worked at the knot in my neck. We talked about friendship and the message of death as we all three felt we had heard it, which was to cherish the living, while you have them. Seize, hold, appreciate. Pure friendship, uncomplicated by romance or blood, is one of the most nurturing human relationships and one of the most easily taken for granted. This was our consensus, spoken and unspoken.

These two plant ecologists had been my dear friends for a few years, but we were never closer than during that drive. Well after midnight, we reached their house in Helena. I slept on sofa cushions. In the morning they got me to a doctor for the paralytic clench in my neck. That was almost ten years ago and I've hardly seen them since.

The fault is mine, or the fault is nobody's. We got older and busier and trails diverged. They began raising children. I traveled to Helena less and less. Mortgages, serious jobs, deadlines; and the age of sleeping on sofa cushions seemed to have passed. I moved, they moved, opening more geographical distance. Montana is a big place and the roads are often bad. These facts offered in explanation sound even to me like excuses. The ashes of the young woman who slipped on the ice have long since been sprinkled onto a mountain top or into a river, I'm not sure which. Nothing to be done now either for her or about her. The two plant ecologists I still cherish, in intention anyway, at a regrettable distance, as I do a small handful of other precious friends, who seem to have disappeared from my life by wind erosion or melting.

Leontiev's Axiom

The ice mass of a mountain glacier flows down its valley in much the same complicated pattern as a river flowing in its bed. Obviously the glacier is much slower. Glacial ice may move at rates between six inches and six feet per day; river water may move a distance in that range every second. Like the water of a river, though, the ice of any particular glacier does not all flow at the same rate. There are eddies and tongues and slack zones, currents and swells, differential vectors of mix and surge. The details of the flow pattern depend on particularities to each given case: depth of the ice, slope, contour of the bed, temperature. But some generalizations can be made. Like a river, a glacier will tend to register faster flow rates at the surface than at depths, faster flows at mid-channel than along the edges, and faster flows down toward the middle reaches than up near the source. One formula the scientists use to describe the relations between flow rate and those other factors is:

$$u = k_1 \sin^3 a\ h^4 + k_2 \sin^2 a\ h^2.$$

Everyone stay calm. This formula is not Leontiev's Axiom, and so we aren't going to bother deciphering it.

Turbulent flow is what makes a glacier unfathomable, in the sense of *fathoming* that connotes more than taking an ice-core measurement of depth. Turbulent flow is also what distinguishes a river from, say, a lake. When a river itself freezes, the complexities of turbulent flow interact with the peculiar physics of ice formation to produce a whole rat's nest of intriguing and sometimes inconvenient surprises. Because of turbulence, the water of a river cools down toward the freezing point uniformly, not in stratified layers as in a lake. Eventually the entire mass of flowing water drops below 32 degrees F. Small disks of ice, called frazil ice, then appear. Again because of turbulence, this frazil ice doesn't all float on the surface (despite being lighter than water) but mixes throughout the river's depth. Frazil ice has a tendency to adhesion, so some of it sticks to riverbed rocks. Some of it gloms onto bridge pilings and culverts, growing thick as a soft cold fur. Some of it aggregates with other frazil ice, forming large dollops of drifting slush. Meanwhile huge slabs of harder sheet ice, formed along the banks and broken free as the river changed level, may also be floating downstream. The slabs of sheet ice and the dollops of frazil ice go together like bricks and mortar. Stacking up at a channel constriction, they can lock themselves into an ice bridge.

Generally, when such an ice bridge forms, the river will have room to flow underneath. If the river is very shallow and the slabs of sheet ice are large, possibly not. Short of total blockage, the flow of the river will be slowed somewhat where it must pass through that narrowed gap; if it slows to less than a certain critical value, more ice will collect along the front face of the bridge and the ice cover will expand upstream. The relevant formula here is:

$$v_c = (1 - h/H \sqrt{2g (p - p_i/p)} h,$$

where v_c is the critical flow rate and h is the ice thickness and everything else represents something too. But this also is not Leontiev's Axiom, and so we can ignore it, praise God.

The Madison River where it runs north through Montana happens to be very shallow. Upstream from (that is, south of) the lake that sits five miles north of Ennis, it is a magnificent stretch of habitat for stoneflies and caddisflies and trout and blue heron and fox and eagles and, half the year anyway, fishermen. The water is warmed at its geothermal source in Yellowstone Park, cooled again by its Montana tributaries like West Fork, rich in nutrients and oxygen, clear, lambent, unspoiled. Thanks to these graces, it is probably much too famous for its own good, and here I am making it a little more famous still. Upstream from the highway bridge at Ennis, where it can be conveniently floated by fishermen in rafts and guided Mackenzies, it gets an untoward amount of attention. This is where the notorious salmonfly hatch happens: boat traffic like the Henley Regatta, during that dizzy two weeks of June while the insects swarm and the fish gluttonize. This is the stretch of Madison for fishermen who crave trophies but not solitude. Downstream from the Ennis bridge it becomes a different sort of river. It becomes a different sort of place.

Downstream from the Ennis bridge, for that five-mile stretch to the lake, the Madison is a broken-up travesty of a river that offers mediocre fishing and clumsy floating and no trophy trout and not many salmonflies and I promise you fervently you wouldn't like it. This stretch is called "the channels." The river braids out into a maze of elbows and sloughs and streams separated by hundreds of small and large islands, some covered only with grass and willow, some shaded with buckling old-growth cottonwoods, some holding thickets of water birch and woods rose and raspberry scarcely tramped through by a single fisherman in the course of a summer. The deer love these islands and, in May, so do the nesting geese. Mosquitoes are bad here. The walking is difficult and there are bleached cottonwood deadfalls waiting to tear your waders. At the end of a long day's float, headwinds and choppy waves will come up on the lake just as you try to row your boat across to the ramp. Take my word, you'd hate the whole experience. Don't bother. Give it a miss. I adore that five miles of river more than any piece of landscape in the state of Montana.

Surrounding the braidwork of channels is a zone of bottomland roughly two miles wide, a great flat swath of sub-irrigated meadow only barely above the river's springtime high-water level. This low meadow area is an unusual sort of no-man's-land that performs a miraculous service: protecting the immediate riparian vicinity of the channels from the otherwise-inevitable arrival of ranch houses, summer homes, resort lodges, motels, all-weather roads, development, spoliation, and all other manner of venal doom. Tantalizing and vulnerable as it may appear on a July afternoon, the channels meadowland is an ideal place to raise bluegrass and Herefords and sandhill cranes but, for reasons we'll come to, is not really good for much else.

By late December the out-of-state fishermen are long gone, the duck hunters more recently, and during a good serious stretch of weather the dark river begins to flow gray and woolly with frazil ice.

If the big slabs of sheet ice are moving too, a person can stand on the Ennis highway bridge and hear the two kinds of ice rubbing, hissing, whispering to each other as though in conspiracy toward mischief, or maybe revenge. (Through the three winters I lived in Ennis myself, I stood on that bridge often, gawking and listening. There aren't too many other forms of legal amusement in a Montana town of a thousand souls during the short days and long weeks of midwinter.) By this time the lake, five miles downstream, will have already frozen over. Then the river water cools still farther, the frazil thickens, the slabs bump and tumble into those narrow channels, until somewhere, at a point of constriction down near the lake, mortar meets brick and you begin to get:

$$v_c = (1 - h/H) \sqrt{2g (p - p_i/p) h.}$$

Soon the river is choked with its own ice. All the channels are nearly or totally blocked. But water is still arriving from upstream, and it has to go somewhere. So it flows out across the bottomland. It pours out over its banks and, moving quickly, faster than a man can walk, it covers a large part of that meadow area with water. Almost as quickly, the standing floodwater becomes ice.

If you have been stubborn or foolish enough to build your house out on that flat, on a pretty spot at the edge of the river, you now have three feet of well-deserved ice in your living room. "Get back away from me," is what the river has told you. "Show some goddamn respect." There are memories of this sort of ice-against-man encounter. It hasn't happened often, that a person should come along so mule-minded as to insist on flouting the reality of the ice, but often enough for a few vivid exempla. Back in 1863, for instance, a settler named Andrew Odell, who had built his cabin out on the channel meadows, woke up one night in December to find river water already lapping onto his bed. He grabbed his blanket and fled, knee deep, toward higher ground on the far side of a spring creek that runs parallel to the channels a half mile east. That spring creek is now called Odell Creek, and it marks a rough eastern boundary of the zone that gets buried in ice. Nowadays you don't see any cabins or barns in the flat between Odell Creek and the river.

Folks in Ennis call this salubrious event the Gorge. The Gorge doesn't occur every year, and it isn't uniform or predictable when it does. Two or three winters may go by without serious weather, without a Gorge, without that frozen flood laid down upon thousands of acres, and then there will come a record year. A rancher named Ralph Paugh remembers one particular Gorge, because it back-flooded all the way up across Odell to fill his barn with a two-foot depth of ice. This was on Christmas Day, 1983. "It come about four o'clock," he recalls. "Never had got to the barn before." His barn has sat on that rise since 1905. He has some snapshots from the 1983 episode, showing vistas and mounds of whiteness. "That pile there, see, we piled that up with the dozer when we cleaned it out." Ralph also remembers talk about the Gorge in 1907, the year he was born; that one took out the old highway bridge, so for the rest of the winter schoolchildren and mailmen and whoever else had urgent reason for crossing the river did so on a trail of planks laid across ice. The present bridge is a new one, the lake north of Ennis is also a relatively recent contrivance (put there for hydroelectric generation about when Ralph Paugh was a baby), but the Gorge of the Madison channels is natural and immemorial.

I used to lace up my Sorels and walk on it. Cold sunny afternoons of January or February, bare willows, bare cottonwoods, exquisite solitude, fox tracks in an inch of fresh snow, and down through three feet of ice below my steps and the fox tracks were spectacular bits of Montana that other folk, outlanders, coveted only in summer.

Mostly I wandered these places alone. Then one year a certain biologist of my recent acquaintance came down for a visit in Ennis. I think this was in late April. I know that the river had gorged that year and that the ice was now melting away from the bottomland, leaving behind its moraine of fertile silt. The channels themselves, by now, were open and running clear. The first geese had arrived. This biologist and I spent that day in the water, walking downriver through the channels. We didn't fish. We didn't collect aquatic insects or study the nesting of *Branta canadensis*. The trees hadn't yet come into leaf and it was no day for a picnic. We just walked in the water, stumbling over boulders, bruising our feet, getting wet over the tops of our waders. We saw the Madison channels, fresh from cold storage, before anyone else that year. We covered only about three river miles in the course of the afternoon, but that was enough to exhaust us, and then we stumbled out across the muddy fields and walked home on the road. How extraordinary, I thought, to come across a biologist who would share my own demented appreciation for such an arduous, stupid, soggy trek. So I married her.

The channels of the Madison River are a synecdoche. They are the part that resonates so as to express the significance of the whole. To understand how I mean that, it might help to know Leontiev's Axiom. Konstantin Leontiev was a cranky Russian thinker from the last century. He trained as a physician, worked as a diplomat in the Balkans, wrote novels and essays that aren't read much today, and at the end of his life flirted with becoming a monk. By most of the standards you and I likely share, he was an unsavory character. But even a distempered and retrograde Czarist of monastic leanings is right about something once in a while.

Leontiev wrote: "To stop Russia from rotting, one would have to put it under ice."

In my mind, in my dreams, that great flat sheet of Madison River whiteness spreads out upon the whole state of Montana. I believe, with Leontiev, in salvation by ice.

Sources

The biologist whose husband I am sometimes says to me: "All right, so where do we go when Montana's been ruined? Alaska? Norway? Where?" This is a dark joke between us. She grew up in Montana, loves the place the way some women might love an incorrigibly self-destructive man, with pain and fear and pity, and she has no desire to go anywhere else. I grew up in Ohio, discovered home in Montana only fifteen years ago, and I feel the same. But still we play at the dark joke. "Not Norway," I say, "and you know why." We're each half Norwegian and we've actually eaten lutefisk. "How about Antarctica," I say. "Antarctica should be okay for a while yet."

On the desk before me now is a pair of books about Antarctica. Also here are a book on the Arctic, another book titled *The World of Ice,* a book of excerpts from Leontiev, a master's thesis on the subject of goose reproduction and water levels in the Madison channels, an extract from an unpublished fifty-year-old manuscript on the history of Ennis, Montana, a cassette tape of a conversation with Ralph Paugh, and a fistful of photocopies of technical and not-so-technical articles. One of the less technical articles is titled "Ice on the World," from a recent issue of *National Geographic*. In this article is a full-page photograph of strawberry plants covered with a thick layer of ice.

These strawberry plants grew in central Florida. They were sprayed with water, says the caption, because sub-freezing temperatures had been forecast. The growers knew that a layer of ice, giving insulation, even giving up some heat as the water froze, would save them.

In the foreground is one large strawberry. The photocopy shows it dark gray, but in my memory it's a death-defying red.

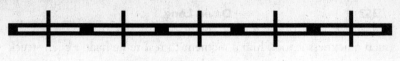

DAVID LONG

The New World

31 October 1940

Toward evening, McCutcheon's cleanup man, an old Swede named Tomasson, stood in the lot behind the store, burning trash in a drum. It would be dark in an hour. The fog would roll back over the valley, as it had each night for a week—by sunrise, hoarfrost would coat the windshields fingernail-deep, the power lines would sag in glinting arcs, as if by some fluke you could see the electricity itself. Tomasson fed in the refuse, spent receipt books and shavings and tiny crushed boxes. He watched it burn, the flecks of ash rising and disappearing against the sky. Now and then he tamped it with the charred end of a pole. Two paperboys, pouches emptied, scuffed out of the alley, caught sight of the fire, and detoured. They eyed Tomasson, but Tomasson only chewed at his upper lip and showed no interest in running them off, so they edged in, and then the three of them stood a few moments, feeling the heat on their faces, Tomasson scarcely larger than a twelve-year-old himself. "Any glass in there?" one of the boys was thinking of asking, hoping for a minor explosion. But before he managed to say this, or anything, Tomasson collapsed. His eyes suddenly crimped, his knees buckled, his hands locked onto the tamping pole—it seemed for a second he'd vault with it, miraculously, up and clear of the valley. But his legs gave, and the pole flew to the side, cracking the nearer boy across the knees with such quickness it took him a moment to realize he hadn't been struck on purpose.

McCutcheon, meantime, was seated in his office at the rear of Sperry Hardware. The door was shut and his forehead lay on a stack of shiny-covered catalogs. Earlier, he'd returned from upstairs, where he'd evicted, or tried to, one of two solitary lodgers (the other being To-masson) in rooms behind the Opera House. Winded, McCutcheon had crouched on the landing and scratched a note against one pant leg and forced it under the door: *Won't carry you one day more. M. McC.* But back downstairs, he felt none of the relief he believed he was entitled to. He sat up, kneading his face. By now the office had grown too dark to be found sitting in. The back window was so matted with alley grit it scarcely let in light—all he saw, dull as November sun, was a glow where the trash fire burned.

McCutcheon's father (known to most as Old Malcolm) had come up the lake to Sperry by steamboat in the year 1900, bearing the proceeds of monies invested down in Silver Bow County. Within days he'd dreamed up the notion of a hall to preside over. He secured land at the corner of First and Montana streets and put up a two-story brick structure: commercial space at street level, Opera House upstairs. Not grand, but a fixture from the first. The high school rented it for the-atricals and winter proms and graduations. McCutcheon, sweating in a wool suit, had been handed his own diploma up on the Opera House stage—so, another June, had Lila Dare McCutcheon, his only child, class of '29.

Old Malcolm had presided with abandon. He offered roller-skating (and sold skates by the bushel basket, the new kind with ball bearings). There were band concerts, wrestling matches, union dances, military dress balls. He brought in road companies from New York and Chicago, presented speakers. And there was the time, long ago, he procured them an elephant. A gray Saturday, spitting snow. The animal was led down the ramp of a freight wagon and up the front staircase of the Opera House, then hidden backstage, where it waited, rocking foot to foot, its trunk letting out a riffled sighing. It was a dwarf elephant, or not full-grown—though its eyes looked ancient, lost in crosshatched smudges. It stood no higher than Old Malcolm's derby, harnessed with red silk, its tail done up in red silk bows. Old Malcolm was delighted.

He loitered backstage, running a hand over the dusty, sour-smelling hide, chatting up the animal's train-weary keepers, and finally demanding that his son be allowed to sit atop it. Though shortly to balloon into a man of Old Malcolm's heft, McCutcheon was undersized as yet, moon-faced, with a fissuring voice. There was no escape; he allowed himself to be hoisted up and led in a tiny circle behind the swaying curtain, mortified.

Old Malcolm was a glad-hander, a booming public man, an optimist. McCutcheon's own view was a man could afford to be cheerful when his life's labors had been rewarded. Even Old Malcolm's death was transfigured into minor legend: by heart attack, while in the bathtub, scrubbing for an evening with a twenty-four-year-old beauty named Cora Baskins.

A neat getaway, people said.

McCutcheon's one dream, when he was young, was to be as well regarded as Old Malcolm, but his own time, the years since Old Malcolm's coronary, was no time for dreams, unless it was the one everyone had, of shucking weight, of finding a place where people weren't so strapped and stooped over. But he didn't think of this often, or with any sense he might actually do it. It was enough keeping the hardware company open, the rest of the block rented. A Hupmobile dealership had gone in and out, ditto a confectionary, a run of other marginal enterprises. Meantime, McCutcheon had lost his wife to Bright's disease, and Lila had careened off into a witless marriage. The high school had added an auditorium with sloped floor, deep proscenium stage, and a thousand velvet-backed seats. Throw in three movie houses and the new Elks, where people went to dance.

Then, three Februaries ago, a short had burned out his stage. McCutcheon was heading home from a card game when the alarm sounded. He ran back, strapped on a cannister, and went after the flames himself. The next day he shut down for repairs. Winter dragged on through March. One of Old Malcolm's compatriots poked his face into McCutcheon's office and said, "If I was you, I'd get up a Friends of the Opera House." McCutcheon felt a gust of fatigue at the thought, and somehow knew, before spring ever blew into the valley, that he wouldn't open again, not anytime soon.

When this mood had visited him before, when he felt as though the next thing would land on his chest and suck the breath from his lungs, he'd haul the boat trailer down to Graves Landing and fish a willow-shaded stretch of river. He'd stay until the light was gone, then drive home and fall quickly to sleep and not wake. Other times he might disappear down to the old Gladstone Hotel in Missoula and be someone else for three or four days. A little poker, a little companionship, no questions asked.

But even diversion felt like work now, felt willed and tainted. The mood didn't go. At forty-eight, he found himself still ruminating on Old Malcolm's life, picking at it for instruction in how to get over center, but the genial, ruddy-faced Old Malcolm grew harder and harder to call to mind. What came instead was the picture of Mc-Cutcheon himself jimmying the bathroom door and finding him with the lather dried on his chest hairs. Each time in this reverie Mc-Cutcheon bent and unstopped the tepid water. Each time his father's huge torso slumped as the water coursed out through the pipes.

Get the hell up, McCutcheon told himself, but before he could stir, before he could take a breath and slick his hair back and go forth between the aisles of useful goods, he heard a pair of boys shouting in the alley, their hands slapping furiously on the steel door.

"You've gone mean and stingy," Lila told him.

Her drinking voice, McCutcheon thought. "Spare us how I am," he said. "Get the radio, will you?"

Lila stayed sprawled in the captain's chair by the fire, arms tossed back over her head, looking so much like his wife it pained him. Rangy as a cat through the midsection, the same sleek nose and squared-off chin, the black half-moon eyes that watched him not straight-on but ten degrees sidelong. What made it worse, Lila couldn't have been more *unlike* his wife if she worked at it, which was possible. Where Hazel Dare had been a serene girl, growing into a steady, unflappable woman (McCutcheon's one joy, his ballast), Lila grew up near-beautiful, short-tempered, and contrary. On her, the off-center stare meant a sizing up, a clenching before she started railing at him, for sins he barely comprehended, the sin of heading the Downtown Boosters Club one year, the sin of giving her hours, of having no imagination—*Jesus*, he thought, *I should be so lucky*.

"What in God's name does she want out of me?" McCutcheon asked his wife. *Patience, Mal*, Hazel told him, as if in due time all would be revealed and put right. But then Hazel was dead. And Lila, whom he'd sent down to Missoula to start music school, was without warning married to a clarinet player in a jazz combo, a man in his *forties*. At first McCutcheon knew only that she was AWOL from the dormitory. A roommate surrendered a few facts, under duress, but it was weeks before he heard from Lila herself, charges reversed from Vancouver, and by then McCutcheon had convinced himself she'd contrived the whole business to get back at him, for a lifetime of seeing to her needs.

"Don't you think about showing up here," he shouted (freezing, only pajama bottoms on, the house dark around him), knowing, even so, he'd receive her without complaint, should it come to that, which of course it did, some months later, 1932, October. No call first, she walked home from the Intermountain depot lugging one pasteboard bag, headed to the kitchen and made supper, eggs and rounds of Canadian bacon, not a word about the clarinet player.

McCutcheon ate, watching her, thinking, *What has to come out, will*, the approach he imagined Hazel would've taken.

Finally he cleared his throat and said, "I'm glad to know where in hell you are."

Lila nodded, carried off the plates, and their truce was begun.

But that wasn't quite right, either. Maybe she was holding her tongue, or maybe she'd just lost the burning need to go after him. He offered to make work for her at the store, but she instead finagled a job at the high school. "Unbelievable," McCutcheon said, hearing this news. "You couldn't wait to clear out of there." Mornings she strode off as she had, but less the green bookbag bouncing at her shoulder, less the cluster of girlfriends. Tuesdays and Thursdays she took in piano pupils, never many, and they were gone from the sunroom by the time McCutcheon got home. Otherwise she read novels from the county library and made sporadic stabs at keeping the house up. McCutcheon believed this would be short-lived, recuperative in a way he didn't wish to explore. But couldn't she start over at the University after that, couldn't she marry again, decently? As for that, Lila didn't go out much—and the men she did date all had something wrong with them. One was recovering from tuberculosis. Another was nineteen.

Somehow, eight years slipped by.

Too, there was her drinking, which waxed and waned in accordance to a cycle McCutcheon never deciphered, something else to either take in stride, or not. Late one night, McCutcheon had been wakened by a farmer in the south valley named Jessup: Lila's Buick had kept on straight where the foothills road made a sharp right at the section line. Heart racing, McCutcheon threw on a jacket, hiked through a misting rain to the store and got the flatbed, and when he arrived at Jessup's saw the tire tracks slashed into the wet lawn and the Buick inert against a wooden flagpole, the top of which had splintered off and struck an upstairs window. Lila was in the kitchen, a towel at her head.

"You all right, honey?" McCutcheon said, trying to pull her hand so he could see, but she shook him off. The man was Tomasson's age, a face he recognized distantly. Once Lila had been taken to the seat of the truck, Jessup followed McCutcheon around to the driver's side and told him, "If it was my daughter, I'd be shamed to death." He walked to his porch and extinguished the light. McCutcheon drove them back, livid—at Jessup. He allowed himself the pleasure of picturing the flagpole's finial busting in and scattering the man's miserly dreams. He made a pact with himself not to give Lila a bad time over this incident, felt a startling surge of well-being overtake him as, nearly home, Lila finally slept against his shoulder.

But he did feel ashamed. He couldn't keep himself from cornering her a few days later, asking, too loud, "What're you doing out on the goddamn foothills road? I mean it, Lila—all boozed up?" The bandage was off, the stitches out, a gap left in her brow where the hair wouldn't grow again. She blew smoke and gave McCutcheon that breathy, self-mocking laugh she'd acquired.

McCutcheon persisted.

Lila glared at him suddenly. "You don't have a clue about me," she said.

McCutcheon wished to say, *Well, that's not entirely true, but why don't you just tell me . . .* but found himself rigid, humiliated. He tore into a speech about how he expected her to pay the damages, and how goddamn fortunate she was Jessup had called *him* and not the sheriff, and was about to say more, all of it best left unsaid, when she rose and trailed from the kitchen. But she did pay, to the penny, and thereafter demanded to pay McCutcheon twenty dollars a month room rent. McCutcheon threw up his hands at this, took the money rather than argue, and tucked it in an envelope inside a book of his wife's still wedged into the headboard of their bed, meaning to give it all back to Lila on some appropriate occasion, though a couple of times he had borrowed against it, most recently to have the roof re-shaked.

Mean and stingy.

He stood, heavily, got the radio himself, and was greeted with the dolorous noise of one of the candidates for district judge.

Tonight's little flare-up with Lila had to do with McCutcheon's saying no, he hadn't planned on driving over to the hospital and looking in on Tomasson.

"I'm not going near that joint," he said again.

And a moment later, "It pains you so awfully much, you go."

Lila didn't move for a while, then stood, slinging the ice cubes from her glass into the fire, where they hissed.

Now Christ, McCutcheon thought. *Why the fascination with Tomasson?*

As for himself, McCutcheon had phoned for the ambulance, then he and Dewey Fritz from the store had waited out back until the old man was lifted to a stretcher and driven off. Fritz had wadded a jacket under Tomasson's head, squatted by him saying, *You just lie still there, Oscar.* McCutcheon stood back. The wind had shifted, blowing a downdraft of putrid smoke into their eyes—finally McCutcheon had to tip the can over and roll it, dribbling ash, out of range. And there, still staring from the corner of the building, was one of those two paperboys. McCutcheon began to raise a hand to shoo him off, but then thought, *Goddamn it, no, have yourself a good long look. . . .*

Monday he took a call from Hy Glendenning, long ago Hazel's doctor, and heard the prognosis on Tomasson, which was bleak, no real chance he'd get back what he'd lost, other strokes sure to come.

What McCutcheon knew about Tomasson amounted to this: He'd shown up one fall day years ago, saying the cook at Currier's had told him to ask Mr. McCutcheon about a room. McCutcheon had been hoping for a younger man, one with a regular paycheck, but let Tomasson the room anyway, and that winter hired him to do light cleanup for a knock-off on the rent. Mornings after some function upstairs Tomasson could be seen sweeping among the chairs, herky-jerk, cap wedged down over his eyes. The next spring he came to McCutcheon and asked if he might be permitted to sharpen knives and saws.

McCutcheon said all right and set him up in the cellar. From his office McCutcheon would catch sight of Tomasson's narrow overalled back disappearing down the shaft of stairs, and find himself wincing at the thought of him down in that rathole, running his files over the sawteeth and thinking such thoughts as McCutcheon couldn't bear to imagine. In all the time since, McCutcheon managed to learn exactly three items of fact about the man: that he'd migrated here from Mountrail County, North Dakota; that he wouldn't take a drink if you held a gun to his temple; and that the finger gone from his left hand had been snagged in a gear sprocket when he was a boy in Sweden. This last, McCutcheon wouldn't have learned at all if he hadn't just asked one morning. The point was, never did he acquire the least fondness for Tomasson, never could he see past his revulsion for the sort of man Tomasson was.

And there can be no greater duty, no greater . . . McCutcheon heard issuing from the Zenith, snapped it off, and stood glaring at the threads in the carpet. An instant later he heard the door of the Buick, then the engine firing under his daughter's foot.

Small to start with, Tomasson had turned into a wizened child, frozen down the right side. McCutcheon had never seen him capless, was startled at the hummock of bald scalp peppered with liver spots.

Lila had shoved a chair beside the bed. She stopped talking, smiled, mock-cheerful. "Look who's come," she said. "Wonder of wonders."

McCutcheon frowned and edged to the foot of the bed, holding his hat. He was flushed from walking, already far too hot.

Tomasson's eyes looked out, rheumy, one blinking like a rooster's eye, the other tearing over and wetting his cheek. Lila bent and dabbed at it with the corner of the sheet.

McCutcheon undid his collar and inventoried the room. A huge weight of a patient lay mounded up in the far bed—asleep, nobody he recognized. The other bed, flanking the window, had been stripped to bare ticking.

Lila went back to talking at Tomasson, asking him things, leaving spaces for him to answer. McCutcheon assumed he could no more do this than backspring down the hall, but suddenly words came—pushed out one at a time, like bits of broken teeth.

"He's worried about his money," Lila said.

McCutcheon palmed the sweat off his temples, and thought, *What money's that?* Tomasson would be the kind who'd trust his backup, what he had, to a Bugler tin, jammed into loosened chimney bricks, down where he sharpened saws.

But what Tomasson was laboring to say had to do with a bank account. Not in Sperry, it turned out, but back in North Dakota. Thirty-three hundred and some dollars.

"Shh, now," Lila said, touching a finger to his lips.

McCutcheon fled to the hall and slipped into the sunroom for a smoke. He stood with his face aimed at the blackened panes, and thought, *Jesus, don't let me ever get like that*, but choked this sentiment off before it could fester, broke away to the stairwell and down to the car, where he waited for his daughter, idling the engine. The fog was back, deep as wool. He lay his head back and shut his eyes. Then Lila was glaring at him through the window, rapping on the glass with her ring.

"I'm walking," she said.

"Get in," he said. "Come on now, Lila," but she was off, striding into the fog.

McCutcheon started after her, but balked. He drove instead to the hotel, where he took a whiskey, then a second, tossed off before anyone could buttonhole him about the state of the world, or (more likely) the state of Sperry's woeful football team. He crossed to the store, rooted in his desk drawer for the master key, climbed the front staircase, and made his way back across the expanse of Opera House. It was cold as sin up there, colder than outside. His breath puffed against the tall, street-lit windows. The burnt flooring had long since been pry-barred up and flung down to a truck, along with the remains of Old Malcolm's maroon velvet curtain, and every functional window propped open to the winter air for days, but still it stank of smoke. Why in hell did he put himself through this?

He swung open Tomasson's door and snapped on the overhead light, expecting . . . he didn't know what. An old man's room, a raft of pathetic debris he and Lila would have to box up and then fight over what to do with. He couldn't have been more wrong. It was sparse as a monk's. Bed made, spare blanket folded at the foot. Razor, hairbrush, styptic pencil laid out by the sink. Good pants hung by the cuffs from the top dresser drawer.

Staring, McCutcheon shivered down the length of him, and didn't venture to touch a thing.

He came down next morning to an empty kitchen. There was coffee on the rear burner, a trace of Noxzema in the air, but Lila was already gone. Five past seven. *What now*, he thought, but rummaging for his good cup, he guessed he knew well enough, and was not at all surprised, a little past noon, when she appeared in his office and slapped down a brown-covered statement book retrieved from Tomasson's sock and long-john drawer.

Plains Guaranty Trust, Stanley, No. Dak. The last balance dated March 1930, in the amount of $3,306.03.

"Ye of little faith," Lila said.

McCutcheon let the book fall, laid an arm on his daughter's shoulder. "What's a man with money doing sweeping floors? An old guy, ask yourself."

Lila scanned the clutter for a place to sit, made a face, then shrugged out from under McCutcheon's arm. "I can see about it myself," she said.

"You know what you're going to find out?" McCutcheon said. "There's not a chance on God's earth that book's any good. It's just something he held onto, you understand?"

Lila looked at him as if he'd made all this up.

"Lila, his mind's not right . . . you can't pay any attention to what he says," McCutcheon said. But he wasn't up to debating her. "Look, go back to work," he said. "I'll take care of it, I'll get the story, okay?"

It took even less time than he imagined, one call to his snotty brother-in-law at the Cripps Bank. Tomasson's bank had bellied up, like so many. "You know when?" McCutcheon said to Lila that night. "The Monday after his last deposit. Can we drop it now?"

Lila ignored this, said, "I'll tell you what else I found."

"Don't," McCutcheon said.

"He owned a bunch of land over in North Dakota." She fanned out a handful of papers for him. "Old tax stuff."

"I wish you'd put that away now," McCutcheon said.

"And look here." She thrust a letter in front of him. The stamp was watery blue, old King Gustav, the handwriting inside minute, spiderish.

Neither understood a word of it. "Except, look," Lila said. *"Broder Oscar . . ."*

"Well, okay," McCutcheon said. "There's a sister." He squinted at the postmark. "This is way old," he said.

"I asked Mrs. Haugen over," Lila said.

Before McCutcheon could say once more, with greater gusto, how it was none of their affair, the chimes rang.

McCutcheon recalled Mrs. Haugen as the fussily braided woman who held forth at music recitals, cantilevered over the lip of the stage, a voice densely Scandinavian. Remembering that, he remembered a Sunday afternoon when Lila (thirteen, fourteen?) had stopped dead a page into her piece. All you heard were folding chairs, pigeons cooing and scratching in the roof gutters. Lila swiveled on the bench and announced, "I've had a change of heart." She'd play Chopin instead. McCutcheon felt his wife's hand on his knee, heard her whisper, *That's not ready yet.* True enough, but Lila stormed through it. McCutcheon sat grimacing, feeling a grudging admiration (maybe she'd grow up with enough of Old Malcolm's effrontery to get by), and also, of course, a wild embarrassment. And he remembered how this Mrs. Haugen had come to the house after Hazel's death, how she'd gotten herself weeping and coughing to where McCutcheon had been obliged to wrap an arm around her shoulder. Mourning had been an utter bafflement. The one time he wanted not to see *anyone*, the house was crawling with sympathizers—and here she'd scarcely known his wife.

McCutcheon straightened and managed a greeting.

Lila hurried her to the table and cleared a place under the light. Mrs. Haugen pulled up a pair of half-lenses and glanced at the envelope. "Oh, Soderhamn," she said. "My brother knew a girl from there." She offered a momentary, close-mouthed smile, cracked back the folds of the letter, and started to read.

"She's telling the kind of summer they were having . . . quite a long part about an anniversary part. *'Etthundra gaster,'* a hundred guests. She wishes he had come."

Mrs. Haugen looked up to check what special meaning this had for her hosts, and asked, "Do you want to hear it all?"

McCutcheon opened his mouth to say, *God, no,* but Lila said, "My father was hoping you could take down a letter to her."

Thus, moments later, McCutcheon found himself standing, hands on the chair back, dictating, while Lila rattled out cups and saucers and a plate of Fig Newtons.

"I'm sorry to be the one to give this unhappy news," McCutcheon started in, faltered, then pushed ahead, cataloging Tomasson's hopelessness. Mrs. Haugen dug into the paper with a wild, looping script.

"There's also," McCutcheon said, "the business of Mr. Tomasson's doctor bills. I'm afraid he's not in any position to take care of them."

McCutcheon avoided his daughter's eyes, which would be on him now. He waited for the writing to stop, added, "As well as other matters you should advise us on."

"Sign it yourself," Lila said.

McCutcheon bent to the table and scratched his name.

"Pieter met this girl on the train coming from the capital," Mrs. Haugen said in that unmoored voice he recollected.

"Your brother," Lila said.

Let's not encourage her, thought McCutcheon.

"She was in a choir," Mrs. Haugen said. "That's all I remember —she'd sung in the capital and was going home. He was in love with her from the first time he saw her. He came into my room, *Tell me what I should write her*. . . . He was so shy, I had never seen him like this. He was asked to her family's house once, it was on the water, a great stone house, so old. . . ."

She sought out McCutcheon's eyes, which had been wandering. "Who can say what it's like now?" she said. "Who knows if people even get their letters?"

"They're neutral over there, aren't they?" McCutcheon said. "There's no fighting."

Mrs. Haugen let her glasses fall. "I should go," she said.

"Your brother and this girl . . ." Lila asked.

Mrs. Haugen rose and accepted her coat from McCutcheon. "It didn't come to anything," she said. "This happened . . . it was just at the time we were coming to this country."

Once he'd shut the door on Mrs. Haugen, McCutcheon stepped around to the kitchen, poured milk in his cup, and dosed it with Seagram's. Lila would be on him now, about the money. He drank, bracing himself. But when he glanced back through the arch he saw her stranded in the foyer, one hand buried in her hair.

"What?" McCutcheon said. "What is it?"

"I don't know," Lila said. "I don't think I can take another winter in this valley."

"Oh, it's that song," McCutcheon said.

Go, then, he was used to saying, believing she wouldn't no matter what he told her. But he didn't know anymore—she and the car could just turn up gone some morning.

"Sit down, Lila," he said. "I'll play you some cribbage."

"Maybe I'll go and see some people," Lila said.

"Who?"

"Oh, nobody."

"Why don't you not," McCutcheon said.

Lila shrugged him a smile and didn't go for her coat, but drifted about the downstairs and shortly later up the front staircase.

Finally McCutcheon killed the lights, checked the heat, and hauled himself up to his own room. Hours later, he woke twisted in his clothes, aware of having dreamed. He'd been in an airplane—hard-rushing wind, sunlight pounding off snowfields. He loosened his shirt and listened to the house: nothing but air purring from the register, then that quit. He scuffed out into the hall. Lila's door hung open a crack, dark. He passed without slowing, without letting his hand swing it open so he could see in to the curved walnut of her sleigh bed and the tossed, vacant covers. But he stalled on the landing between floors, found himself staring out the octagon of leaded glass his wife had so loved, down through the birch limbs to the driveway and the drier, blacker rectangle of pavement where the Buick wasn't. His neighbors' houses crouched under their dark trees, porch lights off. A car inched through the fog, headlamps weak as punks—McCutcheon felt his heart rise, but the car continued past.

That wasn't dreaming, he realized.

Old Malcolm had known a man named Turley with a three-seater Swallow, and one July day they'd rendezvoused up the North Fork road at Cole's Meadow, where bootleggers were said to land by night. Goggled, paired-up behind Turley, they bumped along the strip of beaten-down field grass, lifted up, and banked into the mountain thermals. Old Malcolm with Hazel. McCutcheon's sister, Eve, with her husband, Connie Cripps. Lila with McCutcheon. A deep blue sky, *empty as a baby's heart,* Old Malcolm announced. A day with nothing wrong in it, is what McCutcheon remembered. Here was Hazel clearing the hair from her face, her free hand slipping into Old Malcolm's as she climbed from the Swallow, smiling and breathing hard, her eyes finding his, then Lila's. And later the hampers of food, Old Malcolm astride his camp stool pestering Turley for flying lessons, and Lila, uncontentious for once, trailing off with her aunt to pick early huckleberries in a Maxwell House can. Such a brilliant, mortal day, McCutcheon thought, why trot it out now?

Downstairs, he switched on lights, tore off a chunk of ham in the icebox, told himself to skip the drink, but didn't. It was going on two. He sat and shuffled up the old papers of Tomasson's Lila had left strewn there, and tried stuffing them back in the packet they'd come from. Title and tax statements, old receipts, letters in punked-out carbon. Worthless as the bank book, McCutcheon imagined, as futile a pile of papers as you could find. But then he was looking anyway. Four hundred twenty acres, Tomasson had owned, half a section, plus another hundred. Wheat and barley and hay, a steam thresher . . . McCutcheon stared, stupefied. What was more: The taxes had been kept up, November and May, all the time Tomasson had been gone from it, all that time he'd lodged behind the Opera House.

Up until a year ago, McCutcheon saw. There was a first notice of delinquency, then a second, and another bunch of envelopes Tomasson hadn't bothered to open.

Lila went first, whistling, wearing a slippery rayon number. Blue as a bluebird, as wrong for the hospital as you could imagine.

Tomasson's room was like a Turkish bath.

The big man was gone. Tomasson had inherited the window, but there was nothing to see. Sweating steam on one side of the glass, on the other, night and acres of fog.

"We've written to your sister," Lila said. She loomed over Tomasson, her legs squeezed against the bed linen.

Nothing from Tomasson.

"Juditta? Your sister?"

McCutcheon looked at them, back and forth, his only child and this ruin of a man who was nothing to him. He knew suddenly what foolishness that letter had been. He broke in, "Your sister's passed away, hasn't she?"

Lila gunned him that wild, off-kilter look; it didn't matter, he was right about this. She tugged at her shoulder pad, stepped back, putting a little gap between herself and the bed.

McCutcheon thought, *Isn't life a swell piece of business?*

"When'd you come to this country?" Lila asked Tomasson. "I want to picture it. You were how old—just young?"

"Look now, he's not going to get into a big conversation with you," McCutcheon said. "Don't you see how he is?"

"I'll tell you what I think," Lila said. "I think it took some courage to come over here, to just—I don't know . . ." Her voice had risen, it would now be carrying out into the hall. McCutcheon's head had begun to pound in the heat.

"Mr. Tomasson . . ." she was saying, "some people, I'll tell you, they never do anything like that. Not a thing."

"Lila, come on," McCutcheon said. "You're going to get one of the sisters in here."

"No, I mean, *goddamn it*. Picture you start with nothing—"

"*Enough*," McCutcheon said.

Lila let up for a second, looked at McCutcheon, then Tomasson. Then said, "He's going to take care of all your bills."

"No, now Oscar," McCutcheon said, "I don't know where she got an idea like that."

Lila spun on him. "You're going to," she shouted. "You're fixing it, you're fixing everything."

And then McCutcheon's hand was in the air, fingers balling.

Flushed, chin jutting, she didn't make the first move to cover up, only gulped in a breath, and watched.

But before McCutcheon could learn what his hand would do, there came an upheaval in Tomasson's bed, an eruption of covers, a white stick of arm raking across the nightstand. Water plumed in the air, then slapped down across the front of Lila's dress; the pitcher crashed broadside against the radiator and blew into thick curls of glass that fell spinning to the linoleum.

Lila flung her coat onto the car seat and got in beside McCutcheon. He turned the key and grabbed for the starter button but let his hands fall.

"I'll tell you another thing," he said. "It takes some goddamn courage to stay where you are, too. It takes a goddamn hunk of it."

Lila looked out the window, not letting herself touch the wet place on her front.

"You listen, Lila, we're not all of us Old Malcolm. Some of us . . ."

"Some of us are stuck tight," Lila said. "Tight as corks."

"That's not what I meant," McCutcheon said. But what did he mean? He couldn't bring himself to dig it out. He drove home, creeping, hardly able to see. Over the rise on Third, down crunching into their alley, fingers clamped on the wheel.

"Honey . . ." he started, but Lila jerked the handle and slid out, the rayon sighing across the upholstery.

McCutcheon didn't budge. Soon the lights came on in Lila's dormer. He stared, then broke his eyes away, crammed his fists under his armpits and thought, *You goddamn fraud. What courage does it take a rock to stay where you drop it?*

Then, unbidden as ever, the stations of Old Malcolm's migration sprang to his mind: Marquette to Denver to Leadville to Butte, and finally, an August evening in 1900, to the raucous steamboat landing at the head of the big lake—now just rows of stranded pilings. He'd stepped off and stood beside his trunk and seen the twilight ravishing the Gabriel Mountains to the east, the bottomland running north past the townsite, flat, dusted with haze, and told himself, *Here*, dead certain—this being the heart of all the retellings, all the bluster: his certainty and the bounty that had come of it. Then, dear God, McCutcheon thought, there was Tomasson. How could you not think of him, too? Tempted farther and deeper into this new world, already not new anymore, until he had nothing, and what was the point of all this feverish setting out?

Or, for that matter, of McCutcheon's own *not?*

A nauseating embarrassment spiked through him. How could a man live so long—almost into his *fifties*—and know so little of greater consequence than who owed him for sixty days, and who for ninety, and who'd owe him into the grave? McCutcheon sat frozen, running his hand on Lila's jacket, on the cold fur of its trim. He shot his eyes back up to Lila's window and thought, *Swear to God, I wish it was your mother up there instead of you.*

The sixth of March, 1941. A windy day, almost warm, smelling of saturated earth. Dewey Fritz was there, jowly in his loose-hanging suit; next to him was Lila, then Mrs. Haugen, and finally a big-bottomed waitress from Currier's Café. One short psalm, *The afflicted shall eat and be satisfied* . . . a half-minute of silence for prayer or what-have-you. McCutcheon watched an enormous spray of gulls light on the sodden grass, watched them fan out, flashing like whitecaps among the grave markers. He'd been back to the old man's room after all, by himself, had sat there other nights, reading from the paper or talking as the spirit moved. There were more strokes, *events*, as the doctor called them; it was hard to know if Tomasson was there at all. McCutcheon lingered in the heat and stillness of the hospital room, watching, as if Tomasson might suddenly erupt from this oblivion and regard him with a howling intelligence.

The Monday following the service, as Lila recorded grades at the high school, McCutcheon slipped over to the First Northern Bank and pocketed the last increment of Old Malcolm's bequest, long buried where it could achieve some anonymity, specifically not under his brother-in-law's nose. He walked three blocks south and paid $988 cash for a DeSoto coupe, placed the hardware store in the temporary custody of Dewey Fritz, settled Tomasson's accounts, returned home and composed a one-page note to Lila, mainly instructions, signed it M. McC., struck that out and wrote *Your father*, climbed into the new car, took Idaho west past the sawmill where it became Highway 2, and kept going, spending the first night in Sandpoint, the next in Soap Lake, then on to Portland, and south on Highway 1, aimed for California.

Except for scale, it was like when he'd fled to the Gladstone in Missoula—or so he told himself, driving, though the farther he got from home the less he believed it. The car was a dream. Rocket-shaped, the color of kidskin inside and out, not a whimper of a body squeak. He cranked down the windows, freed his waist button and drove with a straight back, fingers drumming, delighted by the bright strip of beach below the highway, the sight of breakers furling and throwing spray. The radio poured out a flotilla of swing-band tunes. Late morning, shy of the California line less than an hour, he heard the King Sisters come on. *Huuun-gry for your kisses, honey,* Louise King sang. *Huuun-gry for your touch* . . . The harmony behind her was silvery, sharp as engraving. McCutcheon found himself trembling, struck with a violent, unaccountable longing.

He crossed into the city limits of Brookings, Oregon, pulled up and killed the engine. His heart was banging high in his chest. Across the way stood a diner, the Grand Union Luncheonette, chrome and red tin. McCutcheon thought, well, he was just hungry—that was all. Afterward, stuffed with the dollar-and-a-quarter, all-you-can-eat sea bass special, Platte County pie following, he stepped out into the air and ruled out pushing on, drove instead to a bluff overlooking the water, crawled into the backseat and fell asleep, both doors open to the wind.

He took his supper at the same place, the Grand Union, and whereas at home he'd no more cosy up to strangers than vote for a Democrat, here he found himself trading conversation with the people at the next table, a woman roughly his own vintage (her name was Silvie Markle), and her son John, roughly Lila's.

McCutcheon said he'd noticed them there at lunchtime.

Silvie Markle laughed. They'd eaten every meal there for a week. "Kitchen's all torn to pieces," she said, waving a hand. "Utter chaos."

She had a wide, olivy face fringed with pewter bangs, silver-rimmed glasses that rode down her nose. He studied her and thought, *What the hell is it about her?* and realized, besides the friendliness, it was that she didn't remind him of a soul. The son added a nod, mouth full of French bread. He'd toweled his face clean, McCutcheon noticed, but the tops of his ears were still furred with plaster dust.

McCutcheon offered a few words about himself, mainly true. He watched the woman drink her coffee, and after she and her son had paid and left, he found himself staring at the tracing of lipstick on her cup.

Next morning, after idling over his sweet roll in the hotel's airy, near-deserted breakfast room, McCutcheon forced himself to rise and get on with the day, a Friday, bright. He toted his bag to the DeSoto, eyed the street for a filling station, saw a Flying A down two blocks, and thought, *Fine, gas up there.* The trunk slammed with a rich, secure thump. But an instant later he abandoned the car, and took off on foot, up along the storefronts, then back into the grid of neighborhoods.

He was struck by how far along spring was. Tulips were up, the grass shone with shoots of deep color—where Sperry's yards were lifeless yet, mushed-down, long lumps of pitted ice under the driplines of the arborvitae. It took him the better part of an hour to locate the Markles', one of two white-painted relics alone at the end of McKinley, smothered in lilacs and blackberry vines and an insistent, curly-leafed vegetation he couldn't name.

He maneuvered over a berm of torn-out lath on the walkway, and stuck his head in the kitchen door. John Markle was peering into a hole in the counter.

One evening, much later, McCutcheon told Lila: *That was the second time I saw John. . . . He'd just cut the hole for the sink—it was way off. I said, "Too narrow you can fix," and he laughed at himself as if a man's own mistakes were something to marvel at. I suppose I liked him right then. Silvie came out through this drop cloth they'd tacked up to keep the dust confined—they didn't either of them act the least bit surprised I'd turned up at the house. Silvie made some coffee on a hot plate. Funny what you remember . . .*

The same family had built both houses, McCutcheon learned that morning. He trailed after Silvie, stood in the field grass beside her, getting his feet wet, listening, looking back and forth between the green-shingled roofs.

"Quite the family," Silvie said. "Sent someone to the legislature, the whole bit. People named Gilmartin."

"What happened?"

Silvie threw a hand up. "Oh, what happens to people? One thing and another. They petered out."

"Don't they now," McCutcheon said.

"So anyway, John heard these places were going for taxes, and I thought, *Lord hates a coward. . . .*"

"You took *both* of them?" McCutcheon asked.

Silvie shaded her eyes, laughed up at him. "What an idiot, huh?"

If anyone, in his old life, had asked McCutcheon, point-blank, what he had against Tomasson, he would've brushed the question off as nonsense and intrusion. *Jesus*, he might've said, *I can't be picking up everybody's tab*, as if that was all it was, money. He would not have touched on how Tomasson stirred up a host of the rankest feelings in him, or what this disgust (or fear or whatever it was) had to do with his winding up in that freezing Buick, loathing the touch of his daughter's coat, loathing so much as the thought of her gliding around her bedroom peeling off that blue dress. . . .

Until one evening, his first June in Oregon: He and Silvie were at work on the porch of McCutcheon's newly acquired place (later to be guest house), McCutcheon installing fresh screening, Silvie in dungarees, down on the floor prying up rotten jute with a putty knife. Matter-of-fact, her back crossed by bars of shadow, Silvie was telling McCutcheon about her sister's troubles, and happened to say: "You just get to where you can't love anything where you are anymore. You get a crimp."

McCutcheon laid down his tack hammer as if it were made of glass. He leaned his forearms against the top of the stepladder, amazed at how correct this sounded, even more amazed that a run of words could ring in his ears like the blow from a cold chisel.

You get mean and stingy, he thought. The funny thing was, he didn't feel at all that way now.

The barn swallows had come out. Along the edge of the property, the blue spruces were flattening into silhouettes. He watched Silvie's elbow flying to the side, bare and tanned, heard a satisfying rip as the old floor covering tore loose. He felt he knew what would happen next. He'd climb down and touch the shoulder of her workshirt. She'd sit back on her heels (he'd see the denim whitening at her hips), she'd nudge her glasses up and look at him, her lips apart in curiosity, then he'd make his first stab at kissing her, and it would come off with a little grace, or else not, but it gave him an unholy thrill to think of it, even for a second.

"What're you laughing about?" Silvie said.

"Nothing," McCutcheon said. "Can't a man laugh?"

"No, now *what?*"

"Nothing, nothing." He could hardly contain himself.

What if the King Sisters had been doing "Red Sails in the Sunset" and not a song that left him desperately hungry? What if the Markles had spruced up and gone instead to the Brookings Club, or suppose McCutcheon had downed his supper as usual, without a word, face bent to newsprint?

What if Tomasson had fallen straightaway dead?

Imponderables, Old Malcolm would say, which only meant he refused to think of them. But what amazed McCutcheon was his own amazement. That the man he'd become, so late in the game, could wonder at things, his mind bright, not swamped and close.

What if Lila (her heart every bit as crimped as his) had read that gingerly letter he'd banged out on Silvie's machine one evening, and fired back, *Thanks for leaving me all this mess. F.Y.I., Dewey's running the store straight into the ground. . . . We had a big wind last night, that split limb on the Norway maple came down on the Woodcocks' bay window. . . . Look, what kind of stunt are you pulling down there??*

Instead of the reply that had come, a sheet of Hazel's old cockleshell letter paper: *How would you feel about my coming down there for a few weeks. . . . What do you think about August?*

And his own, *Yes, come.*

It occurred to McCutcheon one day—after the war, the house finally reclaimed from vine and damp rot and vacancy—that he'd grown to be a man older than Old Malcolm. And realized the rancor had gone, leached away in the time he'd been with Silvie. It was even possible to daydream about Hazel, to remember her as a young mother, and no longer mire himself in such memories as reaching into their closet and slipping a dress off a hanger—the navy organdy with the white silk flowers—to fold into a bag and give the undertaker.

A good joke on McCutcheon: Brookings turned out to be a town famous for fog. It rolled in off the water prodigiously, mindless of season, dingy as five A.M. He could smell it before he'd opened his eyes, could hear the muffling of the boat horns and the shrieks of the gulls. A walk from the car to the house was enough to glaze the glasses he was now required to wear. He'd stand at the kitchen door, drying them on a shirttail. "*Look* at this!" he'd tell Silvie. "I'm moving to the desert."

"Oh no, you're not," Silvie would tell him.

Because there were days like this one, too—breezy, the air scoured and warming. McCutcheon stepped outside, circumnavigated the house, checking the plum trees, the perennial beds, the height of the grass against his shoe. All was quiet. His boarders were off on their morning rounds. John Markle was framing houses up the coast road, Lila was downtown in the station wagon buying groceries. Silvie had come out onto the porch steps to dry her hair in the sun.

McCutcheon wandered over, hands in his pockets. "You know what I was remembering?" he said.

"The time I seduced you at the luncheonette."

McCutcheon smiled, touched her shoulder. "I was thinking about the Opera House," he said. "I was remembering how Old Malcolm would go in and ribbon us off a string of seats. Right in front, naturally. He'd have us wait in the anteroom so we'd have to parade down the aisle—as if the show couldn't possibly start until everyone got themselves a good look at all of *us*. Hazel and Lila and me, my sister and her girls . . ."

McCutcheon unbuttoned his cardigan, peeled it off, and tossed it over the railing.

"It was exactly how he acted if he'd dragged me off to some big gathering with him. He kept booming out, *You know m'boy here? Maalcom?* I was thinking how much I used to hate it . . . I used to wish I'd never hear it again as long as I lived."

He sat on the step beside her. "What an idiot," he said.

"You're forgiven," Silvie said. "Here." She slapped the comb into his hand and turned her back to him.

And what if he'd never figured out that simplest injunction? *Enjoy your life, take a little goddamn pride. . . .* He worked the comb through the silvery hair, shook the water off, started again at the crown of her head, teasing out the snarls. He could do it all morning. He looked up, past their yard, past the spruces and the tangle of vines, and could see clear out to where the horizon shimmered, faintly blue, empty as a baby's heart.

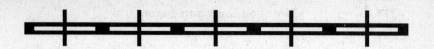

Notes on the Contributors

DAVID LEE

Honored by the Utah Endowment for the Humanities in 1991 as one of the dozen foremost writers in that state's history, David Lee is a poet of wide popular renown, a "pig poet" by self-description. Chairman of the Department of Language and Literature at Southern Utah University, Lee's books of poetry include *The Porcine Legacy* (1978), *Driving and Drinking* (1982), *The Porcine Canticles* (1984)—in which "Loading a Boar" appeared—and, most recently, *Day's Work*, winner of the 1990 Publication Prize of the Utah Arts Council. A descendant of storied Mormon pioneer John D. Lee, David Lee lives with his wife, Jan, and two children in St. George, Utah.

WILLIAM KITTREDGE

William Kittredge has taught in the English Department at the University of Montana since 1969. His first book of short stories, *The Van Gogh Field*, won the Fiction International Prize for 1979. A second book of stories, *We Are Not in This Together*, was published in 1984. *Owning It All*, a collection of essays from which "Home" has been reprinted, followed in 1987. Kittredge's stories and essays have appeared in *Harper's, Outside, TriQuarterly, Rolling Stone,* and other periodicals, and his memoir, *Hole in the Sky,* was published recently.

GRETEL EHRLICH

Gretel Ehrlich was born and raised in California and moved to Wyoming in 1976. A former producer of documentary films, she has written two books of poetry: *Goede/Rock Body* (1970) and *To Touch the Water* (1981). She was a 1982 recipient of a creative writing fellowship from the National Endowment for the Arts. Her collection of reflections on the nature of rural Wyoming life, *The Solace of Open Spaces,* was widely and critically acclaimed, and it was followed in 1988 by a novel, *Heart Mountain.* Ehrlich received a Whiting Award in 1988 and a Guggenheim Fellowship in 1989. "Madeleine's Day" and "McKay" are included in her most recent collection of stories, *Drinking Dry Clouds,* published in 1991.

DEIRDRE MCNAMER

Deirdre McNamer is a native of the Hi-Line region of northern Montana. She has been a reporter for the Associated Press, as well as several western newspapers, and she has contributed periodically to *The New Yorker. Rima in the Weeds* (1991), excerpted here, is her fictional debut. She and her husband, the writer Bryan DiSalvatore, live in Missoula, where McNamer teaches at the University of Montana.

RUDOLFO A. ANAYA

Born in 1937 on the *llano* of eastern New Mexico, Rudolfo Anaya grew up in the town of Santa Rosa. His books include a trilogy of New Mexico novels—*Bless Me, Ultima* (1972), *Heart of Aztlan* (1976), and *Tortuga* (1979)—and a collection of short fictional pieces, *The Silence of the Llano.* He has edited *Voces: An Anthology of Nuevo Mexicano Writers* and *Tierra: Contemporary Short Fiction of New Mexico.* Widely recognized as one of the nation's foremost Hispanic writers and editors,

Anaya teaches creative writing at the University of New Mexico, where he also edits the *Blue Mesa Review*. "Iliana of the Pleasure Dreams" first appeared in *Zyzzyva*.

N. SCOTT MOMADAY

N. Scott Momaday, a Kiowa Indian, is a painter and poet as well as a novelist. *House Made of Dawn* (1968), his first novel, was awarded the Pulitzer Prize for literature. In addition to two books of poetry, *The Gourd Dancer* and *Angle of Geese and Other Poems*, he has published a collection of tribal and familial legends and history, *The Way to Rainy Mountain* (1969), and an autobiography, *The Names* (1976). His second novel, *The Ancient Child*, was published in 1989. "Remote as the stars are his sentiments just now" is a chapter from that novel, a complex blend of Indian lore, western legend, and a lyrical contemporary story. Momaday has received the Premio Letterario Internazionale "Mondello" and is Regent's Professor of English at the University of Arizona. He lives in Tucson with his wife and daughter.

JAMES WELCH

James Welch was born in Browning, Montana, in 1940 of mixed Blackfeet and Gros Ventre parentage. He was educated in reservation schools prior to studying writing in the late 1960s with the late Richard Hugo at the University of Montana. His book of poems, *Riding the Earthboy 40* (1971), was followed by two contemporary novels, *Winter in the Blood* (1974) and *The Death of Jim Loney* (1979). *Fools Crow* (1986), a historical novel that examines a band of Montana Blackfeet threatened with extinction in the early 1870s, received the *Los Angeles Times*'s Book Prize for Fiction, the American Book Award, and the Pacific Northwest Booksellers Award. Welch's tenure as a member of the Montana Board of Paroles was the genesis for his most recent novel, *The Indian Lawyer*, from which this selection is excerpted. Welch and his wife, Lois, who teaches English at the University of Montana, live in Missoula.

PAM HOUSTON

Cowboys Are My Weakness, Pam Houston's first collection of short stories, was recently published. A recipient of a Ph.D. from the University of Utah, she has been a visiting professor of English at Denison University in Ohio. Houston's stories and nonfiction have appeared in *Mirabella, Crazyhorse, The Apalachee Quarterly*, and other periodicals. "How to Talk to a Hunter" first appeared in *Quarterly West* and was included in *The Best American Short Stories, 1990*, edited by Richard Ford. A licensed river guide as well as a writer and academician, she is based in Park City, Utah.

CHARLES BOWDEN

Charles Bowden's books include *Killing the Hidden Waters, Blue Desert, Frog Mountain Blues, Mezcal, Red Line*, and, most recently, *Desierto: Memories of the Future*, from which this selection is excerpted. He has written for *Smart, Buzzworm*, the *Los Angeles Times, USA Today*, and other periodicals. Bowden is based in Tucson, but he spends much of his time in rather more remote locations on both sides of the Arizona-Sonora border.

IVAN DOIG

Born in Montana in 1939, the son of a soon-widowed ranch hand, Ivan Doig left his home state following high school to pursue a journalism degree at Northwestern University. Following the completion of a Ph.D. in history from the University of Washington, he wrote for a number of periodicals before undertaking *This House of Sky* (1978), a memoir of his early life that received a Christopher Award and was a nominee for a National Book Award. *Winter Brothers* (1982), a lyrical history, received a Pacific Northwest Booksellers Award, and his first novel, *The Sea Runners* (1982), was followed by his much-acclaimed trilogy of novels set in Montana: *English Creek* (1984), *Dancing at the*

Rascal Fair (1987), and *Ride with Me, Mariah Montana* (1990), from which this selection is excerpted. Doig and his wife, Carol, a college professor, have lived in Seattle for many years.

THOMAS MCGUANE

Thomas McGuane, a Michigan native, is a former Wallace Stegner Fellow at Stanford University, a prize-winning cutting-horse trainer, and a long-time resident of and rancher in southwestern Montana. His 1971 novel, *The Bushwacked Piano*, won the Richard and Hilda Rosenthal Foundation Award from the American Academy of Arts and Letters, and *Ninety-two in the Shade* (1973) was a nominee for a National Book Award. Those books were followed by screenplays for the films *Rancho Deluxe*, *Tom Horn*, and *The Missouri Breaks*; by *An Outside Chance* (1980), a collection of essays on sport; and by four more novels—*Panama* (1978), *Nobody's Angel* (1982), *Something to Be Desired* (1984), and *Keep the Change* (1989), from which this selection is excerpted.

LISA SANDLIN

Lisa Sandlin came to New Mexico from Texas in 1974. Her stories have received first prize in the *Emrys Journal* fiction competition and the Jeanne Charpiot Goodheart Prize for Best of Issue in *Shenandoah*. Her first collection of stories, *The Famous Thing About Death*, was published in 1991. Sandlin and her son live in Santa Fe.

BARBARA KINGSOLVER

Born in Marlyland and raised in rural Kentucky, Barbara Kingsolver now lives outside Tucson, Arizona, with her husband and daughter. Initially a journalist and scientific writer, Kingsolver's nonfiction has appeared in *The Progressive*, *The Sonora Review*, and *Smithsonian*. *The Bean Trees* (1988), her first novel, was published to wide acclaim, as was her recent novel, *Animal Dreams* (1990). "Why I Am a Danger to the Public" was included in *Homeland and Other Stories* (1989). The story first appeared in *New Times*.

LINDA HOGAN

Linda Hogan is a Chickasaw poet, essayist, and novelist who teaches English at the University of Colorado. She has been the recipient of a National Endowment for the Arts grant, a Minnesota Arts Board grant, a Colorado Writer's fellowship, the Five Civilized Tribes Museum playwriting award, and a Guggenheim fellowship. Her books of poems include *Calling Myself Home* (1978), *Eclipse* (1983), and *Savings* (1988); *Seeing Through the Sun* (1985) received an American Book Award from the Before Columbus Foundation. *Mean Spirit* (1990), from which this selection is excerpted, is her first novel. Hogan and her daughter live in Kittredge, Colorado.

ROBERT MAYER

Robert Mayer was born in New York City in 1939, where he later worked as a reporter and *Newsday* columnist, winning a National Headliner Award and two Mike Berger Awards. Since moving to New Mexico in the early 1970s, he has published six novels: *Superfolks* (1977), *The Execution* (1979), *Midge and Decker* (1982), *Sweet Salt* (1984), *The Grace of Shortstops* (1984), and *The Search* (1986). "The Dreams of Ada," which first appeared in *Vanity Fair*, is an account of murder and the misapplication of justice in his wife LaDonna's Oklahoma hometown. An expanded version of those events, *The Dreams of Ada*, was published in 1987 and was a finalist for the Edgar Award. Mayer and his family live in Santa Fe.

GARY PAUL NABHAN

Botanist and writer Gary Paul Nabhan has been assistant director of the Desert Botanical Garden in Phoenix, Arizona, and was a cofounder of Native Seeds/SEARCH, based in Tuscon. His books include *The Desert Smells Like Rain* (1987) and *Gathering the Desert* (1985), for which he was awarded the John Burroughs Medal for natural history writing. "Harvest Time" is excerpted from *Enduring Seeds* (1989). In 1990 Nabhan was awarded a MacArthur Foundation prize fellowship in recognition of his investigations into and support of indigenous agriculture in North America.

DENISE CHÁVEZ

Playwright, poet, and story writer Denise Chávez is a New Mexico native and a creative-writing protegé of Rudolfo Anaya at the University of New Mexico. Her bilingual plays have been produced throughout the Southwest, and *The Last of the Menu Girls* (1986), whose title story is included in this collection, received the Puerto del Sol Fiction Award. She is currently an assistant professor of drama at the University of Houston in Houston, Texas.

TIM SANDLIN

Tim Sandlin is a native of North Carolina who came west to Jackson, Wyoming, in the early 1970s and decided to stick around in a place he perceives as a kind of wacky paradise. He has worked in Wyoming as a newspaper copyeditor, proofreader, and columnist, a pizza-parlor manager, a dishwasher, elk skinner, and cook, and he has still found time to write three eccentric, spirited, and well-received novels: *Sex and Sunsets* (1987), *Western Swing* (1988), and *Skipped Parts* (1991), from which this selection is excerpted.

RON CARLSON

Ron Carlson was born and raised in Utah. He has taught at the Hotchkiss School in Connecticut and as an artist-in-the-schools in Utah, Idaho, and Alaska. His books include the novels *Betrayed by F. Scott Fitzgerald* (1977), *Truants* (1981), and a story collection, *The*

News of the World (1987). "The H Street Sledding Record," included in that collection, first appeared in *McCall's*. Carlson is director of creative writing at Arizona State University. He lives in Tempe with his wife and two sons. A new story collection, *Plan B for the Middle Class*, was published recently.

JOANNE GREENBERG

Joanne Greenberg has lived in the mountains outside Denver for many years, where she long has been a member of the Lookout Mountain Search and Rescue Team. Her many novels include *I Never Promised You a Rose Garden* (1964), *In This Sign* (1970), *Simple Gifts* (1986), *Age of Consent* (1987), and *Of Such Small Differences* (1988). Additionally, she has produced four collections of short stories: *Summering* (1966), *Rites of Passage* (1972), *High Crimes and Misdemeanors* (1980), and *With the Snow Queen* (1991), in which "Offering Up" first appeared.

TERRY TEMPEST WILLIAMS

Naturalist-in-residence at the Utah Museum of Natural History, Terry Tempest Williams lives at the base of the Wasatch Range, as have many generations of Mormon ancestors before her. She has written for a variety of regional publications and is the author of *The Secret Language of Snow* (1984), *Pieces of White Shell* (1984), and *Coyote's Canyon* (1989). "Whimbrels" is a chapter from her most recent book, *Refuge: An Unnatural History of Family and Place* (1991), an account of her mother's death from cancer and the flooding of the Bear River Migratory Bird Refuge by the waters of Great Salt Lake. Williams and her family live in Salt Lake City.

DAVID QUAMMEN

David Quammen was educated at Oxford and Yale before settling in Montana in the early 1970s. His novels include *The Zolta Configuration*

(1983) and *The Soul of Viktor Tronko* (1987), and he has published two highly acclaimed collections of natural history essays, *Natural Acts* (1985) and *The Flight of the Iguana* (1988). "Natural Acts," his monthly column for *Outside* magazine, received a National Magazine Award for Essays and Criticism. Quammen and his wife, biologist Chris Ellingsen, live in Bozeman, Montana.

DAVID LONG

Born in Boston in 1948, David Long received an M.F.A. in creative writing from the University of Montana in 1974. He has published a book of poetry, *Early Returns*, and two collections of stories, *Home Fires* (1982) and *The Flood of '64* (1987). His stories have appeared in a variety of periodicals, including *The New Yorker*. "The New World" first appeared in *Antaeus* and was named a Distinguished Story of 1989 in *The Best American Short Stories 1990*, edited by Richard Ford. Long, his wife, and sons live in Kalispell, Montana.

FOR THE BEST IN PAPERBACKS, LOOK FOR THE

In every corner of the world, on every subject under the sun, Penguin represents quality and variety—the very best in publishing today.

For complete information about books available from Penguin—including Pelicans, Puffins, Peregrines, and Penguin Classics—and how to order them, write to us at the appropriate address below. Please note that for copyright reasons the selection of books varies from country to country.

In the United Kingdom: For a complete list of books available from Penguin in the U.K., please write to *Dept E.P., Penguin Books Ltd, Harmondsworth, Middlesex, UB7 0DA.*

In the United States: For a complete list of books available from Penguin in the U.S., please write to *Dept BA, Penguin, Box 120, Bergenfield, New Jersey 07621-0120.*

In Canada: For a complete list of books available from Penguin in Canada, please write to *Penguin Books Canada Ltd, 10 Alcorn Avenue, Suite 300, Toronto, Ontario, Canada M4V 3B2.*

In Australia: For a complete list of books available from Penguin in Australia, please write to the *Marketing Department, Penguin Books Ltd, P.O. Box 257, Ringwood, Victoria 3134.*

In New Zealand: For a complete list of books available from Penguin in New Zealand, please write to the *Marketing Department, Penguin Books (NZ) Ltd, Private Bag, Takapuna, Auckland 9.*

In India: For a complete list of books available from Penguin, please write to *Penguin Overseas Ltd, 706 Eros Apartments, 56 Nehru Place, New Delhi, 110019.*

In Holland: For a complete list of books available from Penguin in Holland, please write to *Penguin Books Nederland B.V., Postbus 195, NL-1380AD Weesp, Netherlands.*

In Germany: For a complete list of books available from Penguin, please write to *Penguin Books Ltd, Friedrichstrasse 10-12, D-6000 Frankfurt Main 1, Federal Republic of Germany.*

In Spain: For a complete list of books available from Penguin in Spain, please write to *Longman, Penguin España, Calle San Nicolas 15, E-28013 Madrid, Spain.*

In Japan: For a complete list of books available from Penguin in Japan, please write to *Longman Penguin Japan Co Ltd, Yamaguchi Building, 2-12-9 Kanda Jimbocho, Chiyoda-Ku, Tokyo 101, Japan.*

FOR THE BEST LITERATURE, LOOK FOR THE

☐ **THE BOOK AND THE BROTHERHOOD**
Iris Murdoch

Many years ago Gerard Hernshaw and his friends banded together to finance a political and philosophical book by a monomaniacal Marxist genius. Now opinions have changed, and support for the book comes at the price of moral indignation; the resulting disagreements lead to passion, hatred, a duel, murder, and a suicide pact.   *602 pages*   *ISBN: 0-14-010470-4*

☐ **GRAVITY'S RAINBOW**
Thomas Pynchon

Thomas Pynchon's classic antihero is Tyrone Slothrop, an American lieutenant in London whose body anticipates German rocket launchings. Surely one of the most important works of fiction produced in the twentieth century, *Gravity's Rainbow* is a complex and awesome novel in the great tradition of James Joyce's *Ulysses*.   *768 pages*   *ISBN: 0-14-010661-8*

☐ **FIFTH BUSINESS**
Robertson Davies

The first novel in the celebrated "Deptford Trilogy," which also includes *The Manticore* and *World of Wonders, Fifth Business* stands alone as the story of a rational man who discovers that the marvelous is only another aspect of the real.   *266 pages*   *ISBN: 0-14-004387-X*

☐ **WHITE NOISE**
Don DeLillo

Jack Gladney, a professor of Hitler Studies in Middle America, and his fourth wife, Babette, navigate the usual rocky passages of family life in the television age. Then, their lives are threatened by an "airborne toxic event"—a more urgent and menacing version of the "white noise" of transmissions that typically engulfs them.   *326 pages*   *ISBN: 0-14-007702-2*

You can find all these books at your local bookstore, or use this handy coupon for ordering:

Penguin Books By Mail
Dept. BA Box 999
Bergenfield, NJ 07621-0999

Please send me the above title(s). I am enclosing _____
(please add sales tax if appropriate and $1.50 to cover postage and handling). Send check or money order—no CODs. Please allow four weeks for shipping. We cannot ship to post office boxes or addresses outside the USA. *Prices subject to change without notice.*

Ms./Mrs./Mr. _____

Address _____

City/State _____ Zip _____

FOR THE BEST LITERATURE, LOOK FOR THE

☐ **A SPORT OF NATURE**
Nadine Gordimer

Hillela, Nadine Gordimer's "sport of nature," is seductive and intuitively gifted at life. Casting herself adrift from her family at seventeen, she lives among political exiles on an East African beach, marries a black revolutionary, and ultimately plays a heroic role in the overthrow of apartheid.

354 pages   ISBN: 0-14-008470-3

☐ **THE COUNTERLIFE**
Philip Roth

By far Philip Roth's most radical work of fiction, *The Counterlife* is a book of conflicting perspectives and points of view about people living out dreams of renewal and escape. Illuminating these lives is the skeptical, enveloping intelligence of the novelist Nathan Zuckerman, who calculates the price and examines the results of his characters' struggles for a change of personal fortune.

372 pages   ISBN: 0-14-009769-4

☐ **THE MONKEY'S WRENCH**
Primo Levi

Through the mesmerizing tales told by two characters—one, a construction worker/philosopher who has built towers and bridges in India and Alaska; the other, a writer/chemist, rigger of words and molecules—Primo Levi celebrates the joys of work and the art of storytelling.

174 pages   ISBN: 0-14-010357-0

☐ **IRONWEED**
William Kennedy

"Riding up the winding road of Saint Agnes Cemetery in the back of the rattling old truck, Francis Phelan became aware that the dead, even more than the living, settled down in neighborhoods." So begins William Kennedy's Pulitzer-Prize winning novel about an ex-ballplayer, part-time gravedigger, and full-time drunk, whose return to the haunts of his youth arouses the ghosts of his past and present.   228 pages   ISBN: 0-14-007020-6

☐ **THE COMEDIANS**
Graham Greene

Set in Haiti under Duvalier's dictatorship, *The Comedians* is a story about the committed and the uncommitted. Actors with no control over their destiny, they play their parts in the foreground; experience love affairs rather than love; have enthusiasms but not faith; and if they die, they die like Mr. Jones, by accident.

288 pages   ISBN: 0-14-002766-1